A Remedy for Hurting Hearts

The muscles beneath her hand grew as taut as iron bands, Redmayne so still it was almost frightening. She glanced at his face, saw his eyes shut tight, a knotted muscle twitching in his jaw.

"Did I hurt you? Are you all right?"

"No, damn it. I'm not all right."

"What . . . what is wrong?"

"This." He growled, his hand sweeping up to delve into the damp tangle of her hair. He tugged her mouth down toward his. Her heart slammed against her ribs at the hot intent glimmering beneath his lashes. And Rhiannon wondered if she'd ever have the will to draw another breath as the sensual fullness of Redmayne's mouth closed over hers.

The contact jolted through her as if he'd infused her with the very essence of life—awakened her from a nursery world, all bright smiles and pretty stories, fistfuls of daisies and scuffed play slippers—and suddenly she'd awakened in a realm of legends and lovers, passions and promises.

She should have been shocked, for his was no tentative kiss. It gripped her in a fist of sensation, wild and wonderful and so unfamiliar she never wanted it to end.

Books by Kimberly Cates

Angel's Fall
Briar Rose
Crown of Dreams
Gather the Stars
To Catch A Flame
Only Forever
Magic
Morning Song
The Raider's Bride
The Raider's Daughter
Restless is the Wind
Stealing Heaven

Available from Pocket Books

KIMBERLY CATES

BRIAR ROSE

SONNET BOOKS

New York   London   Toronto   Sydney   Tokyo   Singapore

An *Original* Publication of POCKET BOOKS

A Sonnet Book published by
POCKET BOOKS, a division of Simon & Schuster Inc.
1230 Avenue of the Americas, New York, NY 10020

ISBN: 0-671-01495-1

First Sonnet Books printing June 1999

10 9 8 7 6 5 4 3 2 1

SONNET BOOKS and colophon are registered trademarks of
Simon & Schuster Inc.

Front cover illustration by Fredericka Ribes, tip-in illustration
by Jon Paul Ferrara

Printed in the U.S.A.

To my niece Alyssa Bush, who "would rather read than anything." Thank you for doing me the great honor of dedicating your first book to me. You asked me to put your name in one of my own books. Here it is, sweetheart. This one is for you.

Much love,
Aunt Kim

BRIAR ROSE

❧ Prologue ❧

The pistol ball seared a lightning-hot bolt through flesh, the bitter tang of gunpowder burning in the air, but Captain Lionel Redmayne scarce felt it. Death—every reluctant soldier's lover—was coming to claim him at last on this barren, deserted stretch of Irish road.

Redmayne leveled his own pistol at shadowy attackers who melted into clumps of heather behind outcroppings of rock, seemingly from the mist itself. Three of them. Maybe four. Scenting his blood.

He could almost taste their victory. He'd have to make this shot count. It might be his last. Anyone familiar with a pistol knew as well as he did that it would take precious seconds for him to reload, seconds in which they could close in for the kill. And in the twenty minutes he'd managed to keep them at bay, these men had shown themselves practiced in every method of dealing death.

It was a miracle he'd held them off this long. If he could fight them blade to blade, he might stand some chance. But they had no interest in a fair fight when they'd ambushed him here in the ruins of

Ballyaroon. They didn't want a battle. They wanted a corpse. His.

He objected, of course, though not out of any grand passion for life. He'd been barely six years old when he realized that dying was easy. It was living that was far harder. In his years in the army he had stared into the face of his own death so many times he'd come to dismiss it as a fleeting nuisance, like the faint buzzing of a bee too close to his ear. He just figured this would be a damned embarrassing way to die.

The infamous, terrifyingly omniscient Captain Lionel Redmayne cut down on a deserted stretch of Irish road because he'd been fool enough to travel without a cadre of guards in a land that would sooner have tea with the devil than with the English army. Not to mention the fact that he'd been too distracted by thoughts that tugged at him, troubled him, like importunate children no matter how resolutely he tried to shove them away.

He fired at a blur of movement, heard a cry of pain. At least he'd have company on his way to hell, he thought with some satisfaction, fighting to reload his pistol.

Who the devil were they? he wondered, struggling to jam another pistol ball down the barrel of his weapon. A man liked to know who was shooting at him.

Who hated him enough to hunt him down? Less capable officers he'd tramped over on his way to promotion; common folk caught in a vise between their well-being and his duty; those who feared him, hated him, or saw him as an impediment standing in their way. A grim smile twisted his lips. It would be far easier to sort out who *didn't* hate him.

Yes, there were plenty who wanted him dead—but there was a perilous step from desiring it to making it a reality. And a towering leap from a bullet or sword blade wielded in a fit of passion against an enemy, to the hiring of an assassin. There was something exceedingly cold-blooded in the knowledge that whoever was responsible for this attack might even now be holding polite conversation at a table glittering with crystal, or lounging in a bedchamber seducing some woman.

But it seemed his question would go unanswered.

Only one thing was certain: once this fight was over, there would be no one to mourn him. Lionel Redmayne would slip beneath the silvery surface of life, leaving not so much as a ripple of grief or loss in any other living soul.

It hadn't mattered a damn to him in fifteen years of campaigning. Why did the thought suddenly leave something hollow, aching in the pit of his stomach?

It was this infernal land where passions lay so thick it was impossible to breathe without sucking them in. It was the memory of one moonlit night when flame-red hair tumbled about a woman's flushed face as she danced for another man, love hot in her eyes. A pulsing ember of life so vivid that for the first time in Redmayne's life he couldn't crush it, even in the name of duty. Mary Fallon Delaney had made a glaring mockery of everything he'd believed about himself. Had made him question . . .

Another shot rang out, and he felt the ball tear through his thigh. His eyes swept the village ruins, suddenly glimpsing a ring of ancient stones half-toppled twenty-five yards distant. If he could reach it, he might be able to . . . to what? Escape was impossible, but the stones might provide enough shelter so that he could take yet another assassin with him when he died. That would be reward enough.

Redmayne grimaced, scrambled upward, his thigh

burning, his head swimming with bitter irony. He'd come to Ireland determined to destroy relics of the past like this ring of stones . . . tear them apart and fling them into the sea. That way the infernal Irish could forget . . . the absurd kiss of magic, the tales of long faded glory, the past that was of no use to them. They would accept the future that was inevitable. He'd been so certain he understood the people of this place. He hadn't expected that he could be sucked into their special brand of madness.

His elbow slammed into a stone, pain jolting through him. He gritted his teeth, pushing harder with his good leg, one hand clamped tight over the wound in his other. He heard a shout, glimpsed the pale flash of a man's face. Near. Too near.

They were closing in on him. . . .

The stone ring swirled around him, dark, cool, unearthly, as he dragged himself into a crook between two stones. As if there were anyplace dark enough to conceal him!

Black haze tugged at him, drawing him deeper into cold, still waters. He heard vague shouts of confusion, but it didn't matter anymore. They would find him. And when they did . . . death.

Images swam beneath his half-closed lids. Papa . . . his father's battered doctor's bag, its shiny contents spilled out on a scarred table, useless at last. Fear clamping tight in his belly, the need to tuck his own small hand in Papa's strong one. But Papa's hands were busy holding on to the blue-veined ones of the old woman. *"Reach out your hand, Mary,"* Papa had urged softly. *"They're waiting for you . . . your mama, your papa, the babes you lost so long ago. Everyone you've ever loved. . . . They've come to lead you to heaven."*

Sure, so sure Papa had been. Lionel had believed it

too. Perhaps he still did. But it didn't matter. Couldn't matter for him.

Redmayne winced at the twisting pain somewhere deep inside him where no bullet could touch. No one would come from heaven to take his hand on this barren hill. Even his compassionate father would turn his back on the man his son had become.

Redmayne closed his eyes, fighting back a wave of quiet despair, waiting for the end. He was tired. So tired, the sharp edges of emotions bleeding, his very body seeming to fade away, a piece at a time. Soon there would be nothing left. But then, had he ever really been anything . . . anyone at all?

Redemption—the word flashed through the red haze of his pain, shimmered there, but he turned his face away. He'd be wiser to put his faith in fairies and magic, in destiny and fate, than to believe in forgiveness for a man like him. There would be no hand stretching down from heaven.

"To the devil, then," he muttered in a rasping breath, reaching into the swirl of mist. "Take me, if you dare."

Chapter

❧ 1 ❧

The fairies were whispering the faintest of warnings, which tingled along Rhiannon Fitzgerald's freckle-spattered cheeks and settled deep into her bones. She braced herself against the rocking of her rainbow-hued gypsy caravan and gripped the reins more tightly. Eyes the warm green-gold of a forest primeval searched the wild, rocky landscape swept clean of afternoon mist. The ghostly ruins that had once been the village of Ballyaroon kept unearthly watch over the quiet hills, standing stones with their well-kept secrets, just visible above the verdant green of the next rise.

"Don't let your imagination run wild, Rhiannon," she chided herself, dashing a wayward lock of cinnamon hair from her cheek. "There is nothing amiss. You're only reacting to this place. Echoes of old pain, old sorrows. They grow louder when you're alone." The thought should have offered more comfort.

After all, her reasoning might be valid enough. From the dawning of her first memory, Rhiannon had felt as if an invisible ribbon stitched into her breast bound her to the heartbeat buried deep in these timeless hills, a link carrying piercing sweetness, sorrowful yearning, a joy and a curse. Stark awareness of things seen and unseen beyond the drab veil of most people's reality—ghost-shadows of ages long vanished, silent cries of wounded woodland creatures, the fragrant magic of healing herbs white witches had gathered when the earth was new, and the irresistible pull of tides called destiny.

It was the gift of the fairy-born, her da had told anyone who would listen. Her mother's parting boon before she returned to the magical kingdom of Tir naN Og, leaving her mortal lover and her child behind.

There were times when Rhiannon wished most fervently her mother had seen fit to leave her something a little less troublesome—a pretty locket, perhaps, or a letter Rhiannon could read—precious words that might bring to life the woman she'd never known.

"The least she could have done was leave instructions on how to turn this—this 'gift' *off* once in a while so I can have some peace," Rhiannon complained to the soft-eyed vixen peering between the slats of an overturned basket beside her. But her vague attempt at humor fell flat. The unsettled feelings only intensified as she peered into that pointed little face, so wise yet so vulnerable beneath wisps of russet fur.

"Perhaps I'm just feeling strange because I'm going to miss you, *mo chroi,*" she said, her throat tightening. A sense of pride and impending loss tugged at her as she shifted both reins to one hand and eased her finger into the basket to stroke a silky ear. "Your foot is all mended now. It's time to set you free."

Free. Far away from the foxhounds that had nearly killed her, or their rich masters, chasing after in a mad rush of wind and scarlet coats and blooded horses, delighting in the hunt.

She gazed at the rocky, wild terrain about her, deserted except for ghosts of rebellions past, a place far distant from any of the great houses that would host the blood sports. Not even the most intrepid fox-hunter would dare traverse such rugged land. Out here the little vixen would have a fighting chance to survive.

So just let her go here, now, and turn around, a voice inside Rhiannon whispered. *Don't venture deeper into whatever disturbance is troubling you. What possible dif-ference could a few more miles make?* All the differ-ence in the world. She could always feel when the place was right to release her creatures, sense it, a tingling in her chest. She'd been so certain the stand-ing stones here above the ruins of Ballyaroon would be perfect, felt herself drawn toward them. Was she listening to warning whispers now, or had she merely discovered the handiest way to postpone releasing her little charge for as long as she could? The crea-ture nibbled, delicate as a duchess, on her finger.

Rhiannon blinked back tears. Yes, that had to be what was troubling her. From the time she'd carried her first wounded bird home to be mended, she'd both loved and hated the day she released her charges back to the wild. But it had been different, back at Primrose Cottage. Papa had been there to drive her out to the small parkland surrounding their modest estate in his gig. Her cousins had scampered about, Orla's eyes round with wonder and excitement as she and Triona pilfered the picnic Cook had pre-pared. Warm gingerbread and sour lemonade to take away the bite of sadness Rhiannon felt when she let her creatures go.

Now there was only the wide, empty sky, the whick-ering of Socrates the dray horse, the bumbling of Mil-ton the foxhound as he ran into anything in his path, and the self-satisfied purring of Captain Blood the one-eyed feline with a pirate's heart. The family that had delighted in those soft summer skies was long gone.

No, that wasn't true, Rhiannon thought. She could still feel their presence in the mist. Hear the echo of their laughter in the wind. Sometimes it was almost as if they touched her. Papa, stolen by the hungry waves of the sea. Mama, that beautiful misty woman who lived only in her imagination. But she could call back so many precious memories, finger them like polished stones. And she could visit Triona and her new husband, John, whenever the silence got too loud or the road too solitary.

Her mouth curved, a little wistful at the memory of Triona's pleas that she stay on at the MacKenna farm forever, the worry in her cousin's eyes warming Rhiannon's heart. "You shouldn't be alone out there with Uncle Kevin gone," Triona had said. "Something could happen. You could get hurt, grow sick, and no one might know until it was too late. And there are men— desperate men who might—"

"You know I don't have to be afraid, Triona," Rhiannon had replied. "The fairies look after their own."

Triona's brow had crinkled, troubled. " 'Tis a lovely story, being fairy-born, Rhiannon, but . . . but you can't still believe it's true."

Taken by a mischievous streak, Rhiannon had stared at her cousin with wide-eyed innocence, protesting that she accepted her father's tale as gospel. And yet she'd realized long ago that, pretty as the story was, it was also the perfect way to ease the pain for a little girl whose mama had abandoned her and never looked back. And it *had* softened the pain, at least a little, with glittering magical possibilities.

She had brushed aside Triona's concerns but held fast to the precious gift of love that lit her cousin's eyes. And she tried hard never to forget how very lucky she was.

Besides, she knew something Triona couldn't understand. She was never *really* alone. She smiled, stroking the fox's ear one last time. "One thing I can be certain of, little one. Your basket will be filled before I know it. It won't be long before the fates will put another wounded creature in my path."

With wry humor, she turned her attention back to her driving, uncertain where she would find herself. Socrates was given to taking shameless advantage of his mistress's notorious lack of concentration, veering off course to munch any patch of likely-looking clover he could sniff out. Once she'd been roused from daydreams to find he'd followed a hay cart halfway to Dublin! But in an uncharacteristic burst of obedience, the beast had stayed on track, almost as if he, too, felt the tug of their destination.

She looked up in surprise. The shattered cottages of the village had fallen behind her, and the towering fingers of the standing stones reared up before her, so close she could see the ancient symbols carved into their gray surfaces, hear the echoes of bards' songs still tangled about them.

She'd always felt fascination when stumbling across the fairy forts and dolmens, the passage graves and crumbling castle ruins that dotted the land. But this time there was something different in the haunting melody of the wind, a pulsing rhythm more urgent.

She tried to grasp it, hoped to unravel its meaning, but suddenly Socrates dug his hooves into the turf, balking so abruptly he nearly overset Rhiannon. She clutched at the overturned basket, just managing to keep it from flying off the seat, the vixen darting about in alarm as pans hanging from the ceiling inside the caravan crashed against each other in a resounding cacophony of clangs.

"What in the name of heaven?" Rhiannon choked out, trying to calm the horse as he tossed his head, trying to shy sideways. The unease she'd done her best to explain away flooded back, more insistent than ever.

"Whist, now, Socrates, whist," she murmured in the special voice that had soothed countless wild things. The horse pricked his ears, stood still, but she could see the fine tremor skating beneath his disreputable gray hide.

Carefully she got down out of the cart and tied him to a low-hanging branch. The last thing she wanted was to have to go chasing after him. She doubted he could rouse enough energy to run very far, but there was no point in taking any chances.

She grabbed another basket dangling from the side of the cart. If there *was* something wounded taking shelter hereabouts, she didn't want to give it a chance to slip away. And she'd learned from bitter childhood experience that she wouldn't do the creature any good if she scooped it up with her bare hands and got the blessed daylights chewed out of herself. But even such reasoning didn't ease the trembling in her stomach. She'd made this journey countless times. Why did this time feel so different?

Rhiannon moved toward the ring of stones, her bare feet soft and soundless as the vixen's paws, her gaze searching every clump of gorse and heather, every shadowed nook, looking for the tiniest glimpse of fur or subtle gleam of a wary eye.

But she found nothing, no velvet-eared rabbit, no broken-winged hawk or lame fawn. Then why did she feel so—so odd? Her arm ached. Her left leg threatened to crumple beneath her. And her chest . . . a cord seemed to be tightening about it until it became difficult to breathe, her heart pounding so loud it seemed the birds overhead must hear it.

She frowned, listening for the slightest stirring that might betray a hiding place, but she heard nothing. Perhaps if she climbed to a higher vantage point, she might be able to see better. That overturned slab near the largest crossbar of stone looked like a promising spot.

She moved toward it and was knee deep in a tangle of gypsy roses the glorious mauve of a sunset when she scented something far different from the sweet flower fragrance or the meadow winds. The metallic tang of fresh-spilled blood. Burned sulfur . . . gunpowder. And pain—blinding red.

Caution vanished in its wake. She scrambled toward the stones, certain that something injured lay nearby. Had some hunter found this place? Had his prey eluded him, dragged itself away to die? Wild creatures had a gift for hiding themselves, quietly bleeding to death where nothing and no one could find them. The thought of any living thing suffering alone, possibly dying without so much as a comforting touch to soothe it, ripped at Rhiannon's heart, more than she could bear.

She hadn't spoken the plea since she was a girl, full of rich imaginings, still believing everything her papa had told her. But the aura of pain was so strong, the desperation so fierce, the hopelessness so deep, she couldn't help but use it.

"Help me, Mama," she whispered to the wind. "Help me find—" The words died on her lips. She halted, a cry tearing from her throat as her foot nearly tramped on a man's bloodstained hand.

She blinked fiercely, still scarce believing her eyes. Why in God's name hadn't she seen him from a mile down the road? His red coat gleamed like a fresh wound in the hill. The merest glimpse of the uniform sent spikes of unease shooting through her.

An officer. English. Up here in these wild lands, alone. What could he possibly be doing here? She caught her lip between her teeth, hesitating, wary. Few times in her travels had she been afraid, but twice she and Papa had stumbled across soldiers reeking of whiskey and hostility. The first time Papa had distracted them with magic tricks he'd learned from Gypsy travelers, the second an officer with a Yorkshire accent and the loneliest eyes Rhiannon had ever seen had driven them away before more than a few pots had been broken. And yet she'd never forgotten the bitter taste of fear in the back of her throat, the sense of helplessness.

Yes, an English soldier could be more dangerous than a pain-maddened wolf, and far more unpredictable. For an instant, just an instant, she wished she could turn, run back to her cart. No one need know she had ever found the officer. For all she knew, he deserved the bullets that had wounded him. And yet . . . even as the thought formed, she shook herself fiercely.

He was hurt. Be he human or beast, English or Irish, that was all that mattered. She'd been given the gift of healing, not the power to decide who was worthy of life or death.

Fighting to steady herself inwardly, Rhiannon dropped to her knees beside him, pressing her fingertips to the pulse point of his throat. The faint thrum of heartbeat against her skin jolted through her with the unearthly sizzle of lightning splitting a druid tree. It breached something deep inside Rhiannon, left her shaken.

In that instant his features seared themselves into

her consciousness. Silvery-blond hair tangled about a face no one could look upon and ever forget. Papa had told her once of a prince so beautiful no one could ever tire of looking upon him. They'd buried him in a magical coffin of glass when he died. She'd thought the tale absurd until now.

Power emanated from every line and curve of the man's countenance even in unconsciousness. Strength and intelligence etched the broad brow, ruthlessness and arrogance shaped the angle of prominent cheek-bones, yet there was just a hint of softness about his parted lips, so subtle few would have been able to discern it.

This was absurd! she raged at herself. She had to tend his wounds, see how he'd been injured. Just because he was alive at this moment didn't mean he would remain so while she stood here gawking at him like a dolt.

Scrambling to gather her wits, she searched for the wounds—a torn and bloodied sleeve. Another ragged, glistening tear in his left thigh. The large amount of blood told her that this wound was obviously worse. Cursing herself for her ridiculous hesitation, she ripped off a strip of her petticoat and wrestled with the deadweight of his injured leg as she tried to tie it above the wound to stop the bleeding. Then, fishing in the pouch she ever kept tied at her waist, she took out her papa's penknife and worked to cut the fabric away from the wound.

The slightest groan squeezed from between the soldier's white lips, and he shifted, trying to get away from the pain. If he awakened, the process of baring his wounds would be all the more painful. He might hurt himself or fight her—and he had the look of a man who could overpower her in a heartbeat, wounded or whole.

Voice unsteady, Rhiannon began to sing, low, soft, the soothing song she'd always used to quiet her animal patients. The song Papa had insisted Mama brought from the land of the fairies. Whether it was just another of his stories, Rhiannon was never certain. But the haunting melody did seem to hold its own brand of enchantment. The soldier knotted one of his hands in Rhiannon's skirts, as if to assure himself he wasn't alone. Then he quieted, allowing her to bind the nasty gash in his arm.

She glanced back at the smear of color that was her gypsy cart, uncertain. God above, what was she going to do? She'd stopped the worst of the bleeding, but she could hardly treat his wounds here. What if the men who had done this to him returned to make certain he was dead? She'd have no way to fend them off.

What if you discover he deserved the bullets that felled him? a voice whispered in her head. "That's absurd," she said aloud. "I'd be able to *feel* it." Truth was, she *should* have been able to sense his goodness or wickedness. From the time she was a babe, she'd had that gift as well. She should be able to probe into the essence of his soul with just a touch. But it was as if this place, with its ancient voices, was hazing this man in its mist. Or wasn't it this place at all? Was it the man himself who was so resolutely closed to her, closed to anything or anyone that might breach his defenses? Whatever kind of man he was, she couldn't leave him to suffer.

No one deserved this kind of agony. The only thing to do was to patch him together to the best of her ability.

Climbing to her feet, she stumbled toward the cart, determined to lead Socrates as close as possible. She prayed she could get the officer inside.

She had to lift him into the wagon and then hasten as far away from this place as she could, to someplace where she could care for his wounds, help him regain his strength. Someplace where even the fairies could not find them.

Perhaps the devil was short of assistants, Redmayne thought through a haze of pain. The torturing demons were doing an exemplary job on his thigh and his arm, but the rest of him seemed relatively untouched.

He fought to detach himself from the agony, float above it, beyond the reach of fiery pincers, a ploy that had stood him in good stead during countless other battle wounds. *"Control it, Lionel,"* his grandfather's steely voice reverberated inside his head. *"They can touch you only if you are weak enough to allow them to."* But it wasn't the pain crushing him in its grip this time. It was the barren reaches inside his soul, the overwhelming sense of waste. . . .

What did it matter if he screamed for an eternity? No one would hear him. No one would care.

Fool, he derided himself in disgust. Don't be a fool. Whatever lies beyond this mist, face it like a man. If it's hell you're in, you deserve it. You've earned it.

If they kept a tally of sins in the Dark One's kingdom, Lionel Redmayne's must be long indeed.

With fierce determination, he tried to force his eyes open, the lids so heavy they seemed nailed to his cheekbones. Spears of light screwed relentlessly into the center of his skull, his stomach threatening revolt as he struggled to focus.

What the blazes? The thought streaked through his beleaguered brain. In his famed *Inferno*, Dante had neglected to mention this garish form of torture—hell was decorated in colors that would make any rational man seasick. Bright blue blotched with gold. Sour-apple green and bile yellow with something like red snakes writhing about.

Most alarming of all, bare inches from his nose a single green eye in a distorted, hirsute face peered down at him, unblinking. Instinctively he tried to shift away from it, but it moved with him, inescapable.

Suddenly something swept it out of the way, a voice, a low, scolding murmur, drifting through the haze. Another figure appeared in its place. A soft, pale oval swam before him—large, troubled green-gold eyes, spice-brown hair. A mouth carved with generosity and sweetness. An angel? He marveled. Was it possible?

"Whist, now, lie still." An Irish angel, her voice filled with winsome music, her brow creasing in concern. Heaven . . . was he in heaven? He swallowed hard. There must be some sort of mistake. God knew, when they found it, he'd be hurled down into the abyss. He had to lie still, quiet, not betray the truth about himself.

She leaned closer, her bosom brushing against him, the kind shaped to pillow a man's weary head, soft and inviting and . . . askew. Her lace collar was half turned under one ear, a button had popped off, wisps of hair tumbling in a most troubling disarray. An untidy angel? He couldn't remember any such in the pictures he'd seen as a lad. Every wing feather had been in place with military precision, every golden tress expertly curled. She evidenced a most appalling lack of heavenly discipline.

He tried to speak through parched lips. "Wh-who are . . . Wh-where . . ."

"I'm going to take care of you. I promise," the angel vowed gravely. "It will all be over in a moment."

"Over? Wh-what?"

She drew something from behind her. Redmayne shrank back as he stared at the fire poker, glowing white-hot, coming nearer, nearer.

This must be hell after all!

Her hand was quivering so hard it would be a wonder if she didn't set the whole place on fire—as if the devil needed any assistance. "Forgive my shaking," she apologized, polite demon that she was. "I've done this to several dogs, but never to a man. It must work about the same, don't you think?"

"Torture . . . dogs in . . . hell? What for? Biting masters? Stealing old women's parcels?"

"Hell? What are you talking about? You've been shot. I just mean to cauterize your wounds. It's the only way to make certain they don't putrefy."

He struggled partially upright, his head cracking into something hanging above him. "Cauterize my wounds? That means I'm . . . still alive." He felt no particular pleasure in the realization.

Those green eyes widened with astonishment beneath ridiculously thick lashes. "Of course you're still alive!"

"I prefer to stay that way. Give me . . . that."

"Wh-what?"

"The poker. I'll do it myself."

Horror flooded a face far too tender for such a cynical world. "You can't possibly—"

"I'm afraid I must . . . insist. You're shaking so hard you'll never hit the wound. I prefer only . . . one attempt."

She still didn't look ready to surrender her mission, but he grasped her hand where it was curled around the poker. Warm, soft, capable, her skin shielding him from the hardness of the metal. He steeled himself; then ruthlessly he glared down at the wound in his leg and shoved the hot end of the poker onto the ragged flesh.

Agony seared through every pore in his body, sweat breaking out, but the only cry came from the woman—miserable, soft. He made not a sound, fighting back the sickness from the stench of burning flesh.

Twice more he applied the hot iron to his own wounds before the agony took him to blessed blackness, an abyss of silence. Peace.

Yet even as he let go of consciousness, something pried its way into his mind. Something warm, wet, splashing onto his skin. Tears. The woman bending over him had tears streaking her face. Perhaps she was an angel after all, Redmayne marveled. For only an angel would cry over him.

Chapter

2

Rhiannon hurled the iron poker out the rear door of the caravan, the instrument clattering to the dirt. Horror reverberated in the pit of her stomach. She gripped one of the roof braces to keep her knees from buckling, despising herself for her own weakness.

What right did *she* have to be so shaken? She hadn't had her flesh seared, hadn't felt the piercing of a bullet or the crushing hopelessness as her blood had ebbed into the dirt beneath where she lay. She hadn't waited, alone, for death, like the man whose inert body overwhelmed her small bed.

And yet her nerves were as raw as if she'd suffered that, and more. Her whole body ached from the herculean effort of dragging the wounded officer to the caravan, her nerves frayed by the desperate ride away from the ring of standing stones, her eyes searching the wild lands for any hint of his attackers returning to make certain their quarry was dead.

But most disturbing of all was the memory that had seared itself into her mind—the officer's features when he'd grasped her wrist and forced the glowing point of iron into the raw mouth of his own wound.

If eyes were said to be windows into the soul, the view beyond his was a frightening vista. Terrifyingly cool, his mouth white-lipped, yet curled in something akin to amusement, his voice pain-racked, and yet so—so cynical: "You're shaking so hard you'll never hit the wound. I prefer only one attempt."

What kind of man could be so completely untouched by his own agony? A dangerous man. One completely unpredictable.

She caught her bottom lip between her teeth and turned back to look at him, so still, so seemingly vulnerable, helpless. But he wouldn't be thus forever. Her fingers stole up to the place where her lace collar sagged open, her throat bare. There she touched the fading scars that marred the smooth skin, a tracery of teeth marks that might have ended her life.

She closed her eyes, remembering the wolf she'd once found, so weak it couldn't lift its great head. She'd tended it, trusted it. But the instant it was strong enough, she'd opened its cage, only to have the beast try to tear out her throat. If she hadn't managed to grasp the broom handle, strike the creature in its wounded side, God alone knew what might have happened.

Yet even as Papa had tended the gashes left by the fangs, Rhiannon hadn't blamed the animal. The fault had been her own. She'd known what he was when she took him in.

The wolf she'd been able to lock away in a cage, but she couldn't handle this English officer so simply. The one thing she was certain of was that he was a man wreathed in violence—his very life's work was bound up in hurting instead of healing, imposing the will of a mightier country on a weaker one. And that was not the least of her worries.

One of the first lessons she and her father had

learned on the road was that a traveler depended on the goodwill of the settled people to survive. Even the villagers Rhiannon had come to trust might now become foes because of this Englishman.

She shivered. The wounds from the rebellion were still raw years later. There could be little doubt that she had crossed an invisible line the moment she took the Englishman in. Many in Ireland would see that as treason.

Even once he got well, she could hardly just open the caravan door and set him free the way she did her creatures. God above, what had she gotten herself into?

"Whatever it is, you're in it neck deep," she told herself. "You can hardly dump him in the middle of the road now. Best to do your utmost to make him well and hope that he doesn't leave any teeth marks before he goes."

If that was to be her plan, there was a great deal to do before he awakened again. She had to make him as comfortable as possible now that the first stage of his ordeal was over—after all, an uncomfortable wolf had a tendency to bite.

Steadying herself, she moved toward the bed. She needed to get him out of those bloody clothes, wash them in the stream, bathe the grime and blood from his skin. Poultices to help soothe the cruel burns. And gruel . . . he would need some hearty gruel when he awakened, to help him regain his strength.

More than any of that, she needed a name to call him as she tended him. She doubted he'd appreciate her christening him after some long dead poet or philosopher.

Yet despite all the things she needed to tend to, she hesitated, her fingers gripping the crossbar of wood as she stared down into the officer's face, uncertain as if . . . as if what? He'd snap off her fingers with his teeth?

"This is absurd," she muttered to herself. "Do you want him to awaken and have to endure being shifted around, having his wounds jarred because you were a coward?" Besides, this was a military man. He'd understand her need to discover his identity. It wasn't as if she meant to rifle through his pockets to steal his watch!

But there were things far more precious and sacred than mere bits of gold, private dreamings, tender secrets of the soul. Even English officers had to possess a few of those, she believed, although there were plenty in Ireland who would insist there was nothing but a yawning black cavern where their hearts were supposed to be.

Decidedly uncomfortable, she felt his uniform jacket, hearing the crinkling of paper beneath her hand. Withdrawing an official-looking document, she read the name penned on it so precisely: Captain L. Redmayne.

L. Redmayne. What did the L stand for? She wondered. Linus? Lovett? More likely Lucifer?

Lucifer . . . that most beautiful of all angels, fallen from heaven itself to carve out his own kingdom below. A dark place. A tragic one. She shivered, sensing that this man would have the power to tempt any woman to sin.

She knew nothing of him, only his name, which she'd stolen from the smooth surface of the letter. Knew nothing about the enemies he'd faced in the looming shadows of the standing stones. That information might prove crucial if she tried to protect him during the journey back to wherever he belonged. She glanced down again at the letter she held. Might this missive hold some vital bit of intelligence that would help save both their lives?

She nibbled at one ragged fingernail, uneasy at the prospect of prying into an unconscious man's correspondence. For all she knew, it might be a love letter from a sweetheart or wife far away. Yet wouldn't it be crumpled then? Edges frayed from reading it over and over? This was crisp, the seal new-broken.

In any case, she might need whatever information the letter held if she was to navigate them through the next few days. There was no telling how long Captain Redmayne would be incapacitated by the wounds he'd suffered.

Pricklings of guilt stinging her cheeks, Rhiannon slipped her thumb beneath the broken seal, opening the missive. Holding it to the light, she read: "The most dangerous serpent is the one who sleeps beneath your own roof."

Chill fingers seemed to skate down her spine. She shuddered. A warning—vivid enough. A traitor coiled somewhere within his very garrison, waiting to poison this man with its venom. She read on: "Would you know your enemy's name? Meet me at the town well in the village of Ballyaroon Wednesday next. I will find you among the crowd."

Among the crowd at Ballyaroon? Her brow wrinkled. No one walked there but ghosts. It was nothing but rubble in the middle of nowhere, the town utterly destroyed by the English during the rebellion of 1798. Why would anyone write such a thing? Because he didn't intend a meeting with Captain Redmayne at all—except at the deadly end of a pistol barrel.

She swallowed hard. That had to be it. Ballyaroon might no longer be a village, but it was completely deserted, miles from anywhere, anyone. No one dared stray near it, haunted as it was by screams of those too newly dead. It was the perfect place to lure some-one you intended to murder.

God above, had this man been mad to come here? As if treachery among his own ranks wasn't danger enough, he'd be loathed like a rabid wolf by every Irish-born crofter who crossed his path.

Hatred of the English had been a chronic fever in Irish blood for six hundred years. It surged into vio-lence and then, battered back by British swords, sank beneath the surface again to simmer in the veins until it broke into yet another rebellion. An officer acciden-tally separated from the rest of his men might easily become a target. Captain Redmayne must have known how dangerous it was when he found himself alone.

She folded up the letter again, her fingers plucking nervously at the seal. The good news was that his assailants must know how deserted this place was. Perhaps they hadn't searched for him at all after he was shot. Once wounded, they would believe there was no chance that their quarry could escape alive.

In all likelihood they'd ridden away, certain of their triumph. If not dead already, Redmayne would bleed to death in but little time. No one who knew the iso-lated reaches around Ballyaroon would guess that any living soul would trek up into this fiercely lonely wild place.

He'd been hunted, left for dead. And for some rea-son fate had seen fit to cast him into her path. But Rhiannon was Irish enough to know that fate could be malevolent as well as kind, cruel as well as kissed by magic. Time alone would tell which spirits had been responsible for the outcome of this day.

Returning the letter to Captain Redmayne's pocket, she turned to an equally disturbing task, getting him out of his soiled clothes.

Grasping the heel, she worked the polished boot

from his uninjured leg, then attempted to strip away the other. A low groan tore from the officer's throat. She winced. Only one thing to do. Cut it away, so it wouldn't hurt quite so much. She grasped heavy shears and carefully slid one blade inside the expensive leather. A sheen of perspiration dotted her brow as she wrestled with the recalcitrant leather, even the officer's boot seeming to object to suffering the indignation of such clumsy handling.

The boot thunked to the floor at last, and she glided her hands up the muscled length of his calf to ease down his bloodstained stockings. The instant her fingertips brushed his bare skin, her cheeks tingled and she felt a need to turn her eyes away—an entirely impractical notion—yet this was a man . . . a man's body beneath her hands. A very handsome one at that. Sick or well, she was undressing him.

She swallowed hard. What kind of featherbrained idiot was she, indulging in such nonsensical thoughts? He was injured. He needed her help. And she wasn't some giggling schoolgirl to be reacting this way.

Resolutely she stripped away his other stocking, trying not to notice how strong, how beautifully shaped, his feet were. Moistening her lips, she moved to the red coat. Reluctant again to jar one of his wounds, she took up the shears, making short work of the fine red wool, the dashing gold braid. In minutes it joined the boots in ribbons on the floor.

The shirt he wore beneath was still pristine white where the jacket had protected it, only the ripped sleeve blood-soaked. She slipped her fingers beneath his neckcloth, unnerved by the vulnerability of the skin at his throat, the pulsebeat, faint but steady, the soft stirring of his breath against her wrist as she unknotted the cloth and slid it from beneath his neck.

Then, fearing that she might nick him, Rhiannon

opened his shirt enough to slide her hand inside it, laying the outer edge of the scissor blade against her own palm as she snipped the exquisite linen away. A broad landscape of muscles rippled against the back of her hand. Ridges, hard and powerful, beneath skin like rough satin. Warmth seeped through her, fiendishly intimate, the soft prickle of a silken web of hair roughening the hard plane ever so slightly.

She glanced back up at his face, the aristocratic line of his jaw, the arrogant slash of nose, the chiseled perfection of his parted lips, exquisite despite their pallor, enthralling despite his unconsciousness. What would he think if he awakened to find her handling him thus? The coolness of his eyes, like ice in a mountain stream, flickered into her memory.

The scissors slipped, sharp pain slicing into her thumb. Rhiannon yelped, yanking her hand out from beneath the shirt, thrusting the wounded digit into her mouth, a hot flush of embarrassment flooding her whole body. She was appalling, thinking such things about the poor man while he lay there, helpless!

But she had to admit that it had felt so good to touch someone, to feel human warmth, a need even her precious woodland creatures couldn't fully satisfy. Before Papa died, there had been hugs aplenty— she'd never passed him without his reaching out to tug her curls or pat her cheek or scoop her up in a loving embrace. She'd never realized how much she missed that contact until now.

But this was hardly the same. This man was helpless, in her care. And yet perhaps, hurt as he was, *he* needed the comfort as much as she did. Maybe there was a loved one he was worrying about, missing, someone wondering why he hadn't returned to his post. A sweetheart or a wife, a passel of golden-haired children. Why was it that the possibility stung her so badly? Because once she had dreamed of having her own rollicking brood, one more hope that had faded.

Taking fierce hold of her ridiculous emotions, Rhiannon returned to her task, ridding the captain of his shirt. But as she stripped it away, she discovered something far more unnerving: raised slashes where sabers must have bitten, scars from battles he'd fought, deaths he'd barely escaped. He was a soldier. It shouldn't have surprised her that he carried such marks of his trade.

But no creature so beautiful should have been savaged this way. What had these wounds and the violence they represented cost him? Not only his body but his soul?

Somber, she worked to remove the breeches that clung to the officer's lean hips and steely-thewed thighs like a second skin. Rhiannon eased off his breeches, then took a clean rag, a bucket of water, and began gently scrubbing away the smears of dirt, the dark stains of blood. First, his face—haughty angles, broad brow, stubborn jaw—then down the cords of his throat.

If he'd been Irish, she might have thought him king of the otherworld come out to wander—all powerful, ruthless, perhaps a trifle cruel—come to take a mortal he desired. But he wasn't a man born to standing stones and tales of fairy magic, myths of Cuchulain or Manannán mac Lir, Celtic god of the sea. He was polished to a far different sheen, this man.

Glistening with dampness, scrubbed clean, he seemed like some warrior Caesar, vast empires crushed beneath his heel. A man completely out of place in this humble gypsy caravan, with its bright paint and cramped quarters, sheets so often washed they were worn soft as a baby's cheek.

She drew the sheet up over his body.

"Sleep now. Rest," she whispered to him. "I've got you safe." His eyes fluttered open for a moment, heart-piercingly blue.

"Safe?" He laughed, an ugly sound.

She reached out to touch him.

He stiffened. "No . . . don't . . ." A groan tore from his lips. Then he sagged back, unconscious. Had she hurt him somehow? Jarred his wound? Rhiannon wondered in dismay.

"I'm sorry," she murmured, stunned to find that even though he was still again, his image was branded into her mind. That face, so white, that gaze, so disturbing.

What was it Papa had always told her? There were some deeds so dark that no salvation could touch the sinner; a shadow of the past would always cling to his eyes. To such men, death was a gift.

Rhiannon had wanted so badly to believe that no one was ever beyond hope, beyond help. But as she stared into the chiseled features of the English officer, she wondered if those ice-blue eyes that had pierced her to her soul were the very kind Papa had warned of so long ago.

Redmayne struggled within the red mist, sinking and falling, drifting and sailing, lost in a place woven of shadows. Shadows he dreaded, fought a lifetime to forget. Dangerous. So dangerous to let them in, haunting, crippling, weakening him like a subtle poison. But he was tired, too tired to escape them this time, to lock them back into the darkest reaches of that exquisite hell called memory.

The chamber waited for him—huge and cold and glittering red. Rippling bed-curtains the color of fire materialized out of the mist, unfurling like the wings of some hungry dragon around the vast, heavily

carved bed, swallowing its prey whole. The boy huddled within the belly of the beast, drawing himself
into a ball, his white-gold hair tousled, his small hands
clutching his knees against his chest to hold the sobs
inside. Couldn't let them out. Couldn't . . .

Desperate, he folded himself up inside, ever so
tightly again and again and again, every fear and grief,
every bit of pain or joy. Make it smaller and smaller
until every fragment of himself disappeared where the
man could never find it.

Fire bloomed in Redmayne's shoulder as he stirred,
restless, trying to shift away so he wouldn't have to
see the boy, the glittering chamber, feel the crushing
sense of helplessness.

But he couldn't escape, trapped as surely as the
child was within that hazy world. The gilt door
creaked open, light from it slashing across the mist-
shrouded bed. He could feel the boy's heart thunder-
ing, the fear, the despair clawing in his throat. Footsteps, so soft for such a big man, drummed in
Redmayne's ears.

Eyes like pale stones peered down through the
swirling haze, probing like fingers, as if they could
peel back the top of the boy's head and see inside.
Sweat beaded Redmayne's brow, trickled down his
throat. No! He didn't want anyone to see.

"Papa," the boy cried out. "Papa!"

"Your papa isn't here," a dragon-voice murmured,
so quiet, so cold. "You belong to me now."

Redmayne woke with a start, fighting to shove himself upright. Pain exploded in his shoulder, his arm
collapsing beneath him, hurling him back against the
mound of damp pillows. Knife blades seemed to screw
themselves into his shoulder, but even that breath-
stealing pain couldn't fully banish the icy shadows of

the dragon bed or kill the taste of the little boy's cry on his lips.

Something butterfly-soft brushed his brow. "Captain Redmayne?"

The sweet feminine voice stunned him. He clung to it, trying to wrench himself away from the child and the chamber and the echoes that haunted him there. Sweeping the last webs of unconsciousness from his brain, Redmayne forced his eyes open, staring into a face oddly familiar. Spice-colored hair, freckles, huge worried eyes. He'd thought her an angel. But no self-respecting angel would let her charge stumble into hell.

"Captain Redmayne," she urged gently. "You called for your father just now."

Redmayne stiffened, appalled. Had he called the name aloud? It was contemptible enough to do so in one's dreams, but to voice the name where someone else could hear was unthinkable.

"I'll get word to your father that you've been hurt," the woman said. "Just tell me where I can reach him."

"Six feet under." Redmayne forced his voice into some semblance of his accustomed chill drawl.

The woman looked as horrified as if she'd kicked him in his wound. "I—I'm sorry."

"Don't exert yourself into paroxysms of regret, madam. It happened too long ago to be of any consequence." He grimaced, glancing about. "Who are you, and exactly where am I?"

"My name is Rhiannon Fitzgerald. And you're in my gypsy cart in a glen ten miles from the ruins of Ballyaroon."

Redmayne should have been grateful, her answer scattering the last vestiges of his dream to the winds. Other images flooded to replace them. Deserted roads he'd traversed alone. Battered ruins that had once been a village. The first crack of a shot shattering the unearthly stillness. A trap laid ever so carefully for a fool careless enough to wander into it.

By all logical accounts, he should be on his way to hell now. He could remember his enemies closing in on him. The tramping of their footsteps drawing ever nearer to the ring of stones in which he'd sought shelter until at last it seemed they should be treading on his very hand. And even if he dismissed that extraordinary escape, they should have hunted him down while he lay flat on his back, unconscious. God knew, it should've been easy enough for his enemies to find this monstrosity the woman called a gypsy cart.

If and when they did find him, this time he'd be ready.

Instinctively, Redmayne groped at his waist. "My pistol—where's my pistol."

She looked puzzled for a moment, then sighed. "It's in the clearing where I found you, I suppose."

"Could I trouble you to go and fetch it?"

"I'm afraid it's ten miles away, and growing dark. It could be anywhere between here and Ballyaroon. I was somewhat distracted because of your wounds."

Redmayne's lips tightened. "I see. I suppose it doesn't matter. After all, you must have some kind of weapon hereabouts, traveling the way you do."

"I have Milton." She smiled at him.

"Milton? Is that your husband?" He should have been more relieved at the prospect.

"No. I'm not married." A becoming pink stained her cheeks. The woman was blushing, and a horde of frustrated assassins might be swarming down on the cart at any moment!

Redmayne pressed his fingertips to his throbbing temple.

"If you would allow me to speak to this Milton,

whoever he is, Miss Fitzgerald, I'm certain we can come to an understanding—"

"I don't think it would do much good. You see, Milton is my dog. He takes great pride in guarding the camp. He had a most unfortunate collision with a horse's hoof when he was foxhunting, and ever since then his senses haven't been quite clear. He has a habit of growling at tree roots and missing entirely any rabbits that run beneath his nose. But he tries very hard to be fierce when he isn't stumbling into trees."

Redmayne grimaced. "I hope he writes poetry better than he keeps watch."

A tentative smile curved those too tender lips. For an instant he wondered if he'd ever been quite so innocent. "I'm afraid I named him Milton not because of his literary prowess, but because—"

"Because he can't see well. But I must say, it's obvious even the beast sees things more clearly than you do."

"I don't understand."

"What were you thinking? A lone woman, taking up a strange man in the middle of nowhere—a man who'd obviously been shot and left for dead. Any person with half a wit would have left me there and driven as far away as possible. I doubt the men who did this to me would be averse to putting a few holes in you for good measure while your guard dog attacked his own shadow."

Surprising himself with a sharp tug of impatience, Redmayne struggled to sit up, the fresh-smelling sheet sliding down the plane of his chest to pool against his stomach. He glimpsed the pale tan of his bare skin. What the devil?

He couldn't remember the last time he'd felt bed linen against his skin. He'd slept in his shirt and

breeches as long as he could remember, always prepared to rush from his chamber in a heartbeat. Battles
and ambushes, emergencies of all kinds, didn't keep
regular daytime hours, and a commander would look
dashed foolish running around with a sheet clasped
about his hips.

He raised his gaze coolly to the young woman, intensely aware of his own nakedness, and that she had
seen it. Why should the thought be so unnerving? "My
clothes seem to have gone missing. Don't tell me you
left those back in the clearing, too?"

"Oh, no," she said earnestly. "I washed them in the
stream. They're all dry now."

If Rhiannon Fitzgerald had had time to do all that,
he must have been unconscious for hours. Had he
been muttering in his sleep the whole while? The
thought rose, most unwelcome.

She retrieved a bundle of clothing, presenting it to
him. "They were bloody from your wounds, you see."

"I suppose I should thank you. I abhor disarray."
He looked pointedly at Rhiannon Fitzgerald's decidedly mussed gown. Crumpled and faded, the blue
gown looked worn as soft as satin molded to her generous curves.

He took up his linen shirt, intending to put it on,
then froze in astonishment. The garment hung in pristine ribbons, sleeve slit, front slashed. The uniform
jacket was the same, and his breeches thus desecrated as well. He stared down at them, then raised
his eyes to her face with an expression that had made
battle-toughened sergeants' knees rattle together in
dread. "Do you have such ill luck with all the clothing
you wash, Miss Fitzgerald? Or were you attempting to
wash your breakfast knives at the same time?"

The woman actually smiled at him, heedless. "I

didn't want to hurt you, wrestling you around to get you out of your clothes, so I cut them off."

Redmayne let silence fall for a moment. "I don't suppose you have a spare captain's uniform stashed somewhere in this disarray?" He glanced around the cramped quarters, every inch crammed with God alone knew what.

She flushed. "I'm afraid not. You could wrap yourself in one of my petticoats for the time being. It would hardly matter, since you need to stay in bed."

Redmayne's eyes widened just a trifle. "I doubt the color would suit me. I'm afraid my own garments will have to do." He started to wrap the remnants of his shirt about him.

"But there's no reason you have to dress. You'll hardly offend my modesty since I was the one who"—she had the grace to falter—"who undressed you."

"Your modesty doesn't concern me in the least, madam. My duty does. I have to get back to the garrison immediately."

"The garrison? But the nearest one is—"

"Thirty miles away. I'm aware of that."

"You couldn't possibly walk so far! You'd fall on your face before you got out of the glen!"

"I don't intend to walk. You must have a horse to pull this thing—unless of course, the multitalented Milton is excellent between the traces."

"No. Socrates pulls the cart."

Redmayne grimaced. "No wonder the poor man drank hemlock. Coming down in the world from philosopher to such manual labor must have been most distressing."

"Socrates is my *horse*," she confided with such insufferable earnestness Redmayne ground his teeth.

"Yes. I'd managed to figure that out before now. I'm afraid I'll have to trespass on his good nature, ride him to the garrison. Once I reach it, I'll send a contingent of my men to bring him back to you, laden with a purse large enough to compensate for your trouble and his further humiliation."

"I'm afraid that would be impossible even if you *were* strong enough to attempt it. Socrates won't allow anyone but Captain Blood ride him."

"Captain Blood? You have a pirate stashed beneath the bed? Now I know what happened to my clothing— a round of cutlass practice."

"Captain Blood is my cat." She gestured to a tabby who looked as if he'd ended up on the losing end of a fight. One ear had a decidedly chewed appearance, one eye was missing. "I'm surprised you didn't notice him. He seems to have taken a liking to sleeping on your chest, despite all the times I chased him off."

Redmayne recalled the single amber eye staring down at him when he first stirred into consciousness. Not the devil but a cat. Most embarrassing. "If your cat can ride the horse, I can. I assure you, madam, the mount hasn't been born that I cannot control."

"You've never met Socrates! But even if he were the most docile of beasts, you couldn't manage it. You're injured. Your leg. You couldn't possibly!"

He struggled into his shredded breeches. From the look of them, he supposed he should be grateful her scissors hadn't slipped and nipped off something irreplaceable in her zeal to cut the garment away.

For the love of God, what kind of a woman was she? he wondered as he battled to get himself clothed. He'd bedded his first woman when he was barely fifteen, an apple-cheeked lightskirt presented to him with a sharp command to get the blasted loss of his virginity over with, so he could keep his mind on more important matters. Since then he'd neatly slotted females into certain boxes—dithering ninnies, elegant witches bought for the price of a diamond bracelet, seductresses as greedy for sensation as any man, and decent women, the most boring of all, forever murmuring their prayers and looking at him as if they feared he'd eat them.

Only one woman had refused to be slotted into her proper category and dismissed. There had been just a moment when he almost thought she'd touched that cold, dead thing in his chest called a heart. But she'd married another man—a man of fire and passions seething close to the surface—with an open heart and the courage to lay it before her, no matter what the cost. A man worlds different from the ice-blooded English captain the whole west of Ireland feared. She'd left Redmayne bemused, if not lovelorn, aware that there was a chink someplace in his carefully constructed armor that it was possible for a woman to hammer her way through.

Mary Fallon Delaney had been as different from Rhiannon Fitzgerald as possible, and yet, there was something about Rhiannon's eyes, an eagerness, a whimsy, as if she could see magic beyond the mist— fairy raiders and heroic tales, the same fey elixir in her blood he'd sensed in Fallon. The slightest link between the two females was enough to tighten the bands of unease about his chest. The sooner he got quit of this place and his untidy savior the better.

He staggered upright, the tiny room swimming wildly before his eyes. "My boots, Miss Fitzgerald."

She presented him with the whole boot first, then the second, a lump of mangled leather. Redmayne couldn't suppress a groan.

"This really is a bad idea, Captain Redmayne," she said as he worked to bind the spoiled boot together with strips torn from his ruined shirt. "I wish you would reconsider."

But he was already stumbling outside, bracing himself on the caravan. The most disreputable excuse he'd ever seen for a horse stood a little distant from the cart. The nag paused in cropping grass long enough to give him a sleepy look out of half-closed eyes.

This was the demon horse no one could ride? Redmayne grimaced. The ridiculous beast was so fat he doubted it had ever gone faster than a trot in its whole benighted life.

He worked the bridle into the horse's mouth, then turned to the woman. "I don't suppose the cat has a saddle I might borrow—with the understanding that I'll return it in excellent order, of course."

"There's no point in having a saddle for a horse you cannot ride," Rhiannon insisted so reasonably he wanted to throttle her. "Surely you see this is impossible."

"I'll merely ride bareback. Not the best of situations, but I could hardly look more ridiculous." Doubtless if his assailants saw him on the road, they wouldn't bother shooting again. Why waste lead when they could merely laugh him to death?

He limped over to the horse's side, grasping a hank of mane the texture of broomstraw, then leaned with his left arm against the beast's withers. Redmayne paused, mustering all his strength to fling his leg over its back. But the instant he turned his back on the animal's front quarter, Socrates swung his great head around. To look at the new intruder, Redmayne assumed. A fatal error. Pain shot through Redmayne's hindquarters as those equine teeth sank roundly into his left buttock.

An oath tore from Redmayne's lips. Damned if he'd let a dumb animal get the better of him! With a fierce yank on the bridle, he disengaged the horse's teeth.

Then, sweat beading his brow, he swung up, clinging precariously as waves of agony jolted through his thigh and shoulder, black dots swimming madly before his eyes.

But he'd triumphed. He'd won. He struggled to clear his head, clinging to the sense of satisfaction. Socrates gazed up at him for a moment through a veritable forest of forelock, then, with a gut-splitting sigh, let his knees buckle.

"What the devil?" Redmayne muttered, kicking at the beast with his good heel, but Socrates was oblivious. Ever so slowly, the horse lowered his massive bulk down to the ground with a thud.

Redmayne barely yanked his good leg out from under the horse's belly before Socrates crushed it. Redmayne glared at his nemesis ever so coldly, but the horse was patently unmoved.

"Are you all right? I'm afraid he won't move until you get off." Miss Fitzgerald was wringing her hands apologetically.

Waves of dizziness assailing him, Redmayne surrendered, climbing off of the horse. "Someone ought to shoot you," he muttered.

Rhiannon Fitzgerald hastened over to help him get to his feet, but an unforgivable dimple danced in one of her cheeks. "I suppose I should be grateful I lost your pistol."

Redmayne turned a cold eye on her. "I have to get to the garrison," he said slowly, as if speaking to a particularly dull child. "Have you any idea how dangerous the men who attacked me are?"

"I was the one who found you bleeding." She sobered, something soft and wounded in her eyes. "Perhaps some of the soldiers who came with you got away. They might be bringing help."

"I very much doubt it," he observed wryly.

That tendril-scraggled brow crinkled in disbelief. "But surely you must have brought someone to assist you! You were hunting for information about a traitor!"

Redmayne's gaze sharpened, unease trailing like a blade down his spine. "A traitor? How did you know?" Unless she'd known his assailants . . .

"I read the letter in your pocket—to find out your name," she confessed, as distressed as if she'd betrayed state secrets. No one this flustered over such a minor incident could survive being wrapped up in a conspiracy, Redmayne thought with a touch of grim amusement. Still, the notion of someone prying through his pockets while he was incapacitated was enough to make him most displeased.

"I believe the custom is to write the name on the outside," he enunciated carefully.

"I know. I just . . . I knew nothing about you, and you were so very ill. I hoped that there might be something in the letter that would help me to help you." She looked down at him, sorrow and sympathy haunting those incredibly soft green eyes. "It must have been dreadful, discovering that there was a traitor amid the men you served with for . . . how many years?"

"Three."

"Such a very long time! Perhaps there is someone new among your men, someone you don't know very well."

Three years a long time? It was not even a single grain in the sands of time. She looked as if it were an eternity.

"At least you weren't alone in seeking this villain," she continued, grappling, he could tell, for something brighter, more comforting. "There must have been men you could trust to ride with you."

"No one."

Rhiannon stared at him in surprise, dismayed, uncertain what disturbed her most—that there was no one this man could trust, or the way he revealed it, as if that fact didn't hurt at all.

She'd always abhorred violence, and war was the ultimate obscenity. But she'd assumed that soldiers, embattled, with such a tenuous hold on life, drew closer. Men who trusted each other with their very lives from heartbeat to heartbeat must trust their fellow officers with things even more precious.

"My affairs are none of your concern, Miss Fitzgerald," her patient said with icy calm. "Since your horse will not carry me, there is only one logical choice left to us. Leave me here."

Her eyes widened in horror. "Are you mad? I couldn't possibly!"

She couldn't possibly leave him and preserve her own accursed life like a sensible creature. No, far better to die like an idiot! God save him from the moral pap of do-gooders! "The people who attempted to kill me will very likely strike again. This is none of your affair. Why put yourself in danger? Hitch up your wagon and leave, Miss Fitzgerald. I'd do it if I were you."

"Then it's a good thing you're *not* me. I'll take you to the garrison myself."

"You're not responsible for me or my misfortune. This is no time to be impractical."

"This is no time to be a heroic fool!" she shot back.

"There's nothing heroic in my motives," he assured her.

"As for my not being responsible, Captain Redmayne, you're wrong. I believe that everything happens for a reason, and that if something or someone in need falls into my path, I'm meant to care for it."

"I'm not a head-kicked dog, Miss Fitzgerald."

"No, you take up far too much room on my bed to be a dog, Captain Redmayne. Be that as it may, I found you. You're too weak to tend yourself, so for the time being you belong to me."

"Belong to you?" There was another time those words had iced his blood with terror. This time he choked out a stunned chuckle. "It makes no logical sense to—"

"Captain Redmayne, I have a horse I can't ride and a guard dog who can barely see three inches in front of his nose. Any *logical* person would have drowned them both. You must see how futile it is to try to persuade me to leave you behind. Now you can let me help you into the caravan and back into bed where you belong, or I can wait until you fall unconscious again, break open your wounds, and then I can drag you back into the caravan by your heels."

He looked as if he wanted to argue, but then stark resignation flooded his eyes. "Miss Fitzgerald, permit me to tell you that you make absolutely no sense."

"I take that as a compliment, Captain," she said, looping one arm about his waist. As they started up the steps to the caravan, Milton bolted past them, barking uproariously, as if he'd just noticed a new friend in their midst.

The dog leaped in the air, attempting to lick the captain's face, when suddenly his canine head cracked into the dishpan hanging overhead.

It tumbled down, clanging as it collided with Captain Redmayne's temple. The officer stifled a groan as it bounced off his injured shoulder.

"I'm sorry! I'm so sorry!" Rhiannon apologized, dismayed. "It's just that—that Milton likes you!"

White-faced, Redmayne sank back down onto her

tiny bed, rubbing the bruise the pan had left. "Miss Fitzgerald," he murmured hazily, "no offense intended, but I might have been better off with the assassins."

She almost thought his lips curled into a smile as he drifted back into unconsciousness.

Chapter

3

She was humming, blithely off key. Redmayne buried his face deeper in the pillow. Such an over-abundance of cheerfulness this early in the morning should be made a capital offense. No. Hanging would be much too merciful a fate—but at least it would make things *quiet*.

Surrendering, he shoved himself upright, uncertain exactly why he was wincing. The twinge in his shoulder? The slicing of cat claws as that infernal hell-born feline scrabbled off his chest, or the fact that Miss Fitzgerald had given up humming and actually broken into song!

He blinked like bedamned in an effort to focus his eyes. The woman must have a nice sturdy rope some-place in this caravan. If he couldn't manage to hang her, he might be able to hang himself.

"Good morning, lay-abed!"

Redmayne stifled a groan as she careened into his line of vision like a drunken butterfly, her face wreathed in a blindingly radiant smile.

If he ever did hunt down the traitor, he knew ex-actly what kind of torture he'd inflict to get the man to confess his crimes—lock him in a room with Mistress Sunshine. An hour in her company and he'd be confessing to crimes he hadn't even committed.

"I'm so glad you're finally awake!" she said, energetically stirring something in a blue bowl. "It's so hard to be quiet on such a lovely morning, and entertaining company is so rare here, I hate to waste a moment of it. I've made you the loveliest breakfast. Exactly what you need to strengthen you up."

Perhaps there were *some* benefits to having fallen under her care. He couldn't remember the last time he'd eaten. "I'm most obliged, madam."

She drew a stool near his bed, and before he could object, tucked a napkin under his chin as if he were five years old. For the first time in his life, Captain Lionel Redmayne couldn't think of a single thing to say. Then she plopped down on the stool, bowl cradled in her lap, and took up the spoon. The woman couldn't possibly intend to feed him thus!

"You'll find it quite delicious, I'm certain," she said, scooping up a spoonful of some gray-white speckled glop. Perhaps she was in league with the assassins after all and was attempting to poison him.

"What is . . . this?"

Guileless eyes met his. "Gruel."

Redmayne raised one eyebrow, staring at her as if her hair were afire.

"Miss . . . er, Fitzgerald, I've fallen beneath pistol fire eight times in battle, and *no one* has ever dared present me with such . . . slop."

Her smile faltered. "I made it myself, stirred in some lovely herbs that will help you to heal. You do want to get strong again as fast as you can, don't you?"

"Not if it entails eating that." Most women he knew would either be running for cover, wailing, or raging at him in high dudgeon. Rhiannon Fitzgerald merely sat there, gazing wistfully into the accursed blue bowl. He should have been relieved. He'd taken the bounce out of the woman—that was what he'd desired from the moment he heard her chirping away, wasn't it?

"I didn't mean to offend you," she said. "I tasted it myself, and it was tolerable enough, I hoped."

Redmayne felt a twinge of a most unfamiliar kind. It couldn't possibly be guilt. He didn't believe in it— a waste of time and energy. What was done was done. And yet, as he looked at those downcast eyes with their ridiculously long lashes, he recalled everything the woman had done for him since she'd discovered him bleeding. He stunned himself by growling, "Give it to me."

"Wh-what?"

"The bowl, Miss Fitzgerald."

She grasped the crockery against her middle as if she expected him to snatch it out of her hands. "Don't feel obligated to—"

Obligated? He was obligated to the woman for his very life. If it would please her to see him choke down the odious stuff, he'd humor her. Perhaps he could feed it to the cat when she left the cart. After the claw marks the beast had left, it deserved to be poisoned.

"Miss Fitzgerald, I'll eat it—by my own hand, if you please."

She handed the bowl over, looking so pleased it made the twinge he'd felt all the sharper. "Let me help you out of your shirt. I thought I would mend it."

He didn't like the idea of surrendering anything to the woman, but if it would keep her too busy to think up any more herbal concoctions to plague him with, it would be a small enough price to pay.

She reclaimed the gruel, placing it on a precariously narrow ledge as he tried to wrestle his way out of the garment. But the slashes in the linen and the throbbing wound in his shoulder made the task difficult. Of course, she *would* bustle over to help him.

She'd removed every stitch of clothing he wore while he was senseless, but this time he was aware of her deft feminine fingers brushing his skin, not even briskly, but rather with a kind of inborn tenderness he sensed was as much a part of the woman as the spattering of freckles on her nose. It was an alien thing to him, such gentleness in a touch. Dangerous. Like the juices of the opium poppy, it held the power to numb self-control, dulling a man's will, fettering his independence. It had the power to make even a strong man crave more.

He wanted her to take the garment and go somewhere, anywhere far away from him. But instead of tripping off about her business, she plopped back onto the stool and grabbed up a little basket brimful of sewing gewgaws.

She was threading a needle by the time he recovered from shock. "I thought I would keep you company," she explained. "There's nothing more dreadful than being sick and alone."

She was mistaken. There was something far worse, he thought grimly—the mere idea of letting anyone see him made weak and vulnerable by his wounds. Even animals had the sense to drag themselves off to holes or dens to lick their wounds in private. He schooled his face into bored lines, hiding any evidence of his acute unease. "I wouldn't dream of being such an inconvenience to you. Go about your business."

"How thoughtful of you. But distracting you from your discomfort is my business at present. I confess there's not a great deal to do, traveling about in my little house like this. I tidied up the camp while you were sleeping, and had my breakfast. I even poked about a little to make certain those wicked men who shot you were nowhere nearby." The tiniest of lines at the corner of her mouth betrayed the nervousness she was trying to hide—fear of the men who had hunted him down.

The thought of her running afoul of the assassins made Redmayne exceedingly irritated. "And what would you have done if you *had* found them?" He asked in accents frigid enough to create ice crystals in a pot of boiling water.

"Why, enchanted them with a fairy spell of course," she replied with a wicked twinkle in her eyes. "That is one of the advantages of being fairy-born."

Now he was to be afflicted with her sense of humor? "Miss Fitzgerald . . ." He was going to tell her not to be ridiculous. But didn't even acknowledging such a statement make him seem equally absurd?

"So you see," she went on cheerfully, "I have absolutely nothing to do at the moment but stitch and enjoy your company."

"I take my meals alone."

"Poor lad. Far too busy with your duties to seek out even such small comfort as conversation, I would wager. But there's nothing you can do here, either, so you can just rest."

Perhaps he could drag himself on his belly away from camp, Redmayne considered, even such an indignity looking ever more attractive. Hell might take the form of a talkative angel after all.

"So would you like to tell me about yourself?" she asked. "You must have had many grand adventures."

He'd sooner have been roasted over a bed of hot coals than give her any more glimpses of the man he was. Likely even Mistress Sunshine would be sobered by such enlightenment. If he couldn't dislodge her from his side, his only option was to distract her inquisitive mind. But how? He groped for a moment, then seized on a solution with some reluctance.

"I'd prefer to talk about you, madam." Far preferable to the truth: *I wish you would leave me the devil in peace.* And most people would rattle on about themselves ad nauseam. "What could possess a lone woman like you to wander about in this fashion?"

"Oh, I wasn't alone at first. My papa was with me."

Redmayne spooned up some of the gruel, determined to eat it in record time. There was always the hope that once he was done with the vile stuff, she'd take herself off to scrub the dishes or some such. "Did your father have some sort of itinerant job that made it necessary? A tinker? A peddler?"

"Papa was a barrister."

Redmayne stilled, eyes narrowing. The woman had managed to get his attention. What the devil was a barrister doing wandering around in a painted cart? And yet there was so much about this woman and the contents of her wagon that was inconsistent with the life of a traveler. The cultured tones of her voice, the aura of a lady, instead of the half-wild look he'd seen in the eyes of every Gypsy he'd ever run across. Even the china bowl that he held could have presented itself at any fine dining table without shame.

"When I was a child, we lived in a delightful place, a small estate near Wicklow called Primrose Cottage." Her lips softened into a lost-angel smile. "Rose vines had grown over it for a hundred years, so that the walls were almost covered. And in the summer, when the sun warmed the blossoms, it was like living in a fairyland. There were gardens brimming with every kind of flower, paths weaving through woods so lovely it was easy to believe the lords and ladies of the fairy kingdom held their revels there."

"Why did you leave this paragon of a home?" Another spoonful of gruel—more vile than the last, yet not nearly as unpalatable as making conversation thus. Of course Rhiannon Fitzgerald would open her very heart for his inspection at the slightest prodding. But he couldn't help being a trifle amused at himself. Captain Lionel Redmayne coaxing childhood confidences out of someone. It was like a wolf tenderly inquiring after the health of a lamb. But it was obvious Miss Fitzgerald knew nothing of wolves—dressed in fur or in bright red uniforms.

"Papa was the most wonderful man—full of stories and dreams and love. He opened his arms to the world like a child, always expecting something beautiful to rush into his grasp. He worked very hard, but the cases he took on didn't often make a great deal of money. He had a great hunger for justice, and believed if only he could show people the truth, they would embrace it eagerly."

It was a miracle the man had survived as long as he had, Redmayne thought grimly. There was nothing people loathed more than being shown an uncomfortable truth. They welcomed it about as enthusiastically as they would have welcomed being plunged into a field of nettles. And instead of blaming their own blindness or heedlessness for the discomfort, they were all too eager to kill the messenger, as the Romans had been wont to do.

"Our finances were in some disarray. In an effort to recoup the funds after some costly cases, Papa made some investments with a man he had much faith in. Unfortunately, I'm afraid the man was not to be trusted."

"A great surprise, I'm certain," Redmayne muttered, lips twisting with irony.

"What little savings we had were already strained. We lost Primrose Cottage."

"And the legions of injured parties involved in these just causes your father worked so hard to defend—none of them came to your aid?" Nothing irritated him more than blind idealism, especially when confronted with the victims it could leave in its wake.

Bristling at his sarcasm, Rhiannon Fitzgerald straightened her spine and met his censuring gaze squarely. "Captain Redmayne, most of Papa's clients could barely afford to feed themselves, care for their own families. Several offered to give us a place to stay, but that would hardly have been fair, causing them hardship. Papa refused to accept their help. He said he'd been eager to see the wonders of Ireland since he was a little boy listening to tales of castle ruins and the Giant's Causeway, fairy forts and ancient stone beds where legendary lovers had lain. What better way to see them all than to travel about in a gypsy cart? We'd have a grand adventure, the two of us."

"And your mother? Was she equally eager to set out on this grand adventure?"

"I don't even remember her. It was always just Papa and me."

She'd been left at the mercy of that cloud-brained imbecile her whole life? And at the height of her father's foolery, the man had dragged his daughter out onto the open road? Fed her some ridiculous tale about how wonderful it would be. And then he'd left her alone out here in the midst of nowhere, where any calamity might befall her.

"Your father might have lowered his principles a trifle, taken on a few cases in which he could actually make money—just for a bit of variety," Redmayne observed.

He expected to ruffle her feathers again, see that spark of indignation in her eyes because he'd dared to question her saint of a father. But instead she only picked at a loose thread as if it held the secret to unraveling the universe.

"That was the strangest part." A crease formed between her delicate brows. "As long as I could remember, Papa had been turning away a great many clients. He gave himself to every pursuit wholeheartedly, wouldn't take any case unless he would be willing and able to sacrifice the last drop of his blood for the cause. But in the weeks before we lost Primrose, the people who had been clamoring for his help disappeared as well."

"Trust rats to know when a ship is sinking," Redmayne muttered, more to himself than to the woman.

Her eyes widened. "Odd you should say that. That's exactly how I felt. As if Primrose were a mouse's hole and some giant invisible cat lay in wait outside it, frightening away anyone who might come near. It was so sudden, so complete—the silence, the feeling of isolation."

Redmayne was astonished to feel a stirring of curiosity in spite of himself.

She looked down at the mending in her lap, her voice dropping low. "I wouldn't have minded leaving the cottage so much if I'd felt that the new owner would love it as I had. Care for my mama's roses, take joy in the gillyflowers carved into the mantelpieces. It was a house that had been cherished from the moment it was built. The walls, the very walls, whispered of love." For the first time a wistfulness touched the rare purity of her features, making them even more vulnerable than before. Redmayne's shoulders tightened, but not entirely with impatience. "I knew the house would be lonely after we were gone."

The girl had been packed into a gypsy cart, lost practically everything she owned, not to mention any chance at a decent future—for what kind of man would marry a penniless girl in a garish painted cart?—but as the wagon rattled off into an uncertain future, what had she been worried about? That the house her irresponsible ass of a father had lost would be *lonely*.

Over the years, Redmayne had worked hard to perfect his gift for seeing into other people's minds—into their motives and fears, weaknesses and vices—for to know one's opponent was vital in the vast game that was life. Yet he always viewed whatever he discovered with detachment. Why was it that the picture of Rhiannon Fitzgerald stung? A wistful woman-child's face peering out of the back of the bright-painted caravan, straining to catch a last glimpse of her world before it disappeared?

God's blood, if he didn't feel an uncharacteristic urge to utter some word of sympathy or comfort! Useless rot. It would change nothing that had happened. Still, he couldn't help but wonder just a little about the young girl and her father, cast to the winds of fate on the open road.

"It was difficult, no doubt, wandering about, suddenly paupers."

The woman actually broke into a smile. "I was homesick for a little while, but there was no use in grieving. Parties and beaux, all the pieces of that other life were gone."

Of course any suitors would have abandoned her. It was to be expected. She was a woman without a dowry, whose father was little more than a benevolent madman. What benefit could be derived from taking such a wife? And yet not every suitor would have turned his back on Rhiannon Fitzgerald, Redmayne acknowledged with an unaccustomed twinge of bitterness. There were some noble fools sprinkled in among the ranks of men. Fools like the man who had won the heart of Mary Fallon Delaney, a man who would have slain dragons in her name.

"Once we were on the road, this life grew easier. The countryside was so beautiful, it soothed my spirit. Perhaps I no longer had my mother's roses, but all Ireland was my garden now, Papa told me." Her mouth softened, sweetened, her eyes touched with a faint, pensive shadow. "And I was his briar rose because I bloomed wherever I was planted, and always turned my face up to the sun."

A briar rose . . . it fit her, that sobriquet. Untidy, tangling every which way, petals fragile, and yet too busy thriving to realize it should be battered and withering under such harsh conditions.

Redmayne's own memory stirred, a deep voice, as warm as summer sun, his own father's strong arms outstretched: "Fly to the sky, my little lion. . . ." Even now there were times when he could almost remember what it was like to be tossed high above his father's head, to hear the echoes of his own squeals of delight as he flew, certain Papa would always be there to catch him. Another fairy tale. Another lie. That boy had lost the life he'd known, too. But he hadn't turned his face to the sun.

He shook off the unwelcome memory, wishing the infernal woman would drown the shades of his past in her chatter. But the stubbornly genial companion who had been so talkative moments before had vanished. She'd lapsed into silence, concentrating on threading her needle, her lashes lowered, her full lips pressed together. Tending a quiet heartache, the loss of her father? Why should it matter to Redmayne? Silence was what he craved, wasn't it? Then why the devil was he suddenly prodding her to go on? What was it about her story that sounded all too familiar?

"This man who took Primrose Cottage, I don't suppose he had a name?"

"It was so long ago . . . and Papa didn't speak of it to me. He believed in filling his daughter's head with fairy stories, her arms with flowers, and her skirts with meadow breezes. I knew so little of his business affairs. But I did meet the man once. Paxton, Papa called him. Mr. Paxton."

The hand that held Redmayne's spoon halted midway to his mouth. "It's a common enough name, one would think," he reasoned, loathing himself for his unease.

"Perhaps. But the man wasn't common." He saw a fine tremor work through her. "I glimpsed him once and felt so—so cold. I'd never felt quite so cold. He had the strangest eyes I'd ever seen. Pale and empty, as if—as if there wasn't a soul inside."

"He was an Irishman?"

"No. Nor English either, though he spoke it well enough. It was as if the flavor of half a dozen different languages was still on his tongue. But whenever he came to the cottage, I'm ashamed to admit I did my best to avoid him, ran off to work in the gardens or something. It was too cold with him in the house."

If this Paxton was the same man Redmayne knew, he could understand the urge. How could a starry-eyed briar rose like Rhiannon Fitzgerald know that she could never run fast enough or far enough or hide herself well enough to escape those eyes that had so disturbed her? If Paxton Redmayne wanted to find her, hell itself wouldn't be deep enough to hide in. Or had her father merely been a minor amusement for the old man? Something to allay his boredom until a quarry worthy of his intellect came along? Paxton could never resist toying with people's lives, like a cat with its prey. And yet a country barrister—a bumbling philanthropist, no less—was not his usual quarry. But that was the genius in the old man—that he was as changeable as water, taking on the shape and form of whatever vessel he chose to inhabit at the moment.

God, how the old bastard would laugh if he could see Redmayne here now in this cart with this innocent-eyed woman who had been so desperately wronged. It was the kind of jest Paxton Redmayne enjoyed the most.

Redmayne struggled not to betray the vise of grimness tightening inside him. Why the devil had he been cursed enough to run afoul of the woman? Was this some kind of cruel jest of fate? Or was it the pull of destiny she'd spoken of when she refused to desert him?

He'd been flung in the woman's path. She'd snatched him from the jaws of certain death only to tell him that the dragon who had haunted his boyhood nightmare might have stalked her as well. Might still be stalking her, oblivious as she was to it.

What had she claimed? That the man who had broken her father's finances and taken her cottage away had been called Paxton? The whole affair reeked of his grandfather's ruthlessness. And if the man Rhiannon remembered was Paxton Redmayne, she could have no idea how much danger she might still be in. No game of wits was ever over until Paxton declared it so. No one knew that better than Redmayne. A subtle chill tracked down his spine. He crushed it ruthlessly.

It wasn't that he was afraid for the girl or that he felt responsible for her in any way, he told himself. Whatever disaster her father had gotten her into was purely incidental to him. But there were other matters to consider. He'd never been one to cast away opportunities fate presented him. And the chance to thwart the old man . . . it was a temptation tantalizing beyond imagining.

Perhaps fortune had thrown him into Rhiannon Fitzgerald's path for a purpose. Some small half-forgotten force called conscience winced at the thought, but he crushed it, gaze fixed intensely on the woman now bending over her needlework. If she had run afoul of his grandfather, it was possible, just possible, that she might prove a valuable pawn in the endless game of chess between Redmayne and the man who still haunted his nightmares.

"Captain Redmayne?" Her worried query startled him, drawing him back to the present—the cramped confines of the gypsy cart, the penetrating warmth of her hazel eyes, and the unnerving awareness of his own stupidity. He'd left himself vulnerable during those moments when he allowed his mind to wander.

"What is it, madam?"

"Is something amiss? You look so . . . strange."

Redmayne drew his accustomed cool mask over his features. "A hazard of getting oneself shot, I fear. All that grimacing and groaning, trying to put on a brave face. It gets wearing after a while."

The woman looked so chagrined that any man with a drop of compassion in his veins would have wished the words back. "How utterly selfish of me! Prattling on about things you can have no interest in."

"You mistake me, madam. You've distracted me marvelous well."

Heavy lids drooped low over his eyes, so he wouldn't have to look at Rhiannon Fitzgerald's innocent face. Yes. She'd given him something *else* to think about besides his wounds. For only an idealistic fool would refuse to use a weapon fate might well have cast into his hands.

Chapter

❧ 4 ❧

Night songs drifted in from the distant sea, a fairy murmur beyond the secluded glen. Few could hear it anymore, Rhiannon knew. Not because it was so very difficult, but because they were too busy to listen. It had always comforted her somehow, the bittersweet lullaby of the waves making love to the shore. She'd closed her eyes, sensing generations of women, quiet, pausing still in their busy lives for a moment to listen to the sound of eternity.

But tonight the familiar melody only lapped at the restlessness inside her, not soothing but stirring up so many feelings, so many doubts, so many memories, so many fears.

Emotions awakened by the enigmatic man whose white-gold hair lay tangled upon her pillow. As she sat in the cart, chattering away, she hadn't realized the reverberations he'd managed to set off with his questions, and the merest flickering of an eyelash, or turning of the corner of his mouth.

It was only later, as she went about her tasks, that she became aware of the consequences of their conversation.

Strange, she'd been so determined to leave Primrose Cottage behind her, that life and the starry-eyed seventeen-year-old who had lived it seemed almost spun of fairy tales, belonging to someone far different from herself. She'd made a conscious choice to look ahead in the five years since the gypsy cart had rumbled away from the cottage. She'd vowed to accept life's unexpected gifts instead of yearning for a life that had vanished.

She and Papa had still had each other. That was all that had really mattered. No power on earth could steal away the love that had been the very core of Rhiannon's being. But tonight, tears she'd never shed pressed against her heart, and for some reason, Papa felt very far away.

The officer, Captain Redmayne, had made it seem so. No sympathy in his face, no discomfort at her revelations. Rather, a steady gaze stark with understanding, as if he'd seen past everything, to the most secret, tightly locked box she'd buried deep in her soul, the place where she kept anger and loss, grief and blame, and the haunting image of eyes like cold stones.

Now it was as if his probing had jarred a half-healed wound, made her intensely aware of it when she'd wanted with all her heart to let it fade into a soft-edged dream that could never hurt her.

Milton sidled up, rubbing his great head against her, nudging her hand as if to say, *I'm here. I know you're sad.*

She stroked his silky ears. But even that familiar comfort couldn't still the restlessness, the unease, coiling ever tighter inside her. Always before, the night had seemed soft and full of mystery, a time to stare into the fire and dream. But all that had changed in the hours since she'd discovered Captain Redmayne lying wounded among the standing stones.

Somewhere in that darkness a thousand unanswered questions still lurked about the loss of Primrose Cottage and the man who had stolen it away. Dangers stalked beneath night's black curtain—the captain's attackers wandering about, toasting his supposed death? Or hunting, trying to make certain that their victim was on his way to hell?

Almost more frightening was the knowledge that plenty of Irish crofters between this glen and Redmayne's garrison would be all too happy to give the English captain a helping hand along that deadly journey. She shivered, the night wind turning chill and damp. She was never alone. She'd been so certain of that when she'd brushed aside Triona's fears on the last visit to the farm.

But tonight the isolation pressed against her, the uncertainty, the strain, exhaustion weighing her down like rain-sodden skirts. Quietly she slipped into the caravan and locked the small wooden door. Then she turned in the cramped quarters to where Captain Redmayne lay sleeping on the narrow bed.

She gazed down at him a long moment, needing desperately to . . . to what? Feel even the slightest human touch? An idea flitted into her head as she gazed down at the sliver of mattress not swallowed up by Redmayne's body, and she plucked at some loose trim on her cuff, uneasy.

Triona—and even Papa—would be appalled at the very thought of Rhiannon even *considering* committing such an immodest act. Lying down with any man, especially one she barely knew. But it wasn't as if she wanted to ravish Captain Redmayne, she reasoned, she only needed to sleep. And he had lost a great deal of blood. He'd be in no condition to ravish *her* even if he'd wanted too.

Wasn't that one of the lessons she'd learned on the

road? Not to be tyrannized by other people's arbitrary rules? She was only being sensible. If she slept beneath the wagon, as Papa so often had, she wouldn't hear the injured Redmayne cry out if he needed something.

"Stop rationalizing, Rhiannon," she muttered in self disgust. "Admit the truth. You're afraid. You need this far more than he does."

She eased off her boots, loosened the tightest buttons at her throat, and edged onto the mattress.

It was as if the bed had shrunk somehow, its size devoured by Redmayne's long, lean body. And yet over time she'd grown used to taking up as little space as possible, after nights of keeping baskets of injured creatures close beside her. She would just think of the elegant Captain Redmayne as a particularly large hound.

She might even have managed a smile at her attempt at humor, but Redmayne wasn't any tame hound. More like the wolf she'd tended—fiercely intelligent, untamable, dangerous. His breath stirred the fine hairs at her temple. The warmth of his nearness seeping through the chill inside Rhiannon.

She'd worry tomorrow about being devoured. Tired . . . she was so tired. She curled up on the edge of the bed and let her eyes drift shut.

Redmayne awoke with a jolt, pain shooting through his shoulder as he struggled to get his bearings. Something warm was pressed up alongside him, silky strands of sweet-smelling hair straggling across his jaw, the pillowy softness of a breast nudged his rib cage. Muttering a curse, he propped himself up on his uninjured arm. What the blazes? The woman had crawled into bed with him!

He stiffened, drawing himself tighter against the

outer wall of the caravan in an effort to put some space between them, frustration and something far too similar to alarm reverberating through him. He'd lost his virginity at fifteen, but never once had he spent the night lying beside any woman he'd bedded. Only a reckless fool let anyone see him in the vulnerability of sleep. Sleep . . . the place where nightmares stalked a man, and no amount of steely will could hold them at bay.

And this woman, with her keen intuition, had already learned far too much about him when he was half unconscious, racked with pain, and cried out for his father. The possibility that she might burrow even deeper beneath defenses he'd always thought unbreachable was unthinkable.

There was too much softness about her features, a terrifying tenderness in the full curve of her lips, her eyelashes, absurdly long and curled, lying in rich crescents against her cheekbones. She shivered in her sleep, closing the space he'd managed to put between them, her rosy cheek nuzzled against his bare chest.

When she helped him cauterize his wound with the white-hot brand, it hadn't jolted him this deeply. Instinctively he tried to draw back farther still, but the wall of the caravan blocked any further retreat.

God in heaven, what was wrong with him? He'd bedded his share of women, without so much as a ripple in the surface of his prized self-control. The most beautiful, most accomplished lovers society had to offer had viewed the notoriously omniscient Captain Redmayne as an irresistible challenge. They had amused him—their determination to crack his reserve, drive him to paroxysms of passion. And it had been diverting to observe their varying stages of outrage when they realized how little they had touched his emotions.

Yet never had the most accomplished siren unsettled him the way this lone, tousled, dream-mad little gypsy had managed to. He probed the unaccustomed sensation for a long moment, gazing down into her slumbering features, trying to determine exactly what it was about her that had elicited such a unique response. One couldn't quell unwanted reactions, after all, unless one understood the root of them.

Absurdly quixotic, fiercely innocent, tenacious of joy—Rhiannon Fitzgerald was the sort of woman who should have inspired nothing but ridicule in the cynical captain. Hadn't he learned early that "compassion" was only a prettier name for weakness, that "idealism" was the word used by cowards without the courage to gaze, straight-faced into life?

Why was it, then, that his fingers itched to smooth the strands of hair back from her cheek? An innate need for tidiness, no doubt. Surely nothing more. Forcing his voice into its usual cool tones, he spoke. "Miss Fitzgerald?"

For a moment she groped for the pillow, as if to draw it over her ear, block out the disturbance. Only then did Redmayne notice the dark circles beneath her eyes, the exhaustion draining some of the color from her cheeks. Why the devil should that cause him an unexpected twinge?

"Madam?" he said a trifle more gently. Her eyes fluttered open, confusion and astonishment swimming in their depths. "Wh-what . . . who . . . ?" She scrambled to a sitting position, then seemed to gather her scattered wits. "Are you all right? Is there something wrong?"

"I must confess, I'm not accustomed to waking to find a woman in my bed."

Her cheeks washed so scarlet he couldn't help but be vaguely amused.

"Not that I would object except that you absconded with the pillow."

"I . . . There was nowhere else to—to sleep . . . except outside," she stammered by way of an explanation, "and—and then I wouldn't be able to hear you if you cried out."

Amusement vanished. Redmayne didn't move a fraction, but felt a hardening inside himself, a tightness in his chest. He mustered the tones that had never failed to send the offender scrambling off in retreat. "I won't be subjecting you to any more such nonsense." *I'll cut my own throat first,* he finished grimly to himself.

But Rhiannon's too tender mouth softened, her eyes flooding with compassion. "Once, when I had a nightmare, Papa told me that even the bravest of soldiers needed someone to hold on to when the dragons came at night. Even then I thought a soldier's dragons must be ever so much fiercer and more frightening than mine. I'm glad you had your own father to call for, Captain." She reached out one hand, laid it on his cheek. "You needn't feel ashamed."

Redmayne's throat closed. He forced a sneer onto his lips. "Ashamed? Madam, you obviously have a high opinion of your powers of intuition. This time, however, you are mistaken."

Her eyes glowed with earnestness. "You needn't worry. I'll never tell anyone about the night you cried out. And we don't ever have to speak about it again unless you wish to."

She'd read *his* thoughts? How damnably strange, Redmayne thought with a chill. Not since he was ten years old had anyone been able to unravel the workings of his mind. He'd guarded them far more closely than any miser his treasure hoard. Lucifer was supposed to see into the souls of his prey. They were not supposed to go prying merrily into his.

And as for her vow that they would never speak of his momentary weakness again . . . Bloody hell, he'd never known a woman born who could refrain from ferreting out any intriguing tidbit of information once she'd caught the scent of a secret. Doubtless this woman was just better than most at disguising her intentions. But bedamned if any torture master wielding weapons of steel or of luminous green-gold eyes could wrench any confidence out of Captain Lionel Redmayne.

"Miss Fitzgerald, your vow of silence is immaterial to me. There is nothing more to speak of." He gave a careless wave of one hand.

"You don't believe me, do you? That I'll keep my word?"

Blast if she hadn't managed to disconcert him again! "What I believe is of no importance."

"I feel very sorry for you, Captain."

Pity? That most loathsome of poisons! How dare she! If she were a man . . . what? He'd have found a way to make her pay for such a violation. "Your sympathy is wasted on me."

"How sad. What kind of people have hurt you thus, that there is no one you trust? Someone must have betrayed you. I never will." The stark sincerity in her forest-hued eyes should have pierced clean through to Redmayne's heart. Fortunately he did not possess one. Yet there was something singular about so much earnestness, so much innocence, combined with a fearlessness any soldier on the field of battle would envy. Something that affected Redmayne in a way he couldn't quite name.

A lazy contempt was his usual reaction to too much goodness, and curiosity as to how long it would last if confronted with real pain, real adversity. He'd made a game of estimating exactly how much pressure it would take before virtue snapped. If there was one valuable lesson his grandfather had taught him, it was that a man's powers of deduction needed to be kept honed sharper than his sword. And just as a master swordsman practiced every day the movements of his craft until they were second nature, so the warrior of the mind sharpened his skills at every opportunity.

Only twice had Redmayne been unable to discover a crack in the armor of his opponent—when he'd matched wits with Mary Fallon Delaney, and the man who had risked all to love her. An odd sensation. But not as odd as the one that stole through him now.

He started in astonishment, wrenched from his musings as Miss Fitzgerald wrapped her fingers gently about his. "Sometimes pain can be like a—a gateway, and once you pass through it, you discover something wonderful waiting on the other side."

He should have bristled the way he always did over platitudes, but there was the slightest curve to her mouth, the shadow of her own sadness and loss. Was she saying it to comfort him? Or was it like a mantra she repeated to herself over and over, hoping someday she'd believe it?

Redmayne stared into those blowsy-rose features, the soft oval face, the smudges of dark brow, the halo of flyaway cinnamon curls, and those eyes, those remarkable eyes. It was as if a current passed through her fingers into his, a soft pulsing that warmed places he wanted to stay cold, greening places he wanted to keep deadened and numb.

"I would prefer that you refrain from touching me, Miss Fitzgerald." The words were out before he could stop them, cool and careless, yet revealing far too much for comfort.

She withdrew her fingers, burying them in her skirts almost guiltily.

"We are, after all, barely acquainted," Redmayne said, attempting to deflect that disturbing gaze. "And an officer of my stature must do all he can to protect his reputation—particularly here in Ireland. Stories— especially of English atrocities—grow more swiftly and wildly than a storm at sea. I wouldn't want any- one who heard of our . . . ahem, contact, to miscon- strue my intentions."

She blushed. "Captain Redmayne, I've found that people will believe what they choose to, whether good or ill. There is nothing I can do to prevent that."

An astonishing bit of practical wisdom from Mis- tress Stars-in-Her-Eyes, Redmayne thought as she continued.

"I'm certain that plenty would think the worst not only of you, but of me for helping you."

Something else he hadn't stopped to consider, though no man could serve three days on this island without being aware of the hatred the inhabitants har- bored toward anything English. And if one of their own consorted with the enemy . . . Rhiannon Fitzger- ald was in danger not only from those who had hoped to assassinate him but from those who had been her friends before she took a wounded soldier into her care.

How could he have missed something so vital? His particular brand of genius had been the ability to see every facet of a situation at once, consequences or possibilities beyond the grasp of most men's intellect. But this consequence would have stared the rankest fool smack in the face. Still, he'd overlooked it.

When had his wits gotten so untrustworthy? Per- haps the bullets had put a hole in something far more dangerous than his shoulder. Or was it this shatterbrained fairy maiden who had affected him so strangely? Some charm in one of the bitter potions she'd forced down his throat? He knew he should never have eaten that vile-tasting gruel.

She stood up, tucking a straggly lock of hair behind one dainty ear. She looked lopsided, mussed, creases from the sheet still pressed into her cheek. Why did he feel a ridiculous urge to reach up and try to smooth those faint lines away? Hellfire, forget Miss Fitzgerald's worthless nag, he'd find something to use as a crutch and walk the thirty miles to the garrison. Perhaps he'd get lucky and die of exposure on the way. Far less perilous to be at the mercy of the elements than of one small, untidy Good Samaritan.

"Miss Fitzgerald, it is imperative that I get back to my garrison at once."

"So that whoever set up the ambush that all but killed you can finish the job before you're strong enough to defend yourself? I think not." Her chin jutted up a notch. "I've never yet allowed any of the creatures entrusted to my care to go free before I was certain they were strong enough to survive. I'm not about to begin now."

Redmayne's eyes narrowed. She saw him as one more of her infernal wounded beasts. The knowledge ate like acid into his pride. Something clenched in his gut. Emotion. Anger. Shame.

Fear.

He yanked himself away from it, knowing in that panicked instant that he'd do whatever he had to in order to escape it.

God alone knew what might have happened next, had it not been for a sudden cacophony of baying outside of the caravan. The hound. Milton.

Redmayne froze, instincts honed on countless battlefields sizzling to awareness. Even Rhiannon stilled, her eyes wide, more than a little frightened.

"It's probably nothing," she said, looking completely unconvinced. Who the devil was she trying to comfort? Him or herself?

There was a low murmur of masculine voices, muffled by the walls of the caravan.

Redmayne levered himself up. Excruciating pain shot through his shoulder, a swarm of bright dots swimming before his eyes. Hell, he was as useless as that infernal dog of hers, weak, stranded here without so much as a weapon. Perhaps he could use the remainder of Miss Fitzgerald's gruel to poison the intruder to death. Glancing around, he searched for something, anything he could wield against an enemy.

"Be careful!" she warned. "You'll tear open your wounds!"

"That might be redundant, since there is a more than middling chance that our visitors intend to create a few new ones. Do you have a knife? A fire poker? Anything I can take out there with me?"

"Out there? You're not going out there!"

"Miss Fitzgerald—"

"If those men are the ones who were hunting you, the last thing we need is for you to go charging out, making an even better target of yourself. I'll go alone, try to distract them."

Distract them? The woman was so honest she might as well have the truth emblazoned across her forehead: *"He's hiding under the bed."* It was his pride that made him resolute, not any particular concern for her safety. He'd leave that to heroic fools.

He grabbed her arm so tight it might leave bruises on that lily-fair skin. "Forgive my obstinacy, but I have an aversion to hiding behind a woman's skirts. Superior officers tend to frown on it when it comes time to make promotions."

She glared at him, and he was suddenly struck with the core of intelligence he'd not noticed before beneath the dreamy sheen of her eyes. "I'm certain they'd be as happy to shoot you through my skirts as not, Captain. You hardly think they'd allow any witnesses to live, do you? If I can manage to deflect them, it might save both our lives."

Reasonable. It was so damned reasonable. Then why did it irritate him so thoroughly?

"You can wait in here with the poker and smash it down on their heads if they come searching." She whispered fiercely. "You'll have a much better chance with the element of surprise."

"Where the devil is the poker?"

"I brought it back inside, put it in the corner the morning after we cauterized your wounds."

Redmayne glimpsed the shaft of iron, remembering. It took all of his will to uncurl his fingers, let her go. For a man who, a day before, had suffered little but boredom at the prospect of his death, he was suddenly damned edgy. Doubtless because it was bad form to get even a little shatterbrain killed after she'd saved one's life.

"If you get yourself shot, madam, I shall be most put out." He attempted to speak carelessly, but he couldn't keep the slight roughness out of his tone.

She paused, one hand on the small door, and flashed him a tremulous smile, full of courage, leavened with a humor that pinched in his chest. "So, Captain Redmayne, will I."

Chapter

🍀 5 🍀

A glare of sunlight blinded Rhiannon for a moment as she slipped out of the caravan and shut the door behind her, trying desperately not to reveal the bubble of panic lodged beneath her breastbone. She blinked, attempting to clear her eyes, half afraid of what she'd see. Yet what would it matter? She doubted assassins wore identifying uniforms, after all. She'd have no idea whether she confronted friend or foe until . . . what? One of them leveled a pistol at her?

Her surroundings swam into focus as she stumbled down the narrow steps to the ground, Milton's barking rattling her nerves. The hound was leaping wildly at the roots of a nearby tree, but he hadn't cornered the intruders there. Three men ambled past the dog, two of them in the uniforms of the British army, the other in the threadbare garb of a crofter.

How on earth had they stumbled across the entrance to this hidden glen? In all the times Rhiannon and her father had taken shelter here, she'd never seen so much as a solitary soul, no hoofprints or remains of a campfire. It had seemed possible that papa's explanation was true—that only the fairy-born could enter into the sweet green haven. But there was nothing whimsical about those who tramped across the heather now, no mist of the otherworld about them. They were men like Captain Redmayne, firmly rooted in the present, hard-featured, keen eyed. Intruders in Rhiannon's world.

"Milton!" she called, and the foxhound bounded toward the sound of her voice. She buried her fingers in the bristling fur at the scruff of his neck, trying to take comfort in that familiar warmth. But it was as if she could feel the tension coiling tighter and tighter in the animal, and in the wounded man whose every breath she seemed to sense beyond the bright-painted caravan door.

"Top o' the mornin' to ye, me lovely," the bull ox of a crofter shoved a battered hat back from undeniably Irish features, giving her a mild smile. Rhiannon stiffened, struck by the oddity of it—an Irishman aiding two English troopers. Yet poverty had driven plenty of men and women to betray their own countrymen. A sick wife, a child crying with hunger, a meager room that might be torn down over their heads if rent wasn't paid—such was the price of many an Irish soul.

" 'Tis a terrible fierce watchdog ye have there." The Irishman chuckled.

"He can bite well enough when I point him in the right direction," Rhiannon said. Milton, as if understanding her meaning, sent forth his most fervent growl. The effect would have been far more menacing if he'd managed to aim it at the intruders.

She winced at the rising tide of masculine chuckles.

"Yer beast needn't exert himself on our account," the Irishman said. "We mean ye no harm. I be Seamus O'Leary, o' the Carrickfergus O'Learys, hired t'guide these fine gintlemin through the hills."

"I can't imagine what the 'fine gentlemen' could want in these hills. Since the destruction of Ballyaroon, there is nothing to be found here but stones and heather . . . and ghosts."

"It may very well be a ghost we're seeking." The more imposing of the two soldiers stepped forward with an uneven gait. Rhiannon shivered, and she couldn't help wondering how many enemies he'd sent to the hereafter. He looked as if he might have ridden from the pages of *Sir Gawain and the Green Knight,* a medieval warrior astride a destrier. Military might screamed from every line in the man's body.

Even the bones of his face seemed at war with the flesh that covered them. A lantern jaw thrust out beneath a hawkish nose, deep-set eyes overshadowed by a prominent shelf of brow. A dashing scar hooked along one cheekbone, disappearing into the coarse black hair at his temple. And a sizzling tension emanated from him, but try as she might, Rhiannon couldn't trace its source.

"Permit me to introduce myself," he said in surprisingly cultivated accents. "Lieutenant Sir Thorne Carville, formerly of the Sixty-fifth Cornwall."

"Sir Thorne."

"Mr. O'Leary, Sergeant Barton, and I have been engaged in a most desperate operation these few days past. An officer of the king's army has gone missing."

They were searching for Redmayne. They had to be. She should have felt a rush of relief, flung open the caravan door, and returned the enigmatic captain to his fellow officers. It was the only logical action. Except for the note she'd slipped from Redmayne's pocket and read while he was unconscious. The one that had claimed the traitor he sought could be found among his own men. She bit the inside of her lip, torn by indecision.

"As you know, Miss . . . ?"

"Fitzgerald." Why did she feel as if she had given the man a piece of her soul? "Rhiannon Fitzgerald."

"Miss Fitzgerald." The lieutenant swept her a theatrical bow. "This island can be most hazardous to the health of a lone English soldier. An astonishing number of accidents can befall those who stray too far from their garrison."

"Perhaps it is the mist, Sir Thorne. People have become lost in it for ages past." She attempted to stall, praying that she'd get some sort of insight into Sir Thorne and his compatriots. "Or maybe the fairies stole your officer away. They've been taking mortals prisoner in Ireland since time began."

Thorne's mouth hardened, his eyes narrowing, and in that instant Rhiannon caught a glimpse of what it might mean to have this man as an enemy. "I am a simple soldier, Miss Fitzgerald, given to far more practical answers to such mysteries. Your countrymen are an unruly lot, prone to acts of cowardice, cutting soldiers down with an assassin's blade, a sniper's bullet."

Rhiannon instinctively straightened her spine. "People can become most unreasonable when their homes are pulled down over their heads." It wasn't the wisest thing she could have said under the circumstances, but the words slipped out before she could stop them. She couldn't help glancing again at the Irishman, wondering if one of those shattered cottages had induced him to serve as guide to the enemy. The man winced, then shuttered it away.

As if suddenly aware of his tactical error, Sir Thorne twisted his lips into a grimace of a smile. "You are quite right, Miss Fitzgerald. I beg you to forgive my clumsiness. It is not a soldier's job to question his government's policies in a conquered land, be they fair or foul. We are trained to obey orders. That is all."

That was true enough. And it had often disturbed Rhiannon when she heard hatred of the English poured out more freely than whiskey about hearth fires and crossroads. True, the English government had been brutal, ruthless, in its dealings with Ireland. But sprinkled among the seasoned soldiers who carried out their orders were fresh-faced country boys from Yorkshire and Kent, driven into the army by the same desperate need to survive as the impoverished Irish.

Rhiannon had seen those English boys' eyes grow troubled, filled with regret as they followed their officers' commands. She'd sensed that the things they'd done and seen would haunt them. And as time passed, she'd seen them harden, shut down their emotions as they grew too painful to bear. Enemies, those boys and the Irish crofter's sons, and yet they were more alike than either of them knew.

And men like Sir Thorne and Captain Redmayne were the ones who commanded them to fight each other. Rhiannon's stomach tightened with loathing.

"Miss Fitzgerald." The man Sir Thorne had identified as Sergeant Barton stepped forward. "We are really quite desperate to find this officer. He is a most remarkable man and a brave one." The sergeant's boyish face grew so earnest that for an instant, Rhiannon considered spilling out the truth. Yet, as if of their own volition, her eyes flicked to the rugged features of Sir Thorne.

"I . . . I don't think I can help you," she said. By the gates of Tir naN Og, had she lost her mind? Redmayne was just beyond the door, so gravely injured that it would be best if he saw a doctor. Who could predict whether or not he would spike a fever, the wound turn putrid? Her skills at healing might prove meager indeed if put to such a test.

"Perhaps we could speak with your husband? He might have seen something you missed?" Sir Thorne took a step forward, eyeing the caravan door.

"My . . ." Rhiannon leaned back until her shoulders were flat against the door. "I have no husband."

Something ugly sparked in the lieutenant's eyes. "You are alone?"

The words raked across her nerves. Fool. Stupid fool! To let such a man know she was utterly vulnerable.

"Perhaps you would be kind enough to loan me some char-cloth to start a fire tonight. These hills are intolerably cold and damp." He paced another step forward. "Doubtless you have some inside your caravan."

God in heaven, had she betrayed herself somehow? His intent was clear. He was going inside. Determination carved deep brackets at the corners of his smug mouth.

She scrambled for something, anything that might hold the man at bay. "You can't go in there." She hated herself for the catch in her voice.

Thorne's gaze sharpened. "Why, madam? Have you something to hide?"

"Yes! I—I mean, no! But it's too . . ."

"Too what?"

At that instant her eyes caught sight of a tiny blemish on the sergeant's face. Relief flooded through her as she grasped at one thing that might actually turn this man away. A man unafraid of sword thrust or pistol ball, battle or a swift hero's death. Yet there were other kinds of death that could strike terror into even the staunchest soldier's heart.

"You asked if I had a husband. I don't. But . . . I do have a brother."

Thorne chuckled. "Ready to fight for the glory of Ireland, no doubt?"

"Not now, he isn't. Perhaps not ever." It didn't even take any acting expertise to look worn and worried, as if she'd labored days over a sickbed. "He's ill."

The Irishman took a step back; even the sergeant looked a trifle uneasy.

"I won't disturb him for long," Sir Thorne said. "Barely a moment."

"That will be long enough to put you in danger. You see, he has smallpox."

All three men retreated a step. O'Leary crossed himself, the sergeant letting out a low curse. Even Sir Thorne blanched beneath his ruddy tan.

"Smallpox?" the lieutenant echoed uncertainly, and Rhiannon knew she'd struck her mark.

"He's a mass of bleeding pox. It's horrible, how disfigured his poor face is." She managed a choked sob. "Listen to me, being so absurd, worrying about his face, when he might well be dead before sunset." She looked almost hopeful. "Perhaps one of you would be willing to help me. It's so difficult to move poor Liam. You could lift him from the bed, and I could change the fouled sheets."

Panic streaked across the men's faces, their fear almost comical. "No, madam. We—we need to get on about our own mission." O'Leary was already scrambling toward horses tied at the edge of the clearing.

"But, gentlemen, surely—"

The sergeant edged forward, white-faced. "I suppose I could—"

"Barton, no!" Sir Thorne gripped the man's elbow. "Most unfortunate. My sympathies, madam. But orders to follow. Must see to them." The lieutenant hobbled toward his mount, half dragging Barton with him. Even from that distance, Rhiannon could see sweat beading the man's upper lip.

Her whole body trembled as they wheeled their mounts around, spurring them away. Her knees buckled, and she sank down onto one of the steps, wondering if her heart would ever stop racing.

Looping her arms around Milton, she buried her face in the soft fur of his neck. How long it was she couldn't be certain before the caravan door gently nudged her back. She scooted aside so that Redmayne could swing the door open. She looked up to find the captain braced against the frame, one hand clutching the handle of the poker. He used it like a cane to take the weight off of his wounded leg. Even so, his face was ash pale with suppressed pain, his unfathomable ice-blue eyes surveying the direction in which the soldiers had gone. Yet something that almost smacked of amusement was playing about his white lips.

"You astonish me, Miss Fitzgerald. A tidy bit of lying, that was. Of course I would have seen through it in a heartbeat."

Damn the man for being amused at her expense! She'd probably just shaved ten years off her life, so heart-stopping had that experience been! "Please forgive me!" she snapped. "I haven't had much practice!"

His eyes widened in surprise. "Have I offended you? A thousand pardons. Your performance did well enough for our visitors. I could hear bits of what went on—enough to be most impressed."

Was the insufferable man attempting to poke barbs into her fraying nerves? "I was probably the biggest fool this side of Derry! You could be on your way back to your garrison, to a doctor's care. And I—" she didn't finish. She didn't have to.

"You could have been rid of a most inconvenient guest," Redmayne added for her.

Heat flooded Rhiannon's cheeks at what he'd almost goaded her into saying. "I didn't mean that! I just . . . I still don't know why I didn't tell them you were here. You'd be far safer with an armed guard."

"More likely I would have been dead," Redmayne said quietly. "And so would you."

Rhiannon started, staring at him with round eyes. "But . . . but two of them were soldiers. They spoke about how brave you were. They said the whole garrison is combing the area."

Redmayne grimaced. "I see. It might have been interesting to ask the gentlemen exactly *why,* and what moved them to search hereabouts."

"They were desperate to find you."

"Rhiannon, when I rode out of the garrison, not a solitary soul knew where I was going. These men knew exactly where to hunt."

A stark chill surged through Rhiannon's veins. She pressed a trembling hand to her lips. "Jesus, Mary, and Joseph, you're right! The only ones who could have known . . ."

"They had to be involved in luring me out here to be ambushed."

She swallowed hard. "Then those m-men . . . they intended to . . . to murder you?"

"Not necessarily. They might be merely pawns sent here by whoever was responsible for the attack. I suppose it's possible. But whether they intended to kill me themselves, or unwittingly lead me into the clutches of this elusive enemy of mine matters little. The result would have been the same. Another unsightly hole in my uniform. Most distressing after you worked so hard to mend it."

"When I think of h-how close I came t-to telling

them you were here . . ." Rhiannon pressed one hand against his chest, as if that soft shield could somehow prevent an assassin's bullet from finding its mark.

But there was no scorn in the captain's eyes, only surprise at her touch, and the tiniest quirk of a smile of understanding. "You couldn't have known. Even so, you didn't tell them. You even managed to turn them away. You continually surprise me with new talents, Miss Fitzgerald."

"Perhaps they left this time, but they're still out there. They'll still be searching. It's thirty miles to your garrison, along lonely deserted roads. Plenty of time to find you. And even if I do manage to get you back to your command in one piece, you'll still be in danger. Who's to say someone won't creep into your quarters in the middle of the night and—"

"Don't let your imagination run wild, my dear. I rarely sleep. All those years of campaigning on battlefields."

"But you have to close your eyes sometime! It would take but a heartbeat."

Redmayne stared at her, those uncanny eyes probing with the greatest delicacy, one brow arched in surprise. "So much passion, Rhiannon Fitzgerald," he said softly. "Such righteous indignation. A veritable Galahad in petticoats, you seem."

It should have been mockery. It wasn't.

"May I tell you something?" For an instant he seemed as if he would touch her cheek, but at the last moment, he drew away. "It is dangerous to let yourself care so much. There are far more brutal ends than the swift piercing of a bullet. The piercing of the heart, for example, by hard reality. The death of innocence and tenderness is painful indeed. I would not have you take such a risk on my account."

She swallowed hard, turned her face away. "I would

care about any creature who was being hunted. And I would rather feel that pain than be dead inside."

"Comfort yourself with that thought if you wish," Redmayne said. "But remember that I warned you." He limped down the steps, staring in the direction the soldiers had fled. "Now tell me about our visitors. It is important to know as much as possible about one's enemies."

Rhiannon sucked in a steadying breath. "There were three of them. Seamus O'Leary, an Irishman who was serving as their guide, and two British soldiers— Sergeant Barton—"

"I have only a passing acquaintance with O'Leary, but Sergeant Barton is most familiar to me. A most earnest man. Either he is a pawn or he is far better at concealing his true nature than I would have believed."

"I thought so, too! That he was earnest, I mean. Something in his face made me want to tell him . . . to trust him. He was the reason I almost told them you were here."

"I assume the third man was the reason you did not."

Rhiannon wrapped her arms tight about her own rib cage. "He was . . . disturbing. It was so confusing. Usually I can sense people's essence—goodness, evil, fear, danger—but this time . . ." She shook her head.

"What name did he give you? And, more important, what did he look like?"

"Like a . . . you'll think me silly, but like a knight who had just charged out of the pages of a book. The kind who adored slashing at anybody unfortunate enough to get in his way. He had dark hair, and there was this . . . this tension all around him, as if he were ready to explode at any moment. And a scar. It curved along his cheek."

"Like so?" Redmayne marked the path of the scar along his own aristocratic cheekbone. "Ah, that explains his tender concern on my behalf."

Rhiannon wasn't certain whether she should be relieved or even more frightened. "You know him?"

"Does any man truly know another? Let us just say I am *acquainted* with Lieutenant Sir Thorne Carville. A man of unlimited military brilliance, born to grace the annals of history like a modern-day god of war—at least in his own estimation."

"Were those men your friends? If I run, I might be able to catch them."

"Pray don't exert yourself. And give me credit for better taste, madam. If I ever did stoop to make a friend, I would have much too discerning taste to saddle myself with someone like Sir Thorne and his cohorts. I blush to confess that I am prey to a rather uncharacteristic bout of curiosity regarding the man, however. Tell me, was he limping?"

"Yes."

"Ah, most satisfactory. I thought I'd placed my shot well, but one can never be certain."

Rhiannon was stunned at the coolness in Redmayne's voice. "You were the one who lamed him?"

"On a dueling field at dawn. In all fairness, he shot at me as well, and believe me, madam, he wasn't aiming for my leg."

She'd heard enough absurdly romantic tales. She had to ask. "Why? Did you fight over a woman?"

Redmayne actually laughed. "Do I seem like the type of man to lose his head over some female?"

"Then why?"

"I have an aversion to waste, be it bullets, horseflesh, or soldiers' lives. Lieutenant Sir Thorne did not. Fortunately, when I approached the high command, they shared my view, despite the illustrious military history and not insignificant wealth of Thorne's family. They relegated the gentleman to a relatively harmless position on some general's staff. Thorne objected. You see, it's rather difficult to manage a blaze of military glory when one is thus employed. Thorne sought to repay me for my interference with a bullet. Alas, he didn't succeed in killing me. He did manage a more subtle revenge."

"What did he do?"

"Brought the pressure of his family to bear. The high command appeased the mighty Carvilles by quietly dispatching me to the ends of the earth, breaking my rank, and exiling me to Ireland. My military career was virtually extinguished in the same breath."

She gazed up at him, gladness flooding through her, as if she'd discovered something precious, unexpected. "It was for the soldiers, the innocent soldiers you cared about. What a noble, brave sacrifice."

Redmayne winced as if she'd insulted him. He held up one hand. "No romantic notions, Miss Fitzgerald. My only concern was the depletion of seasoned troops for no good reason. Why run a fine coaching pair of horses to death of exhaustion for no good purpose? If one is going to press them past their limit, one should at least have the brains to do so during a race upon which one has placed a large wager."

If he'd slapped her, he couldn't have had such a terrible effect. She recoiled, repulsed by the philosophy he claimed to have. "You can't possibly mean that."

"Oh, but I do. The lower ranks of soldiers are tools, Miss Fitzgerald, weapons to be wielded by those in command. To become a soldier, one has to face that reality, even if it is only within the most secret recesses of one's mind. I admit that there are officers who have a great love for their men, who suffer great pain at their death. I've seen that hell in their eyes long after battles are finished. But don't make the mistake of assuming I am one of that kind. I have no attachment to anything save logic and intellect."

"If I believed that was true, I would feel very sorry for you. But it makes no sense that you would take such a risk, cripple your own career to save lives unless you cared."

"Ah, stubbornly optimistic to the end. I wish you would quit attempting to look for some good in me. The only result will be eyestrain."

Why was it that his words hurt so deeply? Rhiannon wondered. "I wonder why it bothers you so much," she said, her chin bumping up a notch. "Perhaps you are afraid I might find something you've overlooked."

"You might as well attempt to breathe life into stone, my dear. As for your sympathy, you're wasting it. I prefer my life as it is." He limped down the stairs, paced a little way out into the grass, still bearing the prints of the other men's boots.

Rhiannon was silent for a moment, a little lost, a little desolate. "At least now you know who your enemy is," she said, attempting once more to find something bright in the dark web of danger surrounding them.

"It would seem so at first glance," Redmayne said, his voice totally noncommittal. "I've little doubt the good lieutenant wishes me dead. Were it merely a bullet in the back, I'd have no trouble believing he'd pulled the trigger. However, that he'd have the intellect, the guile, the patience to carry out a scheme cunning enough to fool me—that is hard to believe indeed." He turned back to her, something strange in his eyes. "I need to get back to my garrison at once.

Free myself of any distractions—fairy-born maidens, to be exact, wielding lethal bowls of gruel."

He wanted her safe, Rhiannon guessed. "You needn't be afraid for me."

He sighed. "You *will* persist in draping me with virtues I don't possess. It's a most tiresome habit. You are purely incidental, my dear. My interest is in this coil I've become caught up in. You see, I never could resist a puzzle. And this one grows more intriguing by the moment."

He was talking about his own life, about being hunted, stalked by assassins, men who were willing to betray him, to murder him. Yet his voice was as calm as if he were discussing the guest list for a Saturday evening musicale.

She might even have believed his heart had turned to stone, as he so obviously wished she would, were it not for one tiny flaw in his facade. The echoes of his desperate cries for his father, and the tiniest hint of fear that had played about his mouth when she walked out of the caravan alone to confront the men who might have come to kill him.

He turned away, but she didn't have to look into the handsome planes of Captain Redmayne's face to see.

Chapter

🍀 6 🍀

Redmayne paced off a few steps, grateful for the burning pain in his wounded leg. It almost distracted him, seared away the unfamiliar feelings this woman unloosed inside him. She was the black plague of emotions, virulent enough to be contagious even to him. And he damn well needed to be rid of her. "Hitch up that horse of yours at once," he bit out, trying to ignore her incessant chipping away at the temper he'd almost forgotten he possessed. "We're leaving. Now." He lanced her with a frigid look that should have left her quaking.

Her lips thinned, but that couldn't disguise their softness, the ripe smudge of strawberry pink against the fresh cream of her skin. "We've discussed this before," she said. "These roads are abominable. You are far too ill to be jounced over ruts for thirty miles."

"You mistake me, madam. I am not asking your permission. I am giving you a direct order."

Green eyes peered back at him, so unimpressed by his most chilling glare it was downright embarrassing. "Those men who visited the camp could be anywhere. Don't you think they would become a tad suspicious if I were suddenly to drag my smallpox-stricken brother on a little jaunt across the countryside? Be reasonable, Captain Redmayne." No other admonishment could have insulted him more completely. His temper stopped nudging him. It shoved. Hard.

"You dare to preach reason to *me?* A lone woman who picked up a half-dead stranger after he'd been shot down on the road? And then, as if that wasn't crazed enough, strode out to meet that man's would-be assassins when she was armed with nothing but a pathetic excuse for a lie?"

He was appalled by the tension underlying his voice, the obvious knotting of his muscles. Signs that all but screamed the woman was fraying his nerves. Stunned at such an unheard-of display, he forced ice crystals into his voice. "I am not accustomed to being defied. You *will* do as I command."

"Or else you will do what? Flog me? Break my rank? Have me drummed out of the army?" She reached out and patted his arm. "Don't worry, Captain, there will be plenty of time for that once you are well again."

It took every bit of his will not to grind his teeth—a most annoying habit that he wished he could indulge in. "Madam, do you have any idea who you are dealing with?"

"Quite a clear one, actually." She tossed back a wisp of cinnamon hair, thrusting it into the mass of curls tumbling about her face in disarray. "You remind me of someone I spent a great deal of time with last spring. That was a battle of wills to rival anything you can muster, I assure you."

"You underestimate me."

"*You* underestimate *him!* His name was Icarus—you know, from the Greek myth about the boy who made wings from feathers and wax, then flew too close to the sun. The wax melted, and he plunged to his death.

But I always thought it must have been wonderful soaring while it lasted."

Redmayne clenched his jaw. "Do I look as if I have the slightest interest in mythology at the moment?" he asked very carefully. "It's a pity this Icarus didn't throttle you and save me the aggravation."

"It would have been rather difficult for his talons to reach about my neck. Icarus was a falcon I tended. A boy had broken his wing with a rock, and the bird was a most reluctant patient. He decided it was time for him to go free long before he was properly mended. When I objected, he spent the rest of his convalescence sulking in his cage."

"You dare to compare that bird to . . ." Redmayne began, incredulous, then stopped, glaring. *"I do not sulk."* Devil if his cheeks weren't burning with an angry flush for the first time in twenty-odd years! Perhaps murder was his only option! Damn the woman! Her eyes were actually laughing.

"Captain Redmayne, the similarities between you and Icarus are quite unmistakable. I regret to inform you that you are ridiculously used to getting your own way—by fair means or foul, I would wager. But this time you have met your match. You'll find me unmoved by threats or tantrums *or* fits of the sulks. I know this is difficult for you, but my decision is for the best, I assure you. You might as well resign yourself to it." The empathy in her face was ruined by the slightest hint of amusement and, worse still, understanding. How dare she presume to understand him! He'd spent a lifetime twisting himself into an enigma.

Most aggravating of all, the woman was right! It *would* look suspicious if Sir Thorne and his comrades saw the caravan traveling so soon after their visit. Suspicious enough to bring them all charging down on his head! But that was a risk he was willing to take,

not because he was so eager to ferret out the traitors
who stalked him, or because he was eager to reach
his command, but rather because he would have
charged through the devil's own army to get away
from *her*.

Why display such unseemly haste? For the simple
reason that the woman was driving him mad. Not
since his grandfather had anyone or anything raked
at his nerves this way. He hadn't allowed it. But something about Rhiannon Fitzgerald made him feel closed
in, as if the air had become too thick to breathe, not
unlike the way a falcon must feel, imprisoned by the
bars of a cage, a mocking voice purred inside his
head.

"Captain Redmayne?"

Being jerked back to the present was a most
annoying sensation.

"I know you are not accustomed to taking advice,
but I'm going to suggest this to you anyway." Her
voice lilted with Irish music, yet was more resolute
than that of any besieged soldier he'd ever heard.
"I've been snarled at, snapped at, and bitten more
than once, all to no avail. It would be far more practical to use your energy to get well rather than to attempt to bully me into changing my mind. But it is
your decision."

Was the woman actually *patronizing* him? Captain
Lionel Redmayne? Something hot and uncomfortable
knotted in his gut. Anger? Uncertainty? Maybe a little
of both.

He could scarce believe it. Her eyes met his directly, no fear, no distrust. Didn't the woman have the
wit to realize what he was?

No. She had a clear enough picture. Her observa-
tion echoed in his mind: "used to getting your own

way by fair means or foul." But she was determined to defy him.

So the woman wanted to cross swords with him, did she? She thought herself a worthy opponent? Fine. He'd never been able to resist a challenge. After all, he'd been schooled by the most ruthless man alive.

But how best to defeat her? He mused for a long moment; then his eyes narrowed. Of course. There was only one thing to do. Make his stubborn guardian angel as anxious to be rid of *him* as he was to be rid of *her*.

Yet she was unaffected by the sharp wit and the cold glares that had always been his most finely honed weapons. There had to be another way to break Mistress Sunshine's resolve. How could he horrify her so completely that she would abandon her high principles, happily dump him at the garrison's doorstep, and drive her ridiculous horse and wagon away at breakneck speed?

Redmayne turned toward her, his gaze snagging on the rosy curve of her lips. Generous and inviting, dewy fresh, they shone, glossy in the light of the sun. He would wager his soul that those lips were as untouched by man as the briar roses tangled in a secret glen. What would happen if he plundered them?

It was a despicable plan. Made more loathsome still by everything she'd done for him. He actually felt a twinge. Fortunately, his conscience was so out of practice it was easily silenced. He didn't *really* intend to ravish her, after all, only scare her a little. And whatever his motives, she would benefit from the results as well. Be safer. Released from this crucible of betrayal he was embroiled in, a deadly game in which each move might be the last.

Come to think of it, his plan was fitting, somehow. Poetic justice. She seemed so smug, so certain she

understood every secret corner of her wounded creatures' hearts. It was time to discover whether the lady
had any idea what it felt like *not* to be the savior but
the prey.

Redmayne had always loved the hours before a
siege—time to plan the perfect battle, play out the
scenes in his head again and again until no lives
would be lost to carelessness or flawed logic. Mistakes, costly at any time, were paid in battle with
men's blood. Yet this campaign was different. He'd
never before given a damn about the effect the altercation would have on the enemy. Enemy. A green-eyed
woman with roses in her cheeks and stubbornness
ingrained in every fiber of her being, stubbornness
that had saved his life and tried his renowned
patience.

With every moment that crawled past as the sun
made an agonizingly slow arc across the Irish sky, he
found himself unaccustomedly edgy. He had to wait,
of course. Be patient.

Only a fool would go charging in at once, brandishing either sabres or kisses. Rhiannon Fitzgerald
had a keen enough mind and an uncanny ability to
uncover secrets in a man's eyes. If she got so much
as a hint of what mischief he was brewing, she'd likely
meet his amorous attempts with laughter or with a
blistering scold.

Yes, he knew what had to be done, but in this case
spontaneity was the key. It didn't take a great deal
of plotting. Nor should it take an overabundance of
loverlike skill to singe the hair ribbons off someone as
innocent as Rhiannon. Just cup that soft, impossibly
obstinate chin in the palm of his hand, lower his lips
to hers and taste . . . what? What would she taste of?
Sweet milk and warm honey? Cinnamon?

He grimaced. It didn't matter. He was only going to kiss her for effect, after all. Still, it had been a long time since he'd kissed a woman. He'd have to keep that in mind.

Even the kiss mustn't be too abrupt. He'd have to tease her with hot looks, tempt her with a brush of his hand against hers. And then he'd level her with a lightning bolt of pure sensuality. That should send Miss Innocence diving for shelter. Especially when she came into the caravan to lie beside him in that ridiculously tiny bed. What was it she'd said the night before? She was used to sharing the bed? She'd just think of him as an extremely large hound. He'd wager that would be more difficult after he kissed the blazes out of her.

Impatience stirred, and he arched one brow in surprise at the sensation. He wasn't eager to kiss her, he insisted to himself. It was just that he had too much time on his hands at present. He'd been forever busy, strategizing, planning, working to unravel the secrets that lay in other men's minds. He'd always believed he'd spent most of his life thinking. Strange to suddenly realize it wasn't true.

Here in this tiny glen there was a sudden silence, an unexpected idleness. The sense that he was no longer in control was both baffling and appalling. This lunatic angel of his was far too adept at peeling away a man's defenses to peer inside him. It was one thing to be the probing intellect doing the analyzing. It was another altogether to have some wind-tossed, dewy-eyed little optimist regarding him with enough compassion and understanding to make him want to throttle her.

Rhiannon Fitzgerald's probing was disturbing enough on its own. But equally surprising and unnerving was the knot that had tightened in his gut the moment she mentioned the names of the men who had sought him.

Sir Thorne Carville. There was little to astonish Redmayne there. He'd known from the first he would have to deal with the man again someday. As for the Irishman, it was all too easy to recall how he'd earned the man's enmity. During his first months in Ireland, Redmayne had planned to break the Irish people's ties to their past by destroying the monuments that were a constant reminder of glory long faded. Standing stones and passage tombs, mystic rings of stones and ruins of enchanted castles. The first victim to fall at his orders had been a passage tomb near O'Leary's cottage.

But neither Carville nor O'Leary had disturbed him. He'd had plenty of enemies before and had never allowed that fact to trouble him. It was the presence of the third man that gave him an unexpected twinge.

Barton.

"Were those men your friends?" He recalled the echo of Rhiannon's question and his own hard laugh of dismissal.

"Give me credit for better taste, madam," he'd scoffed. *"If I ever stooped to make a friend . . ."* They'd been nothing but careless words. He knew he never would call anyone by that name. But Kenneth Barton had been too thick-headed to realize it.

Redmayne grimaced. He'd all but drowned in the youth's hero worship when Barton first became his aide-de-camp. An awkward, fumbling, beardless boy who had an irritating habit of dropping things the instant Redmayne entered the room. It wasn't an unfamiliar reaction—Redmayne had always disconcerted those around him. What had unnerved Redmayne far more was the day Barton had stopped dropping things. The day Mary Fallon Delaney and her husband had ridden away from the garrison, and Redmayne had let them go.

It had been futile to pursue the matter any further, Redmayne had claimed. He'd believed that was his reason for releasing them. Barton had not believed it for a moment. And once the whole affair was over, no matter what efforts Redmayne made to push the man back to a comfortable distance, he couldn't escape the knowledge that Barton might yet be awed by him, but that maybe, just maybe, the incomprehensible man also *liked* him.

Even the promotion Redmayne had arranged hadn't sobered the man one bit. Hopeful as a puppy, Barton had always hung about. And Redmayne had had to shove him aside more than once, since dealing him a sharp rap on the nose lacked the dignity required in the army.

From the instant Redmayne had scanned the note alerting him to a traitor in his own garrison, he had thought it was immaterial who had betrayed him. Why did the mere possibility Barton might be involved affect him so strangely?

Doubtless that was Rhiannon Fitzgerald's fault, too. All those sorrowful glances she'd given him beneath those absurdly long eyelashes. The soft ache in her voice, as if she grieved for his loneliness.

The woman should look to her own situation! She talked to animals, for God's sake! She rattled about the countryside in this garish little nutshell of a wagon, totally defenseless. As unfit to be wandering about as a babe who'd toddled off into the forest. She'd lost her home, her father, and the servants who'd doubtless looked after her every need, but she considered herself fortunate, rich. Why? Because she dared to love everything and everyone with the same abandon, from a recalcitrant falcon to a shimmer of mist atop a hill? Because she chose to see what was good—even in a wounded officer who had deadened his heart long ago?

Blast, had she meddled in his mind so much these past few days that he'd begun to sort through his acquaintances, searching for someone who might give a damn if he died?

If he *had* been such a fool, even in his subconscious, then the arrival of Barton had been well timed indeed. An appropriate reminder of why he'd always held himself aloof from his fellow creatures, completely unattached to anyone or anything.

She'd thought he was in pain because he'd been betrayed. But he knew the truth: no one could betray you unless you were foolhardy enough to care about them in the first place. Despite his small stumbles over Mary Fallon Delaney and Kenneth Barton, he was no fool, and not even the softest green eyes in Ireland were going to make him one.

"Captain Redmayne?"

He started at the sound of her voice at his shoulder. He turned to see her standing there with fresh if somewhat threadbare towels draped over her arm and a pot of soft soap in her hand. "Is there anything I can do for you before I go down to the stream? I'll only be gone a little while."

Her cheeks were tinged with pink, her gaze flickering away from his. She was going to bathe, Redmayne realized with a swift surge of satisfaction. What more auspicious opportunity could there be to begin his siege? He would wait a little while, long enough for her to begin, and then . . .

"Captain Redmayne?"

He glanced up at her, hastily concealing any hint of the machinations going on inside his head. But she gazed at him with eyes so guileless, so soft with concern, that he felt as if someone had layered a fine coat of silt over his body.

"I hate to leave you alone." She hesitated.

"Go ahead. I'm used to it." Damnation if that didn't sound a trifle weary, almost wistful. The words, not his tone. He grimaced and said what he'd meant all along: "I prefer it that way."

"I know," she replied, but something about her voice infuriated him. It was not as if she agreed with him but rather as if she knew some truth he wasn't ready to admit to.

He was still attempting to think up an appropriate reply when she started down the grassy bank to where a copse of trees sheltered a bend of the stream from view.

Graceful and light as petals caught on the wind, she glided along, her skirts swaying like the cup of a bluebell, rivers of golden sunlight streaming through the dark flow of her hair. She had none of the elegance of the worldly beauties who had graced Redmayne's bed, none of that practiced perfection, and yet there were men who would think her even lovelier.

In place of satin she trailed an astonishing warmth, a vibrancy in her wake, as if even the sunlight couldn't resist that intangible aura she spun. Instead of jewels gracing her throat and wrists and the tender lobes of her ears, stars sparkled in her eyes. And her hands were scented not with attar of roses but rather with cinnamon and vanilla and something far more rare: genuine compassion.

His hand knotted into a fist. Blast! One would think he'd taken that bullet in his head! He'd never been a man to spin out such absurdities over any woman.

Why, then, did he feel this strange fascination? This need to follow her with his gaze, this anticipation, waiting to see what she would say next? It was merely that she was a curiosity, he assured himself. A woman unlike any he had ever known.

Even Fallon had been all fire and defiance and tempestuous emotions. She was a woman who would keep a man racing in circles just to keep up with her. Rhiannon had the same measure of courage, but there was something else in her—a gentleness, despite her humor, an indefinable quality that invited a man to rest.

He surprised a laugh out of himself, his injured shoulder aching. Rest? The woman hadn't given him a moment's peace since she hauled him into her caravan!

Swearing under his breath, he surveyed the path she'd taken, realizing that sometime during his nonsensical reverie the woman had disappeared from view.

Just as well, he supposed. He'd given her enough time to settle into her ablutions. Half undressed, wet and unwary, she should be vulnerable enough to his attentions. A strange brew of self-disgust and expectation stirred in his belly. Only because he would be meeting her challenge, of course.

In his head he imagined her bare feet padding across the thick carpet of turf, the grass growing damp beside the sparkling water. He imagined how long it would take for her deft fingers to unfasten the army of buttons that marched between the soft hills of her breasts. Doubtless she would pause to study the face of any pretty wildflower that happened to perch on the stream bank. And God help him if some disobliging trout showed her an injured fin. Better to get down there before the woman unwittingly outflanked him again!

Redmayne straightened, limping in the direction

she'd gone, wondering if he'd ever looked forward to crossing swords quite this much.

Even wounded, he was able to move with the stealth of a predator, a skill learned in his grandfather's household, then perfected on scouting missions before battle. He intended to steal up as quietly as possible, give himself time to gauge the best angle from which to "attack." But as the underbrush fell away before him, dappled shadows giving way to the sunshine spilling over the stream, he stopped, all thoughts scattering at the scene before him.

Rhiannon had flung herself into her bath with the same joy with which she faced everything else in her day, wholeheartedly, delightedly, abandoning any lingering fears on the mossy bank along with her heavy skirts. Clad in only her shift, she splashed in the water, hurling cascades of sparkling silver drops at the foxhound gamboling about in a futile effort to find her. Her freshly washed hair clung about her shoulders, and down her back, the thin fabric of her undergarments molding her curves like the hands of a lover.

Rosy patches of her skin glowed through, the dusky circles of her nipples pushing at the fabric, accenting lush breasts. A trim waist and full hips were clearly visible, and a man would have had to be a corpse not to feel a stirring in his loins at the dark shadow of curls arrowing down toward slender legs that seemed to go on forever.

Perhaps he'd managed to deaden his emotions, Redmayne thought, but he still had an appreciation for perfection. Beauty. Yet Rhiannon Fitzgerald's own brand of beauty was fashioned out of a dozen imperfections, flaws that should have made her unappealing, yet instead held his gaze prisoner, made him wonder exactly what it was that compelled him to keep looking at her.

Simple lust, Redmayne reasoned with grim humor. The fact that he hadn't troubled himself to take a woman to his bed since he'd arrived in Ireland. Even the icily controlled Lionel Redmayne's body needed release upon occasion, if only to keep himself from being distracted. Perhaps searing the lady with hot stares wouldn't take much effort after all. And yet . . . the sooner she surrendered, the better. Like all good strategies, there was danger in this one.

He was a man with a man's needs.

And it had been a very long time.

Chapter

7

She sensed his presence mere heartbeats before she saw him, a solitary figure, golden hair sunstruck. Blades of shadow and light hewed his face with the patrician arrogance of the first fairy king who had set forth his royal foot upon the ageless hills of Ireland. Bold, almost too beautiful for human eyes to see.

But a kind of defiance shaped the set of his jaw, an unfamiliar buzz of tension emanating from his lean body in waves that flowed around her, tightening about Rhiannon's breast.

She stilled, tried to suck in a deep breath, chill water running in rivulets down her body. She might have been a stray beggar maid confronting the god of water, her wet hair clinging in a silken web to cheeks already burning with embarrassment, surprise, and something foreign, perhaps a little frightening.

Shoving away the ridiculous sensation, she started toward Redmayne, afraid that something was amiss. The men were returning, his wounds were paining him, while she stood there like a witling gawking at him. "What is it?" she asked, sloshing toward Redmayne. "Is something wrong?"

But at that instant, a miracle occurred. Milton realized one of his most cherished aspirations: he actually *located* what he was searching for. The foxhound launched himself from a patch of mud, his massive paws slamming into Rhiannon's stomach. Her breath went out in a whoosh, the impact hurtling her backward. She crashed down, her mouth filling with a wave of choking water. Her backside slammed into the rock-strewn bottom of the stream, bruising her flesh almost as much as it wounded what little dignity she still possessed.

Sputtering, flailing, she fought to regain her feet, but the tangle of sodden shift and elated canine made it impossible. Milton might actually have succeeded in drowning her, and she might not have objected overmuch, except that a hard hand manacled her wrist, dragging her upright, a deep voice biting out a low command. "Down."

With her free hand, Rhiannon scrubbed her sea-weedlike hair out of her face just in time to see Milton perch obediently on the stream bank, his cloudy eyes fixed with infuriating devotion in the general direction of the man who had dared to discipline him.

Redmayne stood so close to Rhiannon that the heat radiating from his body penetrated her own chilled skin. His low chuckle astonished her, banished her fear that some calamity had overtaken them, yet tightened the net of embarrassment he'd trapped her in.

"Saved from an untimely death. And a most undignified one at that," Redmayne said. "It seems we are even now, Rhiannon."

Her name. He'd merely called her by her name for the first time. But it had changed everything. A strange shiver coursed down her spine, not from the cool of the breeze against her wet skin but rather from the husky rumble of his voice, the hot brush of his breath against her cheek. She tried to swallow, but her throat was inexplicably dry.

"Captain, wh-what . . . what are you doing here?"

"A fine way to thank your rescuer, that. Perhaps you need lessons in the etiquette of a damsel in distress. This is your cue to fall upon me in abject gratitude." He smiled. Her heart stopped. God above, she hadn't even realized the man *could* smile. No one should be given such a lethal weapon to wield against a woman.

"I just . . . I didn't expect—"

"Any company? That is obvious enough, considering your attire."

She skittered back a step, glancing down, agonizingly aware of the thinness of her soaked shift—transparent as morning mist, the curves and shadows of her most secret places visible to Redmayne's all-too-keen gaze.

Any modest, self-respecting woman would have chosen that moment to dive headlong into the water—if it had been deep enough to cover her properly. But Rhiannon was stunned to find herself standing as still as a woodland doe, surprised, curious, trembling just a little at the unexpected sensations rippling through her.

She raised her own gaze to Redmayne's face. Could there be such a thing as hot ice? The piercing blue of his eyes burned. Innocent as she might be, she recognized that heat for what it was, yet she could scarce believe her own deduction. Desire. Was it real? Or as ephemeral as the visions of fairy folk she'd imagined were dancing within the stone circles when she was a child?

She wasn't certain. She only knew that no man had ever looked at her that way before. She scrambled to find her scattered senses.

"Was there something you wanted?"

You.

He communicated it without words, a thick pulse that entered her veins where his fingers were still circled about her wrist. He raised his gaze to hers, and she felt her breath catch as if she'd heard him voice his need aloud.

He cleared his throat, withdrawing his hand. She felt the loss of his touch as if he'd left a wound, and she realized in that instant how much she'd missed being touched.

Oh, Triona and her husband always greeted her with an embrace and a buss on the cheek. Other friends as well were quick to squeeze her hand. But she was on the road so much of the time that she was like someone thirsty, receiving only sips of water when she needed so much to drink deep.

"You asked why I came down here," Redmayne said. "I had hoped that perhaps you would do me one more favor. One of my greatest flaws is that I am somewhat fastidious. I'm afraid my convalescence has left me feeling rather gritty, and a sponge bath is less than satisfactory."

Of course, that was why he had followed her. She should have anticipated that a man like Redmayne wouldn't be satisfied overlong with her halfhearted dabbings with the sponge. "I should have realized that and offered to bring you down here, instead of indulging myself. I just didn't think."

"It's no sin, Rhiannon, failing to anticipate someone else's every need. I'm actually rather glad you can't read my mind." He was mocking her, and himself. Yet she *had* sensed his thoughts a moment ago, and she'd been flustered and delighted and frightened by what she'd found there.

Even more surprising was the captain's other comment: "It's no sin, Rhiannon."

Was he merely teasing? Or had he actually realized the truth? This man of ice, of logic and reason, who claimed to care for no one—was he the first person ever to unearth her most secret vulnerability, the thing that troubled her more than any other failing? That crushing sense of responsibility that had been a part of her for as long as the green of her eyes and the dimple in her cheek.

"Rhiannon?"

The low rumble of her name upon his lips startled her. And she looked up at him, heat stealing into her face.

"If you've got your balance, I'll let you return to your own bath. There is plenty of time later for me to make myself less objectionable."

He intended to leave. It was alarming to realize how fiercely she wanted him to stay.

"Captain, please. I wouldn't want you making such a long walk again on your injured leg. Besides, I'm finished with everything except getting myself dry."

He arched one eyebrow. "You're certain?"

"Of course!"

"Rhiannon, you're not to be trusted. You would say you were finished if you'd barely dipped your toes in the water if you thought someone else needed you."

She should have felt exposed—had it been possible to feel more exposed than she actually was, garbed in her shift. Instead she was glad. "You have your choice, sir." She scooped up the hem of her shift, then crossed to where she'd laid her gown. "Either I can help you with your bath, keeping your wounds at least somewhat dry in the process, or I can leave you to the tender ministrations of Milton."

The dog thumped his tail as if to show that he was more than willing to be of service.

"I much prefer you to your hound," Redmayne said as she grasped her gown. "But—pardon me if I'm being rude—but your dress, there is no reason to put it on and get it all soaked on my account. I'll keep my eyes averted if you wish."

Ah, that was the problem. Wanton as it might be, some part of her wished to remain just as she was. The breeze teasing her bare legs beneath her hem, her hair streaming loose down her back, and this man's hot gaze upon her.

"I think it would be—be best if I . . ."

"Ah, so you are capable of noble behavior, but I am not."

Her brow furrowed. "What on earth do you mean by that?"

"When I was injured, you stripped off my clothing, bathed me, tended me, and I'm certain you observed all the proprieties you were able to."

"Of course I did!" It wasn't exactly the truth, and she was certain he realized it from the guilty fluttering of her gaze away from him.

"Don't you believe me capable of the same courtesy? I am, after all, an officer and a gentleman."

That irresistible light winked in his eyes again. "You wouldn't want me to feel responsible for soiling your gown, would you? I would have to get down on my knees, beat it again with the rocks to get it clean."

"You've never scrubbed anything in your life, I would wager," she said.

"No. Just think of the damage I might do to your gown, and the guilt I might suffer." Why did it seem so strange? His smile, so beautiful, the effort she could sense in him, as he tried to infuse it with warmth. It made her heart ache for the boy she sensed beyond the brilliant blue of his eyes—a boy who had never really had a chance to be. What had happened to him, she wondered, to banish the child in him so completely?

She held on to the soft folds of cloth for one last moment, then released them. Was that triumph she glimpsed curling one corner of his mouth? She couldn't be certain. He turned away, and all she could see was the back of the shirt she'd mended for him, rows of tiny stitches, catching together the slashes her scissors had made. Why was it she was suddenly so certain that whatever scars lay hidden beneath Captain Redmayne's cool facade would not be so easily healed?

Catching her lower lip between her teeth, she crossed to where she'd abandoned the little soap pot and the damp cloth she'd washed with. The man wanted a bath. She should give him one, not waste time trying to pry beneath the mask he kept so carefully in place. *At least, not until he's better able to defend himself,* a voice inside her whispered.

And yet she knew well enough that there were only brief times when the gate to the heart might be open, in wounded beasts and wounded people. And unless one stole inside at the exact right moment, that entrance could slam closed forever. Lost with it, the chance to heal.

Yet wouldn't a man as closed, as fiercely private as this one loathe anyone who saw pain instead of strength? Emotion instead of intellect? Vulnerability instead of invincible control?

Why should it matter so much how he felt about her? She would have him with her for only a little while. He was no Milton or Socrates or Captain Blood, to lounge about, tamed to her hand. He was wilder than her falcon, warier than her wolf, no creature to be kept near her hearth fire, content with her fingers stroking the rare gold silk of his hair.

And yet something inside him called to her, something beyond her need to comfort, to heal. A facet of Rhiannon Fitzgerald she'd thought she left behind forever at Primrose Cottage, sensations packed carefully away with lace fans and satin slippers that had danced their last.

That unique delight, that anticipation, that every schoolgirl cherished in her most romantic dreams—emotions that could be ignited in the space of a heartbeat by a man's smile.

Absurd, these feelings. She was a grown woman with no illusions about the reality of her situation. Balls and beaux were lost to her. And even before she left Primrose Cottage forever, a man like Captain Redmayne would have been far beyond her touch. Ambitious, possessed of qualities of leadership that shone brighter than the gold of his hair, Redmayne was a gifted officer. He would need a wife appropriate for advancing his career. Rhiannon would be hopeless.

Even if she weren't Irish—enough of a strike against her—she would have far preferred mothering homesick boys to courting the favor of pompous generals. She hated formalities that permeated the military, and war, to her, seemed the ultimate obscenity. Hardly a view designed to aid in the advancement of her husband.

Lord, what was wrong with her? The man had been shot, and she'd tended his wounds. He wanted to be quit of her as quickly as possible. Once he returned to his real life, he wouldn't think twice about her except with a vague kind of puzzlement and perhaps a bit of gratitude. In the years to come . . .

But how much time might he have? Weeks instead

of years? Days? Hours? Worst of all, she'd seen the shadow of desolation in his eyes—enough to know that a part of Captain Redmayne might welcome death.

The thought haunted her, hurt her, filled her with tenderness and sorrow. When she turned back to him, she struggled to hide her discomfiture in a flurry of activity.

"Just take off your shirt and we'll make quick work of this before you grow tired."

"Can you help me? I regret the imposition, but the fastenings are difficult, since the wound in my shoulder objects to being twisted in any way."

Such a reasonable request. And she sensed just how much it had cost him. Captain Redmayne was not a man who would ask for help lightly—confess he needed anyone else for anything, even a task so insignificant as unbuttoning his shirt.

She should have felt warmed by even such a small offering of trust on his part. She shouldn't feel the flutter of butterflies' wings in her stomach. After all, she'd performed this task before. Why, then, this sudden hesitation? This awareness of the pale gold expanse of muscle beneath the thin layer of linen, the tingling of her fingers at the memory of how warm, how smoothly muscled his chest had been, the downy gold dusting of curls that had spanned it.

Redmayne's voice startled her out of her thoughts. "If it makes you uncomfortable, I can manage it." Long, strong fingers fumbled with the cloth at his throat. He winced, and Rhiannon could see how hard he tried to conceal it.

The evidence of his pain was like a sharp smack to her senses. Disgusted with herself, Rhiannon lowered the soap and towels onto a tussock of moss, and stood inches away from the captain. She grasped his hand in her own. "Don't. I was just being foolish. I know it sounds silly, but you shrank when you were in my bed."

"I what?"

"You seemed smaller, somehow. More . . . manageable."

For an instant something flickered in his eyes, a wariness, dismay, but it was gone so quickly she thought she must have imagined it. He smiled. "A word of advice, Miss Fitzgerald. You should think twice before using such adjectives in a gentleman's presence. It could do irreparable damage to his pride to be described in such terms upon leaving a lady's bed."

Her cheeks stung, but she managed a smile of her own as she reached for the folds of white linen beneath his chin. Her pulse jumped as the tips of her fingers brushed the corded strength of his throat. "You needn't worry," she said, attempting to sound breezy. "You are back in fine form now. Quite dashing enough to make any woman's heart skip a beat."

A moment of silence throbbed between them, and she could feel his gaze burning into the crown of her head.

"Present company included?" Low, so soft, were his words. She could feel them more than hear them, a sensual vibration of them deep in his throat.

"The state of my heart is immaterial," she said briskly. "You are the patient. My only concern should be nursing you back to health." She rushed down the fastenings of his shirt as if she were charging into the teeth of a rebel army.

"I suppose it should be," he mused. "But I find myself curious."

Why he would be she couldn't imagine. Every brush of her knuckles against his bare chest turned her heart into a battle drum. The words slipped out before she could stop them. "Captain Redmayne, did you stand close to one too many cannons during combat?"

His brow furrowed in confusion. "What a strange question. Why do you ask?"

"Because you must've suffered hearing loss if you cannot mark every beat of my heart."

She surprised another laugh from him, a sound full of astonishment and delight.

It braced her, calmed her at least a little. "I assure you, you don't have to worry that you've lost your effect on women. Now, since we needn't pursue that subject any further, perhaps we can concentrate on giving you your bath?" She gently tugged the shirt off, meaning to bustle about her business, laying the garment out on the rock, helping the injured man with towels and soap and scrubbings. But as she bared the tawny gold of his skin, saw the rippling play of muscles there, her throat went dry.

"Rhiannon," he murmured, "aren't you the least bit curious yourself?"

Curious? About the taste and texture of a man's skin, a thousand subtle differences from that of a woman. Saints above, if he only knew. She lowered her lashes to half-mast to conceal the strange rawness inside her, the sense of loss she'd all but forgotten, packed away, knowing that love was as far beyond her reach now as the moon.

"Curious? About what?"

He answered without a word. Long, strong fingers stroked her thumb, his palm cupping the back of her hand, urging her ever so gently to press it against the place where his heart beat. Sensation jolted through her, her hand resting half upon the bandage still wrapped about his shoulder, half on the hot satin of his skin.

She saw the planes of his face harden, his eyes darkening to midnight blue. Her sensitive fingers felt the quickening of his pulses, a rhythm that matched her own.

She yanked back her hand as if she'd touched a hot coal. He moved swiftly, as if to recapture it, stop her from pulling away, but the action cost him. His breath hissed through his teeth, and he clutched his injured arm tight against his ribs in an instinctive effort to shield it.

"You hurt yourself!" Rhiannon scolded, both relieved and disappointed that she'd been given an excuse to back away from feelings that were too potent, too dangerous, too new. "I knew that would happen! Now, *will* you behave yourself, and let us get on with this bath of yours before you exhaust yourself so badly you fall face down in the dirt?"

For a moment a mutinous spark ignited in Redmayne's eyes. Then he extinguished it. She could feel him release her from the sizzling bond between them as if he'd snipped some invisible thread.

"You would make a formidable drill sergeant, madam. Even a superior officer can tell when it's wisest just to follow orders." With that, he attempted to unbutton his breeches on his own. She almost allowed him to struggle—he'd made her so uncomfortable and, she suspected, committed the far more unforgivable sin of enjoying her discomfiture.

He plunged on manfully, if unsuccessfully, until she relented.

"For goodness' sake, let me do it or I'll get so exhausted from waiting that *I'll* be the one plunging face first onto the ground." But she was in far more danger of her knees crumpling for other reasons. It was one thing to undress such a devastatingly handsome man when he was bleeding, unconscious, perhaps dying. Then she'd had to uncover his wounds to tend them. It was another proposition altogether to undress that same man when he was towering above her, so heart-stoppingly masculine, every muscle taut, every sinew hot with life and the echoes of undisguised male hunger.

She knew she should hurry up and get this bathing affair over with as quickly and efficiently as possible. Concentrate on the task at hand and not get distracted by six feet three inches of dashing English officer. She was concentrating on the task so hard she leaped back in surprise when Redmayne let fly a low curse as her fingers twisted fiercely at a recalcitrant button.

"Rhiannon, I'm aware that a portion of my . . . er, anatomy is causing certain difficulties between us at present, but even so, I'd prefer to keep it in working order for sometime in the future. If you could be a trifle more . . . cautious when you're digging about."

Hot blood flooded her cheeks. "I hurt you! I'm so sorry!" It was instinctive, cultivated through years of soothing injuries and fears, the reflex to reach out her hand, smooth it ever so gently across what pained someone. She was horrified the instant she realized exactly *what* her palm cradled at present. Hot, hardening male.

She jerked back her hand, appalled. "I can't believe I . . . I mean, I didn't intend to . . . didn't think . . ."

"I'm doing enough thinking for both of us right now," Redmayne growled. He turned away, but not before she glimpsed the iron ridge of his jaw. Was it clenched in disgust or in a battle to get his unruly emotions under control? She couldn't be certain.

"We'll just leave the breeches on," he said tightly.

But enough of him was already exposed to set Rhiannon's knees quivering.

In an effort to hide the worst of her humiliation, she grabbed the small cloth, rinsed it in the stream, then dipped it into the soft soap. By the time she turned around, Redmayne had settled himself on a flat rock, putting his body more easily within her reach. He had teased her earlier, taken irritating masculine pleasure in her instinctive reaction to him, like a regal male lion displaying his mane to a lioness. And yet there now seemed to be a difference in the captain, a tension unlike any she'd felt in him before. Frustration, almost. Irritation.

Why? She should be able to get a sense of what was wrong, and yet every time she used her fairy arts to probe into Captain Redmayne's feelings, she felt as if she had stumbled into a choking mist that obscured everything. One of his own construction? A protective veil to guard the heart of a most private man? Or was he hiding something that was truly alarming? A deed beyond forgiveness?

Troubled by her train of thought, she approached him, even her dark musings unable to obscure the way his skin glowed in the sunlight, the smooth expanse marred by a sprinkling of white scars. Once the bullet wounds were healed, they would add to the tally of violence marked there, angry red, fresh, and raw. And then, soldier that he was, Redmayne would march out to court other saber slashes, other pistol balls, wounds to both his body and his soul. It saddened Rhiannon more than she could bear, but it also steadied her hands, softened the jagged edges of her nerves. She wanted so much to break through the barrier he'd constructed, to make this solitary man feel not quite so alone.

"Captain?" she said as she approached him, astonished at the strange prickling of tears beneath her eyelids. "I feel so foolish addressing you that way after we've been through so much together. Would you mind so very much . . . I mean, if you told me your name?"

"My name?" He slanted a glance at her, brows lowered, as if she'd asked him a far more difficult question.

"Yes. Please."

He hesitated, as if the very sound of his own name was strange to his tongue. "I suppose you could call me . . . Lion."

Lion. It fit him far too well—the tawny skin, the gold mane of hair, the quiescent power that could suddenly be transformed into something dangerous. "It's most unusual."

"My father used to call me by that nickname. Lionel, it seemed, was far too much of a mouthful to call a small boy."

"Lion." She tested the cadence of it, smiled. "I like it."

"I am much relieved." He didn't look any such thing. Instead, he seemed clenched inside himself, almost as if she'd stolen something from him.

"Could you lie down upon the mossy part of the rock? That way the water won't run down to dampen your breeches quite so badly while I scrub you. I'd like to keep your leg wound as dry as possible."

It seemed like a good idea until he complied with her request. He eased himself back onto the stone, looking for all the world like a jungle cat, and Rhiannon remembered with stark clarity how she had lain beside him the night before, two strangers, barely touching. What would it be like to feel free to reach out? she wondered. To caress his magnificent body, to warm the cold places inside him with her kiss?

Stop it, Rhiannon. She brought herself up sharply. *You're only making this more difficult.* Warming the cloth between her hands, she leaned over him and gently washed his face—the bold blade of nose, the aristocratic sweep of cheekbone, the rigid line of his jaw. Her fingertips brushed his skin, the silky gold of his hair, his breath heating the tender inside of her wrist.

She moved down his throat, along the strong bow of collarbone, heated dips and hollows where his pulse beat strong. His chest, even swathed in bandages, gleamed powerful, with a stirring masculine beauty.

Despite his complaints, he was so clean it seemed as if she were running the cloth over him for the pure pleasure of it, the way a mediocre sculptress might trace the contours of a masterpiece that could never belong to her.

It was sinful, no doubt, what she was feeling. And yet could anyone blame a scullery maid for running her fingertips across a fold of satin if she had just one chance to touch it? A chance that might never come again.

Succumbing to her own wickedness, Rhiannon let more of her hand slide off of the cloth, come in contact with his skin. The muscles beneath her hand grew as taut as iron bands, Redmayne so still it was almost frightening. She glanced at his face, saw his eyes shut tight, a knotted muscle twitching in his jaw.

"Did I hurt you? Are you all right?"

"No, damn it. I'm not all right."

"What . . . what is wrong?"

"This." He growled, his hand sweeping up to delve into the damp tangle of her hair. He tugged her mouth down toward his. Her heart slammed against her ribs at the hot intent glimmering beneath his lashes. And

Rhiannon wondered if she'd ever have the will to draw another breath as the sensual fullness of Red-mayne's mouth closed over hers.

The contact jolted through her as if he'd infused her with the very essence of life—awakened her from a nursery world, all bright smiles and pretty stories, fistfuls of daisies and scuffed play slippers—and suddenly she'd awakened in a realm of legends and lovers, passions and promises.

She should have been shocked. For his was no tentative kiss. It gripped her in a fist of sensation, wild and wonderful and so unfamiliar she never wanted it to end.

She sensed that he expected her to draw away from him. But her own lips melted deeper into his as he explored the contours of her mouth, tasting, nipping, soothing the tender curves with his tongue. A gasp of pleasure parted her lips, her elbows buckling, until the tips of her breasts, unbound beneath her damp shift, brushed his naked chest.

She felt a ripple of heat radiate through him. His uninjured arm curved around her waist, pulled her down until she lay half across him, a tangle of damp linen, bare feet, and cascading hair.

The intimacy was searing, intoxicating, but he hurled her higher still, his tongue slipping between her parted lips, seeking the warm, eager cavern beyond them.

This was no gentleman's chaste kiss for his sweetheart. This was the kiss of a man, experienced in the ways of the flesh, an expert lover who knew how to stoke the fires he'd started within her.

Hungry. Hot. Insistent. He was all of those things. She should have pulled away. Instead, she opened herself to it with a soft moan.

"Rhiannon . . . you taste so . . . so good. Can't

stop myself." He murmured against her mouth. Even through the haze of passion, his words struck her as odd. This man, so fiercely controlled, surrendering to impulses he didn't wish to. A surrender that thrilled her, and yet had come perhaps too easily to be trusted.

His hand stole up between them, and Rhiannon caught her breath as he teased the tender side of her breast. His fingers shifted until the hot point of her nipple was centered in his wide palm. A low groan reverberated through him, and in a heartbeat he'd opened the tie of her shift, let the fabric drop lower still, gaping open to reveal creamy-soft globes.

He pressed a hot kiss to the curve of her jaw, the pulsebeat at the base of her throat, traced kisses across her collarbone, then down the uncharted expanse of skin to where the hills of her breast began to rise.

It was shocking, indecent, unthinkable, what he was doing, nibbling away her sanity by inches. But more startling of all was Rhiannon's realization that she never wanted him to stop. She wanted more, so much more.

The points of her breasts burned, ached, as he circled hungry kisses nearer, ever nearer her nipple. The secret places between her thighs melted. She drowned in sensation, lost, like a leaf in a storm-swollen river, tossed upon wild currents, a little frightened, yet intoxicated by a power she hadn't ever known existed.

Warm lips drew closer to the tender pink of her areolae, and in that instant, she couldn't stand it any longer, the waiting, the need. Driven by instinct she didn't understand, Rhiannon shifted until her nipple brushed the damp satin of Lion Redmayne's lips.

What did she want? What was she reaching for? More kisses? More husky murmurs? For an instant she could feel it—a glimpse of feminine power, mysterious as the ages, a surging of heat through the man who held her. His lips stirred, parting just a whisper, as if to drink her in. A tiny sound escaped her, half whimper, half cry, and in that instant Redmayne's muscles went rigid wherever he touched her. With a muttered oath he pulled away from her, struggling to his feet as if the rock they'd lain on had suddenly grown white-hot.

Cool air streamed between bodies that had been so close moments before, drenching Rhiannon in reality, the sound of the stream bubbling past roared in her ears. She stared at him, wide-eyed, words and emotions, discoveries and possibilities, a mad tangle in her chest.

White-faced, he glared at her, his features tight with . . . what? Passion? Pain? Disgust?

"Cover yourself." He bit out the words, his voice so harsh it was as if he'd slapped her. A sick knot clenched in her stomach, and she glanced down at the front of her shift as if it belonged to someone else. Thin, damp, the fabric drooped low, revealing kiss-reddened breasts, trembling to the ragged pace of her breathing.

Shame—so fierce, so unexpected—flooded through her, icing the heat of desire, banishing the magic, stripping away half-forgotten dreams, and leaving behind stark reality.

"Rhiannon, do you have any idea what could have happened here?" he demanded, still glaring at her. "Five moments more, and I might have ruined you forever."

Ruined . . . He was right. Why had something so terrible felt so glorious, even for such a little while?

Her fingers numb, she fumbled with the tie of her shift, then hastened over to where her gown lay. She felt so foolish, so reckless, so small. "You're quite safe. I haven't any enraged father or brothers to come demanding a duel to defend my honor."

"I almost wish you had! A nice, swift bullet . . ."

Rhiannon lowered her gown over her head, wishing she could stay drowning in bluebell muslin forever. But that was impossible. Cowardly. She'd made this abominable mess. She'd best face up to it at once.

She glanced at Lion, saw the harsh lines about his mouth, the glint in his eyes—something almost like self-loathing.

"Rhiannon, I'm sorry," he ground out, and she knew instinctively that apologies from Captain Lionel Redmayne were rarer than dragons' teeth and far more costly to the man who gave them.

It would have been so easy to leave it at that, go back to the caravan and pretend the kiss had never happened. Some craven part of Rhiannon wanted to flee even now. But that wouldn't change what had passed between them. It would only make the kiss haunt them both more deeply still. And Lion Redmayne had enough dark secrets hidden away. She couldn't allow him to add this new fragment of self-blame.

"Lion . . ." She took a step toward him, touched his arm lightly, as if it were somehow as fragile as a butterfly's wing. Absurd thought, yet she couldn't help herself.

His fist knotted, but he didn't draw away.

"If anyone is at fault for what happened, I am."

"What the devil?" Redmayne stared at her, aghast—an emotion he could never remember having felt before.

"When you came down here, to the stream, I was scampering around in nothing but my shift—and a wet shift at that." Her cheeks blossomed red, her voice trembling just a little. "I know enough about men to realize that . . . well, that you have certain urges that are difficult to contain."

"Of all the ridiculous rot!" He scowled. "I'd prefer to pass on such a paltry excuse for acting like a lecherous cad."

"You mustn't be so hard on yourself. You're injured and unsettled by everything that has happened to you— someone close to you betraying you, the fact that you almost died. You can't help but be vulnerable."

God above, the woman was apologizing for compromising *his* virtue?

"It's just that . . . once we left Primrose Cottage, I thought I would never know what it was like to kiss a man, to feel all the things I felt when you touched me. You see, I'm not totally blinded by dreams, Lion. There was no sense grieving over something I couldn't change. But when you kissed me and I saw a chance, I just took it without thinking how you might feel afterward."

Something damned uncomfortable unfurled in Redmayne's chest as he looked at her, standing there with her gown still askew, her hair still caught beneath the collar, her face, earnest and ashamed and searingly honest. If she only knew the truth—that he'd planned this little tryst of theirs as if it had been another move in a chess game, cold-blooded, calculated. He'd capitalized on the very innocence that had driven her to pick up a wounded stranger by the side of the road.

He'd done plenty of reprehensible things before, things that were as necessary as they were unpalatable. But he'd never been ashamed—until now. He'd kissed the hell out of her, taken shameless advantage of the situation. And damn it, truth be told, his treachery had allowed him to taste the greatest pleasure he'd ever sampled from a woman's lips. Her mouth had stunned him with its sweetness, its eager clinging.

She'd kissed him, believing that he was worthy of such a gift. But he couldn't escape the knowledge that he'd desecrated something precious, a gift that should have been bestowed on a clean-hearted hero of a man with courage enough to give her an equal measure of his heart in return.

Because, dismiss it as she might, Rhiannon Fitzgerald was not a woman to kiss a man for the sake of experience. Ever since he'd met her, he'd seen her giving away pieces of her heart until it was a miracle there was anything left.

But he couldn't let that make him lose sight of his goal in starting this whole mock seduction: he needed to get back to the garrison. He needed Rhiannon to leave him behind. It would be safer for her, safer . . . for him.

Jaw aching from keeping the truth inside, Redmayne turned and limped toward the little campsite. But he made a vow with each step he took. When tonight came, he'd make certain she had no doubts about who was to blame for what happened between them.

Damn the woman, he'd make her loathe him as much as he deserved, even if it killed them both.

He was soldier enough to know this would have to be his final assault. The risk was becoming too great, the stakes far too high.

But for whom? A voice in his head mocked him. For Rhiannon? Or for the invincible Captain Redmayne himself?

Chapter

&8&

Redmayne prowled around the encampment with the restless tread of a lion expecting a cliff to crumble beneath his feet, the hours creeping past so slowly he wondered if darkness would ever come. How his grandfather would sneer—Lionel, who had been so certain he'd mastered the virtue of patience, pacing like any emotion-drunk fool.

But, damnation, he wanted this whole miserable affair over and done with. He wanted to put Rhiannon Fitzgerald behind him, relegate her seasick-hued gypsy caravan, her absurd menagerie of pets, and the incessant chafing of her kindness to that obscure netherworld of his mind, beyond memory, beyond regret, a place where he wouldn't have to remember how wide her eyes had grown, how trusting.

Blast, he should have known that, with Rhiannon, nothing would turn out as he'd expected. From the beginning the woman had possessed an irritating talent for outflanking him. He'd expected shock, outrage, and the usual posturings of innocence when he kissed her. Who could have guessed that she'd turn to quicksilver in his arms?

If it had been mere desire he'd elicited from her, he would have been surprised yet able to use it to his advantage. A woman's curiosity, too, could be fashioned into a most intriguing weapon, one he'd had in his hands many times before.

But no. Rhiannon had opened her heart to him with a courage and generosity so rare that he'd stumbled from his course.

Hellfire, he'd ridden headlong into the mouths of blazing cannon and never wavered. Why had he faltered before this one untidy Irishwoman? It was enough to unnerve the most seasoned commander, tripping over such an unexpected weakness.

And ever since the debacle at the stream bank, what had his quarry been up to? She'd fluttered about like a drunken butterfly, preparing food, cleaning everything from the horse's hooves to the darkest corners of the caravan.

She had even maneuvered the tiny table out into the sunshine and blanketed it with a lace-edged cloth as out of place here as a silk slipper on a scullery maid's foot. Mismatched yet elegant china was set out in a clutter that should have irritated him, and delicious smells emanated from the cook fire. Bread, hot scones, berries and sugar cooked down into jewel-colored jam, lined a shelf along one side of the caravan.

A less intuitive man might have looked on such preparations as a triumph—the lady's efforts to entice him. But Redmayne knew the woman's doings for what they were—a desperate attempt to keep busy, to bury herself in work so she could forget the damp sweetness of stream-splashed meadow flowers, drown out the pounding of hearts, cool the heat of lips still burning from that first incomparable kiss.

Unfortunately, there was nothing Redmayne himself could do except flash her hot looks from hooded eyes, occasionally pretend to sleep, and when his restlessness grew too unwieldy, pace.

Because he'd made several unwelcome discoveries himself since he'd made his way with such arrogance down the stream bank. He wanted her. Wanted her naked beneath him, those soft hands on his body. He wanted to catch her gasps of pleasure in his own mouth as he kissed her.

Redmayne grimaced. No, it wasn't Rhiannon herself who had unleashed such desires in him. It was merely physical needs held too long in check. His grandfather had been right, that sex was rather like brushing one's teeth—necessary on occasion, with a tendency to become most unpleasant if ignored for too long.

And yet . . . with Rhiannon, there would be none of the detachment that had marked every one of his other liaisons. She would hurl herself into lovemaking with her whole heart . . .

Which was exactly why there would be no real lovemaking. Only the pretense of it—and then the betrayal. The bruising of her tender heart. He regretted it, surprising as that might be. Yet better a bruise of this sort than an assassin's bullet, aimed to silence her.

He was almost ready to pace back to the tree he'd drowsed under several times that day when he glimpsed her coming around the wagon, a wicker basket in her arms. Something was moving inside, a glimpse of bead-like eyes shining out, wary, curious.

"I'll return in a little while. I have some business to attend to," she said, her voice calm, even, yet nothing could stop the flush from blooming in her cheeks.

"What business?" Redmayne inquired. "Extending an invitation to dine to the garrisons of soldiers supposedly searching for me? God knows, you've made enough food to feed half the barracks."

The flush darkened. "It's the week's worth of baking. I didn't . . ." She stopped, as if knowing she was revealing far more to him than she wished. "If you must know, it's time to finish what I came here to do in the first place."

"Now that I think on it, I should have wondered about that. I suppose I thought you'd come to commune with the fairy folk or the ghosts at Ballyaroon."

"I came to release this vixen. She's well enough now to go back to the wild."

"There are plenty of woods closer to civilization, my dear."

"And plenty of huntsmen ready to run her to ground." She clutched the basket tighter against her breast, as if she'd shield the little fox from danger herself, as if it were a babe in her arms instead of a wild thing that might snap off her fingers at any moment.

"Perhaps I should carry it?" Redmayne was surprised to hear himself offer. After all, he reasoned, seduction could be much hampered by a bunch of bandaged feminine fingers.

"No!" she said a little too hastily. "I can do it alone. I wouldn't want you to strain your wounds. I'll return soon enough. Just rest and . . ."

She didn't finish. She didn't have to. He could hear her plea as clearly as if she'd voiced it: *Stay away from me!*

She turned and hurried toward the stream as if she feared he'd catch hold of her skirt and haul her back.

He intended to do as she wished—enjoy the peace and quiet of the camp for a few precious moments, smooth out the ripples the woman was forever stirring up in his mind. But he surprised himself by starting after her, just to make certain she didn't get herself in any more trouble. And perhaps, just perhaps, he could steal another kiss, or manage a brush of fingertips, something to begin the night's onslaught where there weren't dishes to putter about, animals to tend to, or pots to stir.

It took him far longer to trace her path, hampered as he was by his limp. But he took his mind off of the aching by imagining the best tactics to use with the lady—a swift strike, putting both of them out of their misery quickly, or something more subtle?

He'd nearly decided when he glimpsed something—a splash of blue muslin—beyond a tangle of underbrush, heard the quiet sound of a woman's tears.

His pulse tripped, a strange sinking in his chest. He stood still, feeling as if he were prying yet again, peeling back another layer of this woman's soul.

He'd seen her all but naked in her shift beside the stream. But this nakedness of the spirit unnerved him far more. She cradled the little creature in her arms, stroking its russet head, crooning to it, just loud enough for him to hear.

"No more tangling with foxhounds, Duchess," she warned. "Don't let poor Milton deceive you. They're not to be trusted. And don't be casting your heart away on the first handsome male who crosses your path."

The curve of her lips turned wistful, her eyes a little touched with pain, and Redmayne couldn't help wondering about the softness he'd seen in her face, the tenderness just before he'd kissed her.

"Find a mate who will build you a cozy den and fill it with darling little kits. And someday, when my cart comes rattling past, promise you'll bring them out and display the lot of them. You see, I'll never have any babies of my own, so it will be like—like I'm their auntie. Perhaps they can belong to me a little." There was the slightest break in her voice. Redmayne felt it in his gut.

The fox squirmed, gazing up at her with large questioning eyes. It was as if the creature who had been content under her care during her convalescence scented freedom, that most intoxicating of elixirs. Damned ungrateful, Redmayne thought as he watched Rhiannon stroke the pointed ears one last time.

"I'm glad, really I am, that you're all well, and so bright and ready to scamper off. It's pure selfishness, this crying nonsense, because I'll miss you. Good-bye, little one. I'll never forget you."

No, Redmayne was certain she wouldn't—wouldn't brush aside this pain, bury it where it could never hurt her.

She dropped a kiss on the fox's silky brow. Then her grasp on the creature loosened so slowly that Redmayne could feel her reluctance and her exhilaration. No matter how painful the letting go had been for her, there was also triumph in it. Joy.

The fox wandered a little distance away, her delicate body quivering. Then she lifted her nose to sniff the wind. Was she hesitating because of the woman she'd left behind? Jewel-bright eyes glanced back at Rhiannon for a long moment. Then the creature scampered out of sight.

Rhiannon sat there alone, her skirts a pool of blue against the grass, tears streaming down her face as she grieved. For what? For the fox she had tended and come to love? For the barrenness of her own life? The things she couldn't have? Her own cozy den and nest full of kits?

Bloody hell, after having taken in so many creatures, she must know the price that would be exacted of her. If she suffered this much every time she let something go, why the devil take in any injured creatures in the first place? Why leave herself open to this kind of pain?

Some men might have been tempted to go and comfort her. But all Redmayne could think of was how *he* would feel, were he in her place. God's blood, if anyone witnessed him in such a state—stripped bare emotionally, hideously vulnerable—the humiliation would likely prove fatal. Even now, standing here, watching Rhiannon's tears, he felt as if he were violating her. His stomach churned.

Hellfire, Captain Lionel Redmayne had never been tempted to turn tail and run from any field of battle, but now, confronted with one totally oblivious weeping woman, he was coward enough to turn on his heel, ready to beat an ignominious retreat. If only a stick beneath his boot hadn't turned traitor and snapped with a deafening sound.

Rhiannon scrambled about, her green eyes sparking with fear, no doubt thinking that his assassins had returned. He expected her to recoil in horror, to scrub the tears from her face, shamed as if they were a thief's brand. He expected loathing, outrage, any ploy so she might gather the tattered remnants of her dignity about her. But she only looked into his face, tears welling over thick crescents of eyelash, trickling down cheeks a trifle too pink.

Redmayne would rather have faced a horde of screaming Sikhs, brandishing scimitars. He was stunned to hear himself stammering, making excuses. "I was merely stretching my legs."

"You don't fool me, Lion. You were worried about me."

No one had ever accused him of such a motive. He was struck dumb.

"But as you can see, I'm quite safe." Her gaze shifted to the direction the fox had vanished. Her voice sank to barely a whisper. "Do you think Duchess will be?"

Drat the woman! She was looking at him as if he could reassure her. He didn't have a blasted crystal ball. It was a fox, by all the saints. A fox. One she had tended as if it were her own wee babe. He took shelter in gruff levity.

"From what I overheard, you prepared her for her first season as well as any mother could have. Warned her about rogue suitors, advised her as to what a lady needs in a suitable husband. The lack of white muslin gowns and dancing slippers might be lamentable, but she seemed like a most resourceful young lady, and considerable beauty can make a gentleman overlook such a lack of accoutrements."

Her cheeks darkened, and he winced. He might not know the first thing about mopping up feminine tears, but he'd hardly wanted to make things more uncomfortable—for her or for himself.

Why hadn't he pretended he'd heard nothing? Or merely walked away? Why had he stepped on that damned stick? Why had he followed her up this accursed trail? Hell, why had he ever set foot in Ireland where he had run afoul of the woman in the first place? At the moment, he wished himself in Jericho.

But suddenly she managed the most heroic little smile he'd ever witnessed. "I suppose you are right, Lion. I've done all a mama can do. But"—her lip trembled—"sometimes it is so hard to let them go, you know?"

You know? She was looking at him as if she expected him to understand. Hell, he'd never *let* anything go, reluctantly or otherwise. He'd slammed the door in the face of anyone who dared attempt to get to know him. He'd shoved away anything he might get attached to as if it were poison. He'd made certain there was nothing anyone could take away from him. But he just hadn't realized that also meant that he had nothing precious.

Precious as a wounded fox or an almost blind dog, a one-eyed cat, or a gypsy cart. Or a woman's tears dampening his breast as he held her.

Lunacy. This was insane! He'd followed Rhiannon in order to continue his campaign of mock seduction. He'd intended to take shameless advantage of her. To discover any weakness and use it against her. This could have been a perfect opportunity for a ruthless bastard to press his advantage. Perhaps he wasn't quite as ruthless as he'd thought. But no one else need ever know.

Feeling chagrinned, he closed the space between them. Grabbing her hand, he drew her to her feet, wanting to be quit of this clearing, and the emotions he'd witnessed here. "Your skirt is damp from the ground, and I haven't seen you eat a bite of food, despite the fact that you've been cooking all day," he scolded, leading her back toward the campsite.

"I haven't been hungry. I've been too unsettled by our kiss." How could such brutal honesty be spoken so gently?

Redmayne said nothing; his mouth was grim as he retraced his steps. When they passed the shadow of the gypsy cart, she pulled away from him.

"If you wish, I can serve up a feast to you in a few moments."

"What I wish is that you will sit down. The table would be a good place to do it."

"Lion . . ."

"*Sit*, Miss Fitzgerald, or I will make you." He called

her 'miss' in a conscious effort to put some distance between them. It didn't work worth a damn.

She looked as if she wanted to break ranks and start bustling about, serving up the meal she thought he wanted, but she did as he'd ordered, sinking down into the chair with a bone-deep weariness that was all too easy to see. Her fingers curled around a rose-painted teacup, translucent as a ray of sunshine. The only problem was that a chip of china as large as the nail of his little finger was missing from the rim.

Doubtless she had nothing else, and with that irrepressible hospitality of hers would sooner swallow china shards herself than set such a cup out for a visitor to her camp.

Grimacing, Redmayne ladled out a heavenly-smelling stew, balanced breads still warm from baking on the rims of the bowls, and set them on the table, then went in search of the accoutrements to brew tea. Going to the cupboard inside the caravan to retrieve a charming creamware pot with a spout in the shape of a sea monster, he happened to glimpse several other cups with not so much as the tiniest flaw in their rims.

He took one back to the table. "Rhiannon, there are half a dozen of these in the cupboard," he said, reaching for her broken cup. "There's no need for you to—"

She all but snatched the chipped cup to her breast. "I prefer to use this one."

He would never know why he didn't just acquiesce. After all, why should it matter to him if the woman drank her tea out of a broken cup—or out of her Sunday bonnet if she wanted to? But her hands were still slightly unsteady. The fine tremor would put the fragile pink of her lips in imminent danger from the jagged glass edges, a risk that irritated him beyond all reason.

"I regret I must insist. I prefer my dinner partners not to drink from cups that could slice them at any moment. Blood on table linens can be so unsightly."

"You'll just have to risk it this time, Captain. I'm not surrendering." She ran one fingertip tenderly along the unbroken part of the rim. She raised her soft green eyes to meet his gaze. "This cup was my mother's. At least Papa always said it was. Whenever I was sick or tired or sad, he would take this cup down from its special place in the sideboard and let me drink from it—lemonade, cambric tea, fresh milk, or juice from the orangery. It always made me feel better."

"But it's broken." Who in his right mind would hand something so jagged and sharp to a child?

"It's broken because it was loved so much." A shadow crossed Rhiannon's face. "Often the most precious things of all are flawed. That's part of what makes them so rare, so unique. Look at it, Lion. Even broken, it's beautiful, don't you think?" She held it up so that the light filtering down through the branches of the trees shone on the delicate surface of the cup.

He wanted to scoff, to tell her she was being ridiculous. The cup was broken. Broken. But the sunshine illuminated the delicate surface, the painted roses alight with an almost unearthly glow. The way he'd once imagined the Holy Grail must have glowed when Galahad found it at last. He could remember his own father's voice, low and awe-filled, as he read the ancient tale, Mama stitching by the fireside, and Jenny, his sister, her face glowing, seeing far more clearly than any of the rest of them, despite the fact that her eyesight was failing, slipping away a little more every day.

God above, he hadn't thought of that night for so many years, it seemed as if the memory should belong to another man. One buried in the churchyard with the rest of his family an eternity ago.

He knew he should stand up, stride away from Rhiannon's vulnerable eyes and from the wisdom and the pain, the grief and the piercing sweetness of remembering. But he sat as if chained there—by what? His own weakness? Or the strange power of Rhiannon's tale? "It was your mother's. The cup." Redmayne heard himself saying. Why? To fill the silence? Or was there some secret part of him that was envious—for he had nothing that had belonged to his family. Even the few memories he'd once hoarded so carefully were faded and tattered and cast aside.

"Papa said she brought it with her from the land of the fairies when she fell in love with him."

Fairies again! Hadn't he heard enough nonsense about them since he'd been exiled to this infernal place? For an instant, Redmayne almost spoke his thoughts aloud. The people of this island were so certain the place was infested with them, it was a wonder any man could take a step outside his own door without treading on half a dozen of these fairy folk. But something stopped him. The vulnerability in every line of Rhiannon's face? The soft lilt of her voice? Or the way she looked at him, so trusting, so open.

"Every morning, Papa said, they spent an hour together, sipping tea. Mama would tell him tales about Tir naN Og, and the two of them would weave dreams about the future. Mama dreamed me then."

"Dreamed of having children, you mean? It was a logical enough assumption, I would think, after marriage."

"No. Mama knew that I would be born, a girl child. She knew everything about me. What my favorite doll would be, that I would know about healing herbs. That was why I was to be named Rhiannon—the goddess of healing, who either eased the wounded ones or, after death, guided them to paradise, leading them by the hand."

The words were piercing, uncomfortable, the name far too fitting for this woman who sat across from him. Absurd, though, to think that anyone, even a mother, could sense so much about a child before it was even born.

"Mama knew how much Papa would love me and I would love him. It comforted her, Papa said, though he didn't understand why. Only later did he realize that she knew they hadn't much time to be together. Before long, she would have to return to the fairy kingdom and leave us behind."

She was waiting for him to say something. Redmayne could sense it. But he was at a total loss. *No wonder your father lost your home. The man was obviously mad*—would hardly be appropriate. "Uh, I suppose she had some pressing fairy business to attend to. Whatever the blazes that might be," Redmayne began. Then he grimaced, something in Rhiannon's face demanding truth instead of wry humor. "Rhiannon, you don't really believe—"

"Sometimes I do. When I'm alone too long or the night is too dark, I want to believe. It's so much prettier than any of the other tales I could come up with as to why my mother left me behind."

Redmayne didn't expect her words to echo in his own most secret places, the sick clutching of betrayal, abandonment, searching every window, every face in every crowd, desperate to see someone familiar, someone who could scoop you into his arms, tell you it had all been a terrible mistake. Someone to answer the question *why*. . . .

She lowered the cup, strained the tea into it, careful, so careful not to fill it too close to the broken rim. But instead of sipping it herself, she held it out to him across the little table.

"What are you doing?" He eyed the bit of china as if it might explode. "The cup is yours. You need whatever you think the thing possesses."

"Whatever?" She smiled just a little, her lashes dipping over the sea green of her eyes. "Magic, you mean? Fairy magic? Something you don't believe in."

His throat felt raw, his nerves chafed. He forced a laugh. "I'm afraid I'd be drummed out of the army, my dear. I assure you I'll survive without drinking from your magic cup."

"Survive, yes. That is what you're best at, isn't it?" Why did she sound so sad? She peered down into the teacup, the jagged place reflected back at her, broken edges he knew she wanted to mend—in a bit of china or in a man. "Then why am I so certain that you need this right now, Lion? Even more than I do?"

She put the cup back into its saucer as tenderly as a mother might lay a cherished babe in its cradle.

"Rhiannon, the tale isn't true. You know that."

"It doesn't matter whether it's true or not. It's the believing that's important."

She turned and started to walk away. He should have let her go. He wanted her to go, didn't he? Until he could shore up the places inside him she'd managed to chip away at? But he caught her by the arm, drew her back. She turned toward him, and something thudded in his chest.

Dangerous. She was far too dangerous. The knowledge thrummed in his head. Panic tightened in his gut. Didn't she know he had to escape?

"You want to know what I believe in, Rhiannon?"

he growled. "No sip from some enchanted cup. I need *this*."

He meant the kiss to shake her to her core, frighten her enough so she'd back away from him. The taste of her—sweet compassion—had been perilous enough by the streambed. But now it was far more potent.

He could discern the faint taste of grief over the fox she'd set free. He could taste every sip of lemonade she'd comforted herself with as a child, deserted by her mother, blinded by fairy tales she must've suspected were not true.

He'd decimated the resistance of as many women as he had opposing forces. Once he'd chosen the best course, no force on earth could turn him back from it. But as his mouth melded with Rhiannon's, it wasn't persuasion, it wasn't even passion that drove him. Some emotion jagged-edged from disuse as the cup she'd tried to get him to drink from came drifting to the surface. His fingers threaded through the cinnamon silk of her hair, his thumbs against the babelike softness of her cheeks. His lips gentled, and for a moment, just a moment, he knew that emotion for what it was: tenderness.

A sharp stab of something akin to terror pierced his chest. He would have pulled away from her, except that her fingers had found his own face, stroking it with such ineffable wonder that he was stunned, unnerved, intoxicated.

No one had touched him this way since he'd lost the shadowy otherworld that was now as unreal to him as Rhiannon's fairyland. Images too hazy to be called memory—firelight, his father's deep voice spinning the tales of King Arthur. The loving stroke of the hand that had tended so many suffering patients smoothing across Lionel's own hair.

It was unthinkable to allow himself to be drawn

closer to the cliff edge of remembering by such fragile, soft hands, but for some reason beyond his comprehension he followed Rhiannon's lead.

Fire ignited low in Redmayne's belly—a poisonous mixture beyond lust, beyond manipulation, beyond the logic and order that had become his whole reason for being. He kissed her, stumbling into her disorderly world where vines of sensation tangled around even the most resolute, where riotous blossoms tumbled and flourished, where sunlight kissed faces turned up to the sky, where anything imperfect—from a chipped cup to a half-blind dog to a wounded soldier—was drawn into a warm, loving circle, a cherishing place that was half madness, half miracle.

Bloody hell, how he wanted to dismiss what he was feeling, shove it aside. But Redmayne had schooled himself to be as ruthlessly honest with himself as he was logical. She felt so damned good in his arms as he drew her tighter against him, felt the lush pillows of her breasts flatten against his chest. Her waist, narrow and feminine, her hips flaring ever so gently with a womanly curve he wanted to explore slowly, carefully, with a thoroughness that would leave her gasping.

Need. It pounded in his loins with the fierce call of battle drums, irresistible, stirring his blood with heat, with eagerness, demanding that he storm barricades of feminine petticoats and skirts as he'd stormed barriers of stone walls and cannon fire.

His hand slipped up to cup her breast through the fabric, his mind charging forward, imagining peeling away the layers of cloth as if it were the skin of some luscious fruit that he could feast upon.

She whimpered, arching into his hand, and Redmayne couldn't keep himself from unfastening four of the buttons that held her bodice together. Skin—sleek and tender, delicate and blushed with rose—his knuckles brushed it, savored it. His mouth trailed kisses across it, but it was too sweet, too perfect, too tempting. It was almost as if he could taste everything Rhiannon was—things that terrified Captain Lionel Redmayne far more than violent death, sabres, cannons, and hopeless charges into the teeth of the enemy.

He drew away to catch his breath, regain his moorings. Try to recall the reasons why he'd thought it was such a brilliant idea to pretend to seduce this innocent woman.

He might have succeeded in remembering, in rallying his troops if she hadn't caught her lower lip between her teeth and put her trembling fingers on the buttons at his throat. His pulse tripped as he felt the first button tug free.

"Rhiannon." He growled her name, his whole body rigid.

"It—it's all right. I . . . understand," she said in a voice as unsteady as the beat of his heart. "What you want, I mean."

"You don't have the damnedest idea."

"I've been thinking about it all day. And you see, I . . . well, I want it, too."

"It? What the devil?"

"To make love with you." The confession was so soft, so fragile, so impossible that for a heartbeat Redmayne couldn't draw breath into his lungs.

"Have you lost your mind?" he demanded, but she was unfastening the next button and the next, concentrating on them as if the fate of the world were tangled amid the awkwardly stitched holes.

"No. I'm merely being honest."

It was damned disconcerting when the enemy one was laying siege to suddenly began tearing down its own blasted walls. "I think, er, you should take the romantic advice you gave that fox of yours—about not accepting the first male who stumbles across your path."

"Lion."

Blast, why was it that every time she spoke his name it gave him such a jolt? Why had he ever told it to her? He should have told her to call him William or Frederick or James.

"I accepted a long time ago that, living as I do, wandering on the road, there would never be a man I could love—a husband, children, things that I once took for granted I'd have someday."

"Madam, I am far from husband material, if that is what you're thinking."

Her laughter was a little raw, a little sorrowful, a little amused, he could sense, at the discomfort they both were feeling. "I don't intend to force you to the altar, if that is what you fear," she said, sucking in a shuddering breath, and flattening her soft palm against his bare chest. "I know you don't love me. But you *do* care about me. And I care about you. And . . . and you want me."

Want her? He'd never wanted any woman the way he wanted her. That was the infernal coil. It was merely the fact that he'd been celibate so long, combined with his restlessness, trapped here in her little gypsy hell. But his body was clamoring for release, and Rhiannon Fitzgerald was offering it to him, damn her to perdition.

"I know it sounds wanton to you," she said. "Perhaps it is. But just once I'd like to feel the magic of someone touching me, kissing me. Just once, so that I can remember it always." She turned the full battery of those misty green eyes upon him, her very soul stripped bare. Completely vulnerable to him, a man who had plotted to manipulate her, to use her generous heart against her to get his own way. He should have felt contempt at such weakness—his grandfather had all but beaten that lesson into him when Redmayne was a child. Why, then, did he feel something altogether different?

Self-disgust. He'd never bothered much with it in the past. Now it scratched against his nerves, irritating, unfamiliar, mingled with anger, not at Rhiannon so much as at himself, at that part of him that was sorely tempted to take what she was offering.

"From the first I sensed there was something special between us," she was continuing, making the totally irrational seem almost reasonable. "A bond struck before these hills were green. And today at the stream and later, when you found me crying in the clearing and tried to comfort me, I realized what it was—that you were my chance to find out what loving between two people can be."

Destiny again. Gifts from the fates. And a wounded hero, come to give her a dream. Hell, it was a miracle she didn't think he was some sort of apparition from another world. She was gazing up at him as if she believed . . . what? In legend-spun lovers and magical possibilities? More terrifying still, for one paralyzing moment, he wanted to reach out, drag her toward him, close the space between them where doubts and fears and ugly manipulations swirled.

With an oath, he grabbed her arms, this time to keep her from touching him, yanking free what hold he still had on his sanity. "Stop this, damn it," he snarled, furious at himself, impatient with her.

The light in her eyes shifted, from awe-filled eagerness to dark confusion. "Stop what? I—I don't understand."

"That is one thing I'm certain of."

Then he saw that infernal dawning of what the woman thought was understanding, as if she had gauged his motives. "You needn't be noble," she said. "I have no expectations. Only tonight, this one time, this one chance."

"Nobility is the last quality anyone should be fool enough to attribute to me!"

"Then tell me, what is it? What is wrong? You can tell me anything, as long as it's the truth."

"Can I?" he bit out coldly, hiding the panic inside him. Hell, he was as desperate as an animal caught in the jaws of a trap, willing to do anything, even gnaw off its own leg to get free. "Is it the truth you really want?" he demanded. "Fine. This was all a ruse. A ploy. A way to get you to take me back to my blasted garrison."

"Wh-what?" She paled, then tipped up her chin, stubborn. "I don't believe you. You're a good man. I sensed it under the layers of pain. There was something between us. I *feel* these things, sense them."

"Then perhaps your magic powers are a bit off-kilter at present. Did you sense how blasted irritating I find this place? That I'd rather risk an assassin's bullet than stay here another moment? Did your powers even give you a hint that I tried to think of some way, any way, to force you to release me?"

He was hurting her. But, damnation, it would hurt her far more if he let her believe . . . believe what? In some sort of destiny? In one night of lovemaking that would mean nothing to him and everything to her? He might be the cold-hearted monster people claimed, but even he couldn't stomach the thought of this woman carrying an idealized image of Captain Lionel Redmayne in her heart forever because for one insane night his lust had overcome his logic.

"You can't possibly have been so—"

"Cruel? Calculating?" Did the woman even have such words in her vocabulary, he wondered. "I assure you, Rhiannon, I can. It was a clumsy plan, perhaps, but the only one I could come up with under the circumstances. You're impossible to intimidate, to bribe, to bully. And as for reasoning with you"—he snorted in disgust—"I realized that was impossible within moments of regaining consciousness. What was left except to find a way to frighten you into hauling me back to the garrison?"

She was trembling as if he'd struck her. He knew he'd done far worse than that. "You kissed me, touched me, because you wanted to frighten me?" she asked, still unbelieving.

"Yes, damn it. But it didn't work, did it? Who could have guessed an innocent like you would want—" He broke off with a curse. *Want a man who isn't worthy to kiss the sole of your slipper, offer yourself up to him with such courage and generosity it would shatter his resolve and fill him with self-loathing. Who could have guessed that you would taste so right, feel so perfect, unnerve me so completely?*

Redmayne winced. Wasn't it enough, facing Rhiannon, tormenting her, without being tortured by his own infernal thoughts? "What the devil is the point? The whole plan was a disaster anyway." He stalked away, unable to bear the wounded light in her eyes. "I'll be trapped in this Gypsy hell until the end of time."

Disgusted, frustrated, he sank back into his chair, wishing for a moment that he could have temper fits like other men. Break crockery, kick tables, slam his fist against a tree. But instead, he could only sit there, rigid, controlled, balling up all the emotions inside him, smaller and smaller, until they were nothing but a hard lump in his gut.

She should have raged at him, stormed at him, cried and shouted. But she was still standing there, where he'd kissed her, those fingers that had unfastened his buttons limp at her sides. She came to the table, took up the chipped fairy cup in her hands, as if—what?—the infernal thing could make her feel better? Perhaps it might if she used the jagged edge to slash at his heart the way he had slashed hers.

"I suppose it was foolish of me, believing that someone like you could . . . could want someone like me," she said, "but I've always been good at imagining."

She sucked in a deep breath. "What you did was despicable. We'll start for the garrison at daybreak." In a whisper of muslin and sorrow, she turned and walked away.

For a moment he almost called her back. Wanted to tell her that what had begun as a military campaign had ended in surprising pleasure. That he *had* wanted her, more than she could ever imagine. But what would such a confession accomplish except to muddy up the waters even further? No, better to have her hate him as he deserved.

What did any of this matter, anyway? He'd accomplished his goal. She would not be silenced by a bullet. She'd be safe, and he could go back to his well-ordered life. She might not know it, but he'd won a victory for them both.

Victory. Yes. It should have been that simple and logical. It might have been. But suddenly he was certain that some wounds cut far deeper than any bullet could reach and remained long after physical scars had whitened and smoothed away.

He closed his eyes, trying to block out the image of her face, the bruised look in her eyes, the shock and shame that she would carry with her forever.

"Damn it, she should have just let me bleed to death," he muttered. It would have been more merciful than what he was feeling now.

Chapter

❧ 9 ❧

Practical Triona had always claimed it was impossible to die of a broken heart. Now Rhiannon knew it must be impossible to die of shame as well. If she'd managed to survive the past two days, she could survive anything.

She guided the wagon through the wisps of pink-edged mist, wishing she did possess some of her mother's fairy magic—just enough to halt the sun as it sank inexorably toward the horizon.

Darkness would fall soon, forcing her to draw rein, to bring the caravan to a halt and make camp as she had so many times before. It was a ritual she'd always loved—finding a new spot, someplace pretty and inviting to turn into home. Lacy canopies of leaves overhead formed the ceiling; surfaces of silvery lakes became long galleries of mirrors; hollows of green glen or swells of hills formed soft, sheltering walls.

It had never taken much to make a new place feel like home—a bunch of hastily gathered flowers in a jar on the table, a crackling fire, the scent of tea brewing, and the ecstatic sighs from Milton as he slumbered at her feet, his paws twitching, chasing rabbits in his dreams.

Yet nothing she could do tonight would give her even a scrap of that homey peace she craved so deeply. The past forty-eight hours had been a nightmare of tension and strain such as she'd never endured, subtle torture as she and Captain Redmayne had wrestled with the impossible task of existing in such tight quarters without tripping over everything that had happened between them the day before.

He'd been agonizingly polite to her—an officer and a gentleman of the finest mettle. And she'd fought the instinct to avoid him at all costs. She was human enough to want to leave him to his own devices, let him fumble about, tending his own wounds, scavenging his own supper. After all, anyone who could formulate and carry out such a vile, deceitful plan as he had couldn't be so terribly ill anymore. But despite spinning out scenarios of revenge, in the end, she couldn't act on them. She'd suffer for it far more than he ever would if she let his ruthlessness keep her from doing what she knew was right.

Yet she was surprised to discover that, in some ways, treating him kindly was a measure of revenge all its own. At least her behavior kept the inscrutable captain off-balance.

He'd been stunned when she changed his dressings with the greatest of care, even more astonished when, late last night, she'd curled up on the edge of the bed beside him. She hadn't slept, but she'd been near enough to hear his slightest groan.

Unfortunately, that also meant she was near enough to feel the warmth radiating from his body, to perceive the drift of his breath across her cheek. When he attempted to tell her this martyrdom of hers wasn't necessary, that he could sleep beneath the wagon, she'd told him not to be ridiculous. The last thing either of them desired was for him to contract lung fever, a circumstance that would force the two of them to remain encamped together until he recovered.

The night had become a standoff of the grimmest kind, both of them pretending the other didn't exist, both feigning sleep. She only wondered if he had seen what she did, every time she closed her eyes—her own face, that of a dream-blinded fool offering herself up to a man who didn't want her.

The wagon jolted, and she gritted her teeth as pain hammered through her aching muscles. She detested herself for wondering how Redmayne was faring inside the wagon. He'd looked a trifle pale when she stopped at noon long enough to shove some bread thick with butter into his hands. But she'd sensed the eagerness in him to keep traveling—the scarce-leashed energy of a horse fighting the urge to bolt.

She'd taken her own bit of bread back to the seat that swung just above her dray horse's broad haunches, and she'd kept driving, as anxious now to get rid of her passenger as he was to be quit of her.

Yet now it looked as if they'd have to spend another night together before they reached the garrison. It was a prospect most unpleasant.

At that instant the tiny door at the back of the caravan creaked open. She started, feeling as if she possessed the power to summon up the devil.

"Are we there yet?" Redmayne asked, and she couldn't help but be reminded of a recalcitrant school boy traveling home on holiday.

"If we were, the wagon would have stopped," she said with acid sweetness. "It hasn't. We aren't. And we may not be until tomorrow morning."

"There is no logical reason we can't make it to the garrison tonight. I made the calculations, and—"

"Perhaps you should have shared them with Socrates. Obviously his calculations are a bit different. But then, it's harder to count on one's hooves than on one's fingers, I suppose."

"Damnation, I don't want to spend another night here," Redmayne groused.

Rhiannon wished his words didn't hurt so badly. "You needn't fear I'll attempt to ravish you. I'm completely cured of any desire to accost you, I assure you."

"Fine for you, but what about—" Redmayne stopped, glowering, and she wondered what he'd been about to say. She only knew that what came from his mouth next was far different. "What about the men who have been hunting me? The closer we get to the garrison, the more dangerous it becomes."

"And once you're inside the garrison, won't you be in the most danger of all?"

"You underestimate me, Rhiannon. The men who serve under me have a healthy fear of their commander. It is one thing to lure an unsuspecting man out to a solitary death, another to murder him with countless witnesses wandering about. Besides, now I am on my guard."

"I doubt that you have ever been *off* guard in your entire life, but those villains nearly managed to kill you anyway."

She could sense his discomfort in the way he cleared his throat. "Yes, well. Perhaps I was a trifle distracted, but I will not make that mistake again. And once you get me back to my headquarters, it will be immaterial to you. You'll be absolved of all responsibility. Perhaps I can find a kitten with a broken paw or a horse that has foundered to provide you with a distraction."

There was a brittle mockery in his voice, but whether he was mocking her or himself, she couldn't be certain. She wanted to hate him, wanted to rekindle the anger she'd felt at his betrayal. She didn't want to remember the horrible loneliness she'd sensed in him, the heedlessness about his own life, the world-weariness that clung about his mouth when he thought no one could see. She didn't want to hear the echo of his pain-maddened cry, begging for his father.

"Come, Rhiannon, even a saint could not be expected to tolerate a villain like me any longer than necessary. You cannot tell me you won't be relieved to be rid of me after the way I've behaved."

"I'd be mad if I wasn't glad to be rid of you," she said. But why did the thought of leaving him behind make her feel as if she were somehow betraying him? Abandoning him when she should protect him? Protect Captain Lionel Redmayne? By the saints, how he would laugh if he ever discovered she harbored such absurd notions.

She angled a glance over her shoulder. Shadows and light played over his austere features. Was it only her imagination, or did she see just the vaguest hint of regret?

It was over. Redmayne could see the glow of lantern light illuminating the cluster of buildings that had been his headquarters these past three years. He stared down at the garrison he'd become accustomed to, if not enamored of, relieved enough to have this journey nearly at an end.

Yet he couldn't help feeling that in the brief time he'd been absent, everything had changed. The complacency he'd felt for years had vanished, along with the certainty that everything was within his power to control.

Somewhere within the buildings he was so familiar with, among the faces he'd come to know, lurked a coward eager to kill him. A coward who would be far more desperate to finish the deed now that Redmayne had been alerted to his intentions. Nothing drove an assassin to greater lengths than the fear of detection.

But more unnerving still was the effect that one disheveled woman had had upon Redmayne. How much she had altered things with the merest brush of her hand.

Rhiannon, named for the goddess sent to lead a man to another life, to heal him. Was it possible that in some way she already had? No. He was far too dedicated a sinner to be changed in a matter of days. Yet he doubted he would ever forget her. She was rare, his untidy guardian angel. Never had he met anyone with a heart so good, so pure. What poet had written it? "A heart whose love is innocent."

Bloody hell, one could almost accuse him of waxing sentimental. That was cause enough for alarm, but once she was gone, he'd doubtless be cured of it—not unlike the time he'd fought off a bout of the measles on the Spanish peninsula.

He blinked, surprised to note how close they'd drawn to the military installation in the time he'd been lost in his musings. They'd come near enough to see the guards posted, glimpse men going about their business beyond the torchlit gates.

"Halt, ye scurvy gypsy!" the gruff voice rang out—a burly Hampshireman stepping forward, rifle at the ready—Twynham, the man's name was. "If ye've come t'raise yer petticoats, ladybird, ye'd best go 'round t'the back."

"Sir, y-you're mistaken," Rhiannon stammered.

Blast if Redmayne couldn't almost see her blush despite the darkness.

"My name is Rhiann—"

"It matters not who the lady is, private. I am Captain Lionel Redmayne." He bit out the words in his most commanding tones. The soldier froze, whether in horror or shock he couldn't tell.

"The captain is missin', most likely dead! Disappeared days ago." The soldier scrambled to grab a torch from one of the iron torchères bracketing the gate. He thrust it so close to the tiny window in the front of the caravan, it was a miracle he didn't set the whole rig afire. Even the unflappable Socrates managed to muster the energy to shy a bit. The wagon lurched. Redmayne, no longer braced against the swaying, stumbled, his wounded shoulder banging into one of the braces that held up the crescent of roof. He swore under his breath as the Hampshireman bellowed out an alarm.

What the devil? Did he think the Irish rebels had loaded up the gypsy cart like the Trojan Horse? But then, their commander had disappeared, and they'd fallen prey to attack more than once by the disgruntled populace. Within seconds the vehicle was surrounded by grim-faced men, weapons drawn, eyes hard.

"Come out o' there, whoever ye are, hands t' the sky," the private demanded.

Redmayne rolled his eyes heavenward as he made his way to exit the back of the caravan. "If I've come this far only to be shot by my own men, I'll be most put out," he grumbled.

He swung open the door, and limped down the steps.

"Gor save us!"

" 'Tis him!"

A chorus of astonished exclamations rose around him. But as he stepped into the circle of light, every man in the crowd fell silent, half of them looking as if they'd swallowed a prickly pear. Not one face showed pleasure at seeing him alive. Not one man seemed glad he'd returned. He could see them battling heavy disappointment, trying to hide it—as if they could hide their true feelings from him! Once Redmayne would have felt only grim amusement at their reaction, but suddenly he'd never felt less entertained.

"Sir, a thousand pardons, sir," the burly guard stammered as if he expected to face a firing squad because of his mistake. "But who woulda thought that ye would be lookin' like a ragpicker—"

The man nearest the guard jammed his elbow into Twynham's midsection. Redmayne recognized the second man as a rather dull sort called by the name Digger Britch, a man who avoided Redmayne at every opportunity. Perhaps because he'd felt the sharp edge of his captain's tongue with great regularity.

"What Twynham here means, sir, is that you surprised us, that's all." Digger stood by Twynham with the steely resolution of some hero-blind fool guarding a wounded compatriot against a full cavalry charge. Only the tremor in his hands betrayed his nervousness as he faced his commander. "I mean, you, in a gypsy cart, with your clothes all cut up . . ."

So that was what this hubbub was about, Redmayne mused. He'd forgotten Rhiannon's haphazard mending job. He glanced down at his cut-up boot, tied together with a hank of cloth; his shirt was a mass of stitches and slashes the most destitute beggar would have been shamed to wear. Redmayne wanted nothing more than to unnerve the men clustered about him, make them as oddly unsettled as he was.

"Miss Fitzgerald, how did this happen?" he demanded, sounding astonished. "I'm certain I was in full uniform when I left the garrison. Ah, yes. That was before someone shot me and left me for dead." Redmayne searched the faces, probing for even the slightest hint, the tiniest sign that his betrayer was among them.

Outraged murmurs rose. "Irish bastards!" "We'll hunt down whoever dared to do this!" Yet the comments were not bred of any loyalty to Redmayne, rather out of hatred ages old. Redmayne had little doubt they'd be as happy to hunt down the "Irish bastards" with equal vigor simply because the sky was blue or because a footsore peasant had failed to yield the road quickly enough to suit them as they passed by.

He remembered all too clearly Rhiannon's confession, her hatred of war, yet her certainty that the men who fought together, depended on each other for their very life, must share a powerful bond. Truth was, he shared nothing with these men except the walls of his headquarters and the color of his uniform.

Redmayne shoved the unwelcome insight aside. He had more important matters to attend to. After all, he still hoped he might glean some clue from the men as to what treachery was afoot. But suddenly a whirlwind came bolting through the crowd with the most distressing lack of military decorum. Redmayne was surprised to feel something of a jolt as Kenneth Barton broke into the circle where he stood.

"Captain, sir!" the young man gasped, his face waxen, his hands shaking. "They said it was you, but I didn't believe it!"

Why? Redmayne wondered. Perhaps because Barton was one of the men who put the bullets in his flesh? "Barton." He gave the slightest nod of acknowledgment.

"But—but this gypsy cart! I remember . . ." Barton looked up at Rhiannon, still perched on her seat high above him. "Miss Fitzgerald, isn't it? I know you! Your brother . . . There was smallpox in your camp!" The rest of the soldiers drew back, uncertainty and alarm in their faces. It seemed it was rather felicitous to rid the camp of an unwanted officer, but it was another matter entirely for disease to make a random sweep through the ranks.

"Attempted assassination can make one most suspicious, I fear, Barton. Suspicious enough to alter the truth when necessary."

"You were there all along!" Barton dared to look wounded. "At that camp! Why didn't you tell us?"

Redmayne arched one eyebrow at his aide-de-camp's impudence. "I can't imagine why I should be held accountable to you, Sergeant Barton."

The youth paled. "Of course not. But we'd been searching for you. Surely once you realized I was there you knew you had nothing to fear." He looked desperately earnest, searching Redmayne's face.

"Suffice it to say I was in no mood for company." Or for another taste of death spooned up by Sir Thorne Carville, Redmayne thought, but his hidden meaning wasn't lost on Barton. The youthful face fell, like that of a boy who'd suddenly learned he was not trusted by an idolized older brother. But blast it all, hadn't Brutus plunged his knife into Julius Caesar in the end? A knife that doubtless stabbed far deeper than that of any other traitor.

"I suppose my surliness was understandable enough under the circumstances. I had just been shot," Redmayne drawled. "By the way, Barton, do remind me to review with you how to make a thorough search. You seem to have lost that valuable skill—unless, of course, you were looking for something you had no real desire to find."

Barton made a muffled sound of hurt and outrage, but Redmayne ignored it. Instead, he glanced around at the men under his command. The gruff warriors suddenly appeared sheepish as they faced the uncomfortable truth. It took more effort than he ever would have expected to force his mouth into its usual sardonic smile. "I am quite certain you have not misplaced my successor."

"Lieutenant Williams has been half mad searchin' for ye, sir!" Twynham erupted with fierce loyalty.

Williams—the man had been an irritant from the moment he rode into the garrison three months before, the officer of every raw recruit's dream, more devoted to the men under his command than he was to his duty. The man must've been rejoicing at Redmayne's absence. But Williams would be far too *honorable* to admit what Redmayne had known all along—that he'd been hoping to replace the captain permanently.

"Captain," Twynham insisted, "you can't fault the lieutenant! 'Tis nigh impossible to find anything on this infernal island. Can't expect any of the Irish t' help us find a handful o' dirt in the middle of a potato field, let alone an English officer who's gone missin'." Twynham dared to look a trifle disgruntled. "An' besides, how were we t' even guess where t' begin lookin'? Ye never told a soul what direction ye were ridin' off in, nor when ye 'spected to be back."

There was a time when Redmayne might have found such a passionate appeal on the lieutenant's behalf diverting. But tonight, bone-weary, with Rhiannon Fitzgerald's soft green eyes looking on, it made him feel embarrassed and ashamed. The sainted lieutenant, who had arrived three months ago, was so devoted to his men that the soldiers affectionately dubbed him Papa behind his back. Yes, that was the kind of man Rhiannon would understand and admire every bit as much as Redmayne's men did. The notion irritated Redmayne to a surprising depth.

"Private Twynham"—Redmayne made his voice low, silky, dangerous—"do you dare to question my actions?"

The florid face tightened, a trapped light in the private's eyes. " 'Tis just that ye—ye'd be makin' a mistake t' think the lieutenant were doin' anythin' but his duty by ye, sir."

His duty, yes, they'd all do their duty by him, Redmayne thought. But would he ever be able to wring that last drop of courage from their hearts? The drop that made mortal men reach higher, strain farther, fight more fiercely than humanly possible. Out of loyalty. Out of love.

What the devil was wrong with him, dwelling on such sentimental rot? He'd never craved such devotion or the crushing responsibility that came with it. Boundaries, separation, walls—he'd wanted those in abundance. Made certain he had them. Never had he considered crossing those barriers until a cinnamon-haired gypsy had stumbled across his path.

The best way to regain his equilibrium was to send her on her way as soon as possible. To that end, he turned to Britch brusquely.

"See to the provisioning of Miss Fitzgerald's wagon at once. All the foodstuffs she can hold."

"No!" Rhiannon protested. "Lion—I mean, Captain, it's not necessary. I beg of you—"

"Any of my men can tell you how futile that would be," Redmayne said. "Can you not, soldiers?"

"Yes, sir."

"As for the rest of you, go back to your posts,"

Redmayne commanded. "I assume the lieutenant assigned you some useful tasks."

"He did, sir!" a private so young his face was broken out in spots piped up eagerly. "Aye, he did!"

"I am much relieved. Barton, tell the lieutenant I will see him in the map room at once."

Did the soldiers actually look a trifle mutinous? As if they feared Redmayne might . . . what? Punish their precious lieutenant by forcing him to don the slashed and mended uniform and trek about the countryside as Miss Fitzgerald's prisoner?

Redmayne wondered how many of them were wishing they could pack him into the gypsy cart, shove it back outside the gates, and pretend he'd never come wandering back. Hellfire, why should it even matter?

From the instant he'd climbed down from the gypsy cart, the encounter between Redmayne and his soldiers had been absurd. Laughable, really. Then why were his shoulders stiff and his jaw rigid as he watched them wandering away, muttering among themselves? Cursing their ill luck that their captain hadn't had the courtesy to stay missing, no doubt.

Redmayne forced a mockery of his usual smile onto his lips as he turned to face Rhiannon. But the smile turned brittle when he glimpsed her there, gazing down at him with great sad eyes, just a hint of worry playing about the soft corners of her mouth. In that instant *he* was the one who wanted to shove the gypsy cart outside the heavy iron gates, quickly, so she couldn't see how disturbed he was, how unexpectedly raw and tired.

Panic that she might know his weakness poured steel into his spine.

"Miss Fitzgerald, if you would care to climb down, I'm certain a tolerable supper can be thrown together for you before you leave."

"I'm not hungry." She looked bone-weary, more than a little lost, and unhappy. Worse, even, than when she'd bade her injured fox good-bye.

Damnation, had she been fool enough to become attached to *him*, in spite of his villainy toward her?

"Well, then, as soon as Britch brings those provisions I owe you, you can be on your way, I suppose." What the devil was taking the man so long, anyway?

"You don't owe me anything, Lion."

His name. Drat her for using his name—so soft, it might almost have been an endearment. "I owe you my life," Redmayne snapped, his voice rougher than he intended, "though as to its value, there might be a difference in opinion." It was supposed to be a jest, one of the dry witticisms for which he was famous. Why the devil wasn't she smiling?

She climbed down from her high seat, hours of lurching across ruts making her legs so unsteady she stumbled. Redmayne reached out, grasping her waist to steady her, felt the warmth, the softness of her beneath his palm. He should have pulled his hand away the very moment she regained her balance. But what harm could it do to let his touch linger this once? Within minutes she'd be out of his reach forever.

She swallowed hard, gazing up at him. "You will . . . take care of yourself for me? Promise?"

It was a singular request. Redmayne couldn't help but marvel at it. No one in his memory had ever asked such a thing of him. "There is no reason you should trouble yourself about me, Rhiannon."

"I didn't ask you to understand, Lion. Only to promise."

Were those tears glistening in her lashes? Damn, he was the vilest cad ever to draw breath. He could see the reflection of their kiss in her eyes, knew that because of it, she would never forget him. And yet, most villainous of all, he suddenly realized that there was some secret part of him, long buried, that was glad—glad that one soul, at least, would think of him from time to time, one in all the vast impersonal world he'd traveled for so many years alone, untouched.

Tugged by a force he couldn't understand, he raised his fingers to her cheek, meaning to skim across that rosy curve, but at the last moment he rebelled against something too close to tenderness. Instead, he made a great show of straightening the tumbled lace collar at her throat.

"Tell you what, Miss Fitzgerald. We can strike a bargain. I will do as you ask if you promise me something in return."

The glitter had been tears. One trickled down her cheek as she nodded.

"No more tangling with assassins or picking up wounded soldiers by the side of the road. I should be proof enough to you that we're a most unworthy lot." He grimaced. "I suppose it's useless even to attempt to get you to see reason."

"Quite useless." Her voice quavered. "I believe in fairies, you see, so logic is quite beyond my grasp." With that, she strained up on tiptoe and kissed him on the mouth. A quick brush of lips, tear-wet and trembling. It burned into Redmayne more brutally than the iron with which he'd cauterized his wounds.

Never had he tasted someone else's tears. He could barely remember the taste of his own. His throat closed, and he said nothing as he helped her back up onto her seat high above that abominable horse. For an instant he was tempted to offer her one from the garrison stables—the strongest of the cart horses, the most obedient—but he knew she wouldn't take it.

Damn, but the woman picked the most troublesome creatures to love.

Why was it that the insight pierced him, made his hands knot into fists, his breath catch? Redmayne clenched his jaw and he turned away from the soft plea in those green-gold eyes. He strode away across the torchlit road, back to his empty life and the soldiers who feared him, back to the existence that had been his forever.

If only he hadn't been so damnably aware that he was alone again.

Chapter

❧ 10 ❧

Dawn streaked the horizon as Redmayne finally made his way across the compound toward his suite. His wounds ached like fire after endless hours of meetings as he resumed command of the garrison. Exhaustion ground down on him but he kept his shoulders squared with military precision. He could feel eyes boring into him from somewhere in the camp, resentful, mutinous. Some babe-soft private, fresh from Yorkshire and missing his mama, perhaps. Or a more seasoned soldier, one who had learned how to hate, maybe enough to risk luring his commander to a ruined village and a hail of pistol balls.

Redmayne gritted his teeth, forcing himself to take his accustomed long strides, praying with a grim humor that he wouldn't fall face down in the dirt. Damned if he'd let anyone see even a hint of weakness in him.

He couldn't afford it. Especially now, when his troops fairly hummed with discontent, their loyalties obviously fixed on the saintly lieutenant.

Redmayne grimaced. Reluctant though he might be, even he had to give the lieutenant credit. The man had welcomed him with barely a trace of stiffness, only a hint of regret evident in his warm brown eyes. He'd managed things all too well in Redmayne's absence, making small changes that had bettered the lot of the enlisted men. Yet the lieutenant hadn't overstepped any boundaries that would have made him seem to clutch greedily at another man's command. Even so, Redmayne had sensed regret in the man, but not because he'd been robbed of power or control. His regret was more like the reluctance of a superior horseman returning a borrowed mount to its rightful owner, who hadn't the wit or skill to appreciate such an exceptional horse.

The comparison should have rankled. But all Redmayne could think about was that some owners appreciated their beasts far too much—Rhiannon, for example, fawning over that pathetic excuse of an animal that no one in his right mind would call a horse. He'd seen her petting it and crooning to it as though it were something rare and precious, some silver-horned unicorn spun out of legend.

From the window of the map room, Redmayne had glimpsed the gypsy cart lumbering through the gates a mere hour after they'd arrived at the camp, Rhiannon obviously eager to be gone. Even now she might be trying to coax Socrates along, dangling some of the carrots from the garrison commissary in front of the ragamuffin beast's huge Roman nose. Doubtless she'd be singing or chattering or indulging in any number of noisy, irritating habits.

The image should have had the power to amuse him or at least fill him with heartfelt gratitude that she was miles away from him. Instead, it only left him feeling hollow, more tired than before. Because he knew that even if his untidy guardian angel was singing at the moment, she would be sorrowing as well.

Somewhere in that heart, which was far too tender for this world, she would be grieving for him as she'd grieved for the little fox she'd set free what seemed an eternity ago.

He tried to block her features from his memory—the tear-bright eyes, the trembling lips, the quaver in her voice as she'd pleaded with him to take care of himself.

As if he mattered a damn. Yet he couldn't help wondering who would take care of *her.*

"Don't be a fool," he muttered. "She's better off where she is." *Alone, unprotected, on the open road?* a voice inside his head mocked him. Likely one more casualty of his grandfather's cunning and greed. Her home stolen, her most precious treasure a chipped cup? That circumstance was sobering enough, but what about the men who had hunted Redmayne and who might now know she'd rescued him? Lied for him? Sheltered him? What if they decided to make her pay for that folly?

No. He reined his thoughts in sharply. Striking at a lone woman wasn't logical. Why hunt her down when she obviously knew nothing? Assassins would concentrate on sending their main target to the grave. Even the most vengeful of bastards wouldn't waste time on her unless Redmayne himself was dead. The best way to protect Rhiannon was to make certain he was a generous target for them, one that would draw them out from hiding and keep them occupied until he could bring them to justice.

As for his grandfather, there would be time enough to tangle with him as well. He would see to it that whatever treachery Paxton had worked upon Rhiannon's father was undone and as much of her past life restored to her as possible. The thought of her tucked into the rose-draped cottage she'd described tight-

ii, ready to blast his
. At that instant the
spewing forth sparks.
ung awake, poker in
the pistol barrel at
ed cinnamon-colored
ace.
l out her name.
stol barrel to his face,
t army regulation to
rders, Captain?" she

of the cold butt of the
d his finger from the

ened a fist in his chest, awakening something almost forgotten . . . yearning. A wistful wondering of what it might be like to stride through Rhiannon's door in a rainfall of drifting rose petals, sink into one of the chairs at a table she'd weighted down with bunches of flowers gathered from her meadows, while she poured steaming tea into chipped cups, her eyes shining with gladness at seeing him.

Hell, Redmayne thought with a grimace, the pain must be affecting his wits. He no more belonged at Rhiannon's soul-warming table than a feral wolf. But there was *some*thing to be glad about.

With the complicated mixture of assassins, his grandfather's treachery, and regaining a tight hold on his unruly soldiers, Redmayne knew he would have plenty to keep himself occupied in the next few weeks. Perhaps if he kept busy, he wouldn't even think of Rhiannon more than thrice a day.

With grim determination, he mounted the steps to his headquarters, thanking God he'd had the presence of mind to dismiss even his aide-de-camp. Maybe it would be pure hell to tend to his own wounds, worn down as he was, but it was preferable to risking Barton "slipping" with the straight razor, and separating his head from his shoulders. A week ago, the image would have amused him. But tonight it only made his feet feel heavier. Why? Little enough about the garrison had changed since he rode out of here a few days ago, reining his horse for Ballyaroon. The flicker of awe and dread in his men's eyes, the sense of isolation, as if some invisible wall separated him from every other living creature. The boredom, the hints of weariness veiled behind dry wit and mocking humor. Yet somehow everything had changed.

Strange, how cold he felt, knowing that in this

so in another officer
any soldier in Galway
invade Captain Redm
direct order from the

And yet, wasn't it
a more sinister reaso
natural quiet?

He'd never learn t
doorway. With stealt
forays about his gra
door, locked it behin
a malevolent purpose
cape out the door be
question them. And

whole encampment, there was not a single person he dared to trust. In all the world, there was only one . . .

And he'd sent her away.

He fumbled for his keys, relieved that the lieutenant had locked his rooms up the instant Redmayne went missing. It would have been uncomfortable in the extreme to know that anyone had been poking about in his things. Not that there was anything to find there. . . .

Yet as he attempted to push the key into the hole with a hand unsteady from exhaustion, he stiffened, suspicion stirring in his gut. Without turning the key, he pushed down on the latch. The door swung open.

Every nerve in his body tight with battle-readiness, he drew the pistol at his waist, thanking God he'd had the presence of mind to request one from the armory before he left the lieutenant's chambers.

The front room was dark, but he could see a line of candle shine beneath the door to his private chambers. Don't let your imagination run mad, he thought. Perhaps someone had thought to light the fire in his bedchamber. But, no—perhaps they would have done so in another officer's room, yet Redmayne doubted any soldier in Galway would have had the temerity to invade Captain Redmayne's inner sanctum without a direct order from the captain himself.

And yet, wasn't it at least possible that there was a more sinister reason for the flickering light, the unnatural quiet?

He'd never learn the truth standing in the infernal doorway. With stealth born in countless childhood forays about his grandfather's house, he closed the door, locked it behind him. If there *was* anyone with a malevolent purpose about, damned if he would escape out the door before Redmayne had a chance to question them. And if there was only some sleepy-eyed private waiting in the room, Redmayne would feel like such a fool that he might just shoot himself.

Soundlessly he walked toward the door to his bedchamber. One hand on the butt of the pistol tucked in his waistband, he used his other hand to swing the door open. His instincts fairly screamed with the primal awareness of a wild beast whose lair had been invaded.

Candles burned on scattered tables, awash in puddles of melted wax. A fire fought for its life in the hearth, while something merrily burned in a kettle slung over an iron hook above the flames.

The single wing chair was drawn up before it, its massive upholstered back to the door, the sooty point of the fire iron dangling over the chair's arm as if some archer had mistaken the piece of furniture for a promising-looking stag.

At that instant he heard a sound, ever so faint, come from the chair's confines. His eyes narrowed. He slid his loaded pistol from the waistband of his breeches, his finger curling around the trigger. After all, even assassins could fall asleep on the job.

Stealthily he rounded the chair, ready to blast his unwelcome visitor into eternity. At that instant the fire fell apart, hissing, crackling, spewing forth sparks.

The figure in the chair sprung awake, poker in hand. Redmayne stared down the pistol barrel at wide, frightened eyes, disheveled cinnamon-colored hair tangled about a pale oval face.

"Rhiannon!" He froze, choked out her name.

Her gaze flickered from the pistol barrel to his face, and she swallowed hard. "Is it army regulation to shoot people for disobeying orders, Captain?" she asked in a small voice.

Suddenly, horrifyingly aware of the cold butt of the pistol in his hand, he loosened his finger from the trigger, and set the weapon down on the nearest bare surface.

"Damn it, Rhiannon, I could have shot you!" he snapped, astonished at the way his stomach churned. Hell, he'd never bothered to concern himself about things that *hadn't* happened, spinning them out the way some men did, in a string of images that chilled the blood. This one time, though, he saw all too clearly what might have been: a bloody hole ripped in the lace at Rhiannon's soft breast, surprise and pain and sorrow clouding her eyes as life ebbed from her.

"You would never pull the trigger unless you were absolutely sure what you were shooting at. You're far too meticulous about little things to make a mistake in something so important." She spoke with absolute confidence in him. No knowledge of the way fear could quicken the reflexes, distrust tighten the nerves, cloud the eyes. How many soldiers had survived any length of time in the king's service without firing a bullet they wished they could take back? Her naïveté irritated him. Her faith in him chafed. He sought shelter behind an icy voice and a cool glare.

"What the devil are you doing here? I saw you leave the camp with my own eyes."

Dusky roses bloomed in her cheeks, and her gaze flitted away, touching the armoire, the curtained window, the washstand in the corner, touching anywhere except on his face. "I fully intended to leave. I even managed to get half a mile along the road, but in the end I just couldn't do it."

"Do what?"

"Leave you here all alone."

She looked pensive and a little eager, as if hoping against hope he might understand. He did. Far too well for comfort. He shrugged one shoulder, then crossed to the stand where a decanter of brandy stood. He poured himself a glass. "My dear, perhaps you should consider getting a pair of spectacles," he said with far more amusement than he felt. "This garrison is fairly crawling with soldiers. One can scarce take a step without tripping over half a dozen."

"Yes, but not one of them . . ." she began, then stopped, turned away.

He should just let it go, not press her. Whatever she had to say, he doubted he wanted to hear it. Still, he heard the rumble of his own voice. "Not one of them . . . what?"

"Would look after you properly. You'd just glare at them, and they'd flee as if a sea of enemy calvary were swarming down on them. Captain, you are in bad need of someone with the nerve to defy you."

"Such insubordination might be easier to find than you think, since the revered lieutenant has taken command." He could scarce believe he'd spoken the words aloud. It was a confession of vulnerability. And, God forbid, the slightest admission of hurt? "Rhiannon, I thought I made myself clear: I don't want you here."

There was a cruelty in the blunt words. If only she didn't also realize that there was a desperation in them. He wanted her gone more than ever for one simple reason: the unmistakable welling-up of gladness he'd felt in the most secret, hidden part of him the instant he saw her face.

Dangerous . . . it was far too dangerous to allow himself the luxury of such an emotion, a tie to anyone so frail and mortal, fallible and tender.

He expected hurt to wash over her features, making her wilt like the most delicate of blossoms burned by ruthless rays of a too hot sun. But there was only the soft bruising of resignation about her mouth, offset by a recurrent hint of stubbornness.

"I know you don't want me here, but you can't make me leave you."

It was a challenge, no matter how gently spoken. "Oh, can't I? With the snap of my fingers, I can call down twenty men who would be happy to escort you to the farthest reaches of hell if I ordered it."

"You won't do that."

"Whyever not?"

"Because you're not a man given to ridiculous posturing and exerting power where it's meaningless. And to set a guard over me would be futile. They would have to leave me eventually to do whatever duties soldiers do. And the instant they did, I would come back. You'd find me in this same chair with the same fireplace poker."

"Brewing up a bowl of pap for me?" Redmayne was astonished by the angry edge in his voice. "I'm not some puling child who needs a nursemaid hovering over me every second. My wounds are negligible. They'll soon be gone."

"Perhaps. But if you're not careful, you'll have other wounds that won't be so obliging." Her brow creased, and he knew the thought pained her. Astonishing, this heartache over pain not yet felt except in her imagination. "You need someone you can trust to watch your back, Lion," she insisted. "I intend to do it, with your cooperation or without it."

He stared down at her, bemused. He couldn't even remember the last time anyone refused to do what he willed him to do. Any hint of defiance had been quashed easily enough. The slightest glare, the almost infinitesimal tightening of his mouth, the barest flash of warning in his eyes, and his soldiers fairly stumbled over themselves like raw schoolboys. It seemed Rhiannon was impervious to techniques that had brought battle-hardened brigades back to order.

Most astonishing of all was the discovery that the woman was right. If she persisted in her defiance, there was not a damn thing he could do to stop it, short of throwing her in the brig. And if he did that, doubtless she'd have her guards so charmed that they'd not only let her out of her cell but also build her a cozy fire in his quarters so she wouldn't take a chill. Besides, wasn't it possible she'd be safer here, where he could at least keep watch over her?

Excuses, Redmayne thought grimly. He was making up excuses for the first time in his memory. Hadn't he the courage to admit the truth, at least to himself? That he'd been alarmingly glad to see her friendly face? That a kind of unexpected peace had washed over him at her presence, which was welcome, so welcome, in spite of every bit of resistance he could muster. The knowledge tightened something cold and hard beneath his ribs—something almost like fear. He shoved it away so ruthlessly it was as if it had never existed at all. He confronted her, unable for once to keep the fury and frustration from showing in his eyes.

"What the devil do you expect me to do with you?" he grumbled. "We might have managed to share a bed in that infernal wagon of yours, but we can hardly indulge in such an arrangement here without causing some comment. The men were already looking at you with far too much curiosity and speculation for my taste."

That much was true enough. It chafed like nettles beneath his skin when he saw how they stared at her, gauging her beauty, guessing at their captain's restraint, wounded or no. He sensed their curiosity as they imagined their ice-blooded captain with a woman. After so many years in the army, he could envision the jests in the barracks, could almost hear them: "Pity the poor wench if 'e did have 'is way wi' her. Touchin' the captain would be like makin' love t' one o' the stone effigies in the churchyard. Poor lass'd likely get frostbite."

Redmayne's jaw tightened. Absurd, this raw frisson of fury at insults that had been spoken only in his own imagination. Yet the strange bubble of panic was all too real, that someone might scent vulnerability like a wolf scenting blood.

Were there some who could sense the unexpected bond that damnable kiss had struck between him and Rhiannon? He remembered all too well his own intuition three years ago, when he'd seen Mary Fallon Delaney with the man who would become her husband. It was as if an enchanted thread had been strung between the two lovers, if only one had the wit to look for it. And Redmayne had used that bond as a weapon against Mary Fallon and her hero, one far more effective than any clumsy sword. The idea of anyone being able to wield such a weapon against him was anathema.

But no, comparisons between Fallon and her lover and Redmayne and Rhiannon were absurd. He was far more guarded than the impetuous Fallon or her blustering husband with emotion forever naked in his eyes. And after all, Redmayne reasoned, he did not love Rhiannon Fitzgerald.

"You needn't concern yourself about me," Rhiannon interrupted his uncomfortable train of thought. "One of the benefits of traveling on the road as I do is that I have no reputation to ruin. I don't care what anyone thinks of me."

"That's all very well for you, madam," Redmayne growled, very much put out to discover that *he did* care. Captain Lionel Redmayne, who hadn't cared about anything in a very long time. He grimaced, glaring down at her, silently cursing innocence and courage, generosity and warmth—qualities thought to be so pure, treasured. Who could have guessed they could be brewed into simple poison to addle a man's wits, steal his ability to reason, goad him into making mistakes.

He downed his brandy in one gulp, welcoming the fire in his throat. Then he turned back to Rhiannon. "I suppose there is no help for it, then, if you're determined to be unreasonable. You will have to accept my hand in marriage."

It was almost worth all the misery he'd been through just to see the expressions on that soft feminine face, which could hide nothing: shock, disbelief, awe, and alarm. "Lion, you can't—can't be serious. I cannot marry you. I am only offering to stay until things are settled, watch over you until . . . until whoever shot you is caught." Her lashes dipped low, her voice so soft he could scarce hear it. "Besides, you don't love me."

He was overpowered by the very devil of an impulse. He met her gaze with contemptible earnestness. "Love is not necessary in such arrangements as I understand them. Mutual respect, comparable fortunes or family lineage, perhaps."

"We have none of those things in common, either! You can't be serious."

She was right, of course. He'd been a ruthless bastard, teasing her from the first, hadn't he? "No, my dear. I'm not serious." Why was his voice suddenly so rough-edged? "But our supposed betrothal would simplify things for both of us during your stay here at the garrison. Then, in the end, you can jilt me. No one would question your wisdom in doing so."

"But I don't think—"

"We established that the day you first dragged me, bleeding, out of the dust near Ballyaroon." Redmayne was surprised at the near-tenderness in his tone. "You wish to watch over me, Rhiannon, you'll have to allow me to watch over you as well. I know the temper of these men far better than you do. If they thought you a woman of questionable virtue . . ." The mere idea tightened a muscle in his jaw. "You know my passion for order, my dear. You wouldn't want to be responsible for my actions if one of them dared treat you with anything other than respect."

"Only you can be responsible for your own actions, Lion. I can be grieved by them, but—" She stopped, then looked into his eyes, and Redmayne sensed that she saw far more than he would have wished. "Please try to understand. This ruse, this betrothal . . . it seems so deceitful, as if . . ." She looked so miserable he had to knot his fingers into a fist to keep himself from reaching out to touch her cheek.

"As if what?" he asked.

"As if I were profaning something precious."

Blast if he didn't see the flush on her cheek, the reflection of the kiss they'd shared, the touches of fingertips against skin while the stream flowed past them, carrying away wisdom and restraint.

Trust Rhiannon to turn treachery into something bright and fine. Not because she was blind to his original motive—she couldn't be after he'd revealed it to her with all the subtlety of a volley of cannon fire. Rather because she'd seen past his anger and frustration to the more dangerous feelings that had betrayed him: the tenderness he'd fought so hard to hide, even from himself; the pleasure that had rocked him as she'd responded to him with all the generosity of her dreamer's heart. She'd reached into a maelstrom of both ugliness and agonizing beauty, and she'd plucked out only what was good.

It made him ache. Why? he wondered. For her, because of the pain an uncaring world would inevitably force her to face? Or for himself because he would never have the courage to reach out as she did?

"This plan of yours would never work anyway," she insisted. "You see"—she swallowed hard—"I'm not a very good liar." No schoolgirl facing the parish priest for her first confession could have appeared more earnest or chagrined.

This time he couldn't stop himself from touching her cheek, the curve warm, pure, hinting at everything Lionel Redmayne could never be.

"Take heart, Rhiannon," he said, attempting to jest. "I'm a practiced enough liar for both of us." But for once he wasn't amused by the irony.

He wasn't certain what made him avert his gaze, more than a little ashamed. His fingers fell away from her, as if that mere brush of his skin against Rhiannon's could taint her.

"I'll summon one of my men and have him prepare the room down the hall from mine. It is a trifle improper, but considering the attempt on my life, no natural man would question the fact that I'd want to do all in my power to protect my betrothed. Keeping her close by would seem only logical. One of the officers' wives can be pressed into service as your attendant."

"I don't need an attendant. I'm used to being quite independent."

"Rhiannon, we *will* observe the proprieties. If you stubbornly insist on remaining here at the garrison, you will do it on my terms. I won't have half the king's army thinking . . ."

What? A voice inside him mocked grimly. That he

couldn't keep his hands off of his fiancé? That he was slipping into her room like a lovesick youth, taking her in his arms, too eager to wait for the wedding vows, like countless other impatient bridegrooms from the beginning of time.

No. Not even the raw recruit with the wildest imagination would be able to envision Captain Redmayne in such a fevered state. The knowledge should have soothed Redmayne's frayed nerves. Instead, it left him vaguely ill at ease. Why? Because he knew Rhiannon would see it as tragic, not being able to reach out to another human being, regardless of the cost? Yet in Rhiannon's hidden glen hadn't there been a moment, just a fraction of a second, when something uncontrolled had stirred in him, something totally unexpected?

"Lion?"

He started at the sound of her voice, looked down into glen-green eyes.

"I promise you won't regret this—letting me stay, I mean."

"I don't believe in regretting a decision once it is made." He brushed his unease aside, attempting to take shelter in familiar arrogance. But he couldn't help wondering what this decision might cost them both.

Chapter

❧ 11 ❧

It was a hell of a lot harder to sleep alone than it should have been, Redmayne thought grimly as he woke from fitful slumber in the isolation and silence of his own room.

A few days—he'd spent just a few days crammed into Rhiannon's absurdly small bed with her soft, feminine form cuddled close against him. He'd hated the intrusion. He'd been sure he did. Then why was it that all through this endless night he'd tossed and turned, found himself reaching out in his sleep, nerves ragged when he didn't find her?

His concern was doubtless some latent germ of chivalry he'd been infected with. He'd been tormented by hazy impressions that he was still trapped in Rhiannon's wagon instead of safe within his own pristine quarters and, despite his imprisonment, was reluctant to see the woman dumped unceremoniously on the floor. The fear that he'd somehow knocked her out of the bed was the only reason he kept searching for her in his sleep. After all, it couldn't be gentlemanly form to allow the woman who'd saved one's life to bruise herself in such a fashion.

He should have been damned relieved when he awoke to the gleaming bare white walls of his bed-chamber, the spartan-plain armoire standing at attention in the corner. But the night's ordeal had left him exhausted and in a most precarious temper, a decidedly unpleasant circumstance for one who prided himself on both his self-control and his ability to function on impossibly little sleep.

He'd cultivated those two habits since childhood. Paxton Redmayne had stuffed his head from morning till night with unorthodox lessons, pouring insights and information into Lionel's mind in such a relentless deluge that the boy had often felt he was drowning.

Those few precious hours when he was supposed to be sleeping alone in his room had provided the only opportunity for a resentful, hurting boy to concentrate on his own thoughts, formulating complicated plans to defy his grandfather. As for indulging in fits of temper, Lionel had learned early that he couldn't afford that luxury—it made one careless—and carelessness was the sin Paxton Redmayne punished most severely.

Yet even when Lionel's schemes failed, bringing the grimmest retribution, the boy had never regretted the slumber time he lost when other children were dreaming of useless pursuits like catching a fish as big as a round tower, hunting the Minotaur, riding fierce dragons, or playing bold Lancelot to some blushing girl's Guinevere. To a boy who owned nothing except a sharp intellect and the information in his head, the night alone had seemed to belong to him.

Even as a man, Lionel had watched countless moons arc silver across the sky, seen an eternity of stars sparkle, fade, die. Yet after everything that had transpired during the past week, he'd thought for once he would be able to lose himself in oblivion, sleep decently if only from sheer exhaustion and the familiarity of being back in his own bed. Even the threat of assassins shouldn't have had any power over him. He had a warrior's instincts, that lifesaving ability to spring from dead sleep to battle readiness between one heartbeat and the next.

Only one thing had possessed the power to trouble his sleep and turn his feather mattress into a bed that might as well have been stuffed with thorns.

Rhiannon.

Ignoring the throb in his shoulder, Redmayne dragged the back of his hand across his gritty eyelids, and levered himself to a sitting position on the bed.

Blast the woman; her father had nicknamed her rightly. She was the very embodiment of an accursed briar rose, prickling a man until his nerves were raw, yet possessed of the softest, most luminous beauty when it turned its face up, either to the morning sun or to a man's hungry gaze.

And there could be no denying that Redmayne *had* been hungry to see her when she sprang like a startled doe from the wing chair.

But what the devil had he done once he was confronted by her? Had he been sensible? Bundled her off into her cart and lashed that lazy excuse of a horse of hers into a run? No. He'd let the woman outmaneuver him again. He'd set her up in the room just down the hall from his. He'd let her stay.

Let her? Hellfire, as if anyone could get rid of her! The woman was like a case of hives, once one was infected by her, there was no chance of escape. And yet, damn her hide and his own foolishness, some part of him was glad she was nearby. Close enough so that he could keep her safe until those who plotted against him were caught. And close enough so that he could unravel whatever had happened in her past.

Bracing himself for the unpleasant task of working the morning stiffness out of his wounded leg, he swung his limbs over the edge of the bed and got to his feet. The instant he was shaved and changed into fresh clothes he would have her summoned, so that he could lay out some simple rules for her safety. He had no delusions. Rhiannon had the battle instincts of a day-old fawn.

Grimacing, he made his way to his washstand and peered into the mirror. He lowered his eyebrows in puzzlement. Why the devil was he smiling?

Barely half an hour passed before he was ready, garbed in a fresh uniform, one that didn't look as if it belonged in the rag bag. The image that stared back at him from the looking glass was reassuringly familiar. Lean, clean-shaven cheekbones, white-gold hair combed to perfection, ice-blue eyes that betrayed nothing. He could almost believe that his encounter with the assassins' pistol balls and an Irish guardian angel hadn't altered him at all.

Feeling as if he'd regained his grasp on something vital, he strode into his offices. A sleepy-eyed private sprang to attention. "Good—good morning, Captain, s-sir," the youth stammered, knocking a brass candlestick from its stand with his elbow in his haste to salute. Flushing scarlet, he raised his voice above the ringing of the brass. "The lieutenant ordered me to wait for you here. He thought I might be of some service, in case you needed anything."

"The lieutenant is all politeness." Redmayne could almost be amused at the lad's indecision: what best to do—retrieve the candlestick or stand at attention, pretending it had never happened? "Summon Miss Fitzgerald, Private. Tell her I wish to see her here at once."

With another salute and a surreptitious dive for the

candlestick, the lad managed to beat a hasty retreat, his relief so evident that Redmayne could hear his gusty sigh on the other side of the door as it closed. It had always amused him—the effect he had on people. Why was it that the sigh made him oddly weary all of a sudden?

Shoving the feeling away, he began sorting through the pile of dispatches that had arrived while he was away. Most business had already been attended to by the capable lieutenant, but a commander needed to be aware of everything that had transpired in his absence—especially when said absence involved a plot to kill him.

He was absorbed in an order for supplies when he heard the hasty steps of someone running down the hall. His muscles tensed. Such unseemly haste never boded well. Squaring his shoulders, he folded his hands atop the stack of papers, smoothing every ripple of unease from his face until it was undisturbed as a mountain lake.

The private burst in, saluting, his eyes round with distress. "Captain, sir. I went to Miss Fitzgerald's rooms as you ordered. But when I knocked, there was no answer. I—I knew you would be most displeased if I failed to return without her, so I dared to open the door, but—"

A chill trickled down Redmayne's spine, his voice ice-hard. "For God's sake, man, I'm aging here. Just say whatever it is you have to say."

"She's gone, sir."

"Gone?"

The private flinched. "I—I'm afraid so." The man shifted on his feet as if the floor had suddenly become as hot as a frying griddle. "Perhaps she wandered off. You know the Irish are an unpredictable lot, never so much as a by-your-leave and—"

"I hardly think my betrothed needs to ask by-your-leave of any man." Redmayne pierced him with a glare so sharp it should have drawn blood.

"Y—your betrothed?" If the private had taken a dive headlong from the griddle into the fire, he couldn't have looked more aghast.

Redmayne grimaced. It had been close to midnight when he first mentioned his supposed engagement to the few people necessary to prepare Rhiannon's quarters. He'd expected the gossip to rage through the camp like an epidemic. Yet perhaps it hadn't if this fool dared to insult the lady of his captain. "It is true," Redmayne said coldly. "Miss Fitzgerald, be she Irish or no, is to be my wife."

"Meanin' no disrespect, Captain. Even if she is Irish, she must be—I mean, you'd never tolerate irresponsible . . ."

The man seemed, at last, to have the wit to realize he was only digging himself in deeper. He swallowed hard, flinging himself into the fray in one last, desperate gesture. "She—she must be somewhere in the camp, sir. I'm certain she's safe enough. Nothing ill has happened to her."

The fool was a hell of a lot more optimistic than Redmayne was. Even more disturbing was the fact that the private must have seen Redmayne's nervousness or he would never have attempted to reassure him the way he had.

Flattening his hands on the desk, Redmayne shoved himself to his feet with a deliberation that belied the sharp edge of panic carving his vitals.

Rhiannon, alone, unprotected, among a garrison of men trained from the cradle to have nothing but scorn for the "barbarian Irish." Soldiers who had been mocked and spat upon, defied and ambushed by hardheaded fools without the wit to realize they were bleeding and dying generation after generation in a cause that had been lost centuries ago.

As if that wasn't bad enough, Rhiannon would be marked as his lady in a place that probably housed the very men who had tried to kill him. The men she had thwarted. The varlets who would take pleasure in killing her as well.

For a second, part of him clamored to raise a general alarm, have every man in the garrison search for her. But he dared not have even one soldier attempt to find her. To do so would be to reveal a vulnerability that chilled him. Despite the general hatred of the Irish among the troops, no one would dare show the least disrespect to the captain's own fiancée. And as for his assassins—if she was safe now, his excessive reaction would mark her as a certain target next time. Not to mention the fact that once she was found, probably tending a barn rat for colic, the whole thing would be damned embarrassing.

"Remain here, Private, in case my betrothed comes. I believe I will take a tour of the grounds. It seems there was an accident in the wheelwright's shop while I was gone."

"Yes, sir. Old Eli overset a gun carriage he was workin' to mend, but no one was fierce hurt this time, just a few purple fingers an' lots o' swearin', beggin' yer pardon. Not like what happened t' Jemmy Carver."

"The boy who was injured last month."

"Yes. Helping balance a cart when the opposite wheel crumpled. The weight o' the whole fell smack on his leg. Won't be doin' no dancin' again, will Jemmy."

"Perhaps it will be a gift. I loathe dancing myself," Redmayne attempted to seem careless, undisturbed, as he grabbed up his cloak. "Should my betrothed turn up here, Private, you will make certain she remains?"

"Yes, sir."

With a nod, Redmayne strode out into the morning sun. It dazzled him, blinded him for a moment. He glanced around, wondering where the devil to begin looking for one lost woman.

The stables, perhaps? She'd want to see how those ridiculous animals of hers had passed the night. He started in that direction. In the dim, musty confines of the barn, he glimpsed several men cleaning out stalls, another mending tack. In the corner, a frightened stable lad was attempting to tend Socrates, while Captain Blood gazed down with inscrutable feline amusement. The horse bared its teeth at the lad, doubtless waiting for a chance to take a bite.

"Have you seen my fiancée, Private?"

Redmayne's voice so startled the lad that he dropped his pitchfork. Seeing a chance, Socrates nipped him. With a yelp of pain, the boy came to attention well out of reach of those strong equine teeth. Redmayne could have sworn the piratical cat was laughing.

"Y—your lady? Aye, sir. She was here, oh, an hour ago. Kissin' this hell-born horse like it was a newborn babe. An' the other two, that dog and the cat, nuzzled up all night with the horse in the straw, like they'd be happy if ye came in an' joined 'em! That's why I volunteered t' tend t' this horse." The boy gave an injured sniff. "Seemed tame enough. Who woulda guessed?"

"Who indeed," Redmayne drawled with an alarming sense of relief. Rhiannon was safe, just wandering about. He'd put a stop to such nonsense the instant he found her.

"I'd heard tell the mad Irish were nigh magic when

it came t' handlin' horses, but I guess I ne'er quite believed it till now. D'ye think it's a charm she worked on 'im or—"

"Doubtless the poor beast is bewitched," Redmayne said. God knew, the woman had managed to muddle up his own wits something fierce. He grimaced as Captain Blood leaped down from his perch and began doing his best to embed cat hair in every fiber of his captain's uniform. "Did she mention where she was going next?"

"Somewhere on the other side o' the camp. Sergeant Barton was takin' her."

"Barton?" Redmayne's stomach clenched, the vaguest vestiges of amusement dying. Even Rhiannon couldn't be so reckless as to go off with that man, could she? She'd faced him down outside the gypsy cart, seen him with his two comrades. She knew it was likely that Barton, despite his babe-innocent face, was neck-deep in the plot to kill him.

Lionel was appalled to see the stable lad staring at him, an odd expression on his face. "He was showin' her about most gallantlike," the lad piped up, rubbing the sore place on his arm where Socrates had bitten him. "Never need fear for a lady when he's about, sir." Hellfire, the boy was trying to soothe Captain Lionel Redmayne. Had Redmayne really slipped that far? The lad hitched up his sagging britches. "A good sort, Barton is."

Unless he happened to be firing a pistol at someone, Redmayne supposed. Fighting back panic, he shoved the cat aside, then strode out of the stables, his gaze searching the bustle of the army camp. It should be simple enough to pick out a woman in the midst of the soldiers, shouldn't it?

Leg throbbing, pulse far too fast for comfort, Redmayne made his way through the confusion, stopping to inquire here and there. He'd nearly reached the other edge of the camp when someone said he'd seen Barton and a lady going toward the infirmary.

Cursing himself for a fool, Redmayne hastened to the isolated building, constructed far enough away from the rest to guard against contagion. It had been all but empty of late, save for the few injuries that happened about the camp. Quiet, nearly deserted. A place where few would question or be alarmed if they heard a scream . . .

If Barton had dared to hurt her . . . The mere possibility made something poisonous—anger, dread, and resolve—knot beneath Redmayne's ribs. He flung open the door to the building and stalked inside, ready to flay Barton alive.

The instant he entered, his ears were assaulted by a tinkling wave of feminine laughter. Rhiannon. For an instant, he feared he would murder the woman himself.

Forcing every wire-taut muscle in his body to relax, Redmayne paced with lazy stride in the direction of that sound. What he saw was more infuriating than anything he could have imagined. Rhiannon and Barton, arms looped about young Jemmy Carver, were helping him walk with an unsteady gait while three other inmates of the infirmary looked on, their innate loathing of the Irish seemingly forgotten as they teased their comrade.

"She'll have ye dancin' in no time, Jem!" a raspy baritone called out.

"Nay, Jemmy'd be fearful the captain might take his other leg for darin' t'—*oomph!*" A guttural grunt ended the jest as the man next to him jammed an elbow into his gut.

"What the devil ye do that fer?" The grumble ended in a gasp. "Captain Redmayne, sir!" The scramble of white-faced men attempting to struggle to attention bordered on the ridiculous. Most times Redmayne would have enjoyed their discomfiture, passed it off with dry wit. At the moment he wasn't disposed to be so merciful.

"Has Lieutenant Williams instated dancing lessons in my absence, or do you gentlemen need me to add a few more things to your roster of duties to keep you occupied?" he asked coldly.

"No, sir! Beg pardon, sir!" A chorus of stammers rose. Only Rhiannon seemed impervious to his current mood.

"Lion!" she exclaimed with genuine gladness. Redmayne winced at her use of his first name. She paused only long enough to make certain Carver was steady on his feet before she flew to Redmayne's side. "Don't you think Jemmy is improving wonderfully well? Sergeant Barton and I were helping him—"

"Barton, I thought I made myself clear last night when I told you I had no more need of an aide-decamp. Your services are no longer necessary to me or to my betrothed."

Rhiannon's smile died, confusion clouding her face. Barton looked as if he'd taken a pistol blast full in the chest. An apt comparison, Redmayne thought with bitter humor, considering that that was probably where the boy had aimed when he pulled the trigger at Ballyaroon. Damn them both for looking so surprised. After all, there could be no other logical reason why Barton would have been traveling with two of Redmayne's enemies, could there?

"Captain, sir, I thought you just meant that last night you wished to be left alone." Damn Barton for looking so bewildered and hurt. Blast, he couldn't be mourning the loss of his post too grievously. The man had probably been horrified when he first got his assignment to serve the inscrutable Captain Redmayne.

Besides, whatever had happened at Ballyaroon, it was Barton who'd shown up at Rhiannon's caravan door, accompanied by two men Redmayne knew as adversaries. Any sane man would have been suspicious. And suspicion had a strange way of keeping a man alive.

"Lion, please."

His name again. Curse the woman! Her use of it made him feel stripped naked somehow. Rhiannon pressed his arm with one hand, the slender fingers delicate and fragile against the crisp uniform sleeve. "Sergeant Barton has been most kind, showing me all about the camp, telling me how the garrison works, the improvements you've made."

The fact that he might have escorted her ever so chivalrously off the nearest cliff obviously hadn't occurred to the woman. The fact that she was safe should have eased the tightness in Redmayne's shoulders, softened the knot in his gut. Instead, he felt inexplicably angrier than ever.

"I fear I am less than convinced that the sergeant is reliable, considering the fact that he deserted his post for at least a few days."

"I was searching for you, Captain!" Barton cried, hot spots of color on his cheeks. High passion, earnestness, wounded pride? Or was it guilt, a desperate attempt to hide his culpability?

"Indeed. You have found me. Now, if you will excuse us?" He grasped Rhiannon's arm and marched her back to his headquarters without a word, despite her efforts to get him to speak. The last thing he wanted was for anyone to guess his present temper.

The instant the door closed, he rounded on her: "How dare you go traipsing around the garrison without my permission!"

"Your permission?" Her spine stiffened so swiftly it was a miracle it didn't crack.

"What were you thinking? For God's sake, Kenneth Barton might well be one of the men who shot me!"

He expected anger from her, outrage at his scorn. He would have welcomed it, an outlet for the coils of anger and—yes, damn it—fear that still bound him up inside. The last thing he wanted was for her mouth to soften, her eyes to fill with gentle knowing. "I understand now. That is what is amiss," she said almost to herself. She crossed to him, grasped one of his hands in her own.

"Lion, you needn't worry anymore."

"Needn't worry? What the—"

"Sergeant Barton had nothing to do with what happened at Ballyaroon. He would never hurt you." The woman actually dared to smile. "He idolizes you."

He was unnerved by the knowledge that she'd guessed Barton's involvement bothered him. That she seemed to have guessed how deeply his former aide-de-camp's betrayal had cut—that was unbearable. He stiffened, drawing his hand away from her touch. "Did the sergeant tell you this while he was escorting you about the camp? Pardon me for doubting, but I hardly think he'd discuss modern methods of assassination to entertain a lady."

He'd managed to prick her that time! A fierce, defensive light sparked in her eyes. "That boy could no more assassinate you than I could. You ask how I can be so certain? I know it. *Here.*" She struck her fist against her heart. "Just as I knew you were hurt among the standing stones."

For an instant, just an instant, something in him reached out for the certainty that shone in her face, wanted to capture it, hold it. Believe. But thirty-odd years of mistrust were too deeply ingrained. He shoved away that ridiculous impulse.

"I regret to remind you that I do not believe in fairy tales or bewitchings or reading people's hearts by one touch of the hand. And you can hardly expect me to trust your intuition about people, my dear, after you were rash enough to take me into your caravan."

"Lion, you are hurting yourself, and you are hurting that boy by your stubbornness." Glen-green eyes burned with emotion. "Perhaps you can pretend that you have a heart of ice, and the rest of the world will believe you. But I won't!" Her fierce words were lost in a sharp rap on the door. Rhiannon cast a futile glance at it, as if by force of will she could drive away whoever was on the other side. Apparently her mystic powers did not reach quite that far.

Redmayne, on the other hand, was damnably relieved at the interruption.

"Enter," he called. The door swung wide, revealing Lieutenant Josiah Williams. Weariness and resignation tugged at the corners of the officer's mouth, his brown eyes betraying his unease. What the devil was the matter now? Redmayne wondered.

The lieutenant gave a stiff bow to acknowledge Rhiannon. "Beg pardon for the interruption, sir. There is one more matter we need to discuss, something that came up while you were gone." As soon as the words were out, his gaze flickered again to Rhiannon, all that gentlemanly intuition doubtless clamoring an alarm. "It's nothing of importance," the lieutenant said, a flush coloring his cheeks. "We can discuss it at a more convenient time."

"I prefer to discuss it now. Rhiannon, if you will excuse us?" Redmayne had rarely been so glad to dismiss anyone in his life. She cast him a reproachful look, all the more intolerable because it was laced with understanding.

"You will remember what I said?" she pleaded.

"If I forget, I'm certain you will remind me." Redmayne sighed with resignation.

"Captain, sir," the lieutenant said hastily, "in truth, it might be better if your lady remains. This is a situation in which her opinion could be of value."

Rhiannon hesitated, and Redmayne wished both she and the sainted Lieutenant miles away from him.

"I doubt Rhiannon would have any interest in the workings of the garrison," Lionel said.

"No! I find it most fascinating! You see, Lieutenant, Sergeant Barton gave me a tour of the camp this morning, explaining so many things. I got a chance to see facets of Lion that I never could have understood before."

Redmayne was horrified to feel his cheeks burn. Had he ever blushed before? There was no sense arguing with Rhiannon, trying to shove her out the door verbally or otherwise. Once the woman thought she could help someone, she'd be harder to budge than that accursed horse of hers.

Redmayne bit back a sigh. "What is this difficulty you needed to speak of, Lieutenant?"

The man straightened like a freshly cast ramrod. "Captain, sir, first, let me say that I take full responsibility for this situation."

Redmayne rolled his eyes heavenward. "Why is it I doubt such a preface would come before anything I would take pleasure in hearing?"

The lieutenant's Adam's apple bobbed in his throat. "No. But you might not object, considering your own circumstances."

Redmayne groped for patience. "Just say it, man. I

doubt your news will improve no matter how long you stall in telling me."

That goaded the other officer into knotting his fists, resentment glinting in his eyes. "While you were absent, I gave permission for a celebratory dinner of sorts, with dancing, for the soldiers and their wives."

Who would have imagined such a predictably honorable man could actually manage to blindside Redmayne? He paused for a moment, mastering his surprise. "I have heard people display grief in different ways," Redmayne observed dryly. "But to mourn the loss of a commander by hosting a fete seems to me in exceedingly poor taste."

"Surely that couldn't be the reason!" Rhiannon objected, looking most protective of him. Another moment, and she'd be sweeping him behind the shelter of her skirts.

"It wasn't because of you." Williams fairly bristled at Redmayne's insult to his honor. "It was to be for Archibald Whitting and his wife. The ladies discovered that the Whittings have been married thirty years this Saturday."

"Thirty years!" Rhiannon exclaimed. "How lovely!"

"With all the travelling Archie has done with the army, never once have they spent their anniversary together." Fierce defensiveness glinted beneath the lieutenant's eyelids. "The ladies thought we could give them a night they might remember, to make up for it. I thought it was a fine idea and gave my permission. Archie has done good service to the army, often at great cost to his wife."

Redmayne arched one eyebrow, genuinely confused. "The army owes no debt to a man for merely doing his duty."

"Blast it—" The lieutenant started to swear, stopped himself. "The army gives balls whenever it chooses. Why not plan this one to give a man and his wife a little joy?"

"A trifle irregular, what you're suggesting. Officers and enlisted men celebrating together."

"It's been done before. Why not stretch the bounds of protocol for one night? Why not let Archie and fine men like Barton and Jemmy Carver and the like have a bit of pleasure? I even hoped, considering your betrothal, you might be sympath— that you and your lady might like to host it," he amended hastily.

"Perhaps we should inquire after the enlisted men's birthdays," Redmayne observed, so mildly the lieutenant blanched. "Provide a cake, perhaps, or a few presents." He lowered his voice. "We're an army on hostile ground, in case you've forgotten, Lieutenant. We've no time for such nonsense."

His refusal should have been so damned simple, logical. But at that moment he glimpsed Rhiannon's face. Yearning glistened in her eyes, fleeting reflections of grief put aside long ago. Fragile memories of dancing slippers laid to rest, a life of wealth and privilege taken for granted, then lost.

But despite it all, she hadn't lost her joy in life, her hope, her courage. The dreamer's light that no calamity could extinguish shone in her face now, as if she had already come to love Archie and his wife and the magic of a love story thirty years old.

This was madness, Redmayne thought grimly. He couldn't possibly be considering changing his mind! Could he? He stalked over to the window, staring out across the garrison, a beehive of activity in the late morning sun.

A military installation needed discipline, order, not balls and anniversary toasts! A fete would distract the men from their purpose, make them think of their own wives and families far away, sweethearts they hadn't seen for months. Or was Redmayne merely fooling himself? Had he been reckless enough to love a woman who was far away, would anything—from dull peacetime duty to the hideous tempest of full-fledged war—keep him from picturing the perfect oval of her face? Remembering their last moments together? The taste of her lips?

His gaze flashed back to Rhiannon, and he felt an odd wrenching in his chest. She stood, hands folded, in a ray of sunshine, tendrils of cinnamon-brown curls falling in an unruly mass about the pure rose of her cheeks. She'd managed to hide some of her eagerness, but such determined cheerfulness on her part only made things worse.

If she'd ever been foolish enough to love a soldier, doubtless she would have appeared thus as he rode away, wanting her smile to be the last thing he saw, a talisman to carry with him, though her own too tender heart would be breaking.

Damnation!

"All right. We'll have the accursed ball." No one was more astonished at the growled words than the captain himself.

"Oh, Lion!" Rhiannon beamed, her smile so bright it pained him.

"Wh-what?" the other officer choked out. "But I thought you said—"

"You would be ill advised to remind me what I said, unless you have no real desire to honor the gunnery sergeant and his wife."

"No! I mean, yes, of course I won't." The man looked as if the devil himself had given permission for a garden party in the balmiest reaches of hell.

"Perhaps you should go tend to . . . whatever is involved in planning such a fete," Redmayne suggested. "I will offer my felicitations to the happy couple, but I draw the line at ordering up ratafia and lobster salad."

"I will be happy to help!" Rhiannon offered, then looked a trifle uncertain. Her gaze flicked to Redmayne as if asking permission. "Unless . . . well, I've just arrived here, and there is so much for me to learn. Perhaps there's something else Lion would like me to do."

It irritated him and touched him, that she stopped to consider his opinion. There was no logical reason Rhiannon couldn't help the lieutenant if she wanted to. At least if she was busy it would keep her out of trouble, not to mention out from under Redmayne's feet. But he found the idea of Rhiannon under the melting reach of the lieutenant's warm brown eyes an astonishingly distasteful prospect.

He was still formulating an answer when the lieutenant spoke in strained tones. "You needn't trouble yourself, miss. I'll take care of everything." There was a sudden harshness in the other officer, as if he didn't quite trust Redmayne's sudden benevolence and did not particularly like it, despite the fact that it meant the party would go on as planned. No, Redmayne had definitely ruined his perfect record of villainy in the lieutenant's eyes, and the man wasn't enjoying it one bit. If he'd guessed merely consenting to host an anniversary party would disconcert the good lieutenant this much, he might have done it months ago, just for entertainment.

Redmayne was surprised to find his mouth curving in a smile. "Lieutenant, if there is nothing else, you are dismissed."

Obviously vexed, the man offered a rigid salute, then turned on his heel and strode from the room.

The door had barely clicked shut when Rhiannon closed the space between them and hurled herself into Redmayne's arms. "Lion, I knew you would do it! Have the party for the sergeant, I mean!"

Redmayne's arms closed around her—a reflex, merely, to steady her so she wouldn't tumble to the floor. She raised a face shining with pleasure up to his, and he remembered another time when she'd gazed at him in the glen, offering herself up to a man who didn't begin to deserve her as if he were the boldest hero born of legend. *I want to make love to you. . . .*

The memory was agonizingly sweet, unbearably painful, filling him with self-loathing and regret. Suddenly the idea of Rhiannon turning him into some sort of champion over this nonsense was more than he could bear.

"I don't give a damn about the sergeant, his wife, or how long they've been wed," he said evenly. "I merely consented for the pleasure of bewildering the lieutenant."

One soft palm cradled his cheek, the warmth of it seeping into cold places in his soul, her eyes soft and knowing as a sinless Eve's. "You did it for me, Lion. So I could dance again."

Hellfire, hadn't he seen that secret longing in her eyes before he'd made his decision? The yearning for the life she'd known before? Dancing and sipping ratafia, smiling into the eyes of some undeserving escort? Redmayne swallowed hard. She'd read his mind yet again! Redmayne pulled away, tugging at his collar, which suddenly felt too tight. "Don't be absurd," he snapped. "This whole affair will be a good deal of trouble. You'll need a dress. Even if you have one crammed somewhere in that wagon of yours I'm certain it's hopelessly out of fashion."

"I can alter something. I'm a passable seamstress."

"Passable is not acceptable for my fiancée. I shall

order something up myself. And just so there is no misunderstanding, *I do not dance*. I have no desire to be bombarded by pleading glances throughout the infernal ball."

He sounded as petulant as a schoolboy. Rhiannon should have been hurt, angry, or at the very least as disgusted as he was at such behavior. Instead, she cast him a glowing smile.

"It's all right, Lion," she said. "I've probably forgotten how to dance anyway."

It would've been a hell of a lot easier if she had! But as the days passed, every time he saw her there was a new lightness to her feet. As she flitted to the stable, charming every man who crossed her path, banishing generations of hatred with the light of her smile, there was a fresh skip to her step. During her trips to the infirmary to help young Jemmy Carver, there was an airiness about her, as if she were already floating in clouds of dreams.

Even when the dressmakers came, beginning the endless fittings in the next room, Redmayne could hear her feet tapping, as she hummed waltz tunes distressingly off key. He tried his damnedest to ignore her, but in the end there was no escaping the truth.

Rhiannon might well have forgotten how to dance, but blast the woman, she was practicing in her head!

Chapter

❧ 12 ❧

Twilight edged the trees in wisps of ash-gray lace, almost as if night itself were weaving a shroud. Redmayne stared out across the vista of barracks beyond his headquarters window, bemused by the tightness in his stomach. Odd, to feel evidence of emotion after all these years. A little like recalling bits of a language long forgotten, enough to trouble one's peace but not enough to be of any practical use.

Doubtless Rhiannon would be delighted with the news, if ever he went mad enough to tell her what he was experiencing. But tonight he would have preferred to deal with matters in his accustomed way, to be without any feelings at all. At least during the interview that lay before him.

He had to question Kenneth Barton.

Nearly twenty-four hours had passed since Rhiannon's caravan had lumbered into the garrison. Redmayne had taken care of whatever pressing military business had to be transacted. God help any man who claimed Lion had done so in an attempt to avoid the upcoming confrontation.

No, Redmayne assured himself. He'd merely been

gathering his wits, planning the tactics he would use to get the boy to spill any information he might have. An unnecessary effort, Rhiannon would insist. No doubt she believed Barton would work himself to death attempting to aid Redmayne, were he but asked.

"That boy could no more assassinate you than I could," she had said, fierce protectiveness shining in every line of her earnest face. For whom? Redmayne or the earnest youth she had befriended? He felt an odd jab that couldn't possibly be jealousy. Not even an hour had she spent in Kenneth Barton's company, but Rhiannon was damned certain she knew the young man's heart. The way she believed she knew Redmayne's own?

Self-disgust poured through him. God forbid she should ever truly get a glimpse of the cold, dead place in his chest where a heart was supposed to be. Even a fairy-born healer would have to turn away from him, revolted, despairing.

Damnation, what the devil ailed him? Redmayne jammed his fingers through his hair in disgust. He had a job to do—question the young soldier who was his only link to the men who had ambushed him at Ballyaroon.

The task should be simple enough. In his years in the military, he'd become nigh legendary for his ability to pry secrets from the most determined rebels' souls. He'd always discovered just the right leverage, but here, when his own life might well hang in the balance, what was he doing? Nursing something appallingly akin to feelings of betrayal, and imagining the reactions of a woman to whom the concept of logic was as foreign as fairy tales were to him.

Redmayne had to admit his grandfather had been right about one thing. Emotions *were* a curse. In thirty-six years, Redmayne had been burdened with precious few emotions. Once events were over, he turned his back on them, buried them, walked away.

But part of him very much feared he would carry shadows of two recent memories long into the future. The self-loathing he'd felt watching Rhiannon's dreams shatter when he told her his seduction had been nothing but a ruse to bend her to his will. That and the terrible sinking in his stomach when he realized Kenneth Barton stood outside Rhiannon's caravan with the two men who had probably ambushed him at Ballyaroon.

He paced to the window, arms crossed over his chest as if . . . what? he thought in self-mockery. As if he could block any more surprise attacks on his peace of mind?

No possibility of that. At least not in the near future. He glimpsed a familiar figure striding toward his headquarters, defiance and wounded pride in every step. Barton, either already feeling ill-used or preparing to give the performance of his life. Was it possible that a person Redmayne thought of as a guileless boy had the skill of a desperate actor, realizing that he must get into character before striding upon the stage?

Redmayne scanned the room, choosing a chair beside the fire rather than entrenching himself behind the intimidating breadth of his own desk. Harsh tactics would achieve nothing with a man like Barton, except to make his wounded pride harden into something about as permeable as a wall of solid marble.

Carefully, Redmayne curled his fingers about the padded arms of the chair, as if he were no more concerned with this meeting than with those he and his former aide-de-camp had participated in a hundred times before.

But this time *was* different, damn it all.

Within moments Barton was knocking at the door, entering at Redmayne's command. With a salute, the aide stood at grim attention, his jaw raised in the stubborn angle of a schoolboy, wrongly accused, who would sooner take a caning than admit how hurt he was by the injustice.

For an instant, Redmayne recalled Rhiannon's plea on Barton's behalf. Then he shoved it away. "I assume you've been expecting my summons, Barton."

Eyes far too tempestuous for comfort locked on Redmayne's, something distressingly like a tremor managing to work its way through Barton's voice. "I expected you to send for me long ago. Would have welcomed it."

The youth's words nudged a raw place in Redmayne, that secret place where he wondered if he truly *had* been avoiding Barton because he dreaded the boy's answers. Damned if he'd let anyone, especially the aide-de-camp, suspect his own self-doubt.

"Ah." Redmayne pretended to stifle a yawn. "Other affairs had to be put in order before I could tend to this matter between us. A garrison must operate smoothly, even if its commanding officer has been shot by cowards who dared not face him like men." He turned the full force of his piercing gaze on Barton.

A choked sound came from the young soldier's chest. "You cannot possibly— I don't believe you truly think that I—"

"Attempted to kill me? Even you must admit that the evidence is rather damning. Perhaps you would explain how you came to be in that particular stretch of Irish wilderness with those particular men."

"When you disappeared, I was mad enough to think I might be able to find you. After all the time I've served you, I might know your ways while others . . ."

Barton's gaze faltered—the first sign he was hiding something.

"While others what?" Redmayne probed, never taking his eyes off the young man's face. He could feel the dread invading his own body, one breath at a time. He couldn't keep his shoulders from tensing beneath the immaculate fabric of his uniform jacket. "Just say it, Barton, whatever it is," he urged, wanting this over with. "I've been shot, endured the indignity of jouncing across the countryside in a gypsy caravan. Not to mention the fact that your own future hangs rather precariously in the balance. I beg you, have no concern about offending my sensibilities."

"Others might not—not trouble themselves to look terribly hard," the youth burst out, his face washing red.

Redmayne chuckled. "You think this lack of devotion should wound me to the quick? I assure you, it concerns me not so much as *this.*" He snapped his fingers, the crack seeming like a pistol shot in the room. "Your . . . er, devotion, however, does nothing to explain either how you happened to be searching in the area where I was ambushed, nor what you were doing with two men *not* of this garrison. Men who would claim they have good reason to wish me in my grave."

Redmayne was appalled to find some part of him was actually waiting—no, *hoping*—for an explanation. Something to wipe away the ugliness, the suspicion that now tainted three years' worth of Barton's awkward smiles, his clumsy antics, his occasional embarrassing displays of something almost like affection. Only a fool would search for innocence where the stench of guilt was so thick.

He stiffened, resolving to waste no more time and instead to push harder. "I haven't been an easy master. I'm certain there are plenty of men here in Galway who wouldn't blame you for acting against me. Did you plot with those men, Barton? Perhaps take a bribe?"

"No!" Aghast, Barton stared at him with such a betrayed expression that a person would think the aide had been shot in Redmayne's place.

"Then explain how you became entangled in this muddle. It should be simple enough."

Barton's hands clenched into fists, the hard knots of fingers shaking against his pant legs. His eyes glistened, overbright. "Before you turned up missing I was taking your uniform jacket to mend. The letter fell out of your pocket. I caught a glimpse of it. Didn't read it all, just . . . saw something about Ballyaroon."

Redmayne fought to keep the blood from draining out of his cheeks, horrified at his own carelessness. He'd thought the missive had never been off his person. But there had been a short time, when he'd draped his jacket over the back of a chair in order to shave.

Was it possible that he had been so lost in thought, trying to guess who the missive was from, that he'd been distracted? Hadn't noticed Barton's fumblings? No, there was still too much that didn't make sense.

"Do you make a habit of prying into my correspondence?" he demanded, low, dangerous.

"No, but you seemed so strange after you'd read it. I was worried." He flushed. "I felt so guilty about reading the missive, I turned right around and put the jacket back where it had been."

So that was why he'd never missed it, Redmayne thought. "My correspondence rifled and my jacket left unmended. Really, Barton, such a shoddy job in attending to your duties is quite unforgivable."

The young man's chin bumped up a notch. "Perhaps so, sir, but I'm glad I read the letter, no matter what the consequences! At least when you turned up missing I was searching in the right place! If Miss Fitzgerald hadn't found you, I would have."

"And if you suspected I was near Ballyaroon, why didn't you call out half a brigade to comb the hills thereabouts, searching for me?"

"Because you're such a private man. I had already trespassed on your privacy. If there *was* something amiss of a personal nature, I didn't want to betray you. So I went out and searched myself."

Redmayne's jaw clenched. Did Barton understand him so well? The thought was terrifying. "You searched with such energy you were magically transformed into three men? Quite a trick, Sergeant."

"Lieutenant Williams had parties of men searching everywhere. He'd even called in some soldiers from another garrison. When I ran across Sir Thorne and the Irishman, I made an inquiry about you. They told me they, too, were searching. It only made sense to pool our resources. The object was to find you."

"And Sir Thorne and company were as eager to do so as you were, eh, Barton?"

"No. No one was as anxious to find you as I was, sir."

Redmayne knew that another man would be touched by the catch in Barton's voice.

"When you failed to find me, you and Sir Thorne simply parted ways?"

"No. I—I misliked Sir Thorne after a while. There was something . . . when he encountered your lady . . . I realized I'd been foolish to charge off on my own. I left the two men and came here to the garrison, intending to confess to Lieutenant Williams about the letter, your privacy be damned. I had seen blood-

stains by the standing stones in Ballyaroon, and a button I was certain was from your uniform. But before
I could raise another search party, you came rattling
up in that gypsy cart."

"And robbed you of your role as my savior. How
thoughtless of me." The words sounded cruel even to
Redmayne's own ears. He was many things, ruthless
among them, but never could he remember making a
gratuitously cruel comment, especially to someone
with such pitiful defenses as Kenneth Barton. What
the devil had gotten into him?

Cowardice. Despite Barton's words, his earnest explanation, Redmayne didn't dare believe it was the
truth. To believe would mean that the boy had been
fool enough to care for a cold-hearted bastard not
worth half of the anguish spent on him. To believe
would mean Redmayne had wronged the youth in a
way no apology could ever mend. It was far more comfortable to maintain this familiar suspicion of everyone's
motives. It saved Redmayne from questioning his own
too closely.

"When you left Thorne Carville and Seamus
O'Leary, where were they headed?"

"To continue to search for you. But they went in
the wrong direction. I made certain of it."

"You didn't know where I was, Barton. Considering
that, the notion that you could've sent anyone in the
wrong direction is questionable at best."

"I sent them in the only direction I was certain you
hadn't gone. Planted some signs that you'd traveled
that way."

"Because you didn't want them to find me? Steal
your glory?"

"No. Because I couldn't shake this—this strange
feeling—"

God save him, Redmayne thought, repressing a

shudder. Not another person gifted with Rhiannon's intuition.

"It was the way Sir Thorne looked at the Gypsy camp. Something about his face. I think they meant to kill you."

Redmayne stared at Barton's face, probing, wishing for once that he did have the power so many claimed, that he could peer into the lad's head, sift through his darkest thoughts, his guiltiest secrets. See if the tale he'd just told was the truth.

But no man really had that power. Time alone would tell. Meanwhile, both he and Barton would be left with uncertainty gnawing inside them.

"Barton, listen to me. Tell the truth now, whatever it might be. I won't insult your intelligence by telling you all will be well. If you're involved in the attack upon me, you will be punished. But I'll do what I can to ease the penalty if you just tell me who is behind these attacks."

"Sir!"

"Think, Barton. It may mean the difference between being deported to the colonies and dying before a firing squad."

Could the boy's face get any whiter? He looked so infernally young all of a sudden.

"No one in his right mind would believe this story you've spun, Barton. Save yourself. Thorne hasn't the wit to concoct such a subtle plan. O'Leary hasn't the resources, nor have you. Give me the name of the person behind this treachery. Loyalty is for fools. I assure you he'll be happy enough to let you die if by doing so he can save his own skin."

"I told you the truth! I didn't betray you. I stumbled upon those other two men while I was searching. If I knew who lured you out to that place to be killed, I vow, I'd hunt him down. He'd answer to me!"

Why the devil did the lad's impassioned vow disturb Redmayne so? It was almost painful. . . . He held up one hand to stop the flow of Barton's words. "Enough. Such an exuberant defense on my behalf is in bad taste, considering the circumstances. I suppose there is only one thing to do." He laid one finger along his jaw, considering.

Give the boy enough space. If he was indeed guilty, he would bolt. That would be all the answer Redmayne would need. Strange thing was, now that he'd come up with the plan, he had a sudden urge to bind the man to his usual tasks—so close by that Redmayne could hardly move without tripping over him. Blast, wasn't this complex enough without Redmayne sabotaging his own efforts?

"What are you going to do, sir?" Barton asked stiffly.

"I shall wait and see if your story bears out," Redmayne said. "I'm certain that duties can be found for you somewhere in the camp."

Barton swallowed hard. "Captain, sir, please. You have to believe I'm telling the truth. I've tended you for almost three years. I thought we'd begun to—to trust."

"You were mistaken, Kenneth." Why on God's earth had he used the boy's Christian name for the first time? One would almost think it was to soften his words. "I was taught never to trust anyone."

The words must have seemed harsh to the aide, as if Redmayne was brushing him aside. Barton could never guess that he *had* just trusted him, with a truth Redmayne himself had only just come to understand.

Turning away, Redmayne dismissed the aide. He stood for a long time in the growing darkness, candles unlit, as he probed the inner wound he'd exposed, at least to himself.

I was taught never to trust, the words echoed through him. "Aye, Rhiannon," he whispered, the twilight filling with the glow of her eyes. "Nor was I taught to love. I just never knew I regretted it. Until now."

Chapter

❧ 13 ❧

Redmayne paced the confines of his office, cursing his chronic lack of concentration. Barely a week had passed since he'd been mad enough to consent to the dance. A week unlike any other he had ever known.

It would have been easy enough to blame his restlessness on his encounter with Barton or on the effort it had taken to regain control of his troops. There were questions regarding his attackers—more confusing than ever. But those were minor distractions compared to the real problem.

It was Rhiannon who had upset the balance of his existence. Fresh bouquets of meadow flowers crowded surfaces that had once been bare. Laughter and endless chatter broke up the crushing silences of his day. A glowing feminine face greeted him across the dinner table each night—at least those nights when he couldn't think up an excuse to avoid her. Rosy lips curved in welcome, eager to tell him about the goings-on of her day and equally anxious to hear how he'd spent his.

Even late at night, when he dragged himself into

his own quarters, he couldn't escape the evidence of her presence—his coverlets turned down, a fire blazing merrily, a tray waiting, with slices of cake or warm shortbread, little sandwiches stuffed with roast beef, and tea brewed, miraculously, to perfection, no matter what the time. As if she'd been waiting just for him. And on days that had been particularly grueling, there, on the tray, Rhiannon's precious chipped cup, as intimate as a kiss good night.

It was astonishing, terrifying, the expectancy he was beginning to feel, almost as if he needed the things she offered without his ever asking. And it made him fight ever harder to appear unaffected—he would stay later at a meeting over cartwheels or supplies, avoiding her as long as he could resist the pull of her smile.

Perhaps the woman really *was* fairy-born. What else could explain the strange spell she'd cast over the garrison and its inscrutable commander. She'd been among them precious little time, yet already he'd wager half the members of the regiment would gladly lay down their lives for the woman with her heart in her eyes, be she Irish or no.

And because he'd brought her here, even *he* would never be viewed in quite the same way again. He'd been hated, feared, dreaded, grudgingly respected. But Redmayne suddenly realized that never in his life had he been envied—until now.

It was an odd sensation, as if the mere assumption of the other soldiers that he too loved Rhiannon and that, even more astonishing to the men, *she* loved *him*—had forged some sort of bond between the stern captain and his men. Occasionally he even caught the most rash among them smiling in his direction!

Of course, the betrothal was simply a ruse. The men had been duped, if they had but the intelligence to realize it. The love story was all in their imagination. A captain with a heart of ice and an Irishwoman with all the warmth of summer in her eyes—the mere thought of such a union was absurd!

Besides, there should be far more pressing matters for the troops to attend to—stamping out the ubiquitous sparks of rebellion that were forever flaring on this island, for example, or ferreting out the assassins who still lay hidden in the dark. And yet, despite his frustration, Redmayne couldn't blame the men for being enchanted.

She was like a breath of fresh air sweeping the length and breadth of the camp. Lonely men, who hated the oppression they stood for, marooned among a hostile populous, were exceedingly vulnerable to a woman's smile—not the camp follower's brittle come-hither grins, followed by bargains struck and a mockery of love in exchange for coin, but rather the smiles their mothers or sisters or sweethearts might have bestowed on them, filled with warmth and understanding and compassion.

Every man from the lowliest private to the highest in rank craved her attention, whether they would admit it or not. But Rhiannon, forever predictable, was kindest to the shy and the uncertain, the homesick and the injured, the men with troubled faces, who did their duty but hated everything the army sanctioned in Ireland.

He supposed he should be relieved at her popularity from a practical point of view. The men had kept her occupied while he tended to more important matters, but the entire situation had made him edgy, and nothing would please him more than to have the infernal ball over with, the assassins behind bars, and Rhiannon packed up and sent off . . .

Sent off where? That question constantly gnawed

at him. Could he send her off alone again in her wagon, with her horse and her dog and cat and whatever injured creature she happened to stumble across? Humming where no one could hear her. Smiling where no one could see.

It had been difficult enough picturing her continuing in such a life before he'd seen her here. He'd managed to convince himself she enjoyed solitude, as he did. But the woman fairly thrived on the bustle of the camp, the countless hopes and dreams, secret woes and joys of the soldiers. The camp surgeon was ready to canonize her for sainthood. And Lieutenant Williams gazed at her with such sorrow in those spaniel-brown eyes, as if he pictured a cold, miserable future for her, with the icy Captain Redmayne.

At times Redmayne was tempted to tell the man to spare him the despondent looks. He had no intention of carrying Rhiannon anywhere, least of all to his bed.

Redmayne grimaced. It was true enough, he figured, though often at night when he closed his eyes he'd see her, so clearly, as she'd looked during those nights they spent together—tousled, completely vulnerable, the tender curve of her parted lips, the swell of her breast against her nightgown, the whisper softness of her sighs.

He swore under his breath as he felt himself harden beneath the flap of his breeches. An involuntary reflex, he'd learned during studies of anatomy. Still, he hadn't been troubled by such an embarrassing reaction since he was a raw lad. Nothing revealed a man's weakness more clearly.

A sharp rap on the door yanked a grateful Redmayne away from his thoughts. Sitting down behind his desk to hide his discomposure, he bade the person to enter.

Private Twynham saluted smartly. "There's someone here to see you, Captain. Wouldn't state his business, but said you'd know why he was here."

"I believe you've forgotten to enlighten me as to the gentleman's name, Twynham, assuming my visitor *is* a gentleman."

A dull red crept up from the private's collar, but he only grumbled. "Not much o' the gentleman about this man, I wouldn't say. But if a name would help, he calls himself Samuel Knatchbull."

Redmayne stilled. Gentleman? No. He'd agree wholeheartedly with Twynham's estimation of the man's character. But then, that was exactly why the captain had hired Knatchbull. Redmayne affected a bored shrug. "You might as well send him in. Oh, and I have a missive to be delivered to the head groom at once. It seems there was some question about my betrothed's horse running mad. I want to inform the man that he is not to take any rash action without direct orders. If anyone is to have the pleasure of shooting that animal, it will be me." He dug out the note, one that could have been delivered at any time, but would conveniently ensure a quarter hour of complete privacy.

Twynham took the missive and saluted, then ushered Knatchbull into the room, closing the door behind him with a military click. Redmayne surveyed Knatchbull for a long moment. All long bones and loose joints, the man shambled toward him, his face showing not a hint of symmetry, one eye lower than the other, a crooked nose, an overlong mouth filled with imagination and humor.

Knatchbull had never explained the wreck of his face, whether it was a curse from the time of his birth, or a hellish gift from someone's fist. But Redmayne hadn't hired him for his appearance when they'd met years ago. He'd taken Knatchbull into his employ because the man had the most fiercely intelligent eyes Redmayne had ever seen beyond his own mirror.

"Allow me to offer felicitations," Knatchbull said in a baritone so rich and beautiful it might have belonged to an archangel. "I hear you are to be married."

"That is the rumor," Redmayne allowed—the truth, such as it was. "I assume you haven't traveled all this way to congratulate me."

"Hardly. I came for another purpose. I received word that your grandfather is traveling to Ireland."

The boy still buried deep in Redmayne shuddered to life, chilled. He hardened himself against that child's sick loathing, almost supernatural dread. He'd long since discovered that Paxton Redmayne was not the omniscient god he'd delighted in making a little boy believe he was. Rather, he was only a particularly vicious mortal.

"He's to stay in an associate's country house to tie up some rather difficult ends in yet another of his business schemes, the story goes, this one involving shipyards near Belfast."

"Belfast. The other side of the island. That should be enough distance between us."

"I fear he is to be disappointed. The precarious family fortune he was hoping to shatter has taken a sudden turn for the better. It seems they have sparked the interest of an investor. One with enough nerve to board a, ahem, sinking ship."

Redmayne's lips curled in cold pleasure. "One can only hope the investor has the wit to keep them afloat."

Knatchbull met his gaze with complete understanding. "If I were a betting man, I know where I would place my wager. And so, I fear, will your grandfather, the instant he discovers what is afoot. I've heard whisperings that he is most displeased with his luck of late."

"He never was able to endure frustration, though he went to any pains to make certain others suffered it in absolute silence. The Belfast affair should be interesting to watch."

"That remains to be seen. I only wanted to make certain you were aware of his visit. And to deliver these." Knatchbull handed over a pouch full of documents. "More of the usual, I'm afraid. I can stay over until morning, give you a chance to peruse them, sign whatever you wish; then I can carry them away with me, if you prefer."

"Yes. That will be fine. As it happens, there is another matter I want to lay before you. An inquiry of sorts. It has to do with a country barrister who seems to have run afoul of Grandfather. Lost everything, including an estate by the name of Primrose Cottage."

For the first time something akin to worry darted into Knatchbull's sage eyes. "May I suggest that we concern ourselves with that affair somewhat later, Captain? At the moment things are somewhat unwieldy, and I think we would be ill advised to display too much of our hand at present."

"I don't give a damn what else you're roasting over those fiendish fires of yours, Knatchbull. I want this matter delved into, plumbed to the very quick. And I want it done now."

"I wouldn't presume to question your decisions. God knows, you've been a genius thus far. But I tell you, something is afoot. Paxton Redmayne is not a man who enjoys being made to look a fool. There is no predicting what lengths he might go to."

"You needn't fear, Knatchbull. Your fee will be paid regardless of what kind of temper fit Grandfather indulges in. I have provision for you penned neatly in my will."

"That is comforting to know. However, I much prefer you alive. I just want to warn you—"

Redmayne's jaw hardened, bitterness icing his voice. "Trust me, Knatchbull. No warning you could offer would be dire enough where my grandfather is concerned. That is one lesson the old man made certain I understood quite well. The barrister in question is one Kevin Fitzgerald."

"Fitzgerald?" Knatchbull's eyes glittered with interest. "Isn't that the last name of your betrothed?"

"It is. Fitzgerald was pursuing a case. Rhiannon remembers little about it, except that someone was anxious to see his inquiries at an end."

"And all he lost was his fortune and property?" Knatchbull chuckled. "If your grandfather was involved, perhaps this barrister of yours got off lightly. Paxton is more than happy to silence anyone permanently when it suits him."

"I doubt Kevin Fitzgerald was any match for grandfather, if he was anything like his daughter." Redmayne looked away, remembering the love in Rhiannon's eyes, and the grief, whenever she mentioned the father she had lost. Perhaps Kevin Fitzgerald had been a dreamer, head thrust into the clouds, a grown man with the innocence and optimism of a child, one who believed that justice would prevail, that people were innately good. No. Kevin Fitzgerald would have been like a lamb hurled into a pit full of adders.

"Captain, forgive me for prying, but I heard a rumor that you were missing for nigh a week, that you were wounded."

"You heard right. A band of assassins took exception to the fact that I was breathing. They sought to remedy the situation."

"Have you any idea who they might have been or why—"

"My dear Knatchbull, such tender concern for my well-being. It is quite unexpected. No. I can't say I'm certain who is behind the attempt on my life. I recognized three men who were combing the countryside in search of me afterward. Two of the three had a reason to quarrel with me. None of them had the intelligence or cunning to lure me into such a trap."

"Then you still have no idea who instigated the attack?"

"No. The difficulty is that over the years I've made more than my share of enemies, both in the ranks and out of them. I am not a man who inspires devotion."

But wasn't that what Barton had claimed? That his actions had sprung from loyalty? And hadn't Redmayne seen devotion in Rhiannon's eyes when she walked out to confront the three men who might well have come to kill him? A willingness to do battle to keep him safe? Ah, but he would do well to remember that his fairy-born lady was equally willing to risk her life to defend a fox or a wolf or a half-blind hound.

"Where have you begun to make inquiries?" Knatchbull asked. "May I be of service?"

"Perhaps later, after you've discovered who was behind the calamity that destroyed Kevin Fitzgerald."

"But, Captain, the man is long dead, and his daughter is safe in your care, while you are obviously in imminent danger. I beg you, allow me to—"

"Knatchbull, I regret the necessity, but I feel I must remind you that *I* am the one who pays your salary, gives you orders. Do as I bid you. Discover all you can about Rhiannon's father and the treachery that ruined him. Once those questions are answered, you may use your skills to ferret out my attackers, if it will amuse you."

"By that time they might have succeeded in killing you! Captain, this makes no sense. Caution, logic, planning to the minutest detail, and realizing the importance of dealing with everything in its own time— these are the tools that have made us successful thus far. Stray from these principles, and we both know what will happen. It's a dangerous precipice we've been dancing upon. We could slip and fall. And damme, we've both worked too hard to allow that to happen."

"I assure you that I will be the only one to fall. I've made certain you'll feel no repercussions. Let me worry about my own skin, Knatchbull. You do as you are ordered. But I do owe you my thanks for alerting me to the fact that the devil is coming to Ireland. Of course, there are plenty who would claim he has been here since the day we English landed."

"How long has it been"—Knatchbull's voice broke into Redmayne's reverie—"since you actually saw your grandfather?"

"I have not seen him since the day I defied him and joined the army. He had . . . other plans for my future, but even Paxton Redmayne couldn't wrench me from the grasp of the military once I'd taken the king's shilling. I had broken free at last."

"Free? You've spent the past fifteen years attempting to thwart him."

Redmayne opened the drawer of his desk, withdrew a palm-size object. He ran his fingertips over the tiny ridges and hollows that formed the only thing he had kept from the years when he was under his grandfather's tutelage: a chess piece so exquisitely carved it seemed to breathe—the queen, the only woman on the game board. The most powerful piece of all.

"It's a game, Knatchbull. Grandfather would tell you. It's all a game between us, begun when I was but five years old."

"Perhaps it is time you made an end to it," Knatchbull suggested, a touch of sympathy about his long mouth. "Start living in the present instead of in the past. After all, with your marriage . . ." Knatchbull let his voice trail off.

Redmayne looked away, his gaze falling on one of Rhiannon's bunches of flowers. A tangle of bright yellow kingcups and soft brushes of heather. Fresh and vibrant. Alive in a way he had never been. But it was too late. It was impossible to breathe warmth, life, into someone who'd been cold and dead for so long.

"I'm afraid making an end to our game is impossible," Redmayne said. "After all, it's so difficult to find worthy opponents."

"And after one of you dies?" Knatchbull asked, his craggy cheeks pale. "What then?"

Strange. Redmayne had never even considered that. What would he do with his life once the looming specter of his grandfather was gone? For a heartbeat, he imagined a cottage door flying open, Rhiannon rushing out in a swirl of jam-stained skirts and clamoring children. He shoved the vision away, amazed at the pain in it.

"Then it will be finished." Redmayne tucked the chess piece back in the drawer, imprisoning the carved queen under her veil of darkness where no one could see her, touch her, hurt her.

Was that why he had taken the chess piece away from Rawmarsh? Was he so crippled inside, so twisted by Paxton Redmayne's lessons that the only thing he could feel chivalrous toward was a wood-carved lady who could never smile back at him? Never serve him tea in a chipped cup? A lady he could lock away when his emotions were too terrifying or his thoughts too bleak. Banishing her, as he'd tried to do with other images, other memories. Failing, forever failing to tuck them away where they could never find him.

He didn't hear the footsteps in the hall, only the door flying open. Knew before he even turned who it would be. The only person who would dare enter his chambers without so much as a knock.

He turned, full intending to shoot her a quelling glare, more out of habit than any hope it would have some effect. But as she and that gallumphing dog of hers burst into the room, her smile was so piercing, her eyes so bright he felt a pain in his chest instead.

It was amazing she hadn't impaled herself on one of the mass of seamstress pins fastening a patchwork of what would become a gown about her lithe body. Her hands dripped with cascades of lace as delicate as the lashes framing her eyes.

He knew the instant she realized someone else was in the room. Pink stained her cheeks, embarrassment curving her mouth so adorably that any other man would have kissed it.

Redmayne stiffened for an instant, wishing he could warn her as he recalled the reactions he'd seen on other faces the first time they'd glimpsed Knatchbull—shock, a little horror, a desperate attempt to ignore the obvious. Even Redmayne had felt a certain lurch inside, though he'd hidden it well.

He sensed Knatchbull's own effort to brace himself as Rhiannon turned in his direction, Milton scrambling in her wake. Whatever reactions the man had experienced in the past, it was obvious nothing had prepared him for the one he was treated to now.

Rhiannon's features softened, not with pity, but

with warmth and welcome, not attempting to pretend Knatchbull's deformity away as if it didn't matter, but rather accepting its existence, acknowledging in that single glance the pain it had caused him and her regret that he'd had to suffer it.

She crossed to where he stood, and took Knatchbull's gnarled hands in her own, lace and all. "Forgive me. I have an abominable habit of rushing in without thinking. You see, this is the first new gown I've had in, oh, ever so long, and I've not the slightest idea about fashion. Lion is so much better at it that when I couldn't choose which lace, I thought I would ask him."

Knatchbull's eyes, always so sharp with intelligence, gazed at her with such sudden hunger and gratitude that Redmayne was tempted to snatch her hands out of the man's grasp, but the last thing he wanted was for Knatchbull to guess what a ridiculous reaction he was having. Hellfire, even that infernal hound of hers was fairly wriggling with delight as he licked Knatchbull's dusty boot!

Redmayne satisfied himself by saying, "Let me see the lace, then. It would be most vexing if you were still bristling with pins by the time of the fete. Imagine the injuries you would inflict on my soldiers."

She laughed, and Redmayne was appalled at the relief he felt as she turned back to him, spreading the lace maker's wares across his desk.

"Angels or roses?" she asked, frowning down at the delicate netting.

Angels, he wanted to say. *Angels to remind me of you.*

But he didn't dare. He couldn't display such vulnerability in front of Knatchbull, could barely acknowledge it to himself. Where the devil had such a sentimental thought come from in the first place?

From *her*.

"Roses," he said flatly. "Now, if you and that hell-born hound of yours have no objection, might I continue my business?"

Her smile faltered, and he hated the fact that he'd taken some of the joy out of her decision. "Of course," she said, attempting to collar Milton. "How thoughtless of me." The beast made a break for freedom, leaving a paw smudge on the hem of her half-sewn gown. "Thank you for your help," she said as the dog disappeared out the door. "It was lovely to meet you, Mr. Knatchbull. Perhaps you would like to dine with us tonight?"

Redmayne started to protest, but Knatchbull, with the aplomb Redmayne had always admired in the man, saved him the trouble.

"Thank you, Miss Fitzgerald, but I've traveled a long way and am quite weary. A solitary supper and early to bed will be most refreshing for me, though I regret the chance to get to know you better."

Redmayne could tell that the man spoke the truth. No polite nonsense from Knatchbull.

"Will you permit me to leave a tray in your room, at least? Something to nibble on should you get hungry, and a pot of tea. I have a special blend that eases aches and will help you to sleep."

Redmayne looked at the man's ungainly body sharply, noting for the first time a weariness in him. Had it always been there, and had he been too blind to see it? Or had Rhiannon so put the man at ease that he felt safe enough to allow his exhaustion to show?

"I'd not want to put you to any trouble."

"It's no trouble at all. Anyone would be weary after so many hours on horseback."

Redmayne grew still. He'd realized Knatchbull had

come on horseback. If he hadn't been so distracted, he would've thought it strange. The man always lumbered up in a plain black carriage.

Not once had Redmayne considered what it must have cost the man to ride so far on horseback, or why he would have done such a thing—in the interest of saving time. To warn him.

Rhiannon would say it was loyalty, kindness . . . friendship, if he'd only open his eyes to see it.

But then, his briar rose didn't understand the more mundane workings of men's minds: expediency, protecting one's interests, acting out of duty.

"Please, Mr. Knatchbull," Rhiannon urged. "It would please me so much."

Knatchbull smiled with a tenderness Redmayne had never seen before. "Thank you, Miss Fitzgerald. You're very kind."

Redmayne felt unaccountably ill-tempered. Perhaps he should explain to the man the perils of Rhiannon's chipped cup. But it was obvious Knatchbull wouldn't care if the cutlery were bent and all the china shattered. He'd doubtless pick out bits of shortbread from amid the wreckage and claim it was the tastiest he'd ever eaten.

"Good-bye, Lion," she said, casting him one of her questioning looks, soft and probing . . . but damned if he'd let it be healing. A sudden commotion beyond the door rose, a mingling of shouts and howls and barking. Rhiannon's infernal dog.

She rushed out the door, apologizing again for the intrusion while still managing to call her accursed hound. Milton had probably been frolicking in a mud puddle in the few moments since he'd charged out of the office, Redmayne thought, and would be unable to control his delight in seeing his mistress. The ball gown would probably be ruined with paw prints before it was even finished.

He stared at the door where Rhiannon had disappeared, for once not knowing what to say to the man who had been his partner in so much.

"You might very well be the luckiest man I've ever met, Redmayne," Knatchbull said, soft grief in his voice, a wistfulness, a longing for something he might never have.

"Grandfather often remarked on the fact that I had the devil's own luck." But not this time, Redmayne thought. Never this time. With all the best intentions in the world, Rhiannon had only made him see the empty places in himself. The ugliness. The lack.

"If you'll excuse me, Knatchbull, I'll tend to these documents you've brought." Redmayne flattened his hand on the worn leather pouch.

"Of course. And, Captain?" Grim determination twisted Knatchbull's mouth. "I vow, I'll turn all my energies to discovering the link between your lady's father and Paxton Redmayne. The thought of him coming anywhere near her—"

Knatchbull didn't finish. He didn't have to.

"We understand each other, then. I shall depend upon you."

With a nod, the other man limped awkwardly out the door. Redmayne sank down into his chair, ignoring the leather pouch.

Knatchbull had nothing to fear on Rhiannon's behalf. Redmayne would make dead certain that his grandfather would never touch Rhiannon with his evil or his cunning.

He would guard her, as he had the wooden queen for so long. He would find some way to make things right. And then, the instant she was safe, he would do the only rational thing he could do.

He would send her away.

Chapter

❧ 14 ❨

Rhiannon rested one gloved hand lightly on Kenneth Barton's arm, struggling not to let her disappointment show as he led her up the stairs to the room that had been magically transformed into a ballroom.

"The captain sent his regrets, but there was some pressing business that had to be attended to," Barton apologized for the fiftieth time since he'd come to her chamber and broken the ill news.

Lion's absence should hardly have been a surprise. He was forever striding off to attend to some sort of crisis. One would almost think he was doing everything in his power to avoid her. She fought back the sting of hurt.

Ridiculous, that feeling. From the start, Lion had made it no secret of how he felt about her—she was one more nuisance the oh, so capable captain was encumbered with. No. That was her own pain urging her to be unfair. He would ignore the existence of a nuisance. Such an annoyance was too far beneath his dignity to acknowledge. But he was acutely aware of Rhiannon, almost . . . almost painfully so.

She'd glimpsed it in his hooded eyes, sensed it in the rare brush of his fingers against her, noticed it in the lines carved more prominently about his resolute mouth. She'd wanted so much to go to him, ask what was wrong. But she knew him too well to harbor the slightest hope that he might tell her.

Her moroccan heel caught on the slight train of her gown, and only Barton's steady arm kept her from landing in a heap on the floor.

"It's been so long since I've worn dancing slippers," she confided, shaking the billows of fabric loose. "Perhaps I should be relieved that the captain isn't here to see me embarrass myself!"

"Not for a moment, miss!" Barton protested. "I feel sorry for the captain, and I know he regrets missing the chance to escort the loveliest lady in Ireland into the party."

Pale and strained as he was from all that had happened, the young man was so earnest, trying so very hard to please her, that Rhiannon forced a smile. Even so, she doubted she could hide the sinking feeling in her stomach. The loveliest lady? A pleasing fantasy, that. But pure nonsense nonetheless. Two of the young military wives, lively May Weston and merry Sylvie Fordyce, had surprised Rhiannon by charging into the captain's quarters armed with bundles full of rice powder and hair combs, and all the other incomprehensible equipment necessary to turn a woman into a fashion plate.

Laughing with unabashed delight, the two friends had claimed they were thoroughly sick of each other's company, and that the arrival of any young lady of genteel birth was a treat beyond measure. That if Rhiannon would allow them to help with her toilette for the ball, they would be quite overcome with pleasure.

Their offer had nearly undone Rhiannon, her eyes

burning, an unexpected lump forming in her throat. It had been so very long since any woman had offered her friendship. And she'd lost herself in the delightful feminine chaos of what Sylvie called mighty preparations.

All afternoon the women and their two maids had fussed and curled, pinned and plaited. But in the end, even two such renowned military belles couldn't transform Rhiannon into the kind of flawless, elegant beauty Lion would find attractive. The gown—pale green satin, kissed with roses and wisps of lace—already bore the marks of her ineptitude, skirts crumpled by Moll, Cook's six-year-old daughter. The gap-toothed mite had been most grievously offended when Milton mowed her down while chasing an imaginary rabbit. Rhiannon had scooped up the weeping babe, kissing her scraped elbow better, then made a sneak attack on the madhouse of a kitchen to purloin a bit of sugar rock for Moll to suck on.

From the child's point of view, their adventure had been a glorious success, but somehow Rhiannon was certain Lion would not find it so.

She sighed. What was the matter with her? She'd long since given up wishing to be something she wasn't. Even back at Primrose Cottage, she'd seen her own flaws clearly enough, accepted the fact that she would never be beautiful, at least not in the common way, that she would never be elegant or sophisticated.

But at Primrose she'd had her papa's adoration. His assurance that she had her own far more valuable gifts, even if elegance and sophistication were not among them. But Papa had failed to understand that every woman, at some time in her life, wished desperately for beauty and charm, grace and elegance, that ability to dazzle that the darlings of society took for granted. Rhiannon was wishing now.

She felt Barton stiffen into his most military posture as their arrival was announced to the company—which was completely assembled, except for the two of them, Rhiannon realized, more than a little abashed. It seemed the misadventure with Moll had taken more time than she'd thought.

Lieutenant Williams strode over to pay his respects. Sylvie and May rushed over to greet her. She glimpsed Archie Whitting and his wife, their faces glowing with astonishment and love.

And her heart ached.

There had been nights, when her solitary campsite was quiet, and the darkness had fallen, when she'd looked up at the stars scattered across the heavens. She'd imagined this—the shimmering strains of violins drifting on air perfumed by countless velvet-petaled blossoms. Handsome men garbed in their finest, seeking the smiles of ladies aswirl in heavenly gowns. Laughter and endless conversations, girlish hopes and dreams hidden in hearts pounding beneath silver-thread lace.

In her dreams, Rhiannon herself stood among them, her delicate fan clutched in fingers trembling in anticipation. She waited for one man to stride through the crowd, take her hand, and lead her to the floor, knowing it didn't matter to him that her unruly curls were tumbling from their pins, that her gown was smudged, or that she couldn't think of anything bright and witty to say. All he wanted was her face turned up to his, no feminine arts, no flirting or flattering. Rather, something purer, more genuine, a sharing of hopes and dreams, laughter and tears. Love. She'd reconciled herself to the fact that she'd lost all hope of such magic when the gypsy cart rattled down the tree-lined lane, leaving behind Primrose Cottage and the life she'd known. But still, she took the old dream out occasionally, like a pressed flower from a memory box, to hold it, ever so gently, in her hand.

Had some part of her hoped that the fates had given her one last chance to realize her girlish dreams? One night to reach out again for such perfection? If she *had* been naive enough to harbor such hopes, at least now she was realistic enough to surrender them.

For now the mysterious suitor who had haunted her dreams had a face. Arrogant cheekbones, white-blond hair, a jaw chiseled with incredible strength, and eyes sparkling diamond-fire blue with intelligence and secret humor. A mouth held so firm to hide tenderness and longing, terrified of revealing that he needed anything, any*one*.

Rhiannon fought back the sadness, attempting to lock away her crushing disappointment as one of the men led her out to take her place in a cotillion. It didn't matter that her own hopes had been dashed. The soldiers and their wives were so very kind, and they wanted so much to please her. She must never let them know.

Lion wasn't here.

She might as well have been alone on a sea-swept hill, dreaming.

Count on the Irish to be contrary, Redmayne mused, feeling ill-tempered. Forever plotting rebellion, but tonight, when a man could have used the distraction, there wasn't so much as a ripple anywhere on the whole accursed island.

He jammed his hands into the capacious pockets of his jacket, a habit he'd always found appalling. But at least it kept his fingers from picking at buttons or braid or whatever else they could find to occupy themselves.

So this was what a guilty conscience felt like. No wonder the Irish were forever beating a path to the confessional door. If a priest could absolve sin and banish this grinding misery, Redmayne would be tempted to try confession himself—that is, if it weren't for the fact that in his whole life Lionel Redmayne had never once admitted he was wrong to anybody. Not even himself.

But tonight . . . he'd made certain he was neck deep in an altercation with one of the local landowners as the hour of the celebration had approached. He'd goaded the man and strung out the confrontation to ridiculous lengths, grimly wondering if he was attempting to provoke the landowner to murder. In the end, Mr. O'Hara had shown the good sense to stomp off—a most astonishing act of self-restraint—muttering questions about the sanity of the English in general and the captain in particular.

It was an insult that definitely required satisfaction, perhaps a lovely duel set for dawn, but Redmayne had held his tongue. He had an aversion to killing a man for telling the truth. And no one was questioning the captain's sanity more than the captain himself.

He'd merely fled his office, still littered with countless reminders of Rhiannon and how deeply he was going to disappoint her when he failed to appear at the anniversary celebration. Locking the door behind him, he paced out into the night. But still he found no peace.

The camp was quiet, deserted, except for the few unlucky men who had drawn guard duty. He could hear the faint echoes of lilting dance music as it drifted toward him, his imagination filling with the scene he'd witnessed countless times, to his eternal boredom. A military ball. Despite the unusual presence of the rather nervous enlisted men, it was the same game it always was. Constant vying for the most beautiful woman's hand, lust visible in men's eyes, cunning in their ladies', as all sought to better their position. It had wearied him, astonishing as that was, for no one understood better the benefit of using such opportunities to one's advantage.

At least that was what he'd always thought. Now, as he stood in the darkness alone, he wondered if he'd been mistaken. The thing that had wearied him had not been the usual social machinations but rather those few fortunate couples—rare, but ever present—who had smiled into each other's eyes, protected from all that shallowness and petty nonsense by the love that had surrounded them.

Men who would gladly have laid down their sword for the lady who held their heart. Women who would have followed them even if all the medals for bravery and the marks of rank and honor had been stripped away, who would still have gazed at them as if they were the greatest heroes ever born.

Women like Rhiannon, a ruthless voice inside him whispered.

Redmayne swore under his breath, wishing he could kick something and not feel a complete fool. Damn the woman, gazing up at him as if he were a hero wouldn't change anything. It wouldn't wash his soul clean of every vile thing he'd done. Necessary things. Ruthless things. Inevitable things, he'd thought at the time. But vile nonetheless.

He closed his eyes, trying to blot out the sudden, painfully clear picture of her when Barton had gone to fetch her. Confusion, a valiant attempt to hide her disappointment to protect the boy's feelings. She'd smile and dance, but the whole time, she'd be glancing at the door, waiting, hoping. . . .

Better she see him for the blackguard he was. The

bastard who had kissed her, not because he had the wit to appreciate her rare sweetness, but to further his own ends. The son of a bitch who had all but seduced her in an ill conceived plot, then had the temerity to dare to want her, truly want her, after he'd wronged her so unforgivably.

And now he'd hurt her again, hadn't he? Agreed to the dance, ordered the most perfect dress he could imagine for her unique brand of beauty. Then he had failed to show his face at the celebration because he was too much of a coward to . . . to what? To see the shimmering welcome in the most honest eyes he'd ever seen, and to know he didn't deserve it?

Redmayne grimaced, his stomach turning with self-loathing as he remembered countless things she'd done for him, little kindnesses, gentle touches, so many favors he'd done nothing to merit. The whole garrison thought she was his betrothed. If he abandoned her the night through, wouldn't they gossip about it? Not overtly. No, they would not dare. No man in this garrison would dare to question Captain Redmayne. But they'd be *thinking*, God curse them. Murmuring among themselves. Hell, the whispers had probably already begun. And with Rhiannon's sensitivity and strange intuition . . .

Not that he believed in it. Not really. Yet . . .

Perhaps he'd done nothing to encourage Rhiannon's kindness, but she'd certainly done nothing to earn his careless cruelty. How much longer could the infernal fete drag on, anyway? He'd make an appearance for her sake, then leave. Simple. It would be quite simple. He wouldn't even have to dance.

Resolutely, he turned and started toward the music, with the stride of a man marching into battle.

The instant he entered the ballroom, he heard it, a ripple of recognition running through the crowd of soldiers and ladies. A battery of eyes turned toward him. But not with the vulturish anticipation he'd seen in so many other ballrooms—an eagerness to see someone else's humiliation or pain. If he didn't know better, he'd think the lot of them were damned defensive on Rhiannon's behalf, aggravated with the villain who had dared to disappoint her.

He contrived to appear bored, wishing to hell they'd all just go back about their business as his own gaze scanned the crowd. But suddenly he heard a glad cry.

The pleasure in it pierced through him. He turned, to see Rhiannon, abandoning her seat beside lame Jemmy Carver. In a swirl of seafoam green, she hurried across the room toward Redmayne, a halo of curls wreathing her pink cheeks, her smile soft and joyous, so sincere one could almost believe she was a woman in love rushing to greet her betrothed.

Redmayne had rarely loathed himself more than he did at that moment. She'd nearly reached him before he had the wit to go out to meet her. But suddenly he saw new emotions darting across her face—uncertainty, admiration, awe.

He didn't want to see those things in her eyes. They made something twist in the dead regions of his heart.

"I thought you wouldn't come," she said. "That you—you didn't want to."

Trust his briar rose to admit her own vulnerability with complete openness.

"I'm so very glad you changed your mind," she confided.

He bowed low over her hand, not out of politeness, but to master the shame spilling through him. "You should be furious with me, my dear, ignore me most decidedly for my rudeness."

He straightened in time to see her eyes mist, her gloved hand reaching out to catch his.

"What point would there be in that? I've been waiting for you, hoping so much you would walk through those doors. If I pretended to be angry, I wouldn't be able to talk with you. Tell you"—she caught a little breath—"Lion, you look so beautiful!"

She surprised a laugh out of him. He glanced down, aware that sometime earlier, he'd changed into his dress uniform for appearance' sake, though he had no intention even then of suffering through the ball.

"You look so—so perfect. Not a crease or a smudge." Was there a bit of wistfulness in her tone? "You are the most beautiful man I have ever seen. And to think"—a dimple appeared in her cheek— "that everyone here believes you to be in love with *me*. I'm afraid that throws into question the intelligence of your garrison, Captain."

"It does, but not for the reason you think it," he murmured, holding the hand she offered, avoiding the inevitable moment when he would have to draw away. "Rhiannon, you are far too fine a lady ever to stoop to have a villain like me."

"I'm growing rather fond of villains, if you are one."

"Don't." He warned more sharply than he intended. "Even an angel cannot transform a villain into anything worth having. We're dangerous. Self-serving."

"Then why are you here?"

"Because—" *Because I couldn't bear the thought of anyone pitying you. Because I couldn't stop myself from thinking of you dancing in other men's arms. Because I wanted to see you as you must have looked before my grandfather ruined your life—garbed in a gown of the finest satin and lace, your hair all in curls, your eyes shining.*

"I'm here because"—he cast a long-suffering glance across the ballroom—"because I'm a damned fool."

She laughed this time. A soft, wounded sound, full of understanding. "You didn't want me to feel hurt."

Redmayne arched his eyebrows, attempting to hide his alarm. "My dear, you give me far too much credit. I intend to make a base retreat the instant I can arrange it."

She stretched up on tiptoe, kissing his cheek ever so gently before the eyes of every soldier in Galway. "That won't change the fact that you were here," she whispered. Then, as if she understood his discomfort, she sought to ease it with the humor that had always been his refuge.

"Perhaps if you leave quickly enough you won't notice the mess I've already made of my gown, or the fact that even though May and Sylvie drove every hairpin on the west coast of Ireland straight into my scalp, my hair is threatening to tumble down at any moment. I fear I am hopeless, Captain, despite all your efforts to turn me into an acceptable fiancée for an officer of your stature."

He'd heard numerous women angle for compliments, seeking his praise to shore up their vanity or in an effort to use their beauty and feminine wiles to place him under their power. But Rhiannon spoke with wry humor and guilelessness. She was disappointed that she was so different from the brittle beauties whirling about the room in the waltz. It touched him in a way he didn't want to be touched, made him angry at a world that had such limited understanding of the word "beauty."

"Damnation, Rhiannon, don't you know?" he snarled. "You're five times more beautiful than any other woman in this room."

Her eyes widened, as much from his words as from

the savagery in his tone. Disbelief made her draw her hand away from his. Curse it if he didn't feel bereft.

"Lion, don't. You don't have to say things that aren't true. The least we can do is not lie to each other."

"May God split this infernal ceiling and strike me with lightning if it isn't true. In fact, that's a dashed good notion. One way to end the ball."

He'd wanted to please her. Instead, her eyes filled with tears. "You've made your appearance. No one can fault you now. Go ahead and leave."

She started to turn away, offering him the perfect chance to escape.

Why the devil was he charging after her? His fingers closed around the fragile column of her arm. "Wait."

She spun around, and what he saw in her eyes thrilled him, terrified him. A thousand girlish dreams his grandfather had dashed into ruins. Hurt and disappointment, so honestly displayed he could feel it to his very bones. Sweet Christ, you couldn't hurt that way unless you cared for someone. Deeply. The knowledge humbled him as he stared down at her, trying desperately to memorize the look in her eyes so he could recall it when she was gone and he was alone again.

"What is it?" she asked, a fine tremor in her voice. "I have to go take Jemmy some punch."

"Carver will have to wait. I haven't had my dance."

She stared at him a moment, then tipped up her chin with stubborn pride. "I fear I don't feel much like dancing."

Redmayne gritted his teeth. After all he'd been through in this night from hell, the woman was going to dance or be damned. "Consider it a direct order, then."

As if by command of the fairies Rhiannon believed in, the string quartet began the strains of a waltz. To test his resolve, no doubt. He'd always detested the waltz, a dance that forced virtual strangers to come too close, intruding in spaces he preferred no one enter. But it was too late to retreat now.

Rhiannon gazed up at him, still uncertain. He couldn't resist reaching out, touching her cheek. "Please, Rhiannon, dance with me."

"I'll probably tread on your boots, and my heel keeps catching in my train. I—"

He astonished himself by laying his fingertips on her lips to stop the stream of words. Then, giving her no more chance to protest, he gathered her in his arms and guided her onto the floor.

He'd partnered women tutored by the finest dancing masters in Europe, every move they made a study in perfection, but never had he felt such astonishing pleasure as he did now. There was something about the way Rhiannon's hand clung trustingly to his, her teeth catching the dewy swell of her lower lip whenever she missed a count. She felt so warm where his arm cradled her waist, the sweet rose fragrance of her hair filling his senses. She was smudged and tousled and undeniably flawed as she struggled to remember the steps of the dance she'd all but forgotten. And yet Redmayne wondered if he'd ever known any moment as perfect as this.

She stumbled. To shield her from judgmental eyes, Redmayne gathered her closer against him—so close that she would be able to feel every shift of his muscles, his movements, the rhythms and sways, dips and turns.

She gazed up at him in surprise.

"Melt into me, sweetheart. Just close your eyes."

He whispered through the errant curls even now ca-ressing his chin. "Trust me."

Such simple words. People were forever tossing them out as if they were meaningless. Words Lionel Redmayne had never spoken before. Because with trust came responsibility, a bonding he'd always re-sisted. Rhiannon gave him what he'd asked of her with such generosity of spirit that his throat tightened. He could feel her body, stiff with nervousness, softening, relaxing in his arms, could feel Rhiannon surrendering herself to him with an utter faith that humbled him.

And in that moment, it was as if some of Rhian-non's fairy magic had swept them both away from the crowded room and the staring eyes. The mechanics of the dance vanished, the precision with which he'd always marked rhythm and step, until it seemed as if they dipped and swirled on a cloud of Rhiannon's dreams.

The green of her gown, spring soft, matched the hue of her eyes, that miraculous color of new begin-nings, new life. The delicate rose of her lips parted, glistening, tasting of redemption. Her throat, white and pure and graceful as the stem of a lily, disap-peared into the delicate ridge of collarbone, the gener-ous swell of creamy breasts. Breasts he was burning to cup in his palms, not with the selfish fire of lust but with reverence, in supplication, to drink in some of her goodness after being parched and lost for so long.

He glanced down into her eyes, and what he saw there made him catch his breath. Could she see into his most secret thoughts? Reflected there, beneath thick curls of lashes, was breathless longing, her fin-gers trembling in the clasp of his hand. But could his Gypsy angel have any idea what she was inviting, or how unworthy he was, even to take her innocent hand in a dance, let alone take even more?

He clenched his jaw at the memory of that sun-struck day beside the caravan, her fingers unfastening the buttons at the hollow of her throat, her cheeks peony pink, so shy, so brave as she asked him to make love to her.

What would have happened if he'd cast caution to the wind? If he'd laid Rhiannon down upon a bed of flower-spangled moss and stripped away all that lay between them—clothing and secrets, fear and doubt? If he'd drunk in her sweetness, would she have had the power to alter him? In some ways, hadn't she already?

But nothing could change reality. The only way he could hold Rhiannon would be if this waltz lasted forever. And already the notes were fading. The ballroom spun back into focus, the cacophony of chatter too loud, the music too harsh, the lights too garish. He'd always known far more about nightmares than dreams. But as he reluctantly loosened his grasp about Rhiannon's waist, he realized for the first time the fatal flaw that marred all dreams: eventually you had to wake up.

The quartet sent forth a ripple of lively notes—the introduction to a rollicking country dance. But that seemed almost a sacrilege after the closeness they'd just shared. He took Rhiannon's hand and led her off the floor, waving away several young soldiers who headed toward him, doubtless intending to engage him in conversation. They were intelligent enough to make a detour to the punch bowl instead.

"Barton," Redmayne called out at the last moment. "Jem Carver desires a glass of ratafia, if you would be so kind as to get it for him."

Rhiannon stared in amazement, but she was no

more astonished than Redmayne himself was. Yet, truth to tell, he had purely selfish motives. For the time being, he didn't want to surrender his lady or have her worrying about any other man—even a mere thirsty lad she'd befriended.

Drawing her hand through the crook of his arm, he led her through the maze of well-wishers, grinning officers, ladies stammering out compliments: "Never have I seen anything like it! Such graceful dancing!"

He managed to pass them off with clipped comments, steering Rhiannon toward the French doors, swung wide along the portico to let in the sweet, cool breezes. But before he was able to make his escape, two rather portly figures blocked his path: Whitting and his wife, the guests of honor.

"Forgive me, sir," Whitting's sweet-faced lady dared to say, smiling up at him. "But never have I ever seen anything that gave me more pleasure than watching the two of you waltz. It put me in mind of the first time my Archie asked me to dance. So handsome he was in his fine uniform. I feared he'd catch afire from my papa's glaring. But once Archie took me in his arms, I knew nothing would ever be the same again. It was that way with you, wasn't it, sweeting?"

Redmayne groped for something to say, to distract the woman, shield Rhiannon, but as usual, his gypsy angel surprised him. She looked full in his eyes and nodded, her smile wreathed with such ineffable sweetness it stole his breath away.

"You will take good care of her, won't you, Captain Redmayne?" Mrs. Whitting's eyes glowed with dreams decades old, tattered and worn in places, buffeted by life's harsher edges. Redmayne knew Rhiannon would only think them all the more beautiful because of it. "A woman's dreams are so precious, so rare."

Could there be any treasure rarer than the one he'd

found on that bloodstained Irish hill? Yet how could he possibly answer? He couldn't be guardian to anyone else's dreams. He had none of his own.

Rhiannon's voice broke the crushing silence. "Thank you so much for the kind things you've said, Mrs. Whitting. The captain and I wish you and your husband many more years of joy together."

"That we'll have, my dear. The army life can be hard on a woman, especially at first. Wandering about, never knowing where you'll be sent next, or even if you will be able to follow your husband where they've ordered him to go. Loneliness, when he's far away, and you live from one letter to the next. And always the dread of war. And yet in the end you'll find none of the hardships matter as long as you have each other." She leaned over to kiss her Archie's windburned cheek. "I'll be wishing for you the same happiness we've found. I've no doubt you'll have it. There's a heaven full of love in your eyes, child."

A heaven full of love . . . the words lanced through Redmayne, a truth indescribably painful. For even Rhiannon's vast store of love could never be enough, since he had nothing to offer in return.

With a bow, he turned and guided her out the door, grateful for the veil of darkness broken only by circles of light hovering about two torchères. He avoided their glow, as if they'd been placed there by some sorceress, their magic the kind he dreaded most of all. The ability to shine through all his defenses, reveal to Rhiannon all the ugliness inside him. He'd rather suffer any torture than see that heartbreak in her eyes.

So why the devil had he brought her here alone? Why hadn't he offered her a crisp bow and left, as he'd planned to do from the beginning? Why had he been fool enough to dance with her? To hold her so close he could feel her heartbeat against his chest?

Because she made him feel alive for the first time in a very long time, almost as if he were a fallen angel she'd stumbled upon and blessed with her forgiveness. He might know, even if she did not, that the gates of heaven would still be barred to him, that he would wander, an exile, for eternity. But none of that mattered, as long as he could always remember the tenderness, the welcome that had shone for him in her eyes.

And yet he must never be so cruel as to let her know how deeply she'd touched him. For then she'd suffer, too, when he had to wander off alone, even if she had all the glories of heaven around her.

"This is lovely, isn't it?" she asked so softly he scarce heard it.

He looked down at her, glad she'd interrupted his thoughts. "The party? The dancing? You must have missed it very much."

"Oh, it was all beautiful and, well, exciting, since it's been so long. But that wasn't what I meant." She sighed, leaning against the stone balustrade, the gentle breeze tugging at her curls. "Sometimes things get so—so busy with so many people about. I just . . . It's lovely to be alone for a little while, just the two of us. We haven't had much time to talk of late."

He sucked in a breath, scrambling for excuses. "I—"

"It's all right. I know." She cut him off. Was it possible that she *did* know? All the excuses he'd made? His desperate bids to avoid her? Could he have done anything designed to hurt a woman like Rhiannon more?

Regardless, he should just let it go, change the subject and pretend that he hadn't caught her meaning. It was the wisest course. The most logical one.

Instead, he turned his gaze into the distance, where

the darkness lay thick and still. "Forgive me, Rhiannon. I am used to being alone," he said, his fingers tightening on the rough stone.

"I know." Sorrow touched her voice. "It must be difficult, being commander over so many men. You must feel so isolated sometimes, making all the decisions."

"I was alone long before I joined the army, my dear. I can never recall any other way for as long as I can remember."

"But your family. . . . you must have had someone—"

"My parents and sister died in a fire when I was five. My grandfather became my guardian."

"No wonder you were lonely. You were taken from a home that was bustling with your mama and papa and sister. Your grandfather's house would have been far quieter, the household of a lone old man. But I'm certain he tried to make provisions for you, brought neighboring boys to play. Or the servants' children must have been about."

"No. Grandfather abhorred distractions."

"Distractions?"

"Anything that kept me from concentrating on my lessons. Other children, playthings, even books read just for pleasure. He claimed they were a waste of precious time."

"But—but that is absurd! A boy needs someone to laugh with, play at knights and dragons. Surely he couldn't have—"

"I'm afraid he was adamant. You see, my intellect was a thing of endless fascination for him. The chance to shape it offered an irresistible challenge to the old man. I was to be his masterpiece."

"You make it sound so cold. But he wanted to teach you, to share all he had learned. Perhaps he saw that as the greatest gift he could bestow. Maybe it was his way of showing you that he loved you very much in his own way."

No. There had been no love involved, no sharing. Merely the cold calculations as to how much information he could cram into a boy's head before it burst. A chilling experiment to forge a human mind into the most subtle and lethal of weapons to be wielded at Paxton Redmayne's command.

Redmayne started to speak, then stopped himself. Had he lost his wits sometime during that waltz? He'd only wanted to explain to her that he was accustomed to being alone. That it was no flaw in her that drove him away. He hadn't meant to start babbling about things he'd never spoken of before to another soul.

"Do you see your grandfather often?" Rhiannon asked after a long moment.

"No. Grandfather had a great dislike for surprises. When I grew up, I . . . surprised him." Redmayne's mouth curved in a grim smile.

"How?"

"I did not choose the future he had planned for me."

"Not so unusual a sin! Boys and fathers have battled over such differences of opinion since the beginning of time!" She leaped to champion the mutinous youth that he had been. Redmayne explored the odd sensation—someone ready to fight in his defense. It was strange and yet soul-warming, bittersweet after all these years. What might it have meant to him an eternity ago, before he'd ridden away from Rawmarsh, his grandfather's estate, alone? His smile softened as she continued. "After a good deal of stubbornness and great shows of suffering, the two sides usually take a deep breath and mend the rift."

"Perhaps. Or they attempt to forget the other ever existed."

How cold had the words sounded? She looked as if they'd hurt her. "Oh, Lion! That's tragic. Stubborn, clinging to pride, when a simple word of forgiveness would likely unsnarl everything."

"Isn't that just like you, Rhiannon? Certain that with a wave of your hand the ugliest wound should be healed. Some things aren't destined to heal. Other things shouldn't be."

"I don't believe that," she asserted, her chin tipping up. He wished he could kiss her. Turn her mouth up to his and drown in the taste of her, driving back the unsettling thoughts of the life he thought he'd buried long ago. He wished he could believe in Rhiannon's world, where even broken things were cherished, where everyone was worthy of love and needed only to reach out for it. But he'd learned different lessons at his grandfather's knee, lessons he would never forget.

"Lion, perhaps you should try to heal the breach. Your grandfather must be very old. One day you'll awaken and it will be too late. I couldn't bear the thought of you carrying that burden of regret."

Redmayne peered down at her, aching. When had he fallen prey to this desperate need to protect her, shield her? He who had never turned away from ugliness or attempted to evade the truth? Rhiannon, so utterly honest. What would she think if he told her how he'd spent his last night in Rawmarsh? Gripping his fencing foil through the night, imagining his grandfather's eyes widening in surprise, his blood staining the bright blade?

Shouldn't a blood price have been paid, not for the destruction of Lionel's own childhood but rather for the life of the only man who had dared show Lionel a world beyond that brittle cage his grandfather had built around him? Antonio Tidei, the Italian sword master who had taught Lionel for years every secret of the blade. He'd regaled a lonely boy with countless tales of battles fought and won, of a world of adventure far from the tomblike halls of Rawmarsh. Then Tidei had made a fatal error.

He'd dared to suggest that Lionel would make a fine soldier, thereby opening the door to Lionel's prison—and fastening the lid on his own tomb. His was not the quick, merciful death due a man of such incomparable grace and courage. No. The slow, torturous death, not of his body but of something far more valuable to Antonio Tidei: his honor.

Lion winced. What could an honorable man of Tidei's mettle have known of the forces Paxton Redmayne could unleash? Brilliantly forged letters that had made Tidei's hot-tempered best friend believe the sword master was having an affair with his wife—a deception that had destroyed both marriages. The challenge to a duel Tidei refused to fight, and the inevitable label—"coward"—that would shame Antonio Tidei forever.

By the time Lionel had learned of his grandfather's plotting, it had been too late to help the sword master. Only one means of vengeance lay in his grasp—to turn his back on his grandfather, on business interests as vast as any caesar's empire, to leave Paxton Redmayne's theories untested and his dreams unfulfilled, to become the soldier Antonio had been so certain he could be, and to use against Paxton Redmayne the very tools the old man had forced into Lionel's hands.

"Lionel?"

He started, the dark memories swirling away, leaving behind only the faint sickness in his gut, the almost indiscernible sheen of sweat across his upper lip. No, damn it, he wouldn't remember. Wouldn't think about things he'd taken care to bury long ago. He had determined years ago that he wouldn't give his grandfather that power over him. He'd reduce it to a game, cold, calculated, detached from all that had been.

He looked down into Rhiannon's face, knowing with sudden, stark clarity that he'd brought her out here to kiss her. Knowing that chance had slipped through his fingers, as sullied as the night was now by his grandfather's shadow. The old bastard had managed a brilliant countermove without ever touching so much as a pawn.

"Go inside, Rhiannon," Lionel murmured.

"What? What is it? What's wrong?"

"I've stayed too long." Long enough for the ghosts to catch up to him. But then, hadn't Knatchbull brought those shades with him? Hauntings trailing in his wake, despite his effort to give warning.

"Your grandfather is traveling to Ireland," Knatchbull had said, "another of his business schemes . . ." Ah, but no one knew better than Lionel that Paxton Redmayne's business was rarely what it seemed.

"Did I offend you?" Rhiannon asked. "I didn't mean to pry. It's just that, after losing my papa, I know how precious family is. Any family, regardless of mistakes they've made or you've made yourself."

He closed his eyes, the image there as vivid as ever—flowing white hair surrounding a face as white as death, a hawklike nose, a predatory, fiendishly patient mouth, only the eyes burning with life, too hot, too intense, as if the mere touch of that gaze should burn. And hidden behind that gaze? A labyrinth of cunning plotting, the mind of a hellish puppet master, making all those around him dance upon invisible strings.

"I seem to have made one mistake. That's certain," he growled under his breath.

Yes. He should have killed the old man when he'd been so tempted years ago. Before he'd ridden off to the army. If he had, Rhiannon would still be dragging lame animals into Primrose Cottage. Her father might be waiting there, alive, to help her bandage them. She'd still be dancing, or perhaps stealing out onto garden paths to kiss men who were at least half worthy of her.

But if he'd struck with his sword that night, he never would have met her. Rhiannon . . . fairy healer, sunshine pouring through her soul.

His eyelids fluttered open, and he stared down into her face, memorizing every soft curve and sweet tint. For an instant, just an instant, he was villain enough to be glad he'd stayed his hand and let his grandfather live, despite all Rhiannon had lost.

For the one pure moment in Lionel's life had been the moment when he opened his eyes in a gypsy caravan on a deserted Irish hill to find an angel gazing down at him, fairy magic in her eyes.

Feeling the parting like a physical pain, he turned, walked away, off into the solitary darkness where he belonged, leaving her behind, haloed in the glow of the light.

He wondered if she guessed, his fairy-kissed angel, that he'd carried the one thing he feared most with him. Ghosts awakened by the mere mention of his grandfather's name.

Chapter

❧ 15 ❧

Music was still casting its sweet spell, laughter echoing through the makeshift ballroom, but all the luster of this enchanted night seemed to have faded the instant Lion strode down the portico stairs and off into the darkness.

Rhiannon had done her best to keep a smile pasted firmly to her face, passing the endless hours with determined cheerfulness so that no one else at the party might suspect that her heart had been carried away by the tall, lean captain with such enigmatic pain in his eyes. But when she could bear the endless chatter no more, she'd made her excuses and let Kenneth Barton escort her back to the quarters she shared with Lion.

For once, the aide-de-camp was blessedly willing to let silence reign. And as they made their way slowly through the quiet camp, Rhiannon finally allowed herself to take out the memory of this strange, beautiful, infinitely sad night and try to make some sense of it.

What had gone awry? True, Lion had stalked into the chamber with all the good grace of a mutinous schoolboy, forced not only to attend a despised party but also to dance with a loathed neighbor girl. Not that anyone else in the entire garrison would ever have guessed Lion's mood. Only she had known, as she had come to know so often of late, his solitary heartache, his secret fears, his yearnings, all the more heartbreaking because he kept them in silence.

God above, what lay beneath that cool smile? That icy control? A sea of anger and pain and self-doubt so powerful that this man—so courageous, so brave— lived in abject terror as to what would happen if the dams he had built ever shattered, allowing his emotions to tear free.

And if there was some way to help open that gate, to let free whatever poison tortured him, would it be a kindness? Or the most careless cruelty imaginable? Some kinds of pain were too great for anyone to bear. Sometimes that pain was instinctively locked away with savage determination, the only way to keep from drowning in it.

But wasn't Lion drowning now? Sinking beneath the surface with such stoicism she couldn't bear it, as if he believed that he was unworthy of help, that no one would reach out to him.

Whenever Lionel spoke of his grandfather, Rhiannon sensed his inner agony. Guilt because he'd disappointed the old man? Resentment of past wrongs? No, so much more. Things that he would never risk telling her.

"Miss Fitzgerald? We're here. At the captain's quarters." Barton's voice startled her, and she was embarrassed to find that she was still standing before the door.

"I'm sorry, Sergeant Barton. I must have been woolgathering."

"About the captain?"

For an instant, Rhiannon drew into herself, not

wanting to betray that very private man who had trusted her at least a little, completely against his will.

"Miss, I know I've got no call to be telling you anything about him. He's to be your husband, after all. It's just . . . sometimes I know he can seem terrible hard, like ice, as if nothing can ever hurt him. I can't help thinking he's like that because things hurt him far too much."

The young man's insights made Rhiannon's throat tighten. "Oh, Sergeant, I—"

"Whatever is amiss between you, I've seen the way the captain looks at you. As if he's really—really *seeing* someone for the very first time. You've got a warmth about you, a kind of loving way no one can mistake. Please help him, miss, I beg you. He's a better man than he will ever know."

Impulsively she reached out, caught Barton's hand. "You're very wise. And I know how Lion hurt you, believing that you plotted to kill him."

Barton gave a laugh laced with insight and pain. "It was just an excuse, miss, to push me away. See, I cared for him, and that was the one thing he couldn't understand. He hoped that if he shoved hard enough I would hate him."

"But you don't?"

"How could I, miss? When the one Captain Redmayne hurts far worse is always himself?"

Rhiannon stretched up on tiptoe and kissed the boy's cheek. "Thank you."

"For seeing you home?" he asked, startled, pleased, and embarrassed at the same time. "It was no trouble at all! Why, a dozen men would've been happy to cross swords with me for the privilege."

"No. For caring about him. I—I love him, you see."

She'd never even admitted it to herself, a truth so vast it should have been terrifying. Instead, it brought her a sense of peace. She loved him, would always love him. Even if he never let her in his heart, he would feel her love. He would know, and that knowledge had to ease at least a measure of his pain, even if he was alone.

"I will do everything in my power to help him," she promised Barton.

Grim determination tightened the young man's jaw. "So will I, even if he hates us both." With a bow, the youth opened the door, and Rhiannon stepped inside the rooms that held nothing of the spirit of the man she'd come to love. Secrets, closely held, as closely as his heart.

He'd left a candle burning for her, and she took it up as she started for her bedchamber. Not that she'd be able to get out of her gown—it had an army of buttons down the back, and she'd told her maid, Mrs. Webb, to enjoy the dance and not bother returning to help her before bed but to take pleasure in the evening with her husband. It had seemed like a good idea at the time. With wry humor, Rhiannon doubted it would seem quite so brilliant after she'd spent the night trussed up in corset and gown.

She crossed to her own door, put her hand on the knob. Then she heard it—the low, rasping, muffled sound of someone in pain.

Lion! Panic jolted through her, vivid images flashing in her memory—red blood, ugly tears in flesh, his life seeping out onto the hard ground. But she hadn't loved him then.

Casting a desperate glance around, she grabbed up the nearest weapon she could find—one of Lion's swords, lying across his desk. Hefting the heavy weapon before her, she shoved open the door to his bedchamber, ready to face a horde of assassins to save him.

"Lion!" she cried out, her gaze scanning the room, lit only by the hearth fire. The window was open wide, making the shadows dance on the walls with almost manic glee. Some force without substance, dark, heavy, terrifying seemed to press down on her chest so hard she couldn't breathe. But she couldn't see any menacing figure in the room. She rushed to the small stand by Lion's chair, scrabbling to light the candle.

Grabbing it up, the sword in her other hand, she swung around to where low, horrible cries sounded, stifled in the bed.

Still clad in breeches and shirt, Lion lay rigid on coverlets scarce disturbed, unimaginable agony etched on his face, the force of his pain all the more horrible because he fought, even in sleep, to hold it inside.

She should have been relieved, no bright red blood seeped from his body, and yet such wounds of the flesh would have been far easier to bear than these wounds of the spirit, untouchable, unreachable, no matter how desperately she wished to help him.

She put down the sword with trembling hands, tears searing her eyes.

"Please, no!" Lion cried out. "Grandfather, don't! Don't take it!"

She couldn't bear it, went to the side of the bed, knowing how much Lion would hate knowing what she'd seen, what she'd heard. And yet no matter what the cost, she couldn't bear to leave him all alone in his pain.

"Hush, no one is going to—to take it," she said fiercely, not knowing what "it" could possibly be. She laid her hand against his rigid, sweat-damp cheek.

Lion's fingers closed on hers, so tight the bones threatened to snap. She held on, not caring. "Papa's.

It was . . . Papa's," he choked out. "Let me play with it. It's the only thing . . . only thing left."

"I won't let him take it," she vowed, holding him, wanting so desperately to reach into his pain. But he wasn't soothed, wasn't calmed. She could feel the anguish cresting again, rising until it tore from him in another ragged groan.

"I promise I'll forget Papa. Just don't . . ." His voice rose, the desperation of the child he had been echoing through it. Then it ended, sharp, terrible silence dragging her deeper into his nightmare.

A soft voice, so rigid. "No. Can't . . . can't make me! Lock me in here forever . . . don't care! Won't ever do it."

Tears flowed down Rhiannon's cheeks at his broken sob. He lay there, curled up so tight, shaking, white-faced.

"Lion, wake up," she pleaded. "It's a dream, my love. Just a dream."

"No. Real. Come . . . come in the dark. Hear them . . . scratching, hungry like—like me." His fists knotted against his stomach, and he rolled away from her, shame contorting his features. "Sorry . . . Papa, sorry. So hungry . . . I had to . . ." Tears tracked down Lion's arrogant cheekbones, pooling in his white-blond hair. "Take me with you, Papa. Dead . . . I want be . . . dead . . . with you."

She couldn't bear it, leaving him lost, so broken, in his nightmare world. She shook him fiercely, loving him, aching for him. "Lion! Wake up!" she all but shouted, her voice harsh with her own pain. "It's a nightmare! Just a—"

If she lived to be a thousand, she knew she'd never forget his eyes the moment they opened—all defenses torn back, every vulnerability naked, exposed, more agony and desolation than she ever could have imagined.

She expected icy rage, his hands thrusting her away. Fearing that he would hate her forever for what she had seen, she stared into his tortured eyes, all but certain this was the last time she would ever be allowed to look into his beloved face.

But in that frozen instant, she saw something shatter.

"Rhiannon." Her name. Just her name. Her heart broke as Lion raised trembling arms and reached out to her. She bit her lip to suppress a broken cry, knowing it would distress him. She flung herself against him, holding him tight, so tight, knowing he would only let her do so for a tiny, precious fragment of time.

She stroked the damp strands of hair away from his cheeks, felt the warmth, the solidity of his chest. Whatever horrible thing had happened to him, leaving such a terrible scar, he'd found the strength to survive. She had to take comfort in that.

"Did I . . . Did anyone else hear me?" He sounded so uncertain, this man who had always been so confident in everything he said and did.

"No. I told Mrs. Webb to stay with her husband tonight." It hurt her to know that he had no concern for his pain, only for the fact that it had been revealed to someone else.

She felt his rigid muscles ease just a little, felt him suck in a shuddering breath. She felt the shifting in him, braced herself, knowing what would come. Gathering his strength, Lion drew away from her, straightened.

Rhiannon swallowed hard, attempted to explain. "I was afraid someone was trying to hurt you again." And someone had, Rhiannon realized with crushing grief. Perhaps no one had stolen into his chamber with knives or swords, but someone had hurt him far worse than any assassin could have.

He climbed out of the bed, stood at the open window, so stiff, so much alone. "Please accept my sincere apology for disturbing you."

The sudden formality infuriated her. She resolved that she wouldn't allow him to close her out. If he managed to do so now, it would be forever.

"Stop it, Lion!" she said sharply.

He turned, staring at her. "What?"

"You apologize to me as if I were some stranger you've imposed on. Don't you know I would suffer anything for you? If you would let me, I would hold your hand, walk with you into any nightmare you might name."

His eyes widened, pleading, desperate, almost hopeful for the tiniest second. Then his mouth hardened. "Thank you for the offer, but no. If there is one thing I detest it is an overcrowded nightmare."

Rhiannon couldn't stem the tears that stung her eyes. "Lion, don't. Don't try to make a jest out of it. I know how much you are hurting."

"Ah, yes." He gave a brittle laugh. "Fairy magic, wasn't it? The ability to read people's hearts. I'd just as soon you don't go prying about mine. I promise you, you wouldn't like what you find." Desolation shone in every line of his body.

He was trying so hard to pretend, to draw his defenses back into place. Rhiannon stood up and went to him, laid her hand upon the damp layer of cloth that clung to his back. His muscles jumped beneath her palm, but he didn't pull away.

She could feel so much through that little touch. Pain and longing, a desperate effort to hold himself back when he wanted what all creatures wished for when they were wounded, in pain. To have someone hold them, comfort them, heal them. But what had Lion said—that some wounds could never be healed? She couldn't believe that. To believe that might be to lose him forever in the dark wasteland where his nightmares lived.

In that instant Rhiannon took the greatest risk she'd ever dared take in her life. Slowly, she slid her arms about Lion's taut waist, laid her cheek against his back, feeling the dampness of his sweat, hearing the echoes of his terror still reverberating through him, and ever so faintly, perceiving the instinctive reaching-out of his wounded soul to her.

"Lion," she whispered against him, trembling, "whatever happened before, whatever hurt you so terribly, you're not alone anymore. I won't let you be."

"Rhiannon . . ." It was a groan, a plea. "Don't, angel. Even you can't save me."

"I can't believe that. Lion, I love you."

"No!" he snapped, wheeling around, grabbing her arms. His eyes burned with hopelessness. "How can you love me? You don't even know who I am. If you had any idea . . . you'd turn away, sickened, horrified."

"I don't believe that."

"You want to fashion me into some sort of wounded hero? Trust me, you'll only end up hurt, dis-illusioned. I'll destroy you, Rhiannon. Shatter the dreams in your eyes and leave you as barren as I am."

She shuddered, staring into eyes as dark as hell and twice as tormented. She didn't believe him. Couldn't. But that didn't change the fact that he *did*.

"Have you wondered why it's been so difficult to even begin sorting out who attempted to kill me on that hillside? It's because I've done so many things to deserve people's hatred. I've trampled over their lives, destroying whatever I thought I was duty bound to destroy."

"Sometimes people have to make difficult choices. Do things that they regret."

"I've driven families out of their homes, Rhiannon. Shattered the walls so they couldn't crawl back into even that meager shelter. I've offered Judas silver to hungry peasants to tempt them to betray their fathers, brothers, neighbors."

Rhiannon's stomach hurt at the images he spun. Hadn't she seen with her own eyes the suffering the English army had brought to Ireland? Known of the cruelties, the injustice? Her heart had bled for her people. And yet her heart now broke for this man, who had no idea how many shadows those acts had left on his own face.

"Lion, when I found you on the hill, I almost left you there. For just a moment I was tempted. I knew the things you must have done in your king's name. I can't imagine what it must be like to be forced to do such things. To carry such regrets."

"I didn't regret a damned thing I'd done. I told myself it was necessary. The quickest way to eradicate the poison. I didn't realize then that the poison was inside me."

She stroked a lock of hair back from his brow. "How can anyone expect you to care about other people's pain when you can't even feel your own?"

"There is no excuse for what I've done, orders or no. There must have been other ways, gentler ways."

"You'll think of them now. Don't you see, Lion? If you were as hopelessly wicked as you claim, I could never love you."

"You don't. You can't."

"I didn't fall in love with the icy captain, handsome as you were. From the first, I was drawn to the tender places in your soul. The wounded places you hoped no one could see."

"Rhiannon—"

"Don't try to pretend them away. Not anymore. When you touched me, kissed me, when you danced with me, I could feel so much sadness in you, so much yearning. Loneliness. No, I couldn't have mistaken it, Lion. I've been lonely too long myself not to recognize that ache in someone else."

She swallowed hard, framed his face with her hands. "I know you didn't want me to love you. But I couldn't help myself. You kept trying to push me away. But every time you did, Lion, I heard something deep inside you calling me back. I couldn't help but hope that maybe—maybe you needed me as much as I needed you."

"Christ, Rhiannon, the last thing on earth an angel like you needs is a"—he winced, as if sickened—"a scoundrel like me."

"You're wrong. The fairies would never have led me to you if we weren't destined to—"

"The fairies? If they led you to me, sweetheart, they're a damned spiteful lot."

"To some. But never to me. Ever since I was a tiny girl, Lion, I've felt . . . something special, as if a ribbon were strung from my heart to the land of fairy magic. Every time I listened and followed the tug of that ribbon, I found something that healed the ugliness and anger within me."

"Healed you? You're the most perfect creature God ever saw fit to put on this accursed planet. There's never been anything ugly inside you, Rhiannon Fitzgerald. You have such unshakable faith, such courage, such goodness. Don't you see? That is why I could never, never be worthy of even a scrap of your love."

"Is that what you think, Lion? That I'm perfect? That I don't know anger? Hate? The night before we lost Primrose Cottage, I heard a noise. Crept downstairs."

She felt the familiar clenching in her stomach, tasted the bitter tang of regret. It had been such a long time since she'd probed that painful memory, felt the shame of it wash through her. But she would have suffered poring over it a hundred times over if it would wipe away some of the hopelessness in Lion's eyes.

"Papa sat at his desk, his face buried in his hands, crying. It was the only time I ever saw him cry. Over and over he kept sobbing, 'I'm sorry, Moira. So sorry.' The next day, I was going to lose the only home I'd ever had, everything I knew and loved. And there was Papa, crying over my mother. Eighteen years she'd been gone. Gone to the land of the fairies, Papa always claimed. But I'd heard other people whispering that it was all one of Kevin Fitzgerald's ridiculous stories. More likely she'd run off with a lover. Maybe she had another daughter and forgot all about me. Or maybe she was in her grave and Papa just couldn't face her death."

She drew in a shuddering breath, confessing it all for the first time—her own pain, her doubts, her grief, the mocking whispers that stalked her late at night. "The only thing I knew for certain was that she hadn't loved me enough to stay."

"Rhiannon, no one could look at you, even once, without loving you," Lion rasped. "I can't believe she left you behind."

She gave a ragged laugh. "Just then I didn't care if she was on the far side of the moon. I needed Papa. I needed him to tell me everything was going to be all right. The strange thing is that all I had to do was walk through his study door. He would have wrapped me in his arms, soothed me. We could have cried together. But I wanted him to—to choose *me* instead of Mama. I'd been with Papa forever, loved him, taken care of him, while she—"

Rhiannon's voice broke, and she was stunned to feel something warm against her trembling hand— Lion's strong one, covering it with such gentleness, such sorrow for the girl she had been. He didn't say anything. He didn't have to. She felt his anguish in her heart.

"I turned, ran back up the stairs. I had a little box I'd filled with the things I loved best. The fairy cup was on top. I took it, and I . . . I threw it across the room. I'll never know why the cup didn't shatter into a million shards. Maybe fairy magic, or maybe the porcelain was far stronger than it looked. But Papa heard the crash, came running up. The look on his face when he saw the cup, I'll never forget it. He hadn't looked so—so desolate even when he'd first learned Primrose was lost to us.

"He picked it up, touched the broken place in the rim, told me not to worry. Accidents happened, and he was certain I hadn't meant to do it. He carried the cup downstairs, as if it were . . . were something alive, wounded."

"You were barely more than a child. You were afraid."

"I tried to destroy what was most precious to him."

"You're wrong, Rhiannon. The cup was just a memory, a symbol of someone he had loved and lost.

Much as he treasured it, the cup could never run to your father with a broken-winged bird in its hands. It could never fling its arms around his neck or laugh or love him. The most precious possession your father had was your love, and I'm certain that he knew it."

Lionel gave a harsh laugh. "I know it must seem absurd, me lecturing you about the love between you and your father. I've never loved anything. Anyone. I've never dared."

His brow creased, as if he were groping for something, trying to piece it together. "All I do know about love is that someone has to teach you how to love. You can't learn it by yourself. Your father taught you. And your love is so boundless that he must have loved you more than life. And far, far more than a simple china cup."

Hope blossomed in Rhiannon's breast. She clung to his hand. "You're right. After all that pain, all the ugliness of what I'd done, what matters now is that it didn't change the magic of that cup, Lion, or the love I feel whenever I touch it. We all break things, be they china cups or other people's hearts. We make mistakes, hurt each other. Sometimes we even mean to. But we can learn from what we've done. Mend what we can mend. Try to do better."

"You make it sound so simple. I could almost believe—" He stopped, his gaze fastened on their hands, fingers interlaced.

"Believe what?" she prodded, sensing he was balanced on some inner precipice, trying desperately to decide which way to fall.

"From the time I was a boy, I had to learn things, things I never wanted to know, things I hated. But even then, learning was the one thing I was good at.

264 🐾   Kimberly Cates

Do you think that—that if I wanted to . . . if I promised to try . . . you would be willing . . ."

"To what, Lion?"

He raised his eyes to hers, and what she saw there devastated her with hope and joy. "Teach me, Rhiannon," he asked, a lifetime of loneliness and desolation in his eyes. "Teach me how to love."

Chapter

❧ 16 ❧

Lion had seen many expressions steal across Rhiannon's open features in the brief time since she'd burst into his life—tenderness, frustration, confusion, delight, empathy, determination, and grief—but never had he seen such pure joy, such unshakable faith as that which blossomed in her face at his plea.

So powerful was it that for an instant it terrified him, made him want to pull away from her, from the chance that he would fail her, disappoint her, and that his world would be left even more barren than before. For if Rhiannon couldn't teach him to love, he knew with sinking suddenness that he was beyond help, beyond hope. Condemned to a hell far more terrifying than any realm of fire and brimstone that Satan himself could design. Because for an instant, he had tasted Rhiannon's world, harbored the most fragile hope that she might somehow be able to open the gate, let him in.

She grasped his hand in hers, so tight, as if even now she understood his fears, refused to let him slip away. "I'll teach you, my love," she promised, angels in her eyes. "I won't leave you alone."

Her hands framed his face, and she brushed his lips with hers. Rose-petal soft, dewy, and impossibly sweet, her kiss melted into Lion, filling him with the warmth of healing. He groaned, threading his fingers through her hair, cradling the nape of her neck in his palm as he explored her lips, kissing her as if it were his first time.

And it *was* the first time he'd truly kissed a woman—no game of strategy fired by mutual lust, no expediently disposing of inconvenient physical needs, no carefully guarded distance maintained between them despite the intimacy of mouth upon mouth. He came to this kiss more terrified than he had been in his first battle, the smell of gunpowder stinging his nostrils. He came to her far more naked than he'd ever been in his life—a nakedness of spirit.

"Rhiannon . . ." He murmured her name against her lips, *needing* for the first time in his life, allowing himself to tumble deeper, deeper into the sensation. Love—the ultimate recklessness. Nothing made a man more vulnerable. And yet as his mouth moved with heart-hunger over Rhiannon's, the risk was worth the pleasure. A boy's wonder of discovery, a man's first foray into something finer than mere lust. The sensations shook him to the core of his being.

Or was he selfish? Weak? Allowing her to banish his nightmares, his loneliness, take them into herself in an effort to heal him. He didn't deserve her love, her care. Nothing could ever change that.

Though it was like ripping his heart from his chest, Lion loosened his fingers from the silken cinnamon strands of hair, drew his lips reluctantly away from hers.

"Rhiannon, I don't think—"

"You *do* think," she breathed against the sensitive

cords of his throat, "far too much. Love isn't about thinking. It's about feeling. Trusting."

"You'd be a fool to trust me, sweetheart," he confessed. "No matter how much I might wish . . . wish it were different."

"Then you'll just have to trust me." She raised those eyes to his, luminous, a little shy. "Lion, do you remember when we were in the glen? When I was splashing in the water with Milton?"

His mouth went dry. "You'll never know how hard I have to work to *keep* from thinking of it. You looked like a water sprite, droplets sparkling on your face, your chemise soaked through with water, clinging." He swallowed, his voice dropping low, bitter. "But I found a way to crush that vision. I just pictured your face after I told you the truth about why I—"

She stopped the words with the tips of her fingers, laying them across his mouth—such a fragile barrier to hold in something so very ugly. Her lips curved in a trembling smile. "I wanted you to see me that way. To stare at me with that heat in your eyes, almost as if I were beautiful."

"*As if*? God, have you any idea how beautiful you are? You're everything warm and bright and loving. Everything I was so sure I could never have."

A flush stained her cheeks with rose. "But you could have had me. I offered myself to you."

"Damn it, Rhiannon, how could I, no matter how much I might have wanted you? Apparently even I wasn't that heartless. To take such a gift from you, when I could give you nothing in return except pain and disillusionment and regret."

"Is that what you were taught? To give gifts only when you could expect something in return?"

"I never gave anything away, my dear, unless I knew the giving would work to my advantage."

"But in that case, it would have. I mean, I wanted to make love with you. I didn't expect anything from you, Lion, except that one night. It should have been a perfect bargain to your way of thinking. And still you pulled away."

"No, angel. I didn't pull away. I shoved you away from me with all the ruthlessness I could muster, bastard that I am, because"—he sucked in a shuddering breath—"no matter how hard I tried to deny it, you touched something inside me, something buried so deep I wasn't even certain it existed anymore, if it had ever existed at all. The tiniest fragment of—of decency, the barest shadow of what might once have been my heart."

"Even then, dastardly villain that you were, you were trying to protect me, weren't you? A knight-errant fighting hardest against the demons in himself."

"Even an imagination rich as yours will never be able to garb me in the robes of a Galahad. You should have fled while you had the chance, Rhiannon. It would have been better for you, I'm afraid."

"Never. The fairies brought us together, Lion. And the first lesson I'm going to teach you about loving is this one. It isn't always smooth and easy and fair. But once you have it, real love is worth any risk, worth believing in, worth fighting for, even when it seems all hope is lost, because love is the one thing no one can take away from you. My father kept his love for my mother alive for eighteen years after she disappeared from his life. Wherever he is now—in heaven or in the land of the fairies—I'm sure he has that love still. And if you'd succeeded in sending me away from the garrison the night we arrived, I would still be loving you, from somewhere among the green hills, and you would know it, no matter how hard you tried to pretend it away."

He gazed down into her face, so earnest, flushed with emotion, her eyes so bright. Pure love, poured like life-giving water into the hands of a man wandering for an eternity in the desert. Even though he was unworthy to drink it, how in the name of God could he stop himself?

A burning started low in his belly, a fire he'd never felt before—need, pure, unadulterated need—not only of the body but of the very soul. He wanted to draw her into his arms, to strip away the gown that clung like fairy mist to the sweet curves of her body. He wanted to taste every delicate inch of skin he bared.

Hell, he could already remember every sip he'd taken of her lips, even the most careless brush of her fingers—touches that had been so foreign to him before Rhiannon Fitzgerald had stumbled into his life, a tousled fairy maid who brushed aside his fiercest scowls, smiled through his iciest barbs, and dared to do what no one had done before—to see beyond what he was, to look deeper, until she saw all he could be.

Never had he wanted a woman more than he wanted Rhiannon now, and yet . . . didn't he owe her far more than a tumble between his sheets? A quick, fierce bedding in answer to the selfish pounding of his own desire? Shouldn't he wait, make love to her the first time after meeting her at the altar? Lion garbed in his finest dress uniform; Rhiannon glowing and joyous, with flowers twined in her hair? Time. Perhaps she didn't need it, to be certain what she wanted. But he needed it, to know that he might somehow make himself fit to be her husband.

Husband. He'd once briefly considered marriage—an accepted way to ensure one's advancement in the army. Plenty of senior officers were anxious to see their daughters wed. Families to be allied, a favorite weapon of the military dynasties like the kin of Thorne Carville. And yet, in the end the idea of living with anyone, the terror that she might hear his nightmares, discover his secrets, was unacceptable.

Redmayne lifted his trembling hands to her face. "We'll take this slowly, sweetheart." *Even if it puts me through hell,* a voice inside him mocked. "That way we can make certain that I can learn to give you what you need."

"Oh, Lion. I don't need proof that—"

"I do." Was that his voice? So fierce, run through with emotion? "Don't you understand?"

She hesitated for a moment. "Yes. Yes, I do." She touched his cheek, so tenderly, eyes as wise and innocent as Eve's before the fall. Her lips curved in a smile. "Actually there is something I need right now if . . . if you could help me. My buttons. You see, I can't reach them."

Astonished, he watched as she turned her back to him, and with her hands swept up the tumble of curls, exposing the tender curve of the back of her neck. Redmayne could scarce breathe. It wasn't an invitation. She had excused her maid, hadn't she? It was a request bred of simple necessity. Or had the fates designed it to test his resolve to do right by his lady?

Gritting his teeth tighter than when he'd cauterized his wounds, he raised his fingers to the line of tiny buttons and began unfastening them. One after another, he made his way down between her shoulder blades, the fabric gaping open in his path, revealing undergarments gossamer as the wings of a dragonfly.

The finest lace he'd ever seen edged the soft white cloth, but neither soft muslin nor rich lace could hold half the beauty or allure as the lily-fair skin that peeked out from beneath it.

If this was a test of willpower, he was losing, badly. Fingers that should have marched down her back with the single-mindedness of a general taking a hill tarried over the delicate mysteries of undergarments so utterly feminine, trimmed with wisps of lace. Not the rich Mechlin or Brussels lace of women who had been his mistresses, but soft, delicate webs, doubtless fashioned by Rhiannon's own hands. Airy dreams of romance spun by a solitary girl, secret beauty she alone would see. The insight tightened his chest, filling him with the memory of those dreams unleashed tonight at the ball, as she'd spun about, butterfly-free, in his arms.

Had she any idea that she'd loosed dreams inside him as well? Hotter, more earthy dreams, edged with needs fiercer than anything her innocence could imagine and yet softened, gentled with a reverence Captain Lionel Redmayne had never thought to know.

The last button came free, the gown lying open across her back. Swallowing hard, he delved through yet another layer, unlacing the short corset that bound her breasts, his fingers lingering over silky curves and hollows where faint shadows clung. It was nigh more than his senses could stand, that sensation of release as her breasts were freed of their confinement.

Now was the time in lovemaking that they would spill into his hands. He could picture it as vividly as Rhiannon did her fairy magic, and he longed for it with the unforgettable fire of a man who had never allowed himself to want anything that truly mattered.

It was the hardest retreat Redmayne had ever made, withdrawing his fingers from the ivory satin of Rhiannon's skin. But he made it with the fierce resolution of one hopelessly under siege.

"There." His voice gave an uncharacteristic rasp. "You should be able to manage the rest by yourself."

"Yes. I should. Thank you."

He expected her to turn away, float out of his room like the glowing splash of moonlight she was. But there was something strange in her tone. She came about, facing him. Her arms crossed over her breasts, holding up the drooping folds of her bodice, a maddening icing of lace and chemise peeking over the velvety swells. Her gaze clung to his, melting warm, heartbreakingly hopeful, a little afraid.

He saw her hands tremble for a moment, then her slender fingers loosened on the fabric, let it fall free. Soft puffs of sleeve glided down past her elbows, carrying bodice and white waves of undergarments with it, to tumble in drifts about her waist.

Redmayne burned, desire hot as coals in his belly as his gaze devoured the perfect globes of her breasts rising with each nervous breath, the rose-pink of her nipples beckoning him, more delectable than anything he'd ever imagined.

"Rhiannon, don't." He forced himself to reach out, attempt to draw the bodice back into place. "You don't know what you're doing."

"I'm asking you to make love to me, Lion." Her mouth curved in a smile both tremulous and brave. "Asking for the second time I might add."

He winced, all too aware of how much he must have hurt her, humiliated her when he'd turned her away in the glen. How much he'd hurt her even now. To protect her. To keep her safe.

"We can't do this," he ground out. "Damn it, don't you see? I'm trying to . . . to keep you from . . ." He fumbled, sudden, stark honesty raking through him. "What if this is all a mistake? Once I make love to you, there's no taking it back. I won't risk that."

"Lion, I'm not afraid."

Damn her! She should be terrified, putting her trust in a man half of Ireland hated—with good reason, Redmayne thought hopelessly. "I won't ruin you."

"But I know that—that you want me, Lion. I can see it in your face. And I know there have been others for you, before me. It's not as if you haven't—"

"There has never been any other woman before you, Rhiannon," he bit out savagely. "Not one that I've given a damn about. It was all just mutual lust. So easy, uncomplicated."

"I can be uncomplicated too. From the first I sensed you're a man who takes what he wants, Lion. Why not take me?"

Why the devil not? He was half mad with wanting her. Every fiber of his body was screaming with need. Even that imagination he'd kept so firmly under control was in complete rebellion, taunting him with visions of Rhiannon gasping in a wonder of discovery, her hands on his naked body, her hair spilling across his skin in a veil of silk, her thighs parting in welcome as he drove himself home. The gods give him strength, Redmayne pleaded. He'd been lost for so long, and now the fates were offering him such a sweet taste of redemption upon his lady's lips. But no matter how beautiful this loving was to him, for her any union of their bodies could only mean ruin unless they were safely wed.

Hurt was beginning to creep into her eyes. "Lion, I don't understand. Please. I . . ." She hesitated, fretted her lower lip. So innocent. So seductive. "I want you so much."

His resolve almost shattered, and he cursed this sudden plague of scruples that had infected him. She wanted him—this angel with her cinnamon hair and her rose-bloom lips. This woman who had reached into his chest, breathed life into a heart that had been cold and dead for so long. She'd asked so little of him. Not even for the love he wasn't sure he'd ever be able to give. She asked only that he take her to his bed.

But that was why he couldn't scoop her into his arms, take them both where this tide of passion would lead them. She asked so little. She deserved so much.

"Maybe I'm trying to prove something to you, to myself," he admitted softly. "I can't even remember the last time I did anything that wasn't selfish, Rhiannon. I've certainly never surrendered anything I wanted in order to protect someone else. If I can do this, make this sacrifice, keep you safe, even from myself, then maybe I can begin to hope that someday I might almost be worthy of you."

"But, Lion—"

"I won't make love to you until you are my wife."

"Your . . . wife?" she breathed in wonderment. "Lion, is that what you want?"

It was all that he wanted. The wanting filled him so fiercely it hurt. A lifetime of wanting bursting free, shattering him, stunning him. "Yes." It was all he could say. How could mere words ever possibly convey an eternity of need? "But I won't bind you to me until I'm certain I won't hurt you, disappoint you." His voice dropped low, the confession stripping his newfound emotions raw. "I can't fail you, Rhiannon."

She curved her palm against his cheek, her eyes glistening with a sheen of tears he would have paid his life to keep her from shedding. Crestfallen, resigned, she gave a little sigh. "I just . . . Lion, I need so badly to feel your hands on me. I've imagined being with you night after night. Dreamed of it, even when I tried hard not to. I want you so much it hurts."

Blast, how he knew. It was bad enough, being torn

on tenterhooks of desire himself. But to know that Rhiannon was being tortured this way . . .

He captured the hand that lay against his cheek, drew it down between them. Turning her palm up, he stared into its soft hollow. Could he abandon her to her lonely bed, as he had resolved to do? Could he help ease the pain of longing inside her without crossing that fatal line?

He teetered on the brink of a decision, torn. Was he fooling himself? Was this just one more of Lionel Redmayne's famous games of logic, playing with facts, rearranging them to suit his own purposes? Or was he thinking only of Rhiannon?

He gazed down into her upturned face. "Sweetheart, there might be a way . . ." But was he strong enough, selfless enough to show her? "There is a way I can help ease the fire you're feeling if you trust me."

"Of course I trust you." Trust—it was as natural to her as breathing. But did he dare to trust himself? For her—he could do this for her. Ever so gently he reached out, easing the layers of cloth down her hips, thighs, until it fell in a wreath of soft green and rose about her slippered feet.

Her body gleamed in the flickering firelight and the glow of the single candle, slender, graceful as the stem of a lily, all her feminine secrets revealed to his hungry eyes. The rose-tipped mounds of her breasts, her waist, the flare of her hips, the dewy curls that clung at the juncture of her thighs. And her legs, long, shapely, clad in the finest of stockings, ribbon garters tied at their tops.

The vision she made was exquisite, mind-shatteringly sensual, and yet so much more. Something ethereal turned her face luminous, so beautiful that for the first time Redmayne could almost believe in fairy enchantment, and that this remarkable woman had been born of it.

Scooping her into his arms, he carried her to the bed where he'd faced his darkest nightmares alone, fought to stave off sleep. He laid her upon the coverlets, and bent to kiss her.

She tasted of the nectar of every flower-strewn meadow she'd ever run through, her lips parting, seeking his, eager. He skimmed his hands across velvety skin, each brush of fingers and mouth designed to feed the flames now licking their way through Rhiannon's veins.

Torture, such sweet torture, touching her, kissing her. "I love you." She whispered the words again and again, as if trying to make him believe they were true; she instinctively knew how difficult it was for him to do so. Who could have guessed that those words, which had so terrified him with the responsibility they implied and the vulnerability they proclaimed, words that he'd scorned as weakness, would fill him with such awe, such joy. Make him want . . . want all of her.

He held on to that legendary control more fiercely than he ever had in his life, knowing that if he merely rose above her, she would open those pale, soft thighs to cradle him, draw him into her body with all the eagerness, the generosity of her loving soul.

Torture . . . Rhiannon arched her head back against Lion's pillow, drowning in the sensations he unleashed with his hands, with his mouth. Hot, damp, he trailed kisses in a precise line across her collarbone, down to the cleft between her breasts. She trembled, a tiny groan escaping her lips as his mouth edged closer and closer to the burning bud of her nipple, her whole being half mad with a hunger she couldn't fully understand. Mysteries she'd never expected to unravel were revealed to her one finger

stroke at a time as he explored her, a land more wondrous than any tale of fairies or magic or enchanted
kingdoms.

She cried out as his mouth found its goal, suckled
her nipple deep, as if he were drawing life itself from
her body. She threaded her fingers through his hair,
holding him there, against her, heat sizzling from
where his mouth was fastened to her most secret feminine places.

Melting, she was melting in Lion's arms, the power
of his loving turning her wild with craving for more.
Greedy, awed, she flattened her palms against his
shoulders, feeling the tension in him, the questing.
Hating the layers of shirt and breeches that separated
them while she lay there, so open, naked in body as
well as in spirit.

"Y—your clothes . . . Lion, I want . . . I want to
touch you."

He muttered something unintelligible about punish-
ment for past sins. Then he straightened, ridding himself of the white folds of his shirt. His hair glistened
silver-gold around the rigid planes of his face, his eyes
like blue coals, burning, burning as he cast aside the
garment. The landscape of muscle and sinew he revealed all but stole Rhiannon's breath away. She flattened her hands against the hot silk of his skin, her
pulse leaping as she heard him suck in a sharp breath.
His eyes drooped closed, as he instinctively attempted to hide his reaction, but that was impossible.
She could feel the wild current raging between them,
something so right, so perfect, so inevitable, as if this
love had been waiting to be born in ages before
time began.

And she wanted him so badly, all of him, naked as
she was. Her fingertips slid down, brushing the silky
web of gold that spanned his chest, slipping down

toward the band of his breeches. More impatient than she'd ever been in her life, she reached the fastenings, started to undo the first button.

A guttural groan tore from Lion's mouth, and his hand clamped over hers so tightly it hurt. "No, sweetheart," he ground out. "Not this time. Even I don't have that much willpower. Despite all your efforts to reform me, I'm no saint."

"But I want—"

"I know." So much tenderness filled his voice, such wry humor, despite the need she knew was throbbing through him. "You promised to trust me. Trust me in this."

Disappointed, a little chagrined, she sank back onto the pillows, uncertain what she'd done wrong, what to do next. He chuckled, low, soft. "Rhiannon, Rhiannon, you'll never know how much I want what you want."

She started to protest—argue—impossible man. But his lids narrowed, and she saw something almost feral in his eyes before he stole every thought in her head away with a searing kiss. Her lips parted, and she let him swirl her away into a hot cavern, where everything was sensation, and every sensation more soul-shattering than the last. His tongue teased her lips, tormented them. He caught her lower lip gently between his teeth, suckled it once, then with exquisite care slipped his tongue into her mouth. He stroked every tiny, sensitive place inside it, deepening the kiss until she felt almost as if he were mating with her, making love to her with his mouth in a way she'd never dreamed possible.

His hands skimmed down her body, setting brushfires, returning again and again to stir them, his thumbs circling her nipples, the soft skin at the inside of her elbow, then lower, where the top of her stocking still veiled her thigh. She trembled, arching up into every caress, but nothing prepared her for the sudden stirring, like the brush of a feather, against the fragile cove where her thighs clenched together. She whimpered, raised her head in a halfhearted effort to see what he was doing to her.

What she saw sent shafts of pure passion jolting through her. Lion's strong fingers curved around the ribbon of her garter, the wisp of green satin embroidered with tiny rosettes looking impossibly sensual in his powerful hand.

"Pretty," he breathed, gazing down at her body with such heat she could scarce bear the pleasure of it. "So pretty." His lashes drooped, a wicked curl raising the corner of his mouth. "Do you have any idea how beautiful you are, my gypsy maid?"

With excruciating tenderness, he used the end of the ribbon to trace patterns on the pale skin above her stocking, edging higher by the tiniest of increments. Maddening, intoxicating, he whisked the bit of silk against her, every fiber of her being wild with wanting, desperate to know where he'd go seeking next.

She was half crazed, desperate with a wanton need for him to skim the ribbon higher, touch that place burning and damp with need of him. And the instant she could bear it no more, he did what she wanted so badly, whisked the ribbon across the delicate web of her feminine curls. Melting heat washed through that part of her, and she whimpered, unable to keep herself from arching against that torturous caress.

Something shifted in his eyes, the wicked smile fading, replaced by one of almost savage hunger. Dropping the ribbon, Lion threaded his fingers through the curls. Rhiannon moaned as the warm, callused pads of his fingers skimmed slick satin petals where the wildfires he'd set all over her body suddenly seemed to have gathered.

"L-Lion . . ." She gasped his name, half prayer, half plea. "I . . . feel so . . ."

"I want it to feel that way for you," he rasped, stirring his fingers against her. "More than you'll ever know."

She stiffened as he found a tiny, aching point she'd never suspected could hold such a wealth of sensation—pleasure so intense it was nigh agony.

"It's all right, angel. Just trust me. Let me give this to you." He murmured the words, words of praise, a strange mix of urging and comfort as he carried her off into a world so new, so overwhelming.

Exquisite circles, airy brushes, he moved his fingers against her, drawing the coil of pleasure tighter and tighter until she writhed against his touch, reaching for something she didn't understand.

"Please, Lion, I c-can't bear . . ."

"Hush, love. Just let yourself feel it. Know how good you feel against my fingers. Heaven, Rhiannon. Heaven. But there is more. Can I show you?" He gazed so deep into her eyes that it was as if he touched her very soul.

"Anything, Lion. Everything."

He kissed her, hard, drawing his hand away from her. With a whimper of protest, she shifted her body toward him, but he was already moving himself. He slid down her body, kissing her waist, her navel, her thighs. Her legs shifted, restless, her whole body aching.

"I want to kiss you, sweetheart. Here." His thumb brushed the down between her thighs. She gasped, disbelieving, his breath stirring those curls. "Will you let me?"

It seemed so—so decadent and wicked. But he'd

asked her to trust him. Lion, who trusted so little. Who believed so little that he deserved trust. How could she deny him anything he might ask?

She gave him a smile that trembled, then nodded. "Yes, Lion. I love you."

With a low groan, he eased her legs apart, kissed the inside of her knee, swept his mouth upward, kissing, nipping, then soothing each spot with his tongue.

She stiffened, bracing herself, for what, she wasn't sure. Lion curved his hands beneath her thighs, spreading them until she was wide, wide open. Then, with exquisite care, he closed his lips over that tiny, exquisitely burning nub. Rhiannon gasped, arched up, sensation spearing through her—hunger, stripped to its rawest form, need, pulsing so fiercely it blazed behind her eyelids. She writhed, not to escape the sweet, forbidden torment but to urge Lion on, to try to convey what magic she was feeling.

She stroked his hair, crying out broken words of love as his tongue darted out, dipping and circling. Something was building inside her, coiling tighter, tighter, until it was the most exquisite torture, as if, after an eternity of darkness, the brightest of suns danced just beyond her reach.

Every muscle in her body strained toward it, and then, with a flick of his tongue, he sent her hurtling, hurtling through fire-bright sensations, wild and earthy, beautiful and sacred, a breaking apart of body and soul. She shattered, bit her lip to stifle a scream as he drove her pleasure higher, farther, deeper. She gave herself up to it, glorying in his gift.

She wasn't certain how much time passed before the world spun back into focus. Lion's pristine bedroom, everything arranged with military precision. The only thing out of place was the sword she'd carried in to defend him.

It was the same. So familiar. Only one thing was different. Lion.

He leaned over her, one elbow braced on the mattress, eyes still blazing with intensity and need, and yet a wry kind of tenderness, as if some sort of jest had been played upon him.

With obvious reluctance, he grasped the edge of the coverlet and pulled it across her body, tucking it under her breasts. Innocent she might be, but she was enough a child of the wild lands to realize that something was missing in what they had just shared.

"Lion," she said, her cheeks burning, "what about you?"

She could feel the tension in his body, see the hard determination in his face. He was fighting back his own needs, those needs doubtless still pounding through his veins with the same ferocity with which they had pounded through hers before she reached that delicious sense of fulfillment.

"Lion, I want you. I would have welcomed—"

"I know," he said. "But I fear I've stumbled across a most inconvenient case of scruples where you are concerned, my dear. I trust that you won't reveal my guilty secret to anyone."

She buried her face in his shoulder. "Tell that we almost made love?"

"No, sweetheart. That I had you here, naked in my bed and *did not.*" He chuckled, gathering her against him. "It would be most damaging to my reputation, you understand."

"I think I liked you better as a villain," she admitted with a sigh.

He startled her by loosening his arms, sliding from the bed. "I know it is customary to give the bride a betrothal ring. And you'll have one—the finest coin can buy, I promise. But I want you to have something now that you can hold"—he hesitated, crossing to his desk—"to remind you of tonight." He took something out of the drawer. "The night I vowed to wed you, and you . . . you gave me . . . hope." His voice dropped, low, reverent, as he came to place the object in her hand.

She stared down at the most exquisite carving she'd ever seen. A medieval queen garbed in robes so real it seemed they should flutter in the breeze from the open window.

"Lion . . . she's so beautiful."

"It's a chess piece, the only thing I took with me when I left my grandfather's house. It sounds ridiculous, I know. But the old man and I had spent so many hours warring over that chessboard. I'd fought so hard to keep the queen. I just couldn't surrender her, even then."

Rhiannon pressed the wooden lady against her heart, her eyes burning with the knowledge of what Lion had given her—the only possession he'd ever cared about. And a fragment of his carefully guarded past. "I'll treasure her forever. Keep her safe for you."

Fierce intensity darkened his face. Rhiannon stared into his features, realizing she was seeing the real Lionel Redmayne for the first time. The intelligence was there, but without the razor edge that could so easily cut at someone else's confidence, his innate courage and strength honed to a purer, more vivid sheen.

"I . . . care about you, Rhiannon. More than I've ever let myself care about anyone, save that wooden lady. This much I promise you. I will have you one day. And when I do, nothing will stand between us. Not the danger of assassins or shadows from my past or the tiniest hint of dishonor."

She shivered as a cool night breeze blew through the open window, chilling her despite Lion's arms about her. His world waited beyond. A world filled with intrigue and enemies, self-doubt and the nightmare she'd seen reflected in his eyes. Always he'd walked in it alone. From this moment on, she'd make certain they faced it together.

Lionel gathered Rhiannon up in his arms an hour before the camp began to stir. Taking care not to wake her, he settled her into her own bed, draping her nightgown about her body with more tenderness than he'd ever guessed he could possess. Gently he tucked her beneath layers of downy coverlets, then took care to obliterate any evidence of their tryst. The ball gown hung over the chair beside Rhiannon's fireplace, dancing slippers at attention beneath a flounce of hem. Undergarments, still scented with the subtle perfume of her skin, were stacked in a foamy pile to one side. No one would question where she had spent the night.

The wood-carved queen stood in regal splendor on her bedside table, out in the open for the first time in countless years, where Rhiannon would be certain to see it the moment she woke up.

He intended to leave the moment he got her settled so he could put his own room to rights and gather his thoughts. But he lingered, looking down at the wealth of tousled curls against the pillows, the slight smile that curved her lips even in sleep, as if she held a delicious secret close to her heart. Love, he knew. Love for him.

He touched her cheek, as if trying to reassure himself that she was not merely the fevered dream of a man too long alone. Her skin was warm satin beneath his fingertips, her breath, so soft, warm, drifted in precious waves against him. No one knew better than a soldier how fragile life could be, or how fleeting happiness.

He fought back the memory of the lone caravan isolated in that Irish glen, three men striding up to the camp—some, at least, bent on murder. Assassins he should have hunted with his accustomed ruthlessness during the past week. Instead, he'd been far more alarmed by the enemy Rhiannon had loosed upon him—emotions he could scarce remember stirred up in him by her merest smile, touch. Feelings far more terrifying to Redmayne than the paltry threat of his own death. They had confused him, distracted him. He was even shamed to admit that some deep-buried part of him had known why he was suddenly so accursedly inept. He was stalling, as an excuse to keep her near him.

He'd been a fool not to move with lightning swiftness to put everything in order. His first duty should be to make certain she was safe. Now if anything happened to him, she would be just as helpless, as vulnerable, as poor as when he first awakened in her bright-painted cart. A woman alone, cast upon the capricious winds of fate. The thought sent a chill down Redmayne's spine.

No, he vowed. Whatever happened when he confronted his enemies, he would make certain Rhiannon was taken care of. Taken care of . . . Redmayne fingered the strange notion as if it were a pearl he'd found in the sand, something beautiful, flawless, unexpected.

Never in his life had he felt this urge to protect and defend, this almost holy trust inside him, awe-inspiring, terrifying, inescapable. So this was the emotion that he saw burning in the eyes of his men, that indescribable quality he'd examined with such curiosity, used as a weapon when necessary. He'd understood the vulnerability it bred, but never guessed that the wonder in love far outweighed the risks.

Perhaps he would be walking into the flames for Rhiannon by allowing himself to fall prey to these emotions, and yet he was fiercely glad to do it. For when she'd vowed she loved him, her eyes shining with tears, he'd glimpsed for a heartbeat what might wait for him on the other side of the flames.

He straightened with new resolve and stalked from the room. He was garbed in a fresh uniform, ink drying on several letters, by the time there was a knock on the door of his headquarters. He raised his gaze from the missives and glared at the door.

It was time to put an end to whatever game his enemies were playing. The next move was his. It was a crossroads he'd come to countless times during his life. One familiar, almost eagerly anticipated in the past. Why was he suddenly so accursedly unnerved?

He'd never failed before; he had countered every strategy with icy calm brilliance. But one vital thing had changed since Rhiannon Fitzgerald careened into his world. For the first time in his life, Redmayne had something precious to lose.

He closed his eyes, picturing the delicate form of the single chess piece he'd guarded throughout his misspent life. A symbol of what he had never hoped to have until he gave her to his own brave-hearted lady.

A queen for his undeserving heart.

Chapter

❧ 17 ❧

Lion paced the confines of his office, succumbing to a ridiculous show of restlessness for the first time in his life. He couldn't help it, damn it. In the eight days since he'd carried the sleeping Rhiannon from his bed, he'd used every trick in his repertoire to set things in order, flush out the assassins, unearth his enemies once and for all.

He'd even gone so far as to summon Sir Thorne Carville to Galway, intending to confront the man directly. Well-placed questions regarding the man's courage, should he choose not to come, should have sent Thorne bolting to confront his accuser. Lion had been certain he understood this adversary to his very bones. But even the lances aimed at Thorne's prodigious pride had failed to make the man appear.

Even the Irishman who had been Thorne's comrade seemed to have disappeared into the mist, vanishing altogether. Only Barton remained of the three men who had sauntered up to Rhiannon's caravan what seemed an eternity ago.

Frustration gnawed at Redmayne's nerves, loosing an edge of temper he hadn't even realized he possessed. He fought to conceal it, and yet he was appalled to know it was there.

Hellfire, it was one thing to play upon the vast chessboard of life when you didn't care how many pieces you might lose in any gamble. You could play coolly, use your strategies with the greatest of cunning. But the instant one piece became precious, the whole game shifted, became terrifying instead of stimulating.

He paused at the window, where a row of potted flowers now stood, butter yellow in the sun. Another of Rhiannon's gifts, subtly beckoning him to look outside now and then, to tempt him into a world beyond the four walls of this room. Could she possibly guess how much danger might lie in that sun-drenched landscape she so loved? Rhiannon, with her fairy magic, her belief in the goodness of everyone and everything she encountered, couldn't she feel the danger, sense it tightening like jaws about them, its cold teeth gleaming.

Someone was out there.

He could feel it deep in the marrow of his bones where every soldier's instinct for survival lay buried. Was it Thorne? No. He was more powder keg than man, no more able to be silent and subtle under the provocation Redmayne had offered than that keg would be if someone showered it with sparks. The Irishman? Far more likely, and yet, with the extra guards Lion had posted, wouldn't the man have been caught by now? No matter what trap he laid, this person managed to slip through the net as if he had no more substance than moonlight.

He'd spent most of his nights in that odd twilight, not sleeping, yet only partially awake, but these past eight nights had been absolute torture. He couldn't even count the number of times he'd slipped into Rhiannon's bedchamber, damn the presence of her maid a doorway beyond, and had kept watch over her until dawn broke.

Most terrifying of all was the knowledge that no matter what he did, he might not be able to keep his lady safe from whatever peril he sensed circling them like a pack of wolves.

A rap on his door made Lion start. Forcing his face into his accustomed expression of icy calm, he paced to his desk and sat down before bidding his visitor to enter.

Knatchbull, awkward as ever, limped in, his arms full of leather portfolios, obviously stuffed with papers. "Captain." He gave a quick bow, then shut the door. "I came as quickly as I could. Everything is in order—Miss Fitzgerald is made your sole heir."

Redmayne's shoulders sagged a little. That much at least was done. Even if his enemies managed to kill him, Rhiannon's future, at least, was secure. "Thank you, Knatchbull. You are, as ever, efficient. One of your most valuable qualities."

"Sir, there is more." The man hesitated. "I've made inquiries, as you requested, regarding Sir Thorne and the Irishman you suspected of plotting against you."

"And what did you discover?"

Knatchbull's misshapen face fell into miserable lines. "They are both dead."

Lion's blood froze. He stilled a long moment, until he could steady his voice. "How?"

"Thorne drank himself to death one night, raving about you the whole time. The Irishman was trampled by a carriage—one whose driver didn't bother to stop."

"Unremarkable deaths, totally believable accidents, considering their personalities, I suppose. Though strange, so close together."

Knatchbull shifted, obviously damned uncomfortable. "My thought exactly. Something doesn't feel right about it. What about that other boy—Barton, was it? No accident has befallen him, has it?"

Redmayne turned away, rising to pour two snifters of brandy. Why the devil should Knatchbull's query about the boy give him such an infernal twinge? Barton had always bounced about like Rhiannon's accursed pup, eager and bright-eyed. Yet sometime during the past weeks the youth had changed. The incessant chatter had stilled, and Barton had grown edgy, intent, as if waiting for something to happen. Dark shadows smudged cheeks that were once as rosy as any girl's, and his eyes were lost in violet hollows that haunted Redmayne late at night.

A guilty secret? Dark dread? What was the boy afraid for? His life? Had he heard about the fate of his fellow conspirators, and did he now fear that a similar accident waited somewhere for him?

But Rhiannon was so certain of Barton's goodness. She'd defended the boy with such fierce passion that Redmayne, cynical as he was, almost believed, or wanted to believe, what? That Barton was everything he had always seemed? Yet how could Redmayne deny the evidence he saw now with his own eyes, especially when such absurd denial might put Rhiannon in danger?

"Captain, I—I'm sorry to bring such bad news." Knatchbull's voice intruded on Redmayne's grim thoughts.

He turned, snifters in hand, and gave a stiff laugh. "My dear Knatchbull, you know me well enough to be certain I don't believe in killing the messenger. Such a waste, that. And an appalling habit of cutting off one's sources of the most useful information."

Knatchbull's wise eyes clouded with something distressingly like sympathy. "You jest, but I know how disturbing this news must be to you. Have you uncovered any other clues that might lead you to whoever is responsible for all this?"

"No. One of the risks of making so many enemies over the years, I'm afraid. One hardly knows where to begin." The humor faded from his voice. He offered one glass to Knatchbull, then set the other wearily on the edge of his desk. "I wouldn't even mind so much, if I could just be certain my enemy wouldn't grow untidy in his quest for revenge. It's likely that I deserve whatever contempt he holds me in. However, it would be unfortunate if my nemesis should, say, wound some completely innocent person who just happens to be in his way."

"You're speaking about Miss Fitzgerald."

Cold stones seemed to sink in Redmayne's belly, raw horror at what he'd so carelessly betrayed. His worst vulnerability. His most closely guarded secret: love for a woman.

"I've merely been afflicted with a sudden aversion to other people paying for my sins. Perhaps there is hope for my redemption after all."

"Say what you will, my friend, but I know the truth. You are afraid for her. You should be. Someone stirred up the hatred in Sir Thorne and in that Irishman, enough to make them reckless. Not to mention the fact that whoever it was paid them both well. The family of the Irishman was paid enough to book passage on a ship bound for America. Sir Thorne's creditors were no longer banging upon his door. Whoever attempted to kill you has limitless resources and is fatally thorough with anyone who's fool enough to fail him."

Redmayne closed his eyes a moment and saw his grandfather's face hazy in the darkness of his nightmares, white hair sweeping back from a brow broad with intelligence, eyes burning with intensity, ruthlessness. And yet, his grandfather abhorred crude methods as much as Redmayne himself did. Assassins, especially of the caliber of Sir Thorne, were beneath Paxton Redmayne's dignity, were they not? No, he'd choose far more subtle ways—infiltrate those close to his enemy, use them against him with the calm efficiency Paxton Redmayne was legendary for.

"Forgive me, but you do intend to warn Sergeant Barton, don't you?" Knatchbull asked. Redmayne opened his eyes, staring into the tortured shape of the man's face, unease pulsing through his veins. Memories, far too clear, of his grandfather unnerved him. These two men were the kinds of "weapons" the old man would choose—Barton, with his gallumphing appearance of innocence, Knatchbull, who had built trust in business affairs, if little else.

"You've been hired to give me information, Knatchbull, not to question what I intend to do with it." The words sounded cold even to his own ears.

A wounded light sparked in Knatchbull's ages-old eyes. "Perhaps I don't have any right to comment, but this much I can tell you, it would hurt you more than you know if something happened to that boy."

"Not if he's involved in a plot to kill me. I'm afraid I lose all amiability when I'm nearly murdered."

"Do you really believe that Barton was involved?"

"He was there. Perhaps that is all I need to know. Now, unless you have more information, I would like to be alone."

"I hate leaving you like this. I don't—"

"Go. You needn't pretend that you are my confidant. We are business partners. That is all."

"Of course." Knatchbull's gaze sharpened. "The years we've worked together mean nothing. In fact,

it's just as likely that I am in league with your enemies, isn't it? After all, no one is free from suspicion.
Isn't that what Paxton Redmayne taught you?"

"Something to that affect. It's stood me in good
stead all these years."

"Has it? It's kept you from living. You were dead
inside, until that lovely girl refused to be frozen by
your glares, refused to turn away from you."

"Thank you so much for your estimation of my
character."

"I could tell you a hell of a lot more about yourself
than you could ever know, if it would do a damn bit
of good." Heaving a sigh, Knatchbull set the glass on
the table. "If you've ever listened to me, do it this one
time. Don't fool yourself into making a horrible mistake with Barton. Your grandfather has kept you from
trusting anyone all these years. He still controls you,
just as certainly as if you were still a boy locked up
in his attic."

How the devil had Knatchbull known? Had the man
been prying into Redmayne's past? Rage poured
through him, hot and fierce, but before he could
speak, Knatchbull turned and stalked out of the chamber, leaving Redmayne alone with the ghosts that had
haunted him forever.

He paced to the window, glaring out at the
slumped, loose-jointed figure making his way across
the yard. Damn the man, weren't things bad enough
without Knatchbull raking up all this nonsense? Was
Barton the wronged one, the beleaguered—

Blast it! What kind of fool would trust someone who
had been seen with two of his enemies, miles from
anything except the site where he'd almost been murdered? Put not only himself at risk, but his lady . . .

His mind filled with images of Barton's worn features, hollow-eyed, every emotion raw. What could

possibly have caused so tormented a look, save the ravages of guilt? Doubtless Rhiannon could come up with a dozen reasons—a broken heart, for example. But the boy hadn't strayed an inch off the garrison since Redmayne returned, so he could hardly be off plaguing some unfortunate girl with a bout of calf's love.

What the devil was the matter with him? Redmayne wondered. He'd made hard choices in the years of his command. Why was it that this one haunted him despite all logic? Because he'd come to care for the boy just a little, despite his efforts to remain aloof. And yet this time Barton would have to fend for himself. It was the only choice he could make. Wasn't it?

Unable to bear being closed in another moment, Lion got up, strode out into the sunshine. He was merely attempting to get things into perspective. It was only by chance that he came across Barton, more haggard than ever as he tended to his duties.

The lad glanced up, his eyes filling with something unreadable as he saw Redmayne's face. Pain? Loss? Dread?

"Captain, sir, is something amiss?" Barton straightened, his gaze sweeping out behind them, as if searching for something, someone. But what? Who?

"Why?" Redmayne asked softly. "Should there be?"

Barton's gaze flickered away, fastened on the ground. "I don't know, sir."

Redmayne should have walked away. He intended to. He took three steps; then something inside him made him stop, turn, fix a penetrating stare on Barton. "I just received word that two people of interest to you have died."

"Who?"

"Sir Thorne and that Irishman—what was his name?"

The boy's face washed ash gray. "Seamus O'Leary."

"Yes. O'Leary. He was struck by a carriage. While Sir Thorne finally drowned himself in drink, it seems." Redmayne wanted to sound careless, barely interested. Why the devil did his voice betray him, suddenly roughening around the edges. "Be careful, boy."

He cursed himself the instant the words were out of his mouth. Fool—damn fool! *"Never show weakness"*—his grandfather's maxim echoed through Redmayne's mind. For God's sake, Barton might yet prove to be his enemy! Shaken, uncertain, Redmayne spun on his heel and stalked away, hoping to hell he hadn't just made the worst mistake of his life.

"Men are impossible," Rhiannon muttered as she ran the brush down Socrates's flank, wishing she could as easily brush aside the thoughts troubling her. Nearly two weeks had passed since that glorious night when Lion had carried her to his bed, kissed her, touched her with such fevered need, let her peer deep into the most guarded reaches of his heart.

She should be elated, all but drunk with joy. For even though he'd never said the words, no man could show such tenderness unless he loved.

She blushed remembering how fiercely he was fighting to defend her honor, refusing to complete their lovemaking. Foolish man, didn't he know she cared little what the world beyond that bedchamber thought? How could anything so wonderful, so loving, ruin anyone? No, instead it would heal soul-deep wounds like the ones she had seen in Lion's eyes from the first day she'd found him among the standing stones above Ballyaroon.

Yet as the days passed there was no sign of peace

in Lion's face. He worked like a man possessed, a new fever in his eyes. To make it more torturous, he'd barely touched her, stealing only kisses chaste enough to be exchanged before a bevy of nuns.

It was frustrating, infuriating, disappointing, and she sensed it caused him even more misery than it did her.

"I want you so much," he had murmured in her ear, "but I can't have you until this is settled."

Until *what* was settled? This madness about whoever had stalked him at Ballyaroon? The echoes of his past she barely understood? His own raw terror of loving, of trusting? She'd pleaded with him a dozen times, asking him to let her share whatever was troubling him. Offer him comfort, at least, in his bed. But he'd only shaken his head, touched her tenderly, then marched off into his unseen battle alone.

She sighed, then grew still at the sound of footsteps behind her. Barton. She would have been glad to see the youth—he'd been all but invisible the past week—except that he looked so changed. "Kenneth"—she used his Christian name without thinking, laying one hand on his arm—"are you ill?"

An odd smile curled one corner of his mouth. "No, miss, just—just a little tired, I'm thinking."

"Then you should rest. I'll speak to the captain about it."

"No!" He paled, his voice cracking. "You can't do that."

"Whyever not? If you're not ill now, you soon will be if you carry on as you have been. Is something troubling you? Please, let me help you."

"There's nothing you can do. Nothing anyone can do, except me."

"I don't believe that."

Despair and determination warred in the youth's face. He looked away. "It's true. I just have to see this through—" He stopped, alarmed, as if he'd just realized what he'd said to her. Dark color stained his cheeks. "Forgive me for rambling. I need to see to the business that brought me here." He straightened his shoulders with heartbreaking courage. "There is a message just arrived for you at the captain's headquarters."

"But why? No one beyond the garrison knows I'm here. I can't think who would be sending me anything."

"It's an invitation to dine, I think."

"Whoever from?"

"A Mr. Paxton Redmayne, Esquire."

"Lion's grandfather? It must be," Rhiannon said, astounded. She hesitated, remembering Lion's mysterious nightmare, his bitterness toward the man who had raised him.

Barton flushed. "I meant to tell the captain first, but he's off with that Knatchbull fellow. The time is very specific, so I thought you might wish to send an answer as soon as possible. He is staying at Manion House, an estate about six miles from here. If you wish to go, I could see you there."

She fretted her bottom lip. Lion would object to her going to meet his grandfather. There could be no question about that. And yet the old man was his only living relative. If Lion were truly to heal, might not mending his relationship with this man hold the key?

"Thank you, I think I will." She placed the brush back in the bucket, and ran a hand across the top of Milton's sleek canine head. "Will you promise me one thing before we go? You will take better care of your-self, won't you, Kenneth? Once all this nonsense is settled, I'm certain things between you and the cap-tain will be mended, and you'll be back to your regu-lar duties as his aide."

Grief and resignation weighed down the youth's shoulders. "There are things the captain will never be able to forgive or forget. It's not his fault. He's just never learned how. I don't think he can start to learn it now."

A soft glow of happiness warmed Rhiannon, and she laid one hand on the boy's cheek in comfort. "I promise, he'll surprise you, surprise everyone one day. He wants to learn . . ." She stopped, blushed.

What had she almost done? Told Barton Lion's se-cret? That he'd asked her to teach him how to love? Perhaps Lion didn't know it yet, but learning to love also meant beginning to forgive—not only those who hurt you but also yourself.

"I don't think he'll ever forgive me, once he finds out—" Barton's voice broke, and he raised his chin. "But I guess it doesn't matter. I do what I have to do." So much pain in that voice, so much changed from the first time she'd met him. The aura that had been worried, yes, but wide open as a summer field was murky, more closed, as if he were drawing into himself, summoning up every fiber of . . . of what? Strength? Courage? Or was it possible that some-thing darker was at work? What if she was wrong about Kenneth—not about his basic goodness—no, she could never have mistaken an intuition so strong—but the best of men could be trapped into doing things they were ashamed of, could be manip-ulated by those more ruthless, more cruel.

Even her father, with his gentleness, had warned that any man could break, if the right pressure was applied. That was why he had spent so much time, trying to help those who were being crushed by those stronger, trying to keep good people from betraying themselves.

Rhiannon caught her lip between her teeth, remembering the first time she'd seen young Barton, flanked by two others Lion knew as his enemies.

"Kenneth, whatever it is . . . you might feel better if you told someone. Nothing is beyond help, beyond hope. I'm always willing to listen."

For a heartbeat the boy's lean features turned desperate. But after a moment he shook his head. "Thank you for your kindness, miss, but I have to do this alone."

Alone . . . Why was it that men always believed such a thing? As if sharing their heartaches, their pain, was some sort of cowardice? She sighed, saddened not only for Barton but for Lion as well. Both men were trapped by rules that only they could understand.

Fortunately, she wasn't bound by their rules, by any rule except the need to heal, the gift of her mother, fairy-born or no. If Moira Fitzgerald had left her daughter nothing else, she'd left her that inescapable drive. And never had she felt it more strongly than she did for the tall, wounded soldier who had brought true love and passion into her quiet life.

The fates had delivered Lion into her hands, given her the chance to reach the deep, secret places in his soul where wounds still festered, tormenting him with their subtle venom. It was destiny. Certain as the faint whisper of her next breath.

Wasn't it possible that this meeting with Lion's grandfather was another act of fate? One that would purge Lion of that lingering poison forever? No matter what had happened between the two men before, she had to believe it could be mended. Needed to believe it, more than she could ever express.

It marked a place to begin. A place to hope.

No matter how angry Lion might be at what she was about to do, she had to take this chance.

Chapter

❧❧ 18 ❧❧

Rhiannon's hands twisted nervously in the reins, her freshly donned rose muslin gown rippling against the pant leg of Kenneth Barton's breeches as she stared up at the building growing nearer, ever nearer. The gypsy cart rattled and jolted up the wide sweep of carriage circle, a ramshackle interloper in a world she had all but forgotten.

Manion House towered in regal splendor, its entry flanked by grand Corinthian columns, the lion and the unicorn, symbols of England's rule, emblazoned time and again upon the dark gray stone. In her travels, Rhiannon had seen other great houses crowning other green hills, monuments to power built by absentee landlords whose greed and carelessness had bled Ireland white and kept a desperate population dancing upon the knife's edge of rebellion.

In the days before she and her father had left Primrose Cottage, she'd been invited to the occasional ball or musicale in these grand houses. She'd been a handy remedy during those socially distressing times when there weren't enough dancing partners available or when another person was needed to round out an awkward number at the dining table.

But even then, such places had made her feel like a traitor because she couldn't help loving the beauty, the majesty, of the grand estates even though they were exquisite masks hiding inevitable corruption.

Far beyond the gleaming glass windows tiny clay cottages huddled, families with ten, twelve children barely scraping out a livelihood, their meager coin filling the landlord's coffers.

She had paced the marble-lined galleries, disheartened, bemused, and wondered if there were enough magic in the world to bridge the gap between two such disparate worlds, to heal the hatred and pain born of centuries of conquest, oppression, rebellion. Generations of both Irish and English had buried sons and fathers, lovers and children, dreams, and their own fierce pride.

But even these familiar whispers of war in ages past, even the tragedy of hatred that threatened to afflict Ireland forever, had little power to trouble her now.

It was her own actions that unsettled her. The risk she had taken and the consequences that might come of her journey here, to meet a man she'd never seen before.

She swallowed hard. She'd been so certain it was the right thing to do, making the trip to this house. She'd even penned a quick note to Lion, explaining where she'd gone and why, not wanting him to worry. Yet even as she placed the missive on his desk, she'd felt so unnerved she almost threw it into the flames. And with every beat of Socrates's hooves, bringing her nearer her destination, she grew edgier still.

It was only because Lion's trust was so tentative, she assured herself. She feared making any mistake.

This meeting was so important, this chance to heal his old wounds so precious.

Besides, her unease was understandable in these circumstances. Any fiancée would feel nervous, meeting her beloved's family for the first time, especially someone from whom her betrothed had been estranged for many years.

She resisted the impulse to slow Socrates down, knowing she'd feel three times the fool if Lion's grandfather happened to see her approach, perhaps guess she was afflicted with a sudden bout of cowardice.

Far too soon she was reining her disreputable horse and cart to a halt before the vast entryway. The caravan looked as incongruous as a ribbon monger's wares cast into the lap of a queen, its bright colors absurdly garish in such stately surroundings as Barton hopped down from his place beside her.

"You've troubled yourself quite enough on my behalf." Rhiannon gave the haggard young officer a worried smile. "If you like, you may take a bit of a nap inside the caravan until I am finished. It's more comfortable than it looks, I assure you."

"No. I'll deliver you to the old man myself," Barton said with a sudden air of stubbornness. He offered her his arm and guided her up the few steps, to where the towering main door was swept open by a footman. Rhiannon stared in puzzlement—the man looked more like a pugilist than a servant in such an elegant household.

"Miss Rhiannon Fitzgerald," Barton announced, "come to dine with Mr. Redmayne at his invitation." It was as if he were daring the servant to take exception.

The footman's eyes narrowed, a thin gleam of contempt shining beneath his lashes. "We've been expecting you, Miss Fitzgerald. Permit me?" With a bow exaggerated just enough to convey contempt without being a blatant insult, he escorted Rhiannon and Barton deeper into a wonderland of gold leaf and gray-veined marble, gleaming armor and glinting pistols and swords arranged on the walls in graceful fans and circles, lethally artistic designs.

At the end of the long corridor, he gestured to a doorway guarded by two gilt statues—the first, Hercules wrestling the lion, the second showing the majestic beast in death throes beneath his mighty hands.

Rhiannon shuddered at the image, hating the triumph in Hercules' face, the lust for the kill. Was it possible that the statues had some hidden meaning? No. They were ancient, had obviously been in their places of honor for decades. Besides which, Lion's grandfather was only visiting Ireland, was he not? Likely borrowing this manor house merely to be close to his estranged grandson.

She tore her gaze away from the statues and glimpsed the footman watching her, his smirk evident as he sketched yet another bow. "The master will join you at his pleasure. There is a mirror in the corner if you would like to see to your hair." It could have been a kindness, pointing the way to that mirror. A boon gently given. But the man's lip curled with such impudence that there was no way to mistake his contempt.

Rhiannon smoothed the folds of her gown, fighting the feeling that she looked like a grubby scullery maid who had dared to dress up in her mistress's finery. This bout of nerves would never do! She squared her shoulders, determined to carry herself in a way that would make Lion proud of her, striving for comportment worthy of the betrothed of Captain Redmayne.

But the instant the servant left them alone in the

blood-red chamber with its slashes of ice white, she felt strange, completely out of place.

It should have been a beautiful room, every detail the finest, every line and curve of the furnishings a study in perfection. Even the carpets were amazing, embellished with flowers so realistic it seemed you should be able to pluck them and draw in their scent. Oddly disappointed, Rhiannon felt as if it were all some kind of fraud.

A small table, doubtless set up for the occasion, was laden with gleaming silver urns, pots, and platters of every delicacy imaginable. A little distance apart, the most exquisite gaming table she'd ever seen occupied a place of honor on a dais by the window, light streaming across what looked to be a chess set of impossible beauty.

Rhiannon stole nearer, awed. Pieces carved perhaps in the age of Arthur and Guinevere were kissed with such genius they seemed to breathe. Opposing armies faced each other across a battlefield of vari-colored marble squares, pawns like foot soldiers, kneeling with their shields before them, bishops in ecclesiastical splendor, knights on rearing horses, lances drawn. Castles and kings and, on only one side, a queen.

Rhiannon caught her lip between her teeth, staring at the empty space where the other queen should have been. Lion's queen, the one he had given into her keeping the night he had truly asked her to be his wife.

She touched the king who stood alone, the robes so intricately carved, painted with such skill, a perfect match to those that robed the chess piece she now cherished.

Was this not a sign of hope, then? This table, with its pretend armies awaiting combat? Lion had said his grandfather hadn't allowed any distractions, any other children, games, or toys. But the grandfather had obviously spent countless hours teaching Lion this game. Perhaps it was a stern, loveless old man's only way of showing his grandson the affection he'd felt for him. Perhaps his feelings were hidden away, as Lion had hidden his own emotions for so long.

Her throat tightened, and she imagined Lion, a towheaded little boy already so bright, earnestly bent over the game, his blue eyes sparkling. How many hours had Lion and his grandfather spent bent over this game, plotting strategies, attempting to win? Time spent together that must have been precious to both of them, though likely neither would admit it now.

Yet some actions spoke far more clearly than words could have. His grandfather had kept the useless chess game, carried it with him even when he traveled. And not to play with other opponents. No, in all these years, Paxton Redmayne hadn't replaced the queen his grandson had taken.

Rhiannon smiled at the precision with which every piece had been placed exactly in the center of its square, reminding her of Lion's desktop, the top of his washstand—every object lined up as if he'd measured the distance between them. Had Paxton Redmayne taught Lion to be so meticulous? How much of the man she loved would she see reflected in his grandfather?

She glanced at Barton, fretting her lower lip. No matter what she discovered, she owed it to Lion to keep the exchange as private as possible. It was the only way she could keep trust with the man who was to be her husband.

To that end, she turned to Barton. "Please forgive me for my rudeness, Kenneth, but if you could remain . . . er, distanced from the conversation, I would appreciate it. Perhaps you would take a walk about the grounds?"

Strange, he'd grown more nervous as well, the closer they drew to Manion House. Now he looked as if he were perched on some precarious cliff edge, fearing he would fall. An inevitability clung about him, mingling with something like despair. He glanced over his shoulder, through the window, longing clear in every feature.

"Perhaps this wasn't such a wise idea, miss," he said. "The captain . . . he might not like it. We could be back at the garrison before—"

A voice as resonant and unforgettable as that of a modern-day Cicero cut in. "It is not often that men appreciate what is best for them. Do you not agree?"

Rhiannon turned, knew in an instant that she faced the man who had poured steel into Lion's spine, who had honed the ferocious intelligence behind those ice-blue eyes she had come to love.

Garbed in old-fashioned knee breeches and frock coat of the finest black satin, Paxton Redmayne stood like an aging emperor, so imposing he seemed to suck up every wisp of air in the spacious room. Wings of white hair swept back from his wide blue-veined brow and were tied at the nape of his neck with a stark black ribbon and diamond buckle.

Well over sixty years of life had done little to wither the powerful width of his shoulders. They were still squared with the same impossible exactness as his grandson's.

She'd come to understand Lion's rigid carriage as an attempt to control his emotions, to hide any weakness, an important ploy because it guarded a heart that had once been too tender. Were Lion's defenses something this man had taught him? Had the two of them shared that fear of showing vulnerability and that innate tenderness?

If so, she should empathize with the grandfather as well. Didn't such wariness always come from an excess of inner pain?

A smile touched pale lips that held a frightening measure of charm, and Rhiannon was disturbed to think of the pictures of exotic snakes Papa had once shown her in his great book of animals—poisonous yet so beautiful it seemed impossible not to want to reach out and touch their jeweled scales.

She barely noticed Barton slipping from the room as the old man swept her a perfect bow. "Paxton Redmayne, your most obedient servant. And you must be the astonishing Miss Fitzgerald."

She dropped into a curtsy. "Please call me Rhiannon."

"Rhiannon." He turned her name into a purr that slid along her spine like the cold kiss of a blade, the sound reminding her of another familiar, frightening one that still haunted her memory. But how? Who?

"I have been most eager to meet the woman who captivated my grandson." His eyes swept slowly up and down her figure, the gaze so keen it seemed almost a physical touch. "You are, er, not at all what I expected."

She stiffened, knowing exactly what he was thinking—that she was scarce beautiful enough or refined enough for Lion. But she could hardly blame the man for speaking the simple truth. She herself had barely believed that a man of Lion's perfection and discriminating tastes could come to care for her. But now she had the glow of passion that had sparked in Lion's eyes to rob such doubts of their power.

She smiled, recalling the gentle way he'd tucked loose tendrils of her hair behind her ear, kissing the tender lobe. "You are hopeless, angel. Completely hopeless," he'd murmured, but his smile had told her that no angel fallen from heaven could be more perfect in his eyes. "Lion doesn't seem to mind my deficiencies," she said.

The old man started, then smiled a smile that should have warmed away any lingering disquiet. "Forgive me. I didn't mean to imply any dissatisfaction. You surprised me, that is all." He shrugged one elegantly clad shoulder. "I am not used to being surprised. For years I prided myself on being able to anticipate Lion's . . . er, particular tastes. But of late he has proven unpredictable. Doubtless a danger of staying too long in this land. It breeds its own kind of madness, I am afraid."

"Or magic," Rhiannon said, her chin tipping up, more insulted by the slight to Ireland than her own person. "But perhaps you have to be Irish to feel it."

Something flashed in the old man's eyes. He seemed to gather himself up. "I've offended you in every way possible, haven't I? No wonder my grandson hasn't spoken to me for years. After such a display you could hardly blame him."

Rhiannon should have leaped in to reassure him. After all, he'd said so little, made such slight blunders, she shouldn't have been so irritated, should she? But there was something vaguely familiar about him. Something disturbing.

No, Rhiannon dismissed her unease. She felt this niggling doubt only because he was the sort of man Papa had always stood against—a man who thought himself lord of the world, all others his subjects. A hazard of being too well born, too wealthy, she would imagine. But this was hardly the time to drag out old prejudices with a man she'd just met, one who would soon be family.

She looked back at the chess set, trying to catch hold of all she had been so certain it symbolized.

"Miss Fitzgerald, this is far too important a meeting to squander by making mistakes. May I confess to you that my estrangement from Lionel has troubled me greatly. My dear child, may we start again?" Paxton inquired with such politeness it made her uneasy.

What in heaven's name was the matter with her? She'd come here hoping to work out a reconciliation, not to let her imagination run away with her the moment Paxton Redmayne opened his mouth.

This man was Lion's only relative, would soon be her own by marriage. "Of course," she said, suddenly aware of how vast the chamber was, how oddly disturbing without Barton's familiar presence. Paxton drew out one of the gilt chairs at the elegant table, attending to her seating with the greatest of chivalry. Then he sank into the chair opposite hers, his brow creased, eyes sharply probing.

"Miss Fitzgerald, I wished only to meet the woman my grandson selected as his wife. Now that I have met you, I wish to be of service to you." An aggrieved aura pulled at the lean planes of his face. "I taught my grandson not to be careless in his dealings with the ladies, but I fear I must guess that in your case he was—inexcusably so. However, such an, er, mistake can be easily remedied without taking such drastic action as marriage."

Rhiannon stared at him, utterly bewildered. "Mistake. I don't understand, unless"—she faltered—"unless you disapprove of me."

"I disapprove of two young people being trapped when something so simple can remedy the situation before it becomes irreparable." He was watching her face, so intently it was almost painful. "Do you understand my meaning, Miss Fitzgerald?"

"No, I'm afraid I don't."

"You are so different from any woman my grandson would be attracted to, and forgive me, but an officer's wife is vital to her husband's career. She must have a certain air about her and certain abilities."

His meaning was clear enough—abilities she obviously lacked.

"Therefore, I can draw only one conclusion: you carry my grandson's child."

Shock jolted through her, leaving her speechless. If only he knew that she'd be delighted to be with child by Lion. But Paxton Redmayne knew nothing of Lion's self-inflicted torture. He believed pregnancy was the only reason Lion would stoop to wed her. Shame spilled fire into her cheeks.

"I assure you," she said after a moment, "that is impossible. There is no child."

Paxton shook his head. "My dear girl, you needn't dissemble with me. I wish only to help you in your trouble. Allow me to offer you an opportunity to return to your former life." He drew a small vial from the pocket of his waistcoat. "This potion will rid you of the inconvenience and the shame."

As horrified as if there were a child whose life was threatened, Rhiannon shrank back in her chair. "There is no child. And if there were—if there were, Lion would be overjoyed! He would never, never want to—to—" She pressed her fingers over her lips, sickened. She stood, her whole body shaking. "I love Lion, and he loves me so much that he would never . . ." Her voice broke. "This visit was a mistake. I never should have come."

The old man swept from his seat with dreadful elegance, his features blade-sharp, his eyes burning. "My dear, you must allow me to disagree. This is a triumph beyond my wildest imagination. Never did I imagine that Lionel had actually forgotten himself so far as to fall in love. I am . . . overjoyed."

Rhiannon stared at him, wary, still wanting more than anything to leave. Yet was it possible that he truly *was* happy for Lion? Never had she seen more genuine pleasure in anyone's face. Pleasure edged with something enigmatic. Yet hadn't it taken her time, patience, to unravel Lion's closely guarded secrets? Was it so strange that his grandfather should be the same?

A laugh rippled from Paxton Redmayne's throat and echoed through the vast halls. "You'll scarce believe the paradox in this, child. I believe I knew your father. Tell me, are you not Kevin Fitzgerald's daughter?"

Recognition jolted through her, icy cold. No wonder her nerves had been raw from the moment the old man had entered the room! She shivered, suddenly certain she *had* heard that laugh before. In her despairing father's study at Primrose Cottage the day her whole life had crumbled at her feet, lost forever. Even the name was familiar . . . the one she had heard Papa say: Paxton.

"How did you know Papa?" she demanded.

He sketched her an elegant bow. "I, my dear, am the man who ruined him."

Rhiannon backed away, sick dread spilling through her. *That* was why Paxton Redmayne looked familiar. His was that face she'd barely glimpsed as a young girl, the eyes that had so disturbed her she'd done all in her power to avoid him. She had even pretended he didn't exist. "You—you were the one who—"

"It would have been a simple enough legal case—if he'd only chosen to be reasonable. He merely had to close his eyes and walk away. But Kevin Fitzgerald never had the wit to know when he had plunged in over his head. What happened to him was inevitable."

"Why? What could Papa possibly have done to deserve what you did to him?"

Paxton shrugged. "Business interests were involved. A fortune made with another man's money, unbeknownst to his wife, er, his widow by that time. She'd lived in genteel poverty most of her life anyway, robbed by her fool husband's schemes. Her future would merely have been more of what she'd always known. No barrister or solicitor in Ireland was fool enough to take up her cause. But Kevin Fitzgerald came charging into the fray like a thrice-cursed Lancelot, armed with his ledgers and a handful of letters to prove her claim."

That was what she had loved best about her father—his love of justice, the heart so brave, so generous, ready to fight for what was right, no matter what the cost. And this time it had cost him, cost them both everything except each other. "Then Papa had proof. There was nothing you could do."

"Innocent child. You think someone as transparent as Fitzgerald could keep such evidence out of my hands for very long? I found where he had hidden the documents, and I burned them."

Rhiannon reeled. Oh, God, what that must have done to Papa—not only to fail in the case but to see all the evidence destroyed, to know that nothing could ever bring it back from the flames. That he had failed, destroyed the widow's chance of a decent life, and brought a monster like this man down upon his cherished daughter's head. "You are despicable."

"No, my dear. I am thorough. Just as I taught my grandson to be. After all that inconvenience, I made certain no one would ever dare listen to Kevin Fitzgerald's rantings again. All those people he'd fought so hard to help, practically beggaring himself and you in the process, they were too cowardly to cross swords with me. It amused me no end to imagine the paroxysms of guilt they must have suffered, watching the two of you wander off in that ridiculous gypsy cart. But even after you'd been turned into beggars, that fool of a father of yours wouldn't leave well enough alone." Paxton's eyes narrowed, cold as stone. "He traveled from place to place, sneaking off, attempting to unearth more evidence. When he did, it became obvious to me that I had no choice."

Icy claws seemed to crush her throat. "What do you mean?"

"I had to kill him. But I was merciful. They say drowning is pleasant, as deaths go."

Rhiannon feared she'd be sick. Her whole body shook. The thought of Lion as a child in the grasp of this monster was horrifying beyond bearing, and her father—her brave, generous-hearted father who was always looking for what was best and brightest in everyone—to not have known the kind of soulless creature he'd clashed with until it was too late.

Rhiannon squared her shoulders, furious for the child Lion had been, and for her father. "I see now why Lion hates you. You are despicable. I'm leaving."

In a move far too swift for a man of his age, Paxton Redmayne blocked the door. "You can't be fool enough to believe I would let you escape after all the trouble I've gone to to capture you." He smiled, his cold eyes flicking to the chess game gleaming in the sun. "You see, my dear, Lion's queen has finally been delivered into my hands."

Lion strode toward his headquarters, fighting back waves of grim satisfaction. He'd been forced to visit a neighboring estate—an irritating interruption when he had so much personal business to attend to. Yet his military duties couldn't stop just because they were inconvenient, more was the pity.

It had been a routine summons—another nervous landlord, Squire Tuttle, shaking in his boots because he'd heard rebel songs drifting from the cottages of his crofters.

A few less than subtle cautions—that was all that was needed, Tuttle had assured Redmayne. A reminder or two of the fate that awaited those who dared rebel against their social betters. But as Lion had guided his mount among the crumbling cottages, dank with poverty, he fought the unthinkable impulse to hand his own gleaming pistol to one of the hot-eyed men glaring at him from the doorways and instruct the Irishman where to aim at Tuttle for the best effect. Ridiculous notion. The Irishman would only end up dead.

But this seemed a land born for lost causes. Who the devil could blame these people for attempting to drag themselves out of such hopeless desolation? Even if it was only for the briefest flash of glory, futile and foredoomed, for that moment in time, at least, they could feel like men again.

Waste had always infuriated Redmayne, as had carelessness, and this English fool in his fine house was guilty of both those vices, and no doubt countless more. He probably cared for his horses better than his tenants and then was surprised when his tenants didn't thank him for his abuses.

Yet, as ragged and beaten down as the Irish were, they managed to look like captive kings and queens—proud, strong, and far more noble than those who lorded it over them. It was a quality Redmayne appreciated more than they would ever know, one he identified with from the days of his own childhood.

No one understood better than he did how much courage it took to remain defiant even when all hope was gone.

He'd come to Ireland, duty-bound to crush rebellion. When had his sympathies shifted from the occupying troops to the people who were supposedly his enemies?

A gradual thing it had been—the winning of his grudging respect—but he did not have the courage to acknowledge the depth of the change in him until Rhiannon stripped away all his masks and made him stare for the first time into a mirror filled with his own reflection.

These were the people Rhiannon loved, those who had traded her eggs and butter, who had gifted her with stories and songs by their hearth fires, sharing whatever meager stores they had. They had cared for his lady when she was alone. Perhaps that was why he'd returned to the manor house and flayed Squire Tuttle with his acid wit.

It had been almost shamefully easy, intimidating the squire. Lion had used every skill he'd gleaned over the years, every brilliant strategy he'd honed, but this time he'd used it on behalf of someone else, to benefit someone weaker, more helpless. It had made all the difference.

Tuttle had been scrambling to better the lot of his crofters by the time Lion was done with him. Doubtless the dread Captain Redmayne would have to give the squire reminders occasionally, but even that might be amusing. He smiled in anticipation, imagining how pleased Rhiannon would be when he told her about his adventures over the dinner table.

It took infernally little to fill him with joy, with pride, with hope, anymore, just the slightest smile from his lady. He shoved open the door to his office, stepped inside. Devil take it, he wouldn't even wait for dinner. He'd tell her now.

"Rhiannon?" He called out.

A great brown and black mass of canine bounded out of her room—Milton, making a deafening racket, barking. Redmayne rolled his eyes heavenward. He should have guessed he'd never be able to persuade Rhiannon to keep the beast in the stable indefinitely. No doubt the cat would be moving in next. But by God, he thought with a grin, he'd draw the line at that horse of hers!

"Down, you cursed pest," Redmayne ordered, surprised at the sudden sting of affection he felt for the motley creature. Milton leaped on him, crumpling the front of his uniform.

"Blast it, dog. I said *down!*" he said more firmly. "Outside with you, at once." He grasped Milton's leather collar, full intending to haul the dog out, when suddenly, a fierce growl reverberated from the beast's throat.

"What the devil?"

Milton wrenched away, and when Redmayne attempted to grab him again, the dog snapped at him, savage. Milton crouched low, whining, scrabbling with his paws at Redmayne's boots. Something cold unfolded in Redmayne's middle—instinct, nerves tempered in battle, or had he caught Rhiannon's intuition somehow, like a fever? Something was wrong.

"Rhiannon?" He called her name again, more stridently, as he stalked into her chambers. Portly Mrs. Webb was tending to some of the new gowns he'd had made for his fiancée. "Mrs. Webb, I'm searching for Miss Fitzgerald. Have you seen her?"

"Humph! Never knew a lass so given to getting her skirts full of paw prints." Mrs. Webb gave a half-hearted swipe at a sky-colored morning dress. "There was a message delivered, and she went runnin' wherever it bade her, I'd be bound. She was scribbling a note when she summoned me to help her change her gown."

"A note?"

"Left it on your desk, she did. But you needn't worry about her any, sir. Sergeant Barton was with her."

Barton? Redmayne's hands clenched, every muscle in his body wire taut as he remembered how the youth had looked when he told him about the deaths of Sir Thorne Carville and Seamus O'Leary. Barton had seemed desperate, terrified, worn beyond bearing, cornered by forces Redmayne didn't understand. And desperate men did desperate things.

He rushed to the desk, grabbed up the letter penned in Rhiannon's delicate hand. "Lion" was emblazoned on the front, that name, so intimate, so miraculous, so tender when used by his lady. The name no one else had used since those vague memories of his father.

He couldn't still the tremor in his hand as he unfolded the sheet of paper. "My love," she had written. "Please forgive me. I'm about to do something that might make you very angry. I received an invitation to dine today at Manion House."

Dine? And he was supposed to be angry? What the blazes? He read on: "Please try to understand, I want so much to help you, and this might be the first step in healing old wounds. Obviously your grandfather wishes for reconciliation, too, or he would not have invited me."

Redmayne's eyes blurred, his blood turning to ice. His grandfather—Rhiannon had run off to dine with his grandfather? God in heaven, that was like an angel sharing a meal with Lucifer himself!

His grandfather had never done anything without some sinister motive—something dark, something deadly, his victim never suspecting a thing until the noose closed about her neck.

And who had delivered his lady into that bastard's hands? Kenneth Barton. Lion's stomach pitched.

He grabbed up his pistol, stalked out into the yard.

"My horse!" he snapped at the groom. The lad stared at him a moment in abject terror at what he saw in Redmayne's eyes, then bolted for the stables.

It seemed an eternity before he returned, but was only a few moments. Redmayne hurled himself on the horse's back, dug his heels into its barrel.

Tossing its head, the horse blazed from the garrison at a dead run. Every hoofbeat hammered at madness and memory inside Lion, setting them roiling.

God in heaven, Rhiannon, his innocent, brave angel—she had wandered into the depths of his own worst nightmare.

Chapter

❧ 19 ❧

Manion House loomed out of the gathering dusk like a beast fashioned of nightmare, distant walls seeming to jeer at Lion as he drove his horse toward it at a dead run. Memories, like necromancers from another world, swirled their dark magic about him, taunting him with shades of other scenes within the grounds of another imposing manor house across the sea in England.

Rawmarsh—another name for hell. His boyhood prison, the place where everything decent and good inside him had been flayed away by the relentless knife strokes of his grandfather's will.

He'd spent a lifetime trying to forget, but he could still remember it all—his despair, his confusion, then the hopelessness, wanting only to die. Yet in the end he had dragged himself out of the morass of his shattered childhood, determined to beat the old man at his own game.

It had been so easy, when he hadn't given a damn about anything, including whether he lived or died. Cold, calculating, mentally stimulating, their battle of wills had been all those things. But with one glowing smile, one gentle brush of her lips, Rhiannon had changed everything. Life, once shrouded in dull gray, was kissed by his fairy maid's magic spell, a sudden blossoming of every rainbow color imaginable. The most beautiful hue of all that elusive tone known as hope.

And yet he was soldier enough to know that Rhiannon's precious gift to him might be the very thing that tipped the odds in the old man's favor or caused Lion to make a fatal mistake. It was one thing to cast the die for your own paltry life. But to gamble with something so rare, so precious, as his gypsy angel . . .

"Damn it, don't catastrophize," he upbraided himself grimly. "The old man is hardly going to sweep her off to a dungeon or hold a pistol to her head. No, Paxton Redmayne uses far more subtle means against his prey. He's merely probing, to see how best to use her against me."

And yet the very notion made him sick to his stomach. Rhiannon—so open, so honest, so trusting— would be only too eager to spill out every secret of her tender heart in some misguided effort to close the breach between grandfather and grandson. He could picture the scene all too clearly: the old man baiting Rhiannon with that poisonous charm of his, revoltingly sincere as he stole her most private thoughts, all the time laughing at her, mocking her for her vulnerability.

Redmayne pressed his mount harder, rage a thick knot in his chest. It would be a violation of her spirit, what the old man was subjecting her to, every bit as real as a violation of the body. No one understood that better than Lion. He had spent a lifetime attempting to bury the memory of it so deep he'd never again have to feel the sick shame, the devastation of innocence. But it rushed back with the force of a dam bursting, every exquisite shard of pain as fresh and real as it was on the day he first realized what his grandfather had stolen from him.

Secret thoughts, hopes, fears. The very essence of his soul. He had been pathetically easy prey—a child alone, robbed of his family and of all he'd ever known. Need had been wild inside Lion then. He'd felt a desperate craving to trust someone, an inborn desire to bond with him, to share pain and hope, joy and failure, everything it was to be human.

He'd never suspected the depths a person could sink to, the ruthlessness, selfishness. The cruelty. But now he knew, God help him. He knew. And he understood the devastation left behind.

The mere thought of his grandfather prying into Rhiannon's soft heart was enough to drive Redmayne mad. But no, he reassured himself. It had taken Paxton Redmayne weeks to excise Lion's vulnerabilities. Rhiannon had been there an hour or two at most. Lion would grab up his lady and get her the devil out of that old demon's clutches before he could do her harm. He had to believe that, or he'd go mad.

More vital still, he had to get a grip on his own emotions. To charge into Paxton Redmayne's domain in this state—all raw nerves and throbbing fury, the hellish past reflected in his eyes—would be more dangerous than racing afoot into a brigade of enemy calvary without so much as a wooden sword as a weapon.

With more force of will than he'd ever expended, Lion slowed his horse as they came within sight of those in the house. He straightened his uniform and the wind-tossed waves of his hair. But there was one damned inconvenient thing he was discovering about emotions: when they were this real, this vital, this intense, they were dashed hard to shove back into their boxes.

He doubted he could have done so for himself, but for Rhiannon . . . He pictured his lady as she was the night they'd almost made love, her eyes shining with adoration. Not as if he were some perfect Galahad—that was the miracle of it. She looked into the face of all his flaws and loved him in spite of them.

With grim determination, Lion forced his features into their accustomed austere lines, willed ice into the blue of his eyes. But he couldn't suppress the sick jolt he felt when he glimpsed Rhiannon's bright-painted gypsy cart parked before the entry. He drew rein and fought to steady his hands.

No, there was no danger of his grandfather firing a bullet into Rhiannon, but if the old man had managed to plant any seed of doubt, of fear, that would haunt her forever, by God, Lion swore he would kill him.

Dismounting, he handed the reins to a groom and strode up to the door. He didn't bother to knock, merely opened the door and strolled in as if he belonged to a far different kind of family, one that would joyously welcome a wandering grandson home from his travels.

A footman came bolting toward him, scowling. "You'll be leaving at once, whoever you are, or—" the servant began, then stopped, a cunning gleam suddenly sparking in his eyes. It was there for the merest heartbeat—expectancy and recognition—even though Redmayne had never seen the man before.

"I regret my tardiness," Redmayne said, "but there was an invitation to dine waiting when I arrived at my headquarters. Surely it isn't too late to join Grandfather and my betrothed?"

"Late? No, sir. I'd say you've come chasing after

your lady with all haste, you have. Your grandfather will be most pleased at your arrival."

Lion fought to conceal a wince. Perhaps he was tipping his hand by rushing in here, yet what choice did he have? He could hardly leave Rhiannon to his grandfather merely to keep his own guard firmly in place! The thought pierced him like a well-aimed bullet. Hellfire, until now, hadn't he always been willing to do just that? Hadn't he considered protecting his own borders far more important than guarding anyone else's? How much Rhiannon had changed him in so little time, resurrecting what was decent, tending what was good, polishing it to a sheen that drove back the darkness. Gratitude made his throat tighten, as well as his resolve. He would die before he ever let his own shadows overtake her.

"Your weapons, sir?" The footman asked stretching out his hands. When Redmayne hesitated, the servant smirked. "Swords and pistols are hardly appropriate dinner wear."

Lion unbuckled his sword, drew out the pistol at his waist, and handed them to the servant. In Paxton Redmayne's house the social niceties had always been observed, and Lion did not expect to need any weapons. It was merely an excess of caution that had made him conceal a small pistol in his boot. But the knowledge that it was there reassured him.

"If you would follow me, Captain." The footman smirked. "I will show you to the red drawing room."

Red. Lion felt a thin sheen of sweat dampen his palms. So the old man had chosen the setting for his encounter with Rhiannon hoping that Lion would come. That could be the only reason for choosing to borrow a house with so many echoes of his distant boyhood prison. Could Paxton possibly know that Lion still saw the blood-colored walls of Rawmarsh when he closed his eyes, too exhausted from beating back the image to fight any longer? Yes. The cruel bastard had wanted to goad Lion, grind the memory into his face—remind him of the chamber he'd been locked in, left to starve. The horrific shattering Lion had felt inside, breaking apart a piece at a time until at last he'd buckled under the strain and bowed to the sadistic son of a bitch's will. Always intricate plots, shrewd, cunning maneuvers. No, there could be little doubt that the old man had orchestrated this with the genius of a master who was determined to make certain Lion remembered every excruciating detail, especially the boyhood feeling that his grandfather was invincible and that Lion's own battles against him were futile.

But he wasn't a helpless child any longer. That chamber had no power over him anymore when matched against his love for Rhiannon. Love. Yes, damn it. Love. The purest, fiercest passion he'd ever known.

Jaw tightening, Lion followed the servant down the hallway to the room, the footman taking obvious pleasure in announcing him to whoever waited within.

"Captain Lionel Redmayne, sir." Unholy pleasure edged the man's voice, setting every nerve in Lion's body stinging with wariness.

But Lion only strode into the room with the casual gait of a man who had done so a hundred times. Braced as he was, nothing prepared him for his first glimpse of Paxton Redmayne after so many years. Lion suppressed a shudder. The old man looked exactly the same as he had the first moment Lion had seen him. Time and mortality seemed to hold no power over him. Had the wily old demon made a pact with the devil? If so, Lion could almost sympathize with Lucifer. This was one time he would wager Satan could lose his own soul to a mortal's sinister keeping.

"Grandfather." Lion swept him a bow, the slight edge to his voice transforming that term of endearment into a cutting barb. He straightened, leveling his eyes at the older man, giving no quarter, asking none. Hate burned in Lion's gut, made bile rise in his throat. He forced his most sardonic smile. "You haven't changed at all."

The old man gave a snide chuckle. "I wish I could say the same for you, my boy. You have changed a great deal. So much that I would scarce have believed it had I not seen the evidence with my own eyes."

"A hazard of growing up, I would assume."

"I would rather say the tragic cost of forgetting every lesson I ever taught you."

"Not *every* lesson." Lion crossed to where the table was still set, the food untouched, one chair wildly askew, as if flung back in a hurry—but why? Because Rhiannon had been desperate to escape this room and the crafty old spider who played caesar within it? Yet her gypsy cart still stood out front.

She would hardly have set out across the countryside on foot, would she? No. No matter how threatened she felt, a horde of grandfathers couldn't have made her abandon that pitiful excuse for a horse she loved so much.

"You always insisted I not be careless," Lion observed. "And yet, forgive me, but it seems you have misplaced my betrothed."

"Ah, yes, your fiancée. When news of your engagement reached me in Belfast, I couldn't resist seeing her for myself." A smile thin as black ice curled Paxton's lips. "Never fear, Lionel. You cannot believe I would be so careless, once a treasure such as Miss Fitzgerald was delivered into my hands."

Lion fought back a chill. He had heard that tone in his grandfather's voice before, the quiet whisper, as lethal as a Japanese blade cutting to the bone. "Where is she?"

Paxton gave a rumbling laugh. "Why, my dear Lionel, you show a most ungenteel interest in this girl—a mere pauper from what I can tell, of no remarkable beauty or grace."

He wanted to fling the old man's words back into his face, rise to Rhiannon's defense. Paxton Redmayne would never understand how fine Rhiannon was, how rare, worth a thousand of any other woman who ever breathed. But it was obvious the old man had already guessed too much. Damned if Lion would give him any more weapons for his arsenal.

He feigned a yawn. "It is considered very bad form to misplace one's fiancée—especially for an officer. Shows an appalling lack of attention to detail. Now if you will be so good as to tell me where I might find her? In the stables visiting a sick horse? Tending a maidservant's toothache?"

He let his mouth curve into something of a sneer, trying desperately to make the old man believe that the accustomed vein of selfishness still ran deep inside him. He needed the cunning bastard to believe Rhiannon was . . . what? An ornament to further his military career? A necessary bauble, much like a dress sword—relatively useless, a damned nuisance at times, but inescapable just the same.

"I should have guessed such a woman would follow such common pursuits as nursing horses and servants. Doubtless she'll have your commanding officers eating boxty bread and boiled potatoes from your table before long." Paxton heaved a long-suffering sigh. "Lionel, Lionel, we have had our differences in the past, but I never expected to find that you had turned into a fool. Someone should rid you of that common Irish wench before you make yourself the laughingstock of the king's army."

Lion brushed a speck of dust from his sleeve, damned if he'd let his nemesis guess what a tempest of fury and outrage and sick, sinking dread had been unleashed within his chest. "Perhaps I wish to make a fool of myself. How better to make a fool of you? Displaying the degradation of your . . . what was it you once called me—your masterpiece? Your life's work, Grandfather?" Lionel spread his arms in bitter mockery. "What do you think of your efforts now?"

For the barest second something flashed in Paxton Redmayne's eyes, something so savage it made Lion's pulse trip in warning. Then it was gone. "You are a rank failure," his grandfather said. "But then, even the most superior of men fail in their efforts from time to time. It is said Michelangelo took a hammer to one of his sculptures, raging at it because it wouldn't speak to him. An understandable reaction when one has been bitterly disappointed."

"Disappointing you has become my life's work," Lion asserted. "Every man must have a purpose. You taught me that."

"And you taught me to choose a more worthy candidate to use my talents on. I should have guessed that in the end you would be worthless, tainted by the absurd morality of your father, no matter how hard I tried to excise it from you."

"Astonishing that he had any morals at all, with you as his sire."

"I? Your father's sire? Let me banish that delusion. I merely claimed that I was so the French authorities would put you under my guardianship."

Lion was stunned at the numbing wave of relief that swept through him. Had he even realized the subtle horror he'd felt all these years, believing that Paxton Redmayne's blood flowed in his veins? A self-loathing so profound it had shaded every breath he drew. For if he was flesh of his grandfather's flesh, was he not capable of anything? Was he not tainted by evil, poisoned, lost, beyond hope?

His grandfather's low chuckle startled him from his thoughts. "Ah, you feel that I've absolved you now, of some enigmatic sin. But there are stronger bonds than those of mere blood. We are alike, Lionel. I knew it from the moment I first saw you."

"I am nothing like you." For the first time, Lion believed it.

"We are far superior in intellect to the paltry fools who bumble about in our path. Admit it. Has anyone else ever managed to challenge you? Who understands things to the depth you do?"

Lion remembered Rhiannon, the gentle probing of her eyes, the magnitude of her loving. Was there anyone who understood the human heart more completely? Even the battered, pain-deadened heart of the boy Paxton Redmayne had attempted to destroy?

"It is possible to know everything yet understand nothing," Lion said.

Paxton rolled his eyes heavenward. "That sounds like something your fool of a father said to me once. Never did I meet anyone who had squandered such potential. Brilliant he was, but so tangled up in doing good, in caring for the brainless peasants, that he squandered his gifts. He was never more than a paltry country doctor, trading his powders for hen's eggs."

"Then I wonder you had anything to do with him."

"Necessity, boy. Fate. A runaway carriage crashed into a crowd of shoppers on a Paris street. Stephen Kane happened to be nearby. He raced through a hideous tangle of crazed horses, overturned carriages, injured people. He tended everything like a madman—efficiently, brilliantly."

Lion tried to grasp this image of a father he could scarce remember. A good man. A brave man. A decent man, so busy fighting to heal others that he'd ignored the danger to himself.

"Several of the victims would have died without his efforts. I was eternally grateful for their distress."

The strange comment yanked Lion back from the scene playing out in his imagination, the desperate groping for some picture of his father—the shade of his hair, the shape of his mouth. But all he could hear was the echo of that deep voice calling him "my little Lion." "You were glad of their distress? Why? Were you conducting some sort of study?"

"No. The chaos gave me a chance to talk to you. Your father perched you high upon a stack of boxes to keep you safe. You were barely four years old, but you sat there so intent, watching everything. Your eyes were so hungry—frightened, yes, sickened by what you saw—and yet it was as if you were devouring everything with that voracious mind of yours. From the first moment I spoke to you, I knew that you were exactly what I had been searching for."

Lion's stomach turned at the image of the small boy perched on the edge of an abyss more dangerous than he could ever know, while his father, oblivious to the devil who had slipped into their lives, was fighting to save others. It was chilling, the thought that if his father had been just a half an hour earlier in his travels they never would have stumbled into Paxton Redmayne's sight. Things might have been so different. Something buried deep in Lion cried out, reaching for that life that had never been, that father he had known for far too short a time. Love he might have known even before he met his gypsy angel.

But much as he craved knowledge of the family lost in childhood shadows, he needed to find his lady, make certain she was safe.

"You've never seen fit to regale me with such family information before. I have little interest now."

"You have no curiosity about who your parents were or why they were in Paris?"

"Rhiannon is my concern."

"Ah, then you are more like your father than I would have guessed. It took me scarce three doctor's calls to discover that he was nigh out of his mind with worry about your sister, who was going blind, despite your father's best efforts.

"Ah, yes, the great healer was helpless," Paxton mocked with a laugh. "It was quite amusing. He'd cast his practice in Ireland to the winds, couldn't even speak French, but hoped a doctor he'd heard of, a specialist neck deep in research, could save what little was left of your sister's sight." The old man chuckled. "Yes, trust the Irish to be impractical. I should've guessed from the moment I knew Celtic blood ran in your veins that you would be impossible to govern."

"I take that as the highest compliment," Lion said, knowing it was true.

"Your father spent every shilling he possessed before he realized the French specialist was a charlatan whose research was an elaborate fraud. By that time the disease that was stealing your sister's sight threatened to take her life as well." A smug smile curved the old man's mouth. "I knew of another doctor, one who might offer him hope."

Lion's hands tightened into fists, imagining his father's helplessness, desperation. Paxton Redmayne prying through a well of soul-deep pain and grief and using that pain against him. "What did you do?"

"I offered him everything money could buy: life for

his daughter, the possibility she might even be made to see again, and more coin than your father could earn in a lifetime. In exchange I asked that he sell me only one thing: you."

Lion's stomach churned at the impossible choice Paxton Redmayne had offered. And at the horrific certainty that Lion's father had taken it. He must have, for Lion had ended up in Paxton Redmayne's hands. Then why did Lion suddenly find himself asking? "Did he do it? Sell me to you?"

"Your father? He wouldn't be reasonable, of course. No, you were his pride and joy, his little Lion." Paxton sneered at the endearment, the brief phrase that was all Lion remembered from the man who had tossed him high in his arms.

"Then how—"

"I took what he wouldn't give me."

Lion imagined countless scenarios—God knew, he'd seen the lengths his grandfather would go to to get his own way. "Then I have family out there somewhere?"

Paxton made a show of unfurling the ruffles at his cuff. "It would have been most untidy, leaving them alive to search for you. And they would have. They were the sort to turn the world upside down until their dying day. I merely hastened that day, to save myself the inconvenience."

"That day? You're talking in riddles!"

"I told you from the beginning your family died in a fire. I neglected to tell you that I paid someone to set it."

Redmayne's blood ran cold—for the death of the family he'd never had a chance to know, and for other, more immediate reasons. By thunder, why would the old man be babbling about such a thing? Confessing to murder? What possible motive could he have? Lion didn't dare think about it. He'd lose control of his hate, his fear.

"That was all a long time ago," he said. "I'm scarce going to be outraged regarding people I don't even remember, if that was your intent."

"No. I was merely reminiscing about the lesson it taught me, what I had to avoid the next time. The merest breath of parental love can taint a child forever."

Next time . . . The words unnerved him with all they hinted at. But he had to concentrate on finding Rhiannon, sweeping her off somewhere safe. There was no limit to the lengths his grandfather would go to.

"I haven't the time to bandy insults with you," Lion said. "I have duties that await me. Summon Rhiannon, and I won't intrude on your hospitality any longer."

Cunning shone beneath Paxton's lowered lashes. "Are you afraid for her, boy? You needn't be. She's in the tender care of your most trusted aide, Sergeant Barton." The old man caressed the words as tenderly as if he were testing the sharpness of a blade, watching in pleasure as a thin line of blood rose where it touched his skin. "Barton has proved to be a most useful young man time and again. I cannot thank you enough for your astuteness in making him your aide."

There could be only one meaning to that. Barton had been in league with his grandfather all this time. The youth had somehow been shackled into doing the accursed devil's will, and now Barton had escorted Rhiannon into the jaws of one of Paxton Redmayne's diabolical traps.

Lion fought rising panic and hardened his voice. "Where is she, old man? Tell me or—"

"Or what? The first thing I taught you was not to

make threats you cannot carry out. Any move then becomes ridiculous, blustering like a helpless child."

"This is no threat, I assure you. Take me to Rhiannon now, or I'll have to kill you." He made the words sound careless. Could the old man know how many times Lion had imagined killing him late at night, when the horror filled his dreams and slicked his body with sweat? He'd imagined killing Paxton Redmayne as the only certain way to end his legacy of evil.

His grandfather laughed, pacing to a small table that looked frighteningly familiar—the gaming table, set with its exquisite chess pieces. Had the old man carried it with him all this time? "Ah, you are reduced to making threats. What did I teach you? To consider every issue from your opponent's point of view. Think, Lionel. You can hardly blame me for attempting to reclaim what you stole from me the day you left Rawmarsh: the queen."

"Rhiannon is not part of the game."

"Fine, boy. You wish to reclaim your lady? I'll take you to her."

Without another glance, he strode from the room, leaving Lion no choice but to follow. Up the winding staircase, higher, higher. Finally, at the end of a long corridor, Paxton flung wide a door. Rimming the edge of the building high above the stone courtyard was a curved balcony, bound by a waist-high rail of carved stone. Beyond, the Irish countryside undulated like a glorious painting, too vivid to be real.

"What the devil?" Redmayne growled under his breath, every instinct coiling tighter within him.

"You asked for your lady. I merely intend to present her to you."

Lion followed his grandfather around the bend of the balcony, then froze in horror. There, balanced on top of the narrow stone rail, a white-faced Rhiannon stood, bound hand and foot with nothing between her and the deadly fall to the cobbles below.

What held her there, so still? She was pinned between stone and sky by the barrel of the pistol clutched in Kenneth Barton's shaking hands as he stood an arm's length behind her on the broad sweep of the balcony.

Lion's heart stopped. Christ's blood, if she didn't fall off, the accursed turncoat would shoot her, most likely by accident more than intent. What the hell— had the old man gone mad? These were scarce his subtle methods. Nothing could be cruder than a lone woman balanced between life and death this way.

"Lion." She mouthed his name, desolation in her eyes.

It took every bit of strength Lion could muster not to race to Rhiannon, devil take the pistol fire, and snatch her to safety. But that was what the old man was waiting for, hoping for. If this was the hellish revenge he'd arranged for Lion's sins, then the slightest move would set into motion some fiendish trap that would cost Rhiannon her life.

He had to outwit his grandfather somehow. Had to keep his head. It was his lady's only chance.

"C-Captain," Barton stammered. "I—I'm sorry. I had to—"

"My grandson isn't interested in your paltry excuses, Barton. Your true loyalties are evident enough under the circumstances."

Betrayal ripped deep, and Redmayne hated himself for trusting anyone, especially this boy with his spaniel eyes and his weak, traitorous heart. He'd warned Barton about the death of O'Leary and Sir Thorne. God save him, had Redmayne's own words sealed Rhiannon's fate? Had Barton sold her to Paxton Redmayne in a desperate bid to save his own life?

"What did he use to manipulate you, boy?" Lion demanded. "There is still time to tell him to go to the devil."

Barton shook his head, misery etched in every line in his face. "It's too late. You don't understand."

"I understand this much. Only a coward points a gun at a woman, Barton. You want to fire at someone, boy? Shoot me, if you think you're man enough."

A low sob broke from Barton's chest, but the pistol never wavered.

Careless, Lion berated himself. That last comment had been devastatingly careless. Offering himself in Rhiannon's place—he might as well kill Rhiannon himself and be done with it. The old man would know Lion's own death would be easy, whereas the death of the woman he loved . . .

"You are wasting your time berating him," Paxton said. "Barton and I understand each other completely, do we not, Sergeant?"

The youth's Adam's apple bobbed crazily in his throat, his eyes glittered wildly, as if he desperately wished to speak. But Barton only nodded, his jaw clenched white-hard.

Lion couldn't afford any more mistakes. And yet hadn't his grandfather stumbled as well? The old man himself had grown desperate enough to resort to crude methods. Whatever had unsettled him so, precipitated this madness, was chipping away at Paxton Redmayne's legendary control.

Lion had to find a way to use that flaw against him. *Think,* he told himself fiercely. He had to remember everything he'd tried to forget—the hours of plotting strategy, trying to pry into his grandfather's inscrutable mind, exploiting any weakness, digging away at the tiniest chip in his armor.

Only twice in all the games they'd played had his grandfather lost his legendary icy calm—tiny revelations of true emotion that Lion had been discerning enough to see. Both times it had happened because the old man had lost control of the game between them—not the game on the chessboard but rather the grander, larger contest of wills.

Exploit it, damn it, Lion told himself fiercely. It may be Rhiannon's only chance.

With that, Lion chuckled, crossing to the rail, leaning against it with mock negligence. "I can hardly look at this whole scenario without blushing," he said. "Don't you feel a trifle absurd, old man? Such theatrics! It must be dashed demeaning to be reduced to melodrama. You who prided yourself on being so clever, so subtle. Reduced to the most pedestrian villainy."

His grandfather's eyes glinted. "You don't fool me with all your bravado. You never did. I can taste your weakness, the way a wolf scents blood on the wind."

"How unappetizing that must be—especially when sipping fine wine. I should imagine it would quite ruin one's enjoyment. Surely you can pause long enough in this Cheltenham tragedy you've concocted to tell me what has reduced you to such a pathetic level."

"If you only knew."

Lion took heart from the new edge in his grandfather's voice.

"This is yet another stroke of brilliance far beyond your comprehension," Paxton said.

"Yes, yes. No one has ever thought of this before—point a gun at a woman to bend someone to your will." Lion rolled his eyes heavenward. "It's hardly worthy of you. But then, at your age, you are perhaps growing a bit senile, losing some of your wits. Nothing to be ashamed of. It's common enough, I am told."

"Losing my wits? I think not. When I'm rotting in my grave, I will still have three times the cunning you ever did."

"An interesting claim. I'd be willing to test it—right now, in fact, if you'd have the good manners to die."

"You first, boy. Though you've been exceedingly stubborn about it."

Redmayne stared into his grandfather's eyes, saw the truth there. "You. It was you who wanted me dead at Ballyaroon."

The old man didn't deny it. He merely smiled, like a diabolical child caught torturing one of the cats in the stables.

"I probably should have guessed, but the method was so crude I didn't believe it possible. Hired assassins, Grandfather?" Lion said. "It lacks style. In fact, it shows a considerable lack of imagination, not to mention rank cowardice."

"You think name-calling can upset me? As if I cared any longer what you thought!"

"The question is why? Why this sudden interest in hastening my death? True, I've been tampering with your business interests for quite some time, so I imagine you've sustained some losses. But despite my best efforts, your financial empire is hardly ready to tumble down. Forgive my curiosity, but I can't help wonder—"

"You want to know why I wanted you dead?" That ageless face darkened with hatred so intense it struck Lion like a fist. "It is simple enough. What is the first thing I taught you at that chessboard?"

Lion remembered countless punishments, each more grueling than the last, filling him with terror every time he made a move upon the marble board. "Win at any cost."

"I won't lose to you."

Lion stared into the old man's face, realization sweeping through him. "That is it!" he said, astonished. "You know you already have lost, and you can't bear it. In spite of everything you've tried to do to me, every way you've fought to trap me, tangle me up in your twisted plots, I've managed to escape. I won, didn't I, Grandfather? The day I turned my back on Rawmarsh and on you and joined the army."

"No. You were a mere posturing fool. I was certain—" Paxton broke off, eyes narrowing—at what? Lion scrabbled desperately to comprehend his silence. A misstep?

"Were you certain I would come crawling back?" Lion asked.

"I'd made you fit for nothing else. Nothing but matching wits with me. You were mine, to use against my enemies."

"No. I was never yours. You knew it. That was what you couldn't forgive. Years of work. Years you'd invested in me. For what? Perhaps it's understandable, why you would want to kill me. Fine. Do it."

"No!" Rhiannon choked out, stopping his heart as she all but lost her balance. "Lion, don't say that!"

He fought valiantly to ignore her, knowing it was her only chance to survive. Praying for the first time in his life that the angels or the fairies she was born of would protect her, he shrugged one uniformed shoulder. "You want me dead? Go ahead, grandfather," he urged softly. "Have Barton, your toadie, point his pistol at me and pull the trigger. No one knows better than you how little value I place on my life. It is immaterial to me whether I live or die."

God, how his grandfather had taunted him when

he was a little boy, desperate to end his pain, shattered by loneliness, wanting to join his father in heaven. Lion could still hear that mocking voice, insinuating itself into every moment of his day, jeering as he pressed a penknife into Lionel's small hand. "It's sharp enough, if you dig the blade deep. Go ahead, boy. Kill yourself. Show yourself a worthless coward to your father."

Even now Lion could remember the reaching-out inside him, grasping for the world beyond. Peace. He'd wanted peace. But something had risen up inside him, determination not to grant Paxton Redmayne such a victory over his spirit.

But the boy who hadn't cared if he lived or died had vanished, the man who had charged into battle without fear was gone. It was a lie now, his seeming carelessness. A lie. His whole being screamed for life. He had been awakened from a living death by the kiss of a fairy-born beauty. Was it possible the fates had merely taunted him, dangled paradise before him, meaning all the while to snatch it away?

"You say you wish to win at any cost, grandfather. Kill me. Your victory is complete." He wasn't naive enough to believe the old man would ever let Rhiannon live, to be a witness, after all she had seen. But if he could manage to distract his grandfather and unsettle Barton, goad them into making a mistake, he might be able to get the pistol he'd concealed in his boot and blast Barton into eternity while flinging himself at his grandfather and driving him over the ledge.

Death—never in all his years of soldiering had he wanted to deal it out more than he did at this moment.

But he could see the triumph in his grandfather's face, the cunning. "Perhaps I was a trifle hasty in hiring the assassins. I can only thank you for delivering into my hands the chance at a far more poetic vengeance. You see, it's meaningless to steal a life from someone who doesn't mind dying. But if there is someone innocent who might die as well, perhaps that would be the most fitting revenge of all."

Lion winced at the inevitable, his grandfather homing in on his deepest fear. "Killing Miss Fitzgerald? A rather untidy bit of vengeance—"

"But an effective one. However, I can be merciful. She loves you, fool that she is. What think you, Lion? Shall I kill her first? That way, she won't have to watch you die."

Instinctively, Lion started forward.

"Turn your weapon on my grandson, Barton," his grandfather snapped. "He's showing a distressing tendency to interfere."

Ever so slowly, the boy came about. Lion stared, stunned at the torments of hell shimmering in the boy's eyes. He grasped at that last, desperate hope.

"Barton, think," Lion pleaded. "You don't want Rhiannon's blood on your hands."

God help him, even if he managed to reach his pistol and shoot Barton, it would be too late. His grandfather would have shoved Rhiannon, sent her hurtling down to be crushed on the cobbles below. Hopeless. It was hopeless. Still, he had to try. He glanced at Rhiannon, certain his lady must know it, too.

"I love you." Rhiannon's voice, so certain, so sure, her eyes trying to convey something. A message. A warning he could feel like a physical battering in his chest. Her gaze flicked to the bank of windows to one side. Did she see a way out? Some escape that he didn't see? The sun's glare obscured everything beyond the glass. Christ's blood, what was she trying to tell him? There was no time. . . .

Supremely confident, his grandfather paced toward

Rhiannon, bound and heartbreakingly helpless upon the narrow ledge of the railing.

"It will be over quickly, my dear. You'll not suffer long—not nearly as long as you would have had you actually been so unfortunate as to wed my grandson."

Terror clawed at Lion's vitals. "No! Rhiannon—"

Something flashed in her eyes—grief and love and deadly determination. In a burst of insight, Lion realized that she meant to risk everything by hurling herself at his grandfather, knocking him off balance, risking a hideous death to give Lion the slightest chance to fight back. By God, he wouldn't let her!

With a feral roar, Lion launched himself at Barton, but in that heartbeat the boy twisted to one side and fired. Rhiannon's scream pierced the air.

Seconds sped past but seemed to spiral out forever as his grandfather drew a small pistol and aimed it at Lion. Murder gleamed in the old man's eyes.

Lion scrabbled for his own pistol, but it was too late. His grandfather's gun exploded. At that instant a blur of movement lunged between Lion and certain death. His lady? The sound of lead striking flesh sickened him as a cry of pain reverberated through Lion with more force than any bullet.

Lion swung around as Barton stumbled and crashed into the old man, driving Paxton Redmayne hard against the edge of the waist-high rail. For an instant the old man teetered, grasping for anything to hold on to, the stone, Barton's arm, the folds of Rhiannon's gown. But his hands closed on air. He fell with a hellish shriek as Barton crumpled at Rhiannon's feet.

"Lion, the window!" Rhiannon screamed as a shadow moved beyond the glass. Lion drew his own concealed pistol, aimed, fired. A burly servant toppled through the shattered panes, dead, a pistol clattering from his limp hand.

Lion wheeled, half crazed with relief, as he saw Rhiannon safe on the stone balcony, but he recoiled at the sight of her bound arms cradling Barton.

"Barton betrayed us," Redmayne growled. "You don't owe him any pity."

She turned her heartbroken gaze up to him and drew her hands away from the front of the boy's shirt, blood blossoming there, a hellish red. "You owe him your life. Didn't you see, Lion?" Tears coursed down her face. "He hurled himself in front of the bullet your grandfather meant for you."

"The devil he did! I saw—"

"What your grandfather wanted you to see. And you believed it. The man inside the window had orders to shoot me if Kenneth didn't do as he was commanded—play the betrayer, to hurt you, make you careless."

Lion groped for sanity, some logic in all this madness. His grandfather had always been a master at trapping him in illusions. And he'd been fool enough to stumble into another one.

"Then the boy— He didn't betray us?"

"He tried to shoot your grandfather, give you a chance," Rhiannon choked out. "He loved you. Enough to die in your place."

Lion crumpled to his knees, gathering Barton into his arms. Never before had his aide seemed so young. Blood slicked Lion's hands as he fought to put pressure on the wound in the boy's side. "Damn you, boy, don't you dare die! That's a direct order, do you hear me? Keep breathing until I give you leave to stop!"

Fierce, desperate, he willed his own strength into the lad. But what use was it? Strong as Barton was in body, there had ever been a vulnerability about the boy's spirit. A need to be trusted, be accepted, be loved . . . and by whom? The cold bastard of a commander who had been so ready to believe the boy a traitor?

A hundred scenes rushed through Lion's mind— countless signs of Barton's affection, his desperate need to please. Generosity Lion had been too much of a fool to appreciate. If Barton died, *Lion* would be the one who had killed him—his betrayal of the boy far more powerful than any bullet ever molded.

"Help him, Rhiannon." Lion's voice shattered. "You have to heal him. I have to tell him . . ."

"Tell him what, Lion?"

"That I love him. The damned fool . . . The damned *fool!*"

Lion's eyes burned with tears—the first he'd shed since he was a child. They stung at his eyes, diamond hard, as he buried his face against the boy's limp body.

Chapter

❧ 20 ❧

Rhiannon tiptoed into the infirmary, her heart aching at what she saw: Lion, sitting in a chair beside Kenneth Barton's bed. The legendary fastidiousness of Captain Redmayne was gone: his uniform jacket was cast heedlessly upon a table, his shirt hung open at his throat, and his rolled-up sleeves clung to his powerful arms in damp patches from smoothing cool cloths over the boy's feverish body.

She caught her lip between her teeth, fighting back the tears that would only deepen Lion's suffering. For in the week and a half since he'd carried Barton in his arms on the hellish cart journey from Manion House, no man could have suffered more.

Paxton Redmayne's legacy was a vengeance of more exquisite pain than the diabolical man could ever have known. Not once had Lion left the boy's side, willing his own strength into Kenneth with the same grim determination with which he'd spooned broth down the boy's throat, as if Captain Redmayne could force even death into full retreat.

But Rhiannon had seen far too many injured creatures to believe that wanting someone to live, however fierce the desire, would make it so. Imperious death claimed who it would, and abandoned those left behind to grief and guilt and the painful task of putting shattered lives back together a piece at a time.

But this time it wasn't fair, Rhiannon thought sadly. Hadn't Lion been tormented enough? Didn't he deserve this one last chance to be whole? Because if Barton died, Rhiannon knew a part of Lion would die, too. With each breath Barton drew, the boy was fighting not only for his own life but for a life Lion had never known.

Even the lowliest private seemed to sense it. The whole camp was holding its breath, knowing with that all-too-human instinct that no matter what the outcome, nothing would ever be the same. How could it be, when their commander was no longer the man they knew and had feared for so long.

Most astonishing of all, another man had often stood sentinel with Lion through the endless nights, silent, yet strong, bracing. Lieutenant Williams, his ages-old eyes alive with suffering and with an understanding that seemed to say without words, *I know what you feel, what you'll lose with this boy. But the pain is far better than being only half alive.*

A kind of bond had formed between two soldiers who, without the intervention of a twisted old man, might have been far more alike than they knew.

And yet what would happen if Barton died?

Her heart hurt as she crept into the room, laid one hand on Lion's slumped shoulder. He started, glanced up, soul-shattering grief in his eyes. "Tonight." He grasped her hand as if she were the only lifeline in a world gone mad. "The doctor says the crisis will be tonight. If he doesn't wake up, he never will."

"I know." Rhiannon leaned against him, stroking a

lock of hair back from his forehead. "But we have to keep believing."

"You've always been better at that than I am. Give me something to believe in, angel. Don't your fairies have some sort of charm? Magic to make a warrior well? Barton is the bravest lad I've ever known."

Rhiannon wondered how anyone could heal this grief, lashed as it was by self-blame. Death was so dark, so final. From the beginning of time, men had woven tales of other worlds more beautiful than the one they knew, where pain and grief were swept away forever. She kissed the crown of Lion's head, painting such a world for him now. "Here in Ireland some of us believe that the fairies snatch away our heroes. Maybe they'll carry Kenneth off to Tir naN Og, where he'll be forever young. And he'll marry a fairy maid, and live as a hero until Ireland sinks into the sea."

Lion gave a broken laugh. "I fear Barton is from Cornwall."

"So was Tristan, yet he found and loved Isolde, and their love became a legend that has lasted for all time. But if you're so certain that Kenneth won't be given entrance to the land of the fairies, then I suppose the lad will just have to remain here with you."

"I'd sell my soul to see him live," Lion vowed.

"That would hardly be fair, since it seems you've just gotten it back."

Lion drew a shuddering breath. "I just didn't know that it would hurt so much and that I would feel so damned helpless. In my arrogance, I thought by sheer will I could force the fates to do as I pleased. But then you found me and changed everything. Barton hurled himself in front of that bullet, and I knew . . ."

"Knew what, my darling?"

"That nothing else mattered—not control or intellect or power. Nothing was stronger than love."

She knelt down, laid her head upon his lap, her arms curved about his legs. "Then you've learned all there is to know, except for one thing."

He gazed down at her as if she held all the answers in the universe. "What is that?"

"How to forgive yourself." Please, God, Rhiannon prayed, don't let him learn that lesson at Kenneth Barton's graveside.

They kept vigil for hours, watching moon shadows etch silver across the walls, while the valiant boy fought for his life. Dawn streaked the horizon when Rhiannon saw it—a subtle change, the slightest shift in breathing, the tinge of difference in the pallor of his skin.

"Lion," she whispered, clasping his hand.

He stared down at Barton's face, and Rhiannon saw the fear there, so raw, so new.

"Barton?" Lion growled, leaning over the young man. "Barton, open your eyes, boy! That's a direct order."

Rhiannon watched, her heart swelling with joy as Kenneth's eyes fluttered open. His lips curved into a shaky smile. "Captain . . . sir. Never st-stopped breathing," Barton said.

"If you had, I'd have court-martialed you, even if I'd had to track you down in hell, boy."

"It wasn't hell. It was someplace . . . beautiful. Everyone was happy, never sick or . . . or tired. I wanted to stay, but kept hearing your voice, ordering me back."

Lion, holding death at bay by sheer will. Lion, reaching from this world into the next to hold the boy's hand. The image made Rhiannon's eyes burn, her heart burst with hope and gratitude.

"I had to order you back," Lion rasped. "You see, I—I can't manage without you."

"I knew that. That's why . . . tried to keep watch over you and your lady at night. Keep . . . anyone from . . . hurting you."

Redmayne gazed down at the boy, suddenly realizing what Barton had done. He'd stood guard outside the window through countless nights, until he was half sick from the strain of it. "That was why you looked so haggard. You weren't sleeping. I thought . . ." Shame darkened Lion's cheeks. "I thought you were suffering from a guilty conscience."

"I was, when I saw that invitation from your grandfather. I knew you'd be angry if I showed it to Miss Fitzgerald, but I hoped . . . The man was your family. Even if you were estranged, I was certain he wouldn't want you hurt. I thought if I told him what was happening, he could protect you in ways that I never could. I knew I would be betraying you, but I was willing to risk it if it meant you'd be safe. Christ, you should have heard him laugh when I confessed everything to him—my fear for you, the danger you were in. I never guessed that he was the one who wanted you dead."

"Paxton Redmayne has fooled far more worldly men than you. Hell, he poisoned my mind so much I almost didn't warn you when I heard that Sir Thorne and O'Leary had died. That would have left you completely vulnerable, as unsuspecting as a babe while my grandfather plotted to silence you. Damn, what a fool I was! I'm sorry I ever doubted you, lad. Forgive me."

Barton's eyes widened. "But it wasn't your fault. Nothing to blame yourself for."

"You're wrong, boy. I should have believed in you. You'd proved yourself to me time and again, if I'd merely had the wit to see it." Lion hesitated, almost shy. "Perhaps you could find it in your heart to forgive me if I make amends and attempt to show you how much I value you."

"Sir, there's no need. All is forgotten."

"I'll never forget, Barton. All you risked for Rhiannon and me. Please give me a chance to begin again. I intend to wed my lady before the week is out. Do me the honor of serving as my groomsman."

Delight and reluctance warred in Barton's pallid face. "But, sir, it's hardly proper. I'm only a sergeant. I shouldn't—"

"You saved Rhiannon's life. You saved *my* life, though I damn well didn't deserve it. Please, boy. They say the groomsman should be the bridegroom's best friend. You've been my only friend for a very long time. I was just too blind to see it."

"Are you certain, sir? I don't want you to regret—"

"Please, Barton. Say you will."

"Sir, it would be an honor. And, sir, I would never betray you, I swear it."

"I know, boy." Lion said, with certainty in his voice. A victory beyond measure.

Without another word, Rhiannon slipped out of the room, knowing she would never forget the sight of Lion bending over the young man, his face fierce with affection as he grasped Kenneth's hand.

No wedding in the fairy kingdom could have been more magical, Rhiannon thought, her head still whirling with visions of flowers and beautiful gowns, dashing soldiers and heavenly music as she glided the silver-backed brush through her hair. Yet the most magical image of all was that of her husband—so strong, so proud, his love written openly in the warm blue of his eyes.

He'd pledged her his heart, and no lover could ever have taken that vow more seriously than Lion. For the gift he gave her was a heart so new and still so filled with wonder that it awed her, humbled her.

And now, after so much waiting, they were bound together forever, in the way she had dreamed of so many restless nights. She stood, gazing shyly at herself in the mirror. Her hair glistened in a satiny veil that fell to her waist. Her body, scented with lavender, was covered by a gossamer nightgown as fragile as the new dreams just born in Lion's eyes.

She prayed that she could be worthy of the love of this man who was only now beginning to discover who he truly was.

A soft rap on the door made her heart leap, and she turned toward it, her hands trembling. "Come in."

Slowly it opened. Lion stood there, still resplendent, his dashing uniform replaced by a robe of pewter gray. "I wanted to give you enough time to make ready, to do whatever it is you ladies do." His mouth curved in a wry smile. "I'm only beginning to discover that I can be a very impatient man."

Heat stung her cheeks, but she let all her eagerness, her anticipation, all her dreams of what was to come, shine in her eyes. "I'm impatient, too. I've waited so long for you."

"Forever, it seemed." He groaned. "I didn't want to dishonor you. You're too precious, too fine." He crossed to her, gently stroking his knuckles along her cheekbone. "But now . . . now you're my wife, Rhiannon. Mine." His voice roughened, fierce. "It almost makes me believe . . ." His gaze flickered away, a shyness stealing into that face that could be so austere, so controlled.

"Believe what?"

"There has to be magic in a world that could give a fairy maid like you to a man so lost."

"You're not lost anymore, Lion. You'll never be lost again."

"No." He framed her cheeks with his hands, his thumb skimming ever so gently the silky curve of her freckle-spattered nose. "How can I ever be lost again, when the fates gave me my very own light to guide me out of the darkness? A light I can keep forever."

"It wasn't the fates. It was the fairies. They led me to you. But now that we both know you're Irish, I'm not sure who sent them from the land of Tir naN Og—my mother or your father."

"Irish. It's strange, but this land always held a fascination for me. In fact, there was a time when I was chasing smugglers, and led my soldiers down into souterrains—tunnels beneath a ruined castle. Legend claimed the fairies would deal death to any enemy of Ireland who dared tread there. I almost fell, Rhiannon, but something—like an invisible hand—bore me up. Do you think . . ."

"It was your father."

"My father was a doctor, sweetheart, not lord of the fairies."

"But he *was* a hero. Everything your grandfather said made that clear—the way he fought to save your sister and the people in the accident, the way he loved you."

"He must have been—a hero, I mean. I remember so little of him." The grief of that, the loss, would forever be etched in Lion's face.

"But he remembers everything about you, Lion. I'm certain of it. Love never forgets."

He raised his eyes to hers, so uncertain. "Will I, Rhiannon? Will I ever forget the things that happened?"

She wished she could erase all the doubt in that beloved face. "No. I wish I could take away all your pain, but if I could, it would change you, Lion, and I wouldn't do that for all the world. Maybe you would have met another woman, married her, loved her, long before I found you in the standing stones."

"Never. You are the only woman I could love. Didn't you say it was destiny?"

She nodded, overjoyed that he believed it too.

His brow creased. "But my grandfather . . . I can't sort it all out. It's so strange. All those years when I was a boy, he was always there, forcing me to work harder, willing me to be stronger, making me think, no matter how damn painful it was. I've fought him my whole life, hated him. But he's the only family I remember. Now he is dead. Rhiannon, I don't know what to feel."

She closed the space between them, slipping her arms about his waist. "Sometimes feelings are like that. Confusing. Uncertain. In time, you'll sort it out."

Lion gave a humorless chuckle. "Knatchbull visited this morning with some astonishing news. It seems grandfather was so busy attempting to kill me that he forgot to change his will. I inherit everything."

She swallowed hard, wondering what that would mean to this man who was still so tentative, finding his way. She wished she could erase it all with a sweep of her hand—the memories of that evil man, the pain Lion must have suffered deadening his sensitive heart, the loss of the family that loved him so much they would never betray him, no matter how desperate things got. But that was impossible. No matter how one wished it, none of it would disappear. And now he'd been left something tangible that would remind him.

Lion crossed to the nightstand, his fingers caressing the wooden queen Rhiannon still kept there. "I thought perhaps I should go to Rawmarsh. The house

—

where he raised me. Maybe it would help me lay things to rest."

She suppressed a shudder. Return there? To his grandfather's house where he'd been hurt so terribly? What if there was only more darkness waiting for him there? Twisted connivance, traps laid by a man who only knew how to hate?

"I would hate to leave you," Lion said, "but I would never ask you to take a bridal trip into hell."

"Nothing could keep me from going with you, Lion. Don't you know that? I love you. I'd march through hell and gladly at your side."

His lips curved in a smile, unabashedly vulnerable, daring to let her see how much he'd wanted her to go with him, needed her beside him. "I put you through so much, bastard that I was. But I'll spend the rest of my life trying to be the man I see reflected in your eyes."

"I want you, Lion. Only you. Wonderfully flawed, perfect as the fairy cup that once belonged to my mother." She wanted so desperately to drive away every shadow, even the slightest cold whisper of his grandfather's presence—the one stroking darkness into her lover's face. "Make love to me, Lion," she pleaded. "Please. I need you so badly." Rhiannon needed to bind him to her forever in a circle of magic no evil ghost could break. "We'll make our own memories now, love. New ones. Bright ones."

Lion's arms curved about her, drew her tight against him. "I love you, Rhiannon." He kissed her cheek, her temple. "God, what a miraculous thing. To feel it. To say the words aloud. Still, it frightens me. To love anything this much. It's dangerous. If I should lose you . . ."

"That is the most magical thing about loving. You can never lose it if it's real. Even death has no power over it. The love still remains. When I was alone in the caravan, I still felt my papa's love. And you . . . even when that evil man locked you away, Lion, your father's love still surrounded you, made you strong. Kept that spark of light, of goodness, in your heart no matter how hard your grandfather fought to kill it."

"There were times in my dreams when I could almost feel and see my father's arms reaching out for me, hear him calling to me. I thought I was imagining it, that it was wishful thinking. But now . . ."

He shrugged, a man bred to logic, only just glimpsing a magical world beyond it. "I know that if you were in trouble, loving you the way I do, even death could never keep me from reaching out to you, finding a way to let you know I love you. Do you think it's possible that my father did just that?"

"I'm certain of it," Rhiannon said, thanking God that the desperate boy Lion had been had felt that love, though he hadn't quite believed.

Lion looked away. "I wish I had known him."

"We'll find everything we can about your family, Lion. And when our own babes come, we'll tell stories about your father and mother, and they'll live again."

"Babes . . . I'm not certain what kind of a father I'll be, sweetheart. . . ."

"You'll be the father you imagined all those years when you were alone. The father Paxton Redmayne stole from you."

"Yes. I will." It was a vow as precious to her as those he'd spoken in the church. Lion, believing in his power to give love. To have others give it back. "And I'll be husband to you—everything you've ever dreamed of . . . if you'll show me how."

"There is only one thing I want now, Lion." She let a wicked twinkle spark in her eyes. "You in bed."

Lion laughed, the sound so beautiful and free. "I want that too, love. Very much."

He scooped Rhiannon up in his arms, carried her to where their bridal bed stood, sprinkled with rose petals, scented with banks of flowers that filled every vase, gifts from the ladies who had come to love their captain's bride.

His fingers trembled as they started to unfasten the tiny buttons at her throat, but Rhiannon caught his hand, held it. "No, Lion," she surprised herself with her own boldness. "You saw me before, when we almost made love. All this time I've dreamed of seeing you. Please, Lion. Let me, first."

His eyes burned, impossibly blue, filled with a need he didn't try to disguise. He said nothing, only took her hands, placed them on the sash that bound his dressing gown about his narrow waist.

Mouth dry, Rhiannon worked the knot, trembling at the delicious contrast of sleek satin and the skin that had warmed it. Mysteries she revealed one finger stroke at a time. The satin gaped open, and she pressed a kiss against the hair-roughened plane of his chest, reveling in the feel of him beneath her mouth, the scent of him, leather and horses and sandalwood, more intoxicating than any elixir the fairies had ever brewed.

Rhiannon eased the cloth down the slope of his broad shoulders, let it fall to the floor. Golden, heartbreakingly perfect, he stood before her, as beautiful as some ancient god of the sun.

She let her eyes sweep from the arches of his feet, up the long, powerful legs and narrow hips, to the shaft that made him a man. Swallowing hard, she raised her gaze up the flat expanse of his belly, to the swaths of muscle that created the landscape of his chest.

Cheeks burning, she lifted her eyes to his face—the face that had haunted her dreams, carved with the masculine beauty of a fairy-tale prince, frozen by an evil spell. But the spell had been broken. The features that had been like a closely guarded secret were softened somehow, his smile tender, his eyes inviting her in. Into Lion's heart. Into a soul reborn.

Tears stung her eyes as she strained up on tiptoe, pressing her lips against the melting warmth of his. With a groan, Lion slanted his mouth over hers, drinking her in, his lips searching for flavors he knew he would find there—the richness of love, the spice of passion, the indescribable sweetness of new beginnings.

Rhiannon moaned softly, her hands skimming his chest as his tongue slid between her lips, searching out the secret recesses of her mouth. He loved her with a tenderness that made her quiver, his fingers struggling with buttons and waves of fabric as fragile as the wings of a fairy. He caught his breath when he drew away and stripped her nightgown over her head.

Her hair cascaded down about naked breasts, and his gaze darkened, growing hotter still as he stared at her. Deft, strong fingers traced the line of her throat, down to the tip of her breast. "You take my breath away, angel. I don't deserve—"

She stopped his words with her lips, kissing him into silence. "The fairies gave you to me. Who are we to question their wisdom?"

"I know who I am. The luckiest man who ever lived—because you are mine, Rhiannon Fitzgerald Redmayne, to love until the end of time."

The light glowed in his eyes, fierce protectiveness, awe at the miracle that had drifted into his hands. Rhiannon could sense it, feel it echo in the depths of her own heart.

She gasped as he trailed hot kisses down her breasts, his mouth hungry as it fastened on the aching tip, suckling her as his hands explored secrets farther down her body.

With exquisite mastery, he stirred the need that had tormented her for so long, every stroke of tongue and fingers, palms and warm, seeking lips driving her higher, making her need wilder, hotter.

"This time nothing will stop me," he whispered against her hair. "You'll be mine, angel. Mine."

She cried out as his finger eased deeper, slipping inside her, testing her untried opening. She bit her lip and arched into that devastatingly intimate caress as he stroked inside her, his thumb flicking ever so softly against the tiny nubbin hidden within the silky, damp petals of her body.

She felt it again, that primitive pulse, that untamable sense of something building inside her, pushing harder and harder at her control. She wanted it—the sweet, sweet madness she had tasted once before, the wildness of it, the magic. But this time she wanted Lion with her as she plunged into heaven.

"Please, Lion," she gasped. "I need you . . . want you inside me."

He gave a low growl, and she marveled at the depth of the passion suffusing his handsome face—emotion in its rawest form, pure desire, a lifetime of need.

He eased himself between her legs, and she felt the blunt tip of his shaft nudge against her, hard and hot and wonderful, promising fulfillment. He hesitated, kissing her mouth. "Rhiannon, there will be pain. If I could take it for you, I—"

"I want you, Lion. I've waited for you for so long. My whole life. Please, come inside me."

With soul-shattering tenderness, Lion bracketed her hips with his hands and slowly embedded himself deep in her body. The burning pain between her thighs was nothing in comparison to the burning pain in her heart—a loving so complete no tale of magic could ever compare.

He thrust against her in a rhythm so precious it seemed her heart would surely burst. Tears coursed down her cheeks as her body reached for the magic, a magic more beautiful than any she had ever known.

It burst, so bright she was blinded by it, so miraculous she knew she'd never forget this moment, Lion's cry of fulfillment, the arching of his body into hers so deep as he spilled his seed inside her.

She clung to him, stroking his sweat-sheened back, holding him as if she never wanted to let him go. It seemed forever before he lifted his face from the waves of her hair.

"Whatever happens when we go to Rawmarsh, I want you to know this," he murmured, his eyes glistening with tears. "I'm going to make it up to you, everything Paxton Redmayne stole from you. Primrose Cottage is to be your first gift. I'm going to buy it back for you, Rhiannon. Knatchbull is already seeing to it. You'll have a home again."

She smiled, so touched she thought her heart would shatter. "Oh, Lion, it wasn't the walls that made it home. It was knowing someone was waiting for me, eager to see me, to tell me little things—that a new litter of pups had been born in the barn or that a double rainbow shone over the glen. Someone to laugh with over a plate of burned cookies, someone to kiss the finger I blistered when I baked them. Don't you see, Lion? The moment you took me in your arms I was home—the only home I'll ever need."

Lion groaned, holding her tight, so tight. "If that is what home is, my love, I swear you'll never be without one again. My arms will reach out to hold you until the last day of forever."

She clung to him, so fierce, wishing they could stay forever in this bright room, with the soft shield of their love around them. But tomorrow waited beyond the curtained window, and with it the journey to the place where Lion's nightmare had begun.

Chapter

❧ 21 ❧

Lion stared at the portrait, stunned that it still hung in its place of honor in Rawmarsh's blue-and-gold gallery—Paxton Redmayne, dressed as Socrates in flowing Grecian robes, while a slender, pale boy of seven with intense blue eyes and silver-gold hair stood stiffly at his knee, a modern-day Plato drinking in brilliance at the feet of his incomparable master.

It had amused Paxton no end, the tableau he'd arranged. It still showed in the smugness about his mouth, the wicked twinkle in his eyes. Yet there was also a hint of pride in those arrogant features as he gazed down at his protégé.

Wishful thinking on the part of the artist? Lion wondered. Or had there been something more in the man—something that Lion had never seen?

Rhiannon squeezed his arm, her touch warm and familiar in the morass of confusion and ages-old pain Lion had been plunged into the instant he crossed the threshold of his boyhood home.

"How sad," she said softly. "Teaching is the most noble of aspirations, yet he turned it into something twisted, evil."

"When I first came here, I had nightmares that this place was the labyrinth in the Greek myths that Papa had read to my sister and me. This vast, writhing maze of corridors and chambers. There was no escape, and always, waiting within, there was this hideous monster who wanted to devour me. It was so terrifying, Rhiannon. Every step I took, every word I spoke . . . I never knew what would bring that cold rage of his down on my head."

"But you survived, Lion. You escaped the labyrinth, and were so brave and strong that you even managed to free yourself from all the traps he set in your own mind."

"I'll always believe that was your doing, my love. That, or the fairy magic you've spoken of. But now this—it's all so strange."

He crossed to an exquisite globe balanced on the shoulders of a wood-carved Atlas. "The monster is dead."

"He has no power over you. He never really did. Perhaps that is why that pride in the picture turned to something poisonous."

"Master Lionel?"

The voice made him start, turn to see the housekeeper. The woman's face was rounder, more lined with age than when he'd marched away to join the army. Yet there was something different in her eyes— fear—that had always been there. Yet an almost pleading light, an anxiousness, a sorrow. "I hope you've found everything in order."

Lion grimaced. This was Paxton Redmayne's household. Everything had always been agonizingly in order, with a painful precision that left no hint of humanity, not so much as a flicker of warmth. Even the servants who had lined up to greet their new master had seemed as lifeless as the lions carved into the gray stone. Only their eyes betrayed them. Dread, confusion, uncertainty.

Most of them had spent their lives in service to Paxton Redmayne. Now their livelihoods teetered on the whim of the tall young officer who stood before them, a man grown from the boy they had seen tormented so mercilessly.

Despite his own confusion, Lion felt a sharp sting of pity. Did they fear he would take vengeance on them now for failing to help him?

"Mrs. Smith, you needn't hover, nor should you be afraid," he said with that new gentleness in his voice that never failed to surprise him. "Tell the rest of the servants their positions are secure. I realized long ago that all of you were as much his prisoners as I was."

Tears welled up in the woman's eyes. "I always knew you were far too bright for 'im. Too strong. Aye, and too good. That was what he could never forgive you for."

"If there are any people who need to be taken care of—servants too old to do their work, crofters in need of tools or cottage repairs, please let me know. Grandfather had a way of neglecting such things, as I recall. I wish to see that they are taken care of before I go."

"Yes, sir. That's good of you." She hesitated, fretting a bit of braid trim on one of her cuffs. "There is one matter." Her voice tripped with nervousness. "I didn't set it before you earlier because . . . well, there were nothing legal drawn up, and I had to see for myself what kind of man you'd grown into before I . . . I could trust you with it."

Lion winced, thinking how different Mrs. Smith's reaction might have been if he'd strode into Rawmarsh two months ago—a cold, hard man, more dead inside than alive. It was impudent of her to hold something back, but how could he blame her for her caution? "What is it?"

She still looked a trifle uneasy, as if she wasn't certain she'd made the right decision. But then she glanced at Rhiannon and seemed to take comfort. "I knew that Mr. Paxton was up to some devilment. When I heard he'd tried to kill you, I knew the real reason."

Lion swallowed hard, fear stirring in his gut. A reason to kill the man you'd raised as a grandson. One you'd watched grow from a boy . . . Perhaps he didn't ever want to know. Yet Lion hadn't been of Paxton Redmayne's blood. Their relationship had been an illusion, hadn't it? And wouldn't understanding the hate that had finally pushed Paxton Redmayne over the edge help Lion put this to rest?

Mrs. Smith sucked in a steadying breath. "If you and your lady will follow me, I'll show you."

Lion nodded, and with Rhiannon on his arm, went after Mrs. Smith. But as she left the gallery and made her way to the rear of the house, his muscles tightened, his own steps slowed. Winding stairs spiraled up, dark stairs he'd climbed many times. He wished to God he could tell her to stop, turn, and run back out into the sunlight where he could breathe again. But Rhiannon's hand on his arm, the love radiating from her touch, sent her strength flowing through him, her complete faith in him, her healing of both body and heart.

"These were my chambers when I was a boy," he explained, fighting to keep his voice steady.

"Yes." She looked up at him, sorrow and complete understanding in her eyes.

At the top step, Mrs. Smith fetched a heavy key from her vast ring, slipped it into the lock. "Sir, I did what I thought was best, hiding what I did."

What the devil was it? Some information about his family? Some shard of his past?

"Open the door, Mrs. Smith," Lion said, wishing he could bar the portal forever.

Her hand trembled as she shoved the door open. It was the same, Lion thought numbly. All the same, as if he'd just left the schoolroom for a lesson in swordsmanship with Signor Tidei. Lion stepped into the chamber where he'd spent countless hours, the walls lined with books, maps pinned on every empty surface. His heart wrenched in pity for the boy he had been.

"I see nothing different," he said. "Where is this great revelation, Mrs. Smith?"

"Hidden away, sir, where you tried to hide when you were a wee lad."

The tiny cubbyhole under the eaves; he'd folded himself up tighter and tighter inside the place, trying to disappear. But it was futile to attempt to hide from Paxton Redmayne. Lion had always been found.

Slowly he crossed to the hidden nook, leaned down to peer into it. His heart stopped, his breath caught in his throat. "Christ's blood!"

A small, pale face peered up at him, round-eyed with fear.

"A child!" Rhiannon gasped, disbelieving.

"The master brought him here two months ago, poor mite. Vowed he'd not make the same mistakes he made with you, sir. That this time, he'd not be so soft."

"No. God, no." Lion couldn't bear the pain of it, the hideous wrenching of staring into that small face that reflected all his terror, all his confusion, the pain of the boy he had been. The thought that someone else had suffered at Paxton Redmayne's hands made

Lion's knees buckle. He knelt down before the shadowy nook.

I should have killed the old man years ago, so he could never hurt anyone again, his own guilt screamed in his head. *I should have killed him.*

"Sir, the lad is that terrified, he is, of gentlemen. They hadn't many but fearsome cruel ones in the poorhouse where the master found him."

A poorhouse. So the child had exchanged one kind of hell for another. Lion wished to God he had Rhiannon's gift for healing, for soothing pain. He should step away, let her reach out to the child with that incredible gift she possessed. But his own understanding of the child, terrifyingly complete, held him there, gentled his voice.

"What is your name, boy?"

"T-Tommy, sir." His whole little body shook.

"Tommy. Don't be afraid, lad. No one is going to hurt you ever again."

Big eyes stared in disbelief.

"I know how frightened you've been," Lion said. "There was a time when I was frightened, too."

The lad pointed a stubby finger at Lion's uniform. "You're a soldier. Soldiers are never afraid."

"That's not true. I've been afraid many times as a soldier. And even more times as a lad. You see, this was my room when I was a boy."

Tommy's mouth dropped open displaying two missing teeth. "You—you're *him?* The other boy that used to belong to Mr. Redmayne?"

"Yes." Lion glanced up at Rhiannon, drew strength from the love in her gaze. She stood a little apart, trusting him with the boy. She had complete faith in his power to help Tommy, Lion realized, even if he had none.

"You killed Mr. Redmayne," Tommy said. "Mrs. Smith told me."

"He tried to kill me, Tommy. And my wife."

"Because he knew if you found out 'bout me, you'd come an'— an' you wouldn't let him keep me. He told me all 'bout you."

So that was the reason for the hired assassins, the clumsy plots. Yes, the old man had known that Lion would come.

Lion winced, wondering what the old man had said to Tommy—lies, the most loathsome kind, no doubt, to twist the boy, terrify him. "Why don't you get to know me yourself, Tom, and then decide what you think about me?"

"I already know. I heard the servants whisperin' how brave you were. How hard you fought 'im. It made me think . . . well, he couldn't take everything in my head unless I let him."

"That's right, boy. You were right."

"But it got terrible hard. He locked me up in this room, all red, and I was so scared an' hungry."

A hot ball of rage shoved at Lion's ribs, seared his throat.

"But then . . . then I found something, an' I wasn't so scared anymore. Mrs. Smith said it b'longed to you."

Tommy scooted out; he was so thin, his face pale, his eyes old. He stood in front of Lion, the image of everything Lion had been. Tommy dug one hand into his pocket.

Ever so slowly, he unfolded his fingers from bits of gold, tiny gears, the bent hands of a watch. Lion's father's pocket watch.

He reeled, staring down at it, remembering the hideous sound as he had crushed it beneath his own boot heel, the devastation as the last link with his family shattered. In the middle of the night he'd crept out of his bedchamber and found the pieces of the watch in the rubbish heap, hidden them away. Years later he'd meant to go back to Rawmarsh for them, but it had hurt too much whenever he thought of it, and his guilt and shame had kept him away. In the end he'd folded up the memory so tight, buried it so deep, he'd all but forgotten it. He wanted to forget it.

"It's broken," Tommy admitted, abashed. "I didn't break it. I swear."

"No," Lion said, aching. "I did. Crushed it beneath the heel of my boot. I still have nightmares, remembering." He glanced up at Rhiannon, remembering his humiliation the first night she'd heard him crying out as he relived the watch's destruction. "Grandfather wouldn't let me out of the Red Room until I destroyed the watch."

Lion heard Rhiannon's soft gasp of horror, sorrow, felt the brush of her fingertips against his shoulder.

Tommy looked up at him, so sad, so knowing. "Why did he make you do that?"

"The watch belonged to my father. I loved him, you see." Lion reached out with a finger to touch a tiny gear. "Father gave it to me to play with. That night someone set our house afire. My father, my mother, and my sister all died. This was the only thing I had left to remind me of them."

"He wouldn't like that," Tommy said with a shudder.

"No."

"Mr. Paxton, he kept askin' an' askin' 'bout my father an' such before he took me from the poorhouse. But I never had a father. Never had a mama, either. If I did, it would hurt terrible bad to break something they gave me. Now your papa's watch is ruined," Tommy said, stirring the pieces with his finger.

"No. You see, that's what I didn't understand then. We can take all these pieces, Tommy, and put them back together again. We can fix it."

"Will it be just the same?"

"No." Lion admitted. "It will never be just the same. But in a way, it will be even better."

"That's impossible."

Lion studied little Tommy's face, seeing the intelligence his grandfather must have seen, and the promise. But even more clearly Lion saw the sensitivity that not even the brutal denizens of the poorhouse had stolen from his baby-pink lips, the desperate need to trust, to believe. Thank God that in the two months his grandfather had kept the boy, he hadn't managed to crush him.

"You see, Tommy, the watch will be even stronger because it survived in spite of everything it went through. My wife taught me that." He glanced up at Rhiannon, saw tears shining in her eyes. "You are just like this watch, Tommy. You'll be even stronger, even braver, when we fix what grandfather tried to do to you."

The boy caught his lower lip between his teeth. "Maybe I'm too bad to fix. The man at the workhouse said my mama threw me away, just like my papa did. Mr. Redmayne was the only one who ever wanted me."

The boy's words clawed at Lion's heart. He glanced up at Rhiannon, a desperate plea in his eyes. She understood him, answered him without a word. Only a tearful nod that offered everything, not only to Lion but to the little boy standing before them, so alone.

Lion turned back to Tommy. "I want you." His voice broke. He reached out, touched the boy's cheek.

Hope flared in Tommy's eyes; then wariness shadowed it. "But what about her?" He pointed at Rhiannon.

Lion laughed, gathering Tommy into his arms. "I'm certain she wants you. She's always finding things nobody else wants to love. She has a horse no one can ride, and a dog who runs into trees. And she found me, Tommy, when I was broken and alone."

Rhiannon stepped forward, knelt down. "You see, Lion and I just got married, and there's only one dream left that I have that hasn't come true: to have a little boy of my own."

Joy blushed the boy's cheeks, squeezing Rhiannon's heart. All her life creatures in pain had come to her, sought her healing, that warmth something she had always cherished, always known.

But it was Lion whom Tommy turned to. He flung his arms about Lion's neck, so tight, so trusting, as Lion carried him away from the dark room and out into the light.

It was near midnight when Lion came to bed, weary, yet miraculously at peace. "The watch is all but mended. It needs only a piece of glass to cover the face. Tommy helped. He's as smart as a whip, that boy."

"He is."

"Rhiannon, you don't mind— Perhaps it wasn't fair of me to ask you to decide about the boy so swiftly."

"I knew I wanted Tommy from the beginning. The instant I saw your face as you looked into his eyes."

"You've taught me so much, lady. How to open my heart. I was so certain I didn't deserve love. Even when you cared for me, I thought it was because of your generosity, your goodness, not because of anything worthy in me. But Tommy—I think he's beginning to love me, too. So there is a chance that I might be someone worth loving after all."

Rhiannon slipped her arms around him, held him tight. "I knew that all along, from the first moment I looked into your heart."

"I didn't want you to," Lion confessed. "Didn't want anyone to. I was so afraid of what you would find."

"I found something more beautiful than any dream I'd ever dreamed, Lion." She smiled, loving him. "And no one has ever had more practice at dreaming than I have."

Lion had learned to love. Her gallant, battered knight had broken the evil spell at last. And now he would teach another boy who needed love so badly.

Her heart nearly burst with joy as Rhiannon raised her lips for her husband's kiss, certain that in all the world of fairies and legends there was no greater magic than this.

UNDER THE BOARDWALK

Linda Howard, Geralyn Dawson, Jillian Hunter, Mariah Stewart, and Miranda Jarrett

A DAZZLING COLLECTION OF ALL-NEW SUMMERTIME LOVE STORIES

○ **Under the Boardwalk**
Coming in July 1999

Kimberly Cates
□ **Briar Rose** (now available) 01495-1/$6.50

Laura Lee Guhrke
○ **Breathless** Coming in July 1999

Andrea Kane
□ **The Gold Coin** Coming in August 1999

Tracy Fobes
○ **Heart of the Dove** Coming in August 1999

Sonnet Books
Proudly Presents

LILY FAIR
KIMBERLY CATES

Coming Soon
from Sonnet Books

Turn the page for a preview of
Lily Fair. . . .

The wild Irish hills seethed like a giant's cauldron, a baffling mixture of rugged stone, lush green meadow, and lacings of mist broken by patches of sky that glittered as bright and blue as a fairy's wing. Even the trees seemed human, reaching their roots like fingers into earth pulsing with the passion and pain of a land at war with itself.

Legend claimed the Tuatha de Danaan, the fairy folk who had once ruled the island, had lost a great battle but defeated their mortal enemies in the end by melting into trees and hillsides, stones and streams, fleet red deer and the most cherished reaches of people's memories.

Now another battle was being fought for Ireland—a war between druid gods of earth and saints' God in heaven. Yet, though Caitlin of the Lilies had been raised within the holy confines of the Abbey of Mary of Infinite Mercy and loved the sisters there—their gentleness, their faith—she understood a truth they could never comprehend.

No matter how many saints hallowed Irish ground, no matter how many monks inscribed manuscripts of impossible beauty upon the island's seaswept shores, Ireland would always have a pagan heart.

She could feel its steady throb no matter how determinedly she bent her head in prayer, the voice of the land calling to her, wild and sweet. *You can never be like the rest of them, Caitlin of the Lilies, for you belong to me.* She had fought it, sometimes feared that indefinable *something* that made her different from all the others. In the end she had surrendered to the invisible barrier that separated her from the practical world of the nuns. And yet never once in twenty years of life had she been able to deny that it existed.

Whatever spell had been cast upon the night she was abandoned at the druid altar was real. And never had she felt its pull more strongly than she did today. *Her* day. The day twenty years ago when Reverend Mother had found her, a newborn babe wrapped in the robe of a chieftain.

Caitlin glanced back at the walls of the abbey, knowing that there were plenty among the Reverend Mother's pious flock who disapproved of her yearly pilgrimage to the block of stone with its ancient writings. They charged her to spend the day fasting and in prayer, to resist her shameful link to things heathen. Yet how could she? It was the one time in the year she had something to hold, something to touch, to assure herself that the voices in her dreams were real. . . .

She shivered in anticipation, her bare feet light on the cool moss as she raced through the trees, certain the yearly offering would be there. She could almost feel it—the cool stem of one perfect lily between her fingers. She could nearly smell it, the fragrance whispering sweet possibilities. The precious knowledge that someone beyond the abbey walls still cared for her.

Whoever had abandoned her had not forgotten her. And somewhere in the wide world Caitlin had never seen, a mother, a father, a whole family might wait to claim her.

She could not suppress a sting of guilt, a sense that she was ungrateful. No mother, real or imaginary, could have loved her more than the mistress of the abbey. And yet, had not Reverend Mother been the one who first guided her steps along the path to the druid stone, with a secret sorrow, a wistfulness in the nun's mist-gray eyes, as if she knew that this was where Caitlin belonged, no matter how much Reverend Mother might wish otherwise?

Caitlin felt a twinge, but she promised herself that after she delighted in the lily and the wondrous imaginings it always brought, she would go to the Reverend Mother's cell and show her the perfect flower. She would lean against the older woman's knee as she had every night since childhood and wrap herself tight in real love that never faltered. *Love that should be enough,* a voice inside Caitlin whispered.

Nay, she would not tarnish this day with regrets or self-recriminations. Reverend Mother always wished her to feel joy on these journeys. From the beginning, she had understood the questing spirit in Caitlin, the restlessness of a young girl who had never seen the wonders of the world that lay beyond the abbey.

How many times had the prayerful lips curved with indulgence as she told Caitlin her own memories of the outside world? The great fortress where she had grown up, favorite daughter of a mighty warrior. The thrill of cattle raids, the adventures spun by bards about the hero Cuchulain. She had said other things as well, confided her regret over the heartbreaking rift between her and her beloved father when she had refused to marry any one of a dozen suitors, choosing instead the life of a nun. Reverend Mother had hinted quietly of different dangers that were transformed by the whisperings of other nuns into wickedness and sin, horrors so unspeakable that women had fled to the abbey to escape them.

Yet in spite of all the tales she heard, Caitlin had fashioned the Irish wilds into an innocent girl's dream where all women were brave and every man a hero, and each year a perfect lily drew her closer to that magical place.

Caitlin grimaced. Not that she had had much success imagining the bold, handsome heroes. From the beginning, the abbess had told her it was possible that one day she would leave the abbey, that it was even possible marriage might be her destiny.

Yet the only example of a man Caitlin had ever seen was Father Columcille, a wrinkled gnome with a bulbous red nose and rheumy eyes she had watched with great interest as a child, certain they would pop out of their sockets at any moment.

In the end, the men in Reverend Mother's tales had become creatures elusive and mysterious, as deliciously fantastic as the pagan gods Cuchulain had fought. But it did not matter, Caitlin thought with a toss of her head. It was *her* world, *her* imaginings, and today was the one day in all the year she could venture beyond the abbey's stone walls to taste the magic of that world just a little.

She rounded a tussock of heather, saw the trees thinning, the sun falling across her in great bars of light. Suddenly she slowed her steps, uncertain why. Did she feel the reverence in this old and holy place? Was she hoping that perhaps this time the mystery of her birth might be revealed? Or was her hesitation something simpler—the knowledge that once she walked through the last archway of oaks and crossed to the great slab of stone to claim her lily, the enchantment would be over for yet another year?

One hand smoothed a cascade of raven locks. The other settled the folds of her simple robes about her, but no power on earth could ever tame the exhilaration sparkling in her fairy-blue eyes.

Intent on making the delight last as long as possible, Caitlin fastened her gaze on the ground, carefully placing her bare feet in an effort to avoid spring's first blossoms that scattered the seldom-used path.

Her fingers tightened in the rough cloth of her robes, and she caught her bottom lip between her teeth as she glimpsed the base of the massive stone. Ever so slowly she let her eyes trek up the gray surface, past intricate carvings she could not decipher. Sucking in a deep breath, she raised her gaze higher, to the broad top of the druid altar, the rugged cradle in which her lily had always lain.

Caitlin froze. She could not speak, could not breathe. There, upon the altar, lay a man, his dark lashes pillowed against high-slashed cheekbones. Did he sleep? Or did he lie here in some sort of fairy enchantment? Part of the magical spell that had bound her from her birth?

He might have been Cuchulain, called back from the land of heroes, so powerful was the long sweep of his body, rugged planes and hollows, corded muscles barely disguised by the linen of his shirt and the thick wool folds of the garment wrapped around him.

Hair the sleek brown of a stag's coat was threaded with strands of fiery red that snagged the sun. The waves glowed rich and thick against the tanned planes of a face as fiercely beautiful as any peregrine's. His nose, an arrogant blade, was strong as the shortsword bound at his waist, his cheekbones carved in a high, proud arch. But it was his lips that held

Caitlin transfixed. Lips impossibly soft, unspeakably sensual, unbearably masculine, above a stubborn jut of jaw. The mouth of a poet, a bard, captured in the face of a warrior.

She swallowed hard, drinking in the sight of him, certain that if she gazed at this man for an eternity she could never have her fill. One glimpse, and her world had altered utterly, forever.

Was this what the lilies had promised? The mysteries that had always surrounded her? Was this, then, her destiny? This man?

Or *was* he a man, built of bone and sinew? Was he mortal at all? She trembled at the thought. Could it be possible that he was something far different—an offering from the ancient ones who had melted into the trees and the mountains, setting Ireland aglow in countless shades of green, feeding the island with the life in their souls? Could this magnificent creature be woven of that beautiful magic? For her?

The thought was terrifying in its sweetness. Yet could this encounter have any meaning besides fate? Every year there had been a lily waiting for her on this day. Now he lay in its place. . . .

Filled with wonder, she reached toward the hard column of his arm, but it seemed wrong, a cold way to begin an enchantment. Moved by an instinct she barely understood, she leaned toward him, felt the heat of his breath against her own cheek. He was real, she thought numbly. Real.

Closing her eyes, she pictured his awakening when she brushed the hot satin of that poet's mouth with her own. Summoning up her last bit of courage, Caitlin lowered her lips to his.

A roar shattered the clearing, a flash of sinew and hard, grasping hands catching her in a bruising grasp. She tried to scream, but in a heartbeat she was sprawled on her back on the stone, a crushing weight pinning her down. Caitlin struggled, tried to scream, but a hard hand crushed down on her mouth.

Balling her hand into a fist, she swung with all her might, catching her attacker on one high cheekbone, her knee driving instinctively for the vulnerable flesh between his thighs. With a grunt of surprise and pain, the beast rolled off her. "Hellcat, you all but unmanned me!" a rough voice snarled.

Her vision cleared, and she found herself staring into a face as fierce and pagan as any warrior god the druids had ever dreamed. She felt a horrible sense of loss. The sleeping hero she had found vanished forever.

Green eyes pierced her so deeply that she could not breathe. "I thought your Christian God said to love thy enemy," the man sneered with a scornful glance at her habit, "not knock him senseless."

Caitlin scrambled back, her legs so tangled in her robes she could not get to her feet. "Wh— who are you?"

"They call me Niall." His mouth hardened further still. "Niall of the Seven Betrayals."

What kind of man could he be? One whose very name proclaimed his infamy? Caitlin's gaze flicked to his, and she saw her revulsion register in those fierce green eyes. His lips curled in the harshest smile she had ever seen.

"You are wise to be wary of me, madam."

She hated him for sensing her fear, hated herself for letting it show, no matter how well founded that fear might be. Drawing the tattered remnants of her pride about her, she tipped her chin up in what Reverend Mother always called her fairy queen expression—one that, at the moment, made it evident that she wanted nothing more than to command some minion to cut off his head.

"Did you steal my flower?" she demanded, as incensed as if he had robbed the treasure of Tir naN Og itself.

If nothing else, she had set him off-balance. "Steal?" he echoed. "A flower? What the devil for?"

"It is supposed to be there. On the druid stone."

"Let me assure you that if I ever decided to turn thief, I would not waste my time stealing an accursed *flower*. Why the blazes it should matter so much to you, I cannot begin to guess." His eyes flicked down the coarse homespun of her clothes, and he laid one powerful finger alongside his jaw. "Then again . . . perhaps I can. Meeting a lover, are you? I wonder if your abbess would approve."

"I— I am not! She— she would—" Caitlin cut off her stammerings, her cheeks burning with embarrassment and indignation. She wanted nothing more than to slap the smug expression off the man's face.

"So you *are* from the abbey. You might be of some use to me yet." Something in his voice terrified her. "I have ridden three days without sleep searching for the abbey of St. Mary's. Could not find the accursed thing. Finally fell asleep on that rock of yours. Perhaps it was fate. Now I will not have to stumble about, searching, any longer. You can show me the way."

Caitlin stared in disbelief. This warrior, intimidating enough in a chance meeting, was far more frightening seeking the abbey. And he wanted *her* to lead him to the walls?

She shuddered, thinking of the Sisters who had raised her—so gentle, so compassionate, so trusting in the protection of their God. She reeled from the sudden realization that all the things she loved about them left them terrifyingly vulnerable.

She struggled to keep from imagining what sort of damage this giant of a man—this warrior—could do to a flock of defenseless women. "What business could you possibly have at the abbey?" she demanded.

Disgust and impatience sparked in the warrior's hard eyes. "I come to claim a wench."

Caitlin crossed herself. "G-God help her."

Niall gave a snarling laugh. "She will need far more help than your puling God can offer."

"Wh-who . . ." The question snagged in Caitlin's throat, a hard, barbed thing. She knew before he spoke, felt it—a horrible sinking in the pit of her stomach.

"They call her by some absurd name. Caitlin of the Lilies."

"Nay!" Caitlin gasped, foolish childhood dreams crumbling into nightmare. "That is impossible!"

Holy Mary, why had she not guessed? Why had she not suspected that what the other sisters had warned her of, feared, was true? That the lilies were sweet poison luring her to disaster instead of a fragrant path to some wondrous destiny?

Terror drove sudden strength into her limbs, her hands tearing loose the tangled skirts as she scrambled to her feet. One last glimpse of that implacable face burned itself in her memory; then she ran, back to everything she had loved yet so long taken for granted.

But no matter how fast her feet flew, Caitlin knew the truth. The abbey walls could not bar a man like that forever. Tears streaked her cheeks, hot, hopeless, sick with certainty. Even Reverend Mother's love could not protect her now.

Caitlin felt countless eyes upon her as she ran through the gate, the bevy of sisters gaping when she dragged the heavy bar across it as if an invading army marched against the abbey. Sister Luca, a plump woman who often nodded to sleep over her prayers, dropped the bundle of carrots she had been clutching and hastened toward her, alarm in her moon-shaped face. "By Jesus, Mary, and Joseph, child, what has happened?" she asked, brushing the dirt from stubby fingers. "You look as if a horde of devils is at your heels!"

"N-not a horde." Caitlin shuddered. "One is enough!" She was shamed by the tears that stung her eyes, but she could not stop them. "Wh-where is Reverend Mother?"

Luca's cheeks went white. "In her chamber, I think. But she had some private meditation to attend to. She asked not to be disturbed."

Caitlin cast a glance back at the wooden gates, half expecting to hear the thunder of a battering ram, the bellow of the devil's voice, at any moment. A man of the sort she had found in the druid grove would be wise enough to follow her to the abbey. And once he found it, he would not be thwarted by such a paltry barrier as the abbey gates for long.

Caitlin grasped the old nun's sleeve. "Whatever happens, Sister Luca, do not open the gates. You cannot let him in! I beg of you!"

"Let *him* in? A . . . a man?" The old woman crossed herself with fierce resolution. "Never, by the sacred blood of St. Patrick!"

A little comforted, Caitlin wheeled and raced into the ancient stone building. She wound through chambers where she had skipped as a child, played hoodman blind, learned to recite her prayers. A place where danger had never even dared scratch at the window in the form of a childish nightmare.

Her hands shook. Her heart thundered. Reverend

Mother would make everything all right. Forever calm, infinitely wise, she would think of some way to help her.

Caitlin rounded a corner, plunged into the Reverend Mother's cell. She froze, the sight so blessedly familiar, the place so filled with peace it seemed almost possible that the scene in the druid grove had been nothing but a wicked dream.

Fine boned as the most fragile bird, yet exuding incredible strength, Reverend Mother leaned over a humble wooden chest, holding something up into the brightest shaft of light from a sliver of window, doubtless so she could see it more clearly with her failing eyes.

Caitlin was stunned to realize that it was the robe she herself had been wrapped in as a babe: folds of white linen, exquisitely embroidered with birds and horses, interlacing designs worked with thread of gold. Caitlin had thought it had been given away to the poor years ago, like every other worldly possession that came into the convent.

Reverend Mother straightened, doubtless alerted by the sound of footsteps that she was no longer alone. The saintly woman turned, her cheeks pink as if she had been caught in some dark, indulgent sin. Her eyes glowed, misty with memories, proud and a little sad. But the moment her gaze locked on Caitlin, she dropped the robe back into the little chest, the fragile folds tumbling in a disordered heap like a broken rainbow.

Her brow creased with worry, the abbess crossed to her, framing Caitlin's cheeks in her callused palms. "Caitlin, child? Whatever is amiss? You look ill."

It was harder than Caitlin could have imagined, shattering the older woman's peace, but there was no help for it. "I . . . I went to the grove."

"Did you injure yourself? Parts of the path are rocky—"

"Nay. But my lily . . . it was not there."

Relief smoothed the creases bracketing the Reverend Mother's mouth, a soft empathy gleaming in her mist-colored eyes. "I know you are disappointed, my dove. Perhaps some woodland creature ran off with it. You and I can go search for your lily together."

"Nay!" The idea of the Reverend Mother going out into the woods, facing that beast of a man, was unspeakable. "There was . . . was something else in the lily's place." Caitlin was trembling now. She could not stop. A sob broke from her lips. "A monster—a horrible beast of a man. He grabbed me and . . ."

Reverend Mother paled, stricken as if someone had plunged a dagger into her breast. But she seemed to draw on her wealth of inner strength—of faith—to shore her up. She gripped the lid of the chest with one hand to steady herself. "Caitlin, you must tell me what happened," Mother insisted in a calm, bracing voice. "Everything, child. Did this man . . . touch you in ways he should not have?"

"Aye! He did! He did!" Caitlin saw the aged nun curl tight inside herself as if she had taken a physical blow. "Look at my arms!" Caitlin shoved up the sleeves, displaying the beginnings of bruises on her lily-pale flesh. "He grabbed me! He shoved me down onto the stone and . . . and he *bellowed at me!*"

The abbess went still, hope sparking in her eyes. "That is all? You are certain?"

Indignation shot through Caitlin. *"All?* No one has—has ever done such unspeakable things to me before! I struck him in the face. Kicked him. I got away."

The nun actually smiled! "Of course you did, my bold, brave girl! Thanks be to God." Reverend Mother gathered her in her arms, stroking her hair.

"I always feared this day would come. Knew it would. The robe . . . it was so fine, the lily left for you every year. I tried to prepare myself. And to prepare you." She turned, an expression Caitlin had never seen before on her face, a fierce, almost feral love, the earthy love that made a mother fling herself before a charging stag to save her child.

"But this I promise you, Caitlin, my own. My soul will be damned before I let some cruel brute drag you away from here, despite the claims of fate and destiny!"

Caitlin swallowed hard, whispering words she had never spoken before. "I am afraid."

Look for
LILY FAIR
**Wherever Paperback Books
Are Sold**

**Coming Soon from
Sonnet Books**